MANDATORY FLIGHT

to Linda

JAMES CAMPBELL

Mandatory Flight

ISBN: 978-0-9966076-2-9 (print)
ISBN: 978-0-9966076-3-6 (ebook)

MANDATORY FLIGHT

PROLOGUE

Ile-a-Vache, Haiti

Cloaked in darkness and just out of sight, he silently watched the house as he hid behind a small group of palm trees. The party had been in full swing for hours, and the music was so loud he could feel the rhythmic thump of the bass beating through his body. His tired legs ached, but being a professional, he had learned to ignore the discomfort, knowing it was crucial to stay alert. His client was an important man and did not accept failure. He had never failed his client, and tonight was not going to be the exception.

The layout of the house and the number of guests concerned him. He knew the floor plan and escape routes well, but with the volume of people, it would be impossible to monitor the vast estate. Adding to the problem, the host had set up an impromptu dance floor on the outside patio, surrounded by vines of bougainvillea. The dense, colorful flowers blocked his view of the mingling guests, who kept disappearing one by one into the darkness, absorbed in conversation on their cell phones. It was difficult to keep track of them and make sure they reappeared. He thought about how much simpler it had been before the damn cell phones were invented. He also worried that he might be getting too old for the job. When the time came to achieve the night's objective, he wondered if his skills would be sharp enough to complete the task.

While watching the flow of people leave the patio to smoke or use their cell phones, he caught a quick glimpse of unexpected movement by the shoreline. He was instantly concerned since no one from the party had walked in that direction. He scanned the area under the light of a full moon, anxiously trying to identify the subject. He saw nothing, but something was there. Normally he would investigate, but without backup he couldn't leave his post. He realized he should have recruited more help for the evening. Something wasn't right, and he had a bad feeling—but in his business, he always had a bad feeling.

With dinner, awards, and dancing, the party lasted well into the night. The air had become damp and he could feel the morning dew condensing on the ground. He could also feel an arthritic throbbing in his right knee. Years earlier he had taken a bullet, and the night air never agreed with the old wound.

Patiently, he waited. Around two o'clock, the party began to wind down, and by two thirty, the band and the guests had departed and his subject was finally alone.

He watched the lights go out in the house and prepared himself for what he knew was about to happen. She exited through the back door and, with the aid of the moon and the soft light from the torches surrounding the patio, he watched as she walked toward the beach. Taller than most of the girls on the island, she was a natural beauty with long black hair flowing smoothly off her café au lait shoulders. She had a tantalizing presence that caught the attention of all men and most women. That way she had about her of making people notice had always caused him some concern. With that thought, he instinctively reached for his chest and felt the reassuring lump of the weapon tucked away in his shoulder holster.

She leisurely made her way to the beach and after walking a few feet, paused in the sand before moving to an old tree that, despite being dead for years, still stood proudly, its limbs hardened by the wind and salt air. She cautiously scanned the area.

Trees from the edge of the beach cast shadows over the sand and rocky outcrops. A sudden breeze in an otherwise calm evening made the branches sway. He wondered if that was what he had seen earlier. She studied the shadows closely, having been taught to be observant.

—

Moving toward the trees, she thought about the stressful weeks she'd spent planning all the details for that night's fundraiser. It had been a great success, raising more money than expected for a grassroots project that she had started as a child. She had always dreamed of making a significant, positive impact on the disadvantaged inhabitants of the island, which she now did with her foundation. With the recent funding from her benefactors, things were moving in a positive direction. Unfortunately, not everyone shared her sentiments. Her increasing popularity with the masses was becoming a constant threat to those who did not want her to succeed.

The private beach appeared empty, as she had expected. Having the only house on the long stretch of beach, she rarely saw anyone. The only thing visible was the smear of white lights from the vodoun ceremony being performed at a community center about a quarter of a mile down the beach. She recalled that it was a "year and a day" commemoration for one of the local Mambos, and in the distance she could hear the songs of celebration. The practitioners of vodoun revere death and believe it to be a transition from the current way of being to the afterlife. Some believe that after the spirit leaves the body, it's trapped in the physical world for a period of one year and a day.

After that period, a ceremony is preformed that celebrates the release of the spirit into its new form. It's considered an honor and obligation for family and friends to help the spirit transcend its earthly bounds. After a year and a day, the spirit will manifest itself somewhere in the realm of nature. It can become the howl of the wind or maybe the rustling in the trees.

She felt a sudden chill thinking about the abrupt breeze that had rattled and moved the now still trees. She did not participate in vodoun, but with it being a rich part of the island's culture, she had grown up around the beliefs and could not help but wonder about the coincidence.

Comfortable that she was alone (or at least not in the presence of anyone in the physical form), she began removing her clothes for her nightly swim. It was a long- held symbolic custom on the island to swim uninhibited by clothes—at least in private. She had been doing it since she was a child, and it seemed to be the one thing that could take away the daily pressures that so often consumed her. Hanging her towel and dress on the limbs of the old tree, she noticed the moonlight reflecting off her body and knew that someone else was probably seeing it as well. She smiled, knowing he was trying his best not to.

—

He was indeed trying to watch but not to see. He had been the girl's bodyguard since she was twelve and regarded her as family. When she became an adult, she had felt she no longer needed his protection, but her over-protective father had insisted that he continue to watch and protect her. Unfortunately, the previous year, a tragic, violent act involving her husband had proven the father's instincts to be correct. Although the incident had not directly involved her, it had been a wake-up call that times were changing and that desperate people were doing whatever it took to maintain their agendas—even if it meant murder.

As she eased into the water, he reluctantly left the beach to patrol the property. She usually swam for fifteen minutes, giving him just enough time to make his nightly rounds and respect her privacy. This particular night, he felt uncomfortable leaving his post. He had thoroughly vetted the guest list and, knowing or being familiar with everyone on the list, he had no concerns or suspicions that he could give a name to. Maybe the feeling was because of the earlier movement on the beach or the way that she had slightly stumbled while walking toward the water; he wasn't sure.

Hastily, he conducted his patrol and made his way back to his post. The first thing he noticed was her dress and towel still hanging from the old tree, blowing in the breeze. He looked at his watch. It had been at least fifteen minutes since he'd started his patrol. As was the routine on most nights, he expected her to be finished by then and back at the house. A feeling of panic washed over him as he scanned the well-lit ocean for her. Nothing but sliver light reflected off the calm, clear water. She was nowhere in sight. His mind raced with indecision. He thought about running to the house, but she would not have left her towel and dress hanging on the tree, and she definitely would not have gone for a walk without her clothes.

Needing to act fast, he rushed toward the water and frantically jerked his flashlight from his vest, shining it up and down the beach and across the water. She had vanished and he feared the worst. He knew she had been drinking, which was uncharacteristic of her. He cursed himself for not staying with her. As he splashed frantically into the water, he pulled his cell phone from his pocket to call for help. It was the last thing he remembered.

CHAPTER ONE

The Next Day—Colby

A s I sped down the narrow road at over 150 miles an hour, the dangerous sharp left turn was only seconds away. I had to make a decision, and it needed to be quick. Everything outside of my tunnel vision was a fast-moving blur. Immediately to my left was another car caught in the same desperate situation. If there was any hope of surviving the upcoming turn, one of us would need to lift off the throttle and apply the brakes—but no one was lifting. There was only enough room for one car to squeeze through the tight turn, and if we arrived at the same time, it would end catastrophically. The emergency helicopter loomed at the top of the hill as an iconic omen, waiting for daring drivers who held the red mist in their eyes. That's what we call it when a driver's expectations exceed his abilities and his emotions cloud rational thought or logic. The symbolic warning of the helicopter was heeded by few, and those few were the ones who usually found themselves at the back of the pack.

Gripping the steering wheel tightly, I held my breath and stood on the brakes—but only after the driver next to me had relented and hit his. The downforce of gravity pinned me to the seat, and all my senses were collectively trying to transition the car from the braking zone into the quick turn. I could feel the sweat pooled in my leather gloves as I reluctantly willed my foot off the brakes and, barely hugging the track, slid all four wheels through the turn.

Coming out of the turn, I pressed the accelerator to the floor and cleared him by mere inches. Not happy with the outcome, the driver filed in behind me and gave me a not-so-gentle "love tap" on my back bumper. With twelve more turns to go at the famous Road Atlanta racetrack, there was a good chance that within the minute and a half it took to complete the 2.54-mile circuit, I would find myself in this same position several more times.

Leaving turn 10-B, we sped up the track with only the dark, gray horizon in our windshields. It had rained most of the day, but neither of us paid heed to the wetness of the track. Blindly cresting the hill and building speed, we shot down the turn and entered the long front stretch. Nearing the start-finish line, I could see a man in a white official's suit leaning over the rail, aggressively waving a white flag. Within seconds we would again be nearing 150 miles an hour and facing another battle on turn one. A look in my rearview mirror revealed an empty track. In an epic fight for first place and the regional championship, we had left the entire field at least a quarter of a lap behind.

It was just the two of us on the last lap of the last race in a season that had seemed to last forever. I was the current holder of the regional championship, and it was obvious the driver of car number 57 wanted to take the title from me. Not ready to relinquish the championship, I kept my right foot firmly planted on the accelerator.

Along with my gloves, my race suit and helmet were soaked with sweat. The ice had long since melted in the cooler in the back of the car that pumped cold water through a myriad of lines to cool my race suit and helmet. It was pumping hot water now, but nothing could shake my concentration.

Entering the braking zone into turn one, I glanced quickly at my competitor through the passenger-side window. Through the limited view of his checkered window safety net, I could sense his determination and knew he was not going to relinquish the turn. To win races and championships, one must learn to read the language of a car and the mind of its driver. If he's indecisive, the car will signal that with quick, jerky movements. If he's confident, the car will move with fluidity and balance like a thoroughbred racehorse. I knew all too well that the driver who had just pulled up beside me was confident and ready to claim turn one—and maybe the race and championship as well.

As we sped toward the corner and closer to the point of decision, I had a bad feeling and knew I should give up the turn. There would be eleven other turns, eleven other chances to plot a strategy before we reached the finish line—but I couldn't let it go. I had been seriously considering retiring from racing and this could very well be my last race. If I gave up the turn and allowed car 57 to take the lead, I would never get it back. He wanted it too badly.

Deep into the braking zone before the turn, neither of us blinked, and we were still accelerating. I had chosen the outside line, giving myself more space to take the turn at a faster speed. The trade-off was giving him the opportunity to set the point of entry from the inside position. If I were to overdrive the turn, I would just spin off the track and end up stuck in the sand—suffering nothing more than a bruised ego and the loss of the race and championship. If he overshot the turn, his car would slam into mine, pushing us past the sand trap and into the deadly concrete retaining wall. As we closed in on the turn, we realized at the same moment that we had gone too far. We both locked up our brakes—but it was too late. Smoke from my protesting tires immediately filled my car, blocking my view of the impending disaster.

Violently, number 57 slammed into the passenger side of my car at close to a hundred miles an hour. Locked together, we slid to the edge of the track where the pavement met the grass. Through the wear of countless drivers miscalculating the turn, the edge of the track had developed a trench that dropped a few inches lower than the pavement. As my wheels dug into the ditch and with the weight of the other car pressing against me, I was instantly catapulted into the air.

The immediate spinning and negative force of gravity felt like a nightmare roller-coaster ride. I had seen enough accidents to know the one I was currently involved in would not end well. After hitting the ground and flipping several times, the car gained enough momentum to again become airborne. As I sailed over the concrete wall, I caught glimpses of the colorful metal and rubber scars of drivers who had been in similar situations—but had been stopped by the wall. As the trees spun past, I wondered what was on the other side.

It suddenly became dark as the car dipped below the horizon and began to fall into what appeared to be a ravine. At that moment, I felt disconnected from the racetrack and far away in another realm. The flight ended with the car crashing to the ground and rolling down a steep embankment. Strapped into my safety harness, I could feel my body being shaken, and then everything went black.

—

Disoriented, I could barely hear Aubrey's voice in the distance. "Come on and wake up. You need to get up." She kept telling me the same thing over and over again. I felt like I was trapped in a dream and couldn't get out. I finally opened my eyes, expecting to be staring into the fluorescent lights of a hospital-room ceiling, hearing beeping and suction noises while bound in a body cast—but fortunately that was not the case.

To my surprise, I was in my own bed with Aubrey propped up beside me. She was holding two cups of coffee and impatiently shaking me with her foot. Instead of a body cast, I was wearing the silly red pajamas decorated with dog prints she had given me for Christmas. I could swear the coffee smelled like burning tire rubber, but thankfully it had all been a dream. Aubrey handed me a cup of coffee and ran her hands through my hair. "Your hair is soaking wet. You okay?" she asked.

It took a second to get my bearings.

"Why are you sweating?" she asked.

I was now awake, and my mischievous mind was fully alert. "Well, I was actually at the climactic point of a very racy dream. Maybe you could give me about ten more minutes of sleep so I can make it to the finish line?" I asked, jokingly closing my eyes in satisfaction and leaning back against my pillow.

Not happy with my reply, she pinched me on the sensitive area underneath my arm. "Is that right? So just who was this racy dream about?" she asked, tilting her head to one side. Aubrey and I never missed an opportunity to have a little fun.

"Well, she was a sexy, beautiful, lean machine. A little fast at times and hard to handle, but when caressed just right, she'd do most anything I wanted," I replied, describing the Porsche I'd raced when I lived in Winnipeg. I hadn't been able to part with her, and I brought her with me on my move back to Georgia. I'd been spending a lot of time with her lately, and thinking about maybe racing again. It was the only thing that made Aubrey jealous.

She shook her head and dropped her shoulders in mock defeat. "It's that damn race-car mistress, isn't it? You wait until I get my hands on that four-wheeled tramp! I'll cut all her hot and sexy wires," she said with a pout. "Maybe you need reminding who cost you less money and keeps you warm at night," she said while moving closer. I had a good idea where things were going and took both coffees and set them on the bedside table. I knew this was going to be a very good morning.

She swung herself on top of me and pushed my shoulders toward the mattress. With her long legs straddling my hips, she slowly peeled off her gown, revealing a firm figure that immediately got a response from me. Slowly, she leaned down and softly kissed my neck. Her wild long auburn hair swept across my face, and her scent filled the air. I pulled her closer and breathed her in.

"Can your little race car do this?" she asked as she eased me out of my pajamas. With her eyes locked on mine, she began doing things to me that a race car could never do. After an intense ten minutes, she took two long gasps and held her breath. Grabbing and squeezing my hands as hard as she could, she closed her eyes and exhaled with pleasure.

Only seconds behind her, I found an ending that was much sweeter than the dream she'd interrupted.

Content, she collapsed and curled up beside me. It was the perfect moment leading up to what I hoped would be the perfect day.

It was Saturday, June twenty-first, the summer solstice and the longest day of the year. Aubrey and I had chosen it for that very reason to be our wedding day. We wanted the day to last as long as possible.

—

The heat I'd felt in the bedroom seemed to be just as intense outside. From the cool, air-conditioned house, I peeked out the window and could see waves of heat forming in the air. It was only ten o'clock and the mercury in the thermometer, visible on the porch, had already risen to ninety degrees. The high of the day was expected to reach a hot and humid one hundred. This would not have been an issue if we had planned to have the wedding inside like most couples do with summer weddings in the South. But for very special reasons, there was only one spot we had ever considered.

Aubrey and I had met more than thirty years earlier in a little town set on the rocky shoals of the Ogeechee River. Jewell, Georgia, if for no other reason, measured up to its name by being the place where I met the girl who was never far from my thoughts and permanently embedded in my heart. Introduced by way of a friendship between our fathers, we spent many summer days swimming and fishing on the shoals of the Ogeechee and many evenings of teenage discovery on a small dock that hung over a patch of the muddy, slow-moving river. Sitting on that dock during the summer we both turned sixteen on the exact same day, I gave her a small gold ring with a speck of an emerald to show her that I loved her. Just recently on the same dock, I gave her another gold ring with a diamond to show her I had never stopped.

Until a few years before, we had not seen each other for the better part of those thirty years. Our lives had gone in different directions during our college years, and it was not until I moved to Madison, Georgia that we reconnected. Not only did we reconnect, but we soon found ourselves in the middle of a bizarre and twisted tale of murder and mystery. In a classic case of truth that was stranger than fiction, our love was reignited when we were pulled into a race to stop a psychopath. It's a complicated story. Let me just throw out a few phrases: water supply, poison, major US cities.

Our story, which involved the CIA, the FBI, and Homeland Security, ended with the bad guys being killed. The government decided to keep the case classified; everything was hidden neatly from the public, and life got back to normal—well, a new kind of normal.

Up until the fateful day when Aubrey became involved in the almost crime of the century, she was working at a small-town antique market as an artist and furniture builder. After the disaster had been averted, I fully expected her to continue with her art while I went on with my retirement. I'd sold a logistics company that I had owned in Canada and was very content waking up each morning with the weather as my only worry. Our plans were to spend weekdays in Madison and weekends at either her family's river house in Jewell or my farm in nearby Warthen.

Unfortunately, our lives took another turn. According to the CIA, the little artist who had previously made her living recreating old furniture had a knack for working clandestine operations. I was immediately opposed to her being involved in anything dangerous, believing we had probably used up most of our nine lives during the ordeal the previous year. Plus, I was just a little jealous that, with my proven accomplishments as an experienced pilot and the pyrotechnic skills I'd learned from the boys in Winnipeg, they had not offered *me* a job.

My buddy Nathan from the CIA, who'd shared in our previous adventure, assured us she would only be doing minor consulting jobs and would primarily be working with him in safe situations. So far, that seemed to be the case, but she and Nathan had recently traveled outside the country on a job or mission or whatever it was they called it. I was not cleared to have information, so I had no idea where they went or what they were doing.

When Aubrey had gone for her initial month of training, we were only allowed to talk once a week and she was not allowed to reveal her location or discuss her training. I was not happy about the arrangement, and Nathan loved to tease me about it. He constantly rubbed it in that he talked with her every day. He said that she was doing great, that she was a star. One day those two will need me and I will get the pleasure of throwing their "need to know' attitude right back at them. My pride has never let me ask either of them the first question about their work.

It was approaching noon and time to make the short drive from Warthen to Jewell. Aubrey fed the dogs a few treats and gave them big hugs before getting in the car. She'd wanted them to be part of the ceremony, but thankfully her mom had quashed the idea. Aubrey had attended a wedding where the couple's dogs had been part of the ceremony as the ring bearers or flower dogs or something silly like that. After that, she brought up the idea of having Hannah and Savannah do the same at our wedding. But our hound dogs had never left the farm and had not been privy to dog cotillion classes or etiquette training. Their only skills were begging for food, barking at two in the morning, and scratching and licking. I was in full agreement with Mrs. Reese that they needed to stay at the farm.

Aubrey's parents had spent the week in Jewel making sure everything was just right. A few years earlier, the Reeses had moved to Augusta, and now they only came back to the river house for an occasional weekend or family gathering. As was the tradition, Mrs. Reese had planned a little luncheon at the house for Aubrey and her friends, and Mr. Reese was taking Nathan, me, and a group of my friends on an afternoon fishing trip.

After a twenty-minute drive through the rolling, sandy hills of the coastal plain, passing a state park and the little community of Rock Hill, we arrived and pulled up the gravel driveway. Starting up the drive and seeing the big house on the hill reminded me, as it always did, of the first visit my father and I made to the Reeses' house.

—

It had been just after dark that long-ago day when we turned off the main road and started up the long driveway. I could see at the crest of the hill a tall, majestic house lit with soft, glowing lights. That fall, Dad and I had joined a hunting club and were dropping by the Reeses' to pick up a map of the hunting property. I'd met Aubrey earlier that day at the hunting club and was nervous about seeing her again. Expecting to see a crowd of boys at the clubhouse after the morning hunt, I'd been surprised and disappointed to see only a girl dressed in camouflage, freckle faced with her hair tucked under a hat. She stood next to her dad, shouldering a Marlin 30-30—the gun I had been saving for all year. I had a paltry single-gauge shotgun that in my hand suddenly seemed like a toy. I felt slightly intimidated and embarrassed. I was a city boy, and she eyed me with suspicion and didn't have much to say.

We walked up the sidewalk to the house and Dad clanked the door knocker, which was shaped like a bird dog. Aubrey answered, no longer dressed in camouflage. She was wearing blue jeans and a flannel shirt, and her long auburn hair fell across her shoulders. She asked us to come in, but I could hardly move. She was the prettiest girl I had ever seen.

Sensing my nervousness, my father placed his hand on my shoulder and eased me forward. Mr. Reese met us at the door, and the two men walked to the den, leaving Aubrey and me standing in the foyer.

After a few awkward moments, we found that neither one of us knew much about hunting, we both liked sports, and we shared the same birthday. We walked into the den and sat on the couch talking until my dad told me it was time to go. We made a connection that day that would last a lifetime. It was also the day that changed my life.

Now, thinking about it on our wedding day, I looked at her and smiled. Seeming to know what I was thinking, she squeezed my hand and smiled back.

At the house, we found her parents standing on the front porch, waving with big smiles, having already come outside, anticipating our arrival. I think they were as excited about the wedding as we were.

Sadly, my dad would not be there, and the reason why still brought back the emotions of that day. After thirty-five years with the railroad, he'd traded in that life for the retirement of his dreams. He bought a large tract of hunting land in Warthen, which I refer to as "the farm," and spent his days walking the marshy bottom of Williamson swamp and traversing the hickory hills, searching for signs of deer. Deer hunting was his passion, and no one was more excited about opening day than Robert Cameron. It was his passion for hunting that had circuitously led me to Aubrey. Thirty years later, it would lead to a wedding.

In only his fifth year of retirement, tragedy struck one cold, rainy winter's day. I remember the weather because I was the one who found him, wet and shivering, in his deer stand. It was only a few weeks before I was to leave for Canada to start my own career. We had arranged to have dinner at his house that evening to celebrate my move and to say our goodbyes. We shared a tight father and son bond and, realizing it might be a while before we saw each other again, we wanted one last night together.

Earlier in the day, I'd tried unsuccessfully to reach him on his house phone. It was in the days before cell phones, and if you didn't reach my father by six-thirty in the morning, it would be late into the evening before you had another chance. Arriving well after dark, I was surprised to see the house unlit.

As kids, we had called Dad the "light warden." He was always coming up behind us, turning off the lights. I can't remember how many times he threatened to make us pay the light bill. Still, I was shocked to see no lights at all. It was at least an hour after dark and he should be sitting in his rocking chair by the fire, sipping on his nightly glass of bourbon. I wondered if he'd shot a deer and was looking for it, but at the same time I felt anxious.

I entered the house and turned on all the lights. After a nervous few minutes, I grabbed a flashlight and hopped on a four-wheeler to go find him. There were so many places he could have been, but I knew his favorite deer stand and decided to check there first.

I pulled up on the power line to a small stand he referred to as a "rain stand." As he'd gotten older, he'd quit climbing trees and only hunted from the ground. He'd built half a dozen blinds with three short walls apiece and tin roofs to keep him out of the elements. Shining my flashlight into the stand, I found him slumped over in a chair. I immediately yelled his name.

I reached into the stand and pulled him up. He was wet and shivering. His face was pale and his eyes looked weak and glassy. He tried to speak but winced in pain instead. Over the past few weeks, he'd been complaining of a tightness in his throat that made it hard to swallow. We assumed it was an infection or a cold, but we would later learn it was a classic symptom of a heart attack.

I was in a panic and was not sure what to do, but I knew I had to act fast. I thought about running back to the house and calling the

EMS, but there was no way I was going to leave him alone. I lifted him from the chair and lowered him onto the seat of the four-wheeler. He reached out for the handlebars to balance himself, but the effort was too much. He slumped back against me, and I put my left arm around him to hold him close to me. He seemed almost lifeless, and I pleaded with him to hang on. The cold rain had turned to sleet, stinging my face as we flew back to the house on the ATV. I drove with one hand and held my father with the other.

At the house, I ran inside, put my father on the couch and grabbed some quilts from a trunk to tuck around him. He was shivering uncontrollably, which I took as a good sign. I lifted his legs up onto the arm of the couch to keep the blood supply close to his heart. I had heard somewhere that's what you were supposed to do. I found the phone and dialed 911. Being that we were back in the woods and off the main road, I gave them detailed directions to the house.

I ran back to his side and, through tears, told him all the things a son would say to his dying father. I held his hand and could feel a gentle squeeze of acknowledgement.

It seemed like it took forever, but the paramedics finally got there and loaded him for the trip to the hospital. On the way, I frantically called my sisters and mom with the news. They left Atlanta immediately. I followed the ambulance to the hospital and through the light from the back door-window, I could see the EMTs frantically working on him. I prayed out loud that he would make it to the hospital alive.

We pulled up to the emergency room and I jumped from my car and stood waiting for the ambulance's door to open. To my surprise, when they opened it, Dad was awake and talking to the EMTs about—what else? —deer hunting. It gave me a glimmer of hope.

The doctors stabilized him the best they could but said he had experienced a very serious heart attack and would need to be transported to Augusta by a life-flight helicopter. They had already dispatched the helicopter and it was on the way.

Standing by his bed, waiting for my mom and sisters, I had precious minutes to talk with my dad. He told me how proud he was of me and how I had been the best son he could have ever hoped for. Tears ran down my face as he spoke. With a weak voice, he told me that he hoped that I would find love and one day be a father. He said I would make a good one. He also told me to be happy and to have no regrets. I told him how much I loved him and needed him and to please hang on. With one last squeeze of my hand, he smiled and closed his eyes.

Dad left us that cold winter evening, but his warmth has never left my heart.

—

In her mid-eighties, my mom is still fiercely independent and lives by herself in a large two-story house in Oxford, near where I grew up. Her passions are her yard and flowers, which beautifully reflect the hard work that has made her the envy of the local garden club. As she has gotten up in years, we have suggested many times that she let us hire a landscape company to help her tend the yard, but she'll have none of that.

One afternoon, I stopped by for a visit. I knocked on the door several times and when she didn't answer, I used my key to let myself in. It was not uncommon for her not to hear someone at the door. It was a big house, and she had become a little hard of hearing. I found her sitting in the front parlor with a heating pad pressed against her shoulder.

"What happened to you?" I asked, walking over to her chair. She waved her hand and casually said, "Oh, nothing."

But I knew it was something. I pressed further and finally got an answer.

"I fell out of that damned tree in the front yard, trying to cut a limb."

It would have been pointless to chastise her, so I just asked her how.

"Well, I'd cut a limb just above it last year, and when I grabbed hold of the old stub to support myself, it broke and I fell off the damn ladder. Next time I'll remember not to grab some old stub," she said, as if to reassure me.

I just shook my head and laughed. There would not be a next time because before I left, I intended to sneak that ladder into the back of my truck. I had to admire her spirit and hoped I was still climbing a ladder at eighty-three.

She was looking forward to the wedding and had called a few days earlier to tell me how happy she was that I had finally come to my senses. She also said that she was expecting grandkids. I laughed and told her that ship had long since sailed.

My sister Nell had flown in from Cincinnati and spent the day fussing over my mom, trying to get her dressed and ready for the wedding. My mother, like most older Southern ladies, took weddings and funerals very seriously. Everything had to be perfect. After a stop in Covington to pick up my other sister, Gay, Nell gave me a quick call to tell me they were on their way and to have a strong drink waiting.

—

In the small pasture alongside the gravel driveway, there were about fifteen cars parked in a row. It appeared the guests for the luncheon and the fishing trip had arrived. I saw Nathan's old Ford pickup backed in between a few pine trees, separated from the rest of the vehicles. Being the paranoid one, he always planned for a fast retreat.

I pulled my truck in front of his to block his exit. The opportunities to get one over on him were few and far between.

Before getting out of the truck, Aubrey turned toward me and put her hand on my arm. "Are you sure you're ready for this?" she asked.

It had taken a long time to earn her trust after I broke her heart all those years before. I knew she had forgiven me but maybe not totally forgotten about our college years. I'd let other things take center stage back then and lost what was most important: the most amazing girl I'd ever met. She knew by then that I would love her forever, but I think it was just something she had to ask.

"I'm ready, and don't be thinking about trying anything funny. I brought a shotgun in case you considered changing *your* mind," I said, smiling as I got out of the truck and walked around to open her door.

She jumped out, gave me a reassuring peck, and ran up to the porch to see her mother. They had always been close, but after the ordeal the year before, Aubrey had made a point to see her much more often.

Hearing the clanging of horseshoes and laughter in the backyard, I gave the Reeses a wave and headed off to greet my friends. That's when something near the edge of the woods by the well house caught my attention. It was Nathan, leaning against a pine tree and smugly watching me. It was just like him to be off hiding somewhere. I walked over and he just stood there with a crooked grin.

"What the hell are you looking at?" I asked.

"At a man who's been single for most of his life and is about to lose his freedom. I don't know who to feel worse for, you or Aubrey," he said, offering his hand to shake.

I grabbed his hand and pulled him in for a hug. "How long have you been here?" I asked.

"Long enough to have a nice conversation with the Reeses and watch them wonder why in the world the two of you are so close with an old man they barely know anything about. I also think you threw them for a loop, choosing me to be your best man instead of one of those beer-drinking horseshoe players," he said, gesturing toward the backyard. That was Nathan. He never gave anyone a straight answer.

I looked around to make sure that no one was nearby. "Maybe I should tell them you're a CIA operative who not only recruited their daughter into your shady little world but could kill both of them with your hands in a matter of just seconds," I said, speaking in an almost whisper. I folded my arms across my chest, feeling good about getting the best of him.

"You ready for today?" he asked, turning serious. It was the second time in the last few minutes I had been asked that question.

"As I'll ever be," I said as Mr. Reese approached.

He greeted me with a handshake and an earnest look. "Colby, son, are you ready for this?" he asked.

Well, damn. That made three!

"Yes sir, I am. I'm pretty sure your daughter is making a big mistake, but what can we do?" I said with a shrug.

He laughed and gave me a pat on the back. "Yeah, that's exactly what her mom said."

"Really, that's what she said?" I asked, alarmed.

"No, son, I'm just kidding. You know that Mary loves you," he said as he laughed and punched Nathan in the arm. Mr. Reese was a big bear of a man with a soft, loving heart. He and my dad had been close friends, and I knew he missed him and wished he could have been there for that day. "Let's go get them city boys before they hurt themselves with those horseshoes," he said. "I believe it's time to fish. There's a great little catfish hole about a mile up the river on the Hancock County side, and it's full of fish just waiting to be caught." He headed back to retrieve the loud crew in the back.

I walked into the kitchen to ice down a cooler of beer, knowing that would most likely be the only part of fishing that would interest that group of guys. They only had a few hours before their wives would arrive and begin to curtail their drinking.

But, as I was about to find out, there was to be no fishing on that day.

CHAPTER TWO

It took a few minutes, but Mr. Reese finally got my slightly ine-briated friends from the backyard to the driveway. Mrs. Reese and a few of Aubrey's friends were on the front porch, laughing and pointing at us. Well, *Aubrey's friends* were laughing and pointing. Mrs. Reese had her arms folded across her chest and a stern look on her face. I can only imagine what might have happened in the back-yard. Of the six guys who were there, four were from my years at the University of Georgia, and two were friends from Covington and Madison. All six had a wild streak that always kept things interesting.

Mr. Reese corralled the boys into his 1978 Suburban, and Nathan and I rode in his truck. Of course, I had to move my truck so he could get out. I thought about asking to drive the old Willys Jeep that Mr. Reese had owned since I was a teenager, but I was told to get in Nathan's truck and that I had to hurry. It seemed Mrs. Reese's patience had run out and he wanted us all out of there.

We left the house in a cloud of dust and made a right turn onto Georgia Highway 16. I was a bit confused, being that the acclaimed fishing hole and Hancock County were in the opposite direction. I started to ask Nathan where we were going, but I knew he would answer in some sort of riddle or long parable and I still wouldn't know.

After a few minutes, we crossed the Ogeechee River and turned down a familiar road. In the distance I could see our non-fishing destination at the foot of a hill. I should have known.

We pulled into a gravel parking lot and the doors of the Suburban flew open before Mr. Reese could get it stopped. Laughing and hollering, the guys made a beeline to the entrance of the dilapidated building. Mr. Reese walked back to my side of Nathan's truck and stuck his head in the window. "You didn't really think we were going fishing, did you?" he asked.

"Well, actually, I did," I replied.

"Son, you should've known that crew had zero interest in anything to do with fish. They'd not been at the house five minutes before pulling me aside and asking the location of the closest bar. They said it was their duty to uphold some kind of custom or tradition of getting the groom *comfortable and prepared* before the wedding."

"Mr. Reese, I know you didn't fall for that?" I asked.

"Of course I didn't, son, but if all they wanted to do was drink, I didn't want them messing up my fishing hole," he said. "Go inside and have some fun, and we'll have ourselves a fishing trip when you get back from your honeymoon. This ol' bar has not seen much excitement lately. I know Ms. Jean will be glad to have the business. I think she might have called in a few lady friends to add a little spice to the occasion." He glanced toward a car that had just pulled in.

I looked over and saw a group of girls spilling out of an old Buick Regal painted in three different shades of gray primer. It was bouncing to some kind of music I couldn't identify. The girls were wearing cutoff blue jean shorts, tight shirts, boots, and cowboy hats and were all laughing as they walked to the door. Things were about to get interesting.

"I assume that Mrs. Reese and Aubrey don't know about the change of plans?" I asked.

"Well, I saw Mary nosing around the truck before we left, and she's smart enough to know that it's hard to catch a fish if you don't have any gear. I'd bet money she's already called to see if we've arrived. But don't you worry, son; she won't say a word. She's just glad to have us gone so she can get on with her little hen party at the house," he said with a chuckle.

We walked into the unpainted concrete block building, which was topped with a rust-covered tin roof. The windows were blacked out and covered by bars, giving the place a look that didn't scream out *welcome*. Inside, that was not the case. The walls and floors were lined in heart pine, and the twenty-foot bar was crafted out of teakwood and topped with a half-inch layer of high-gloss polyurethane. Underneath were arrowheads, shards of Indian pottery, political buttons, old coins, and all sorts of treasures from the past. Behind the bar was a large shelf stocked with as many brands of spirits as you could imagine. A large mirror reflected scattered neon beer signs and old ceramic-coated advertising pieces that covered the opposite wall. There were several pool tables and, of course, a jukebox.

The guys had already bought a few buckets of beer and commandeered the pool tables and the jukebox. The girls must have chosen the music, because it was the same thumping sound that I'd heard when they pulled up. They started dancing and were pulling a few of the guys from the pool table to join them. Nathan, Mr. Reese, and I found seats at the bar and ordered a few Pabst Blue Ribbon beers—the only kind sold—from Ms. Jean, the fragile old lady who owned the bar. Ms. Jean looked like the Sunday school director at the local Baptist church, but that was deceiving. If one acted up or caused a ruckus in her bar, they found out real quick that she was anything but a Sunday school teacher. A sailor would be more accurate.

"Colby, you sure you're ready to get married?" she asked while she poured.

"Actually, Ms. Jean, I was thinking about calling off the wedding and was hoping you and I could run off together," I said. "You know I've always had a thing for you. What do you say? You up for it?"

What she did next was quintessentially Ms. Jean. She stopped pouring my beer, took off her apron, walked over to the breaker switch, and cut off the power. The place went dark with the exception of a little light coming from the exit signs.

"Place is closed. Everybody's got to leave," she yelled.

Everyone was silent, wondering what the hell had just happened.

"Come on, let's go; everybody out," she called. "Colby and I are escaping from this hell hole and running off to Mexico."

After a second or two, the lights and jukebox came back on. The first thing that I saw was the sly grin on the owner's face. The place erupted into laughter.

"Sorry, Colby, but I could never do a thing like that to Aubrey," she said. "You'll just have to follow through and think about me in your dreams." If Ms. Jean was not pushing eighty, she might have been serious.

We spent the next couple of hours drinking and playing pool. The guys kept shoving me shots of something brown, and I secretly passed them back to Nathan, who poured the liquor out and handed me back the empty shot glasses. The music from the jukebox seemed to be getting louder, and the dancing had moved from the floor to the tops of the pool tables.

More girls arrived and were immediately charmed by the city boys from Atlanta—or more likely they were charmed by the bills flowing from their wallets. Thankfully, the crew soon forgot about their mission to get me good and drunk and seemed to attach that goal instead to themselves and the girls. Nathan and Mr. Reese were consumed with military talk about their time in Europe and Southeast Asia, so I took the opportunity to slip outside.

The weatherman had gotten it right for once. The air was hot and humid, and my shirt immediately turned wet and clung to my back and chest. It felt good after being in the cold air of the bar. I looked at my watch and it was already four. The wedding was at seven, and I thought we probably should be leaving. I grabbed my phone from my pocket to check for messages and had to resist the urge to call or text Aubrey. I could not wait to tell her about our "fishing trip."

Of course, there had been times when I'd been right there in the middle of the fun. In my day, I'd danced on more than a few pool tables, but times had long since changed. My only interest now was in building a life with Aubrey.

After a few minutes, I heard the door open and turned to see Nathan walking toward me.

"Three hours until you get to make the best decision of your life," he said.

"I couldn't agree more," I replied.

Nathan paused for a second and then looked at me with a warm expression. "Colby, I want you to know what a privilege it is to have you and Aubrey in my life," he said. "I'll never forget the day you showed up at my door with Aubrey in your arms. That girl was in bad shape. Your blind trust in me that night really meant a lot. What we went through that next week helped me to form the kind of bond that I didn't think I could. With very few exceptions, I don't let anyone get close. An occupational hazard, I suppose. But the two of you have renewed my faith that trusting someone else is something I can do. I love you both and hope to never disappoint you or Aubrey either."

I could have sworn I saw a little misting in his eyes.

I didn't know what to do except to grab him into a big hug. Although Nathan was only about fifteen years older than me, he felt like a father. Whenever I was upset and needed someone to talk with, Nathan was always there. I was sure the quick hug made him feel a little bit uncomfortable, his generation being strictly the type to stick to shaking hands.

Suddenly the door of the bar burst open, and in a flash my friend Kyle was in the parking lot. He was shirtless, missing his shoes, and wrestling to pull his pants up. Right on his heels was a short blonde, who was missing her shirt as well and cussing him every step. It was only seconds before the rest of the guys and girls made it outside and the scene escalated. Beer bottles and cans were being thrown in all directions.

Mr. Reese ran out amid the commotion and jumped into the Suburban and fired it up. He blew the horn and the guys ran over and jumped in, but not before one of the larger girls kicked my buddy Alan in the seat of his pants as he was diving into the back. She high fived one of the other girls, and laughing, they headed back into the bar.

Nathan and I glanced at each other, confused, then jumped into his truck and followed Mr. Reese out of the parking lot and up the road.

"I don't know what happened, but it definitely wouldn't be a good idea to take that crowd back to the house," I said. "I hope Mr.

Reese has a plan because Mrs. Reese will kill him if they show up like that."

Nathan just shook his head.

It was not two seconds before my phone rang. It was Mr. Reese.

"Hey, what happened back there?" I asked.

I could hear the boys laughing in the background, and Mr. Reese had to raise his voice to speak over them. "One of the girls dared your friend Kyle to get naked on top of the pool table," he reported, laughing. "After he complied, he dared her to get naked too. She took off her clothes, and your buddy didn't let any time go by before he grabbed her boobs, and she slapped him so hard he fell right off the table. He managed to get half his clothes back on before he got kicked out the door. I think you saw the rest."

"Is Ms. Jean mad?" I asked, concerned.

"Not at all," he said. "I think she actually put the girl up to it. That old lady has a lot of spunk. She yelled out at the guys to come back anytime."

The laughing got louder in the background, and I knew it must be awfully rowdy in the truck.

"What are you going to do with them?" I asked. "You can't take them back to the house."

"I'm going to run them over to the clubhouse at the hunting land and try to get them settled down," he said. "As soon as I tell them their wives will be arriving in an hour or so, I'm sure that they'll be fine. You and Nathan go on back to the house and start getting ready."

"Thanks, Mr. Reese. See you in about an hour, and cut off their drinks right now!"

That was never going to work, but I had to at least say it.

"I'll take care of them, son. You go check on the women," Mr. Reese said as he was hanging up.

Nathan and I arrived back at the river house and could see the yard had filled up with cars. We pulled up and Nathan backed his truck into a spot that, as usual, was chosen with an eye toward a quick getaway. It looked like the luncheon had ended, and the women were all on the front porch, lively with libations. I could only imagine what would happen if Aubrey's friends and my cretin groomsmen got together before the wives made it to the house. I looked around for Aubrey but didn't see her. I was sure that Mrs. Reese had her upstairs, fussing with her dress, hair, and makeup.

Nathan saw his wife's car in the parking lot and disappeared to find her. It was just two hours before the wedding and I could feel the excitement in the air.

Needing a little time alone, I took a walk down the bank of the river and reflected on some of the wonderful memories that had led me to the evening.

Looking over the swimming hole, I remembered how a teenaged Aubrey used to tease me until I found the courage to take the fifteen-foot jump off of the big rock into the muddy water. I also remembered the last time that my father visited the Reeses and we all ate lunch on the dock.

Memories, both sad and sweet, are links to our past that help define our future. In less than two hours, Aubrey and I would complete the circle that had begun so many years before.

CHAPTER THREE

All the guests had arrived, and the crimson sun was beginning to set over the slow-moving river, painting a perfect backdrop for the wedding. The ceremony, of course, was being held on the dock. Mr. Reese had hired a company to set up rows of chairs at the top of the bluff overlooking the river. Big white tents were spread across the yard, in place for the reception, and flowers lined the walkway leading from the house to the dock. The invitation list had about two hundred names, and I think almost everyone had shown up.

Nathan and I were in the small guesthouse getting dressed when the rowdy six, along with a few other friends, barged through the door. Nathan flinched and immediately reached into his inner-jacket pocket. *Great,* I thought. All we needed was for Nathan to pull a gun on one of my drunken friends. He quickly regained his composure and disappeared into the kitchen. Thankfully, no one noticed.

"Colby, we came to give you one final chance to get the hell out of here and avoid the misery of marriage—like the rest of us poor bastards should have done!" This was incoherently and dramatically stated by my friend William, who himself was on wife number three.

"Thank you for your concern, William, but if you want to warn someone, it should be Aubrey," I replied.

"We tried, but her old mama wouldn't let us anywhere near her," my buddy Alan said with a slur in his voice. They all got a big kick out of that and fell on each other laughing. Kyle pulled out a large bottle of rum that was still half full. He twisted off the cap, which he threw in the trash.

"I think we need a toast," he proclaimed, unsteady on his feet. All the boys collectively replied with a "Hear, hear" and started passing around the bottle. I looked back to see Nathan standing in the kitchen, shaking his head. After the bottle had been passed around twice, they forgot about the toast and stumbled out the door. It was great to see them having so much fun. They all had stressful jobs and complicated lives, and it was nice to see them unwind. They might regret it in the morning, but for now, they were having a big time.

It was approaching seven o'clock and time to head to the dock. I was a bit nervous, but not about getting married. For Aubrey, my mom, and her parents, I wanted everything to go smoothly and as planned. I hoped I would get all my words right and that one of my foolish friends wouldn't fall head-first into the river.

As we walked toward the dock, the scene was magical. There was a light breeze coming off the water, and the clouds reflected the sunlight in a brilliant, colorful display. The band was playing soft music, and the trees seemed to be swaying to the beat. We still had about fifteen minutes before the ceremony, and I could not wait to see

Aubrey in her wedding dress. I noticed that the bar was the center of attention and that Aubrey's friends and mine had finally connected. Seeing them together made me think about the wild scene at the bar.

I suddenly had a horrible image of the small blonde girl with no shirt and her friends rolling up to the wedding in the thumping Buick. I was sure that one my drunken groomsman had invited them. It would have been hilarious if they had shown up at anyone else's wedding, but not mine. I had enough to worry about and quickly dismissed the thought.

With ten minutes to go, Nathan, the preacher, and I walked down the steps to the dock. Mrs. Reese had the rails intertwined with white ribbons and bows, and on each post was an assortment of colorful summer flowers. I looked up the bluff, and every chair was filled. The colorful summer dresses and hats blended with a sea of seersucker suits. The scene was certainly apropos for a Southern summer wedding.

The preacher asked Nathan if he had the ring, and Nathan patted the side pocket of his jacket, indicating that he did. I wanted to ask him if he had his gun in the other pocket to see the reaction from the preacher, but I thought better of it. The preacher was an old family friend and was sneaking up on ninety years old. We had to help him down the steps, and I leaned over and instructed Nathan to be sure to help him back up after everything was over.

All of a sudden, everything got quiet. The band started playing, and the wedding party began their trip down the steep steps to the dock. Earlier, I had designated a few of my more responsible friends to escort my mom and Mrs. Reese down the steps. They both made it to the bottom and were full of smiles.

With almost two hundred people watching, I held my breath while the inebriated groomsmen prepared to escort the bridesmaids down the steps. I noticed Aubrey's friends were more than slightly drunk. It was hard to watch. We really should have gone on that fishing trip.

They were side by side, arm in arm, and had made it about half-way down when one of the girls began to sway. Her mouth was wide open, and I was not sure if she was going to throw up, fall down, or both. She was near the back of the group, and if she fell forward, it would be like a row of tumbling dominos. Nathan was about to run up the steps and help when I saw Trey, who was behind the girl, grab hold of her waist and steady her. Somehow the group made it to the dock, giggling all the while. I took a quick glance up toward the bluff, where the wives were lined up in the front, fanning themselves and fuming. I couldn't help but laugh.

The mood immediately changed and everyone grew silent as the band began playing Wagner's bridal march. I was so nervous that my knees began to shake.

And then the moment came. I glanced up toward the top step, and there she was. There was Aubrey coming toward me. I know every groom has said this, but she was the most beautiful bride I'd ever seen. She looked stunning in a white gown with a low, plunging neckline and a long slit to show off her leg. (I helped her pick out the dress.) Her long auburn hair curls fell across her shoulder and her chest. She looked like an angel.

As the music rose to a crescendo, a proud Mr. Reese walked Aubrey down the steps and onto the dock where it had all begun. As she approached the platform, I glanced at the post where many years ago we had carved a heart along with our initials. We had to have only been fourteen or fifteen years old. After what seemed like a lifetime of being away from her, our lifetime together could now start.

Mr. Reese brought Aubrey to my side and placed her hand in mine. He had tears running down his face as he leaned toward me. "Son, please take care of her," he said.

That's when I let go, and I could feel my own tears cascading down my cheeks. What I told him then came straight from my heart. "I've loved her since the day we met and will spend the rest of my life showing her how much. I will always take good care of her."

Mr. Reese gave me a big hug and stepped back to join Aubrey's mother. It was time to get to the business of taking myself a wife.

The preacher smiled at me and Aubrey, then looked up toward the guests. "I've been waiting a long time for this day," he said. "I can remember the first time Aubrey brought Colby to church and I had the pleasure of meeting this fine young man." He placed his hand on my shoulder. "Through Sunday school, prayer meetings, and Sunday-afternoon suppers, I've had plenty of opportunities to spend time with these two and watch them fall in love. If two people were ever meant to be together, it's the two of them. I guess God works in his own time and figured that time was now. I'm honored that Aubrey and Colby asked me to officiate what will be my last and most anticipated wedding. Now, if I may ask, will you please bow your heads?"

We all bowed our heads and hearts.

"God almighty, through this union you have answered a prayer that many of us have prayed for many years. I feel blessed to have been chosen to bring this couple together by your grace and through your love. Please bless them and watch over them. They are very special. I also know that Robert Cameron is in Heaven, smiling down upon us on this momentous day."

I looked over at Aubrey, and tears were rolling down her cheeks. It was a joyous, emotional occasion, and everyone seemed to be sniffling. My bride and I said our vows, repeating the preacher's words. Then we finally said, "I do." I kissed my wife with a passion that had been building for more than thirty years, and the whole world seemed to stop. For a brief second, my mind went back to that exact spot where we'd had our first kiss as teenagers. I snatched her up with the energy of a sixteen-year-old and carried her up the steps.

We spent the next thirty minutes taking pictures and then we had our first dance. The song was "The First Time Ever I Saw Your Face" by Roberta Flack. She sang about finding someone and loving them until the end of time. Well, I was going to do just that, and then when time was over, I planned to keep on loving Aubrey.

After the traditional dances with the parents of the bride and groom, it didn't take long for things to heat up. The band played a few songs for the old crowd and then it was time for them let loose. The dance floor came alive with the aid of the liquid courage being poured at the bar. Aubrey and I danced some, but mostly sat back and laughed at our friends. The pinnacle of the entertainment was watching William and Alan dancing together and trying to sing "Whiskey River" by Willie Nelson. I made sure someone got a video of the dance—or whatever one might call it.

About an hour into the reception, Nathan walked over, kissed the bride, and gave me a handshake and a hug. He said he'd gotten a phone call and had to leave a little early. I asked if everything was okay, and he replied with a smile, "Oh, of course it is." I sensed that it wasn't, but this was Nathan, so who knew?

Around midnight the party was breaking up, but only because the band had to go. A few of the guys, not wanting the night to be over, offered money for them to stay, but it was late and everyone had a long drive back to civilization.

Someone had the idea to move the party to the clubhouse on the hunting property. That suited Mrs. Reese just fine. She didn't want all the drunks laid up in her house. The clubhouse was just a few miles down a dirt road that connected with the driveway and was big enough for the crowd to stay the night. The guys and girls loaded up a few coolers of beer and wine and headed to the clubhouse. I could hear them hollering all the way down the road.

Before they left, I heard William loudly whispering to Kyle that he had the number of one of the girls from the bar. The wives had already left, so anything could happen. If William wasn't careful, I thought, he might be staring down the barrel of wife number three and not live long enough to make it to number four!

As for me and my bride, we were headed back to the farm. I had a special little surprise, and it was going to be quite a night.

Chapter Four

I woke up before Aubrey and took a few minutes to watch her sleep. The morning light revealed her smooth, lean profile, and I could not resist the urge to run my hand over the length of her hip and into the slender curve of her body. She began to stir and her breathing became heavy. With my mind still on the long night of pleasure we'd enjoyed the night before, I slid up next to her, wanting more of that. I kissed her softly on her parted lips and she opened her eyes at last.

"You can't be serious," she said.

I knew where that was going and eased away with a guilty look.

"Oh, Colby, I would love to," she said, "but I think you broke it. I don't think I can move! Go get me some ice!" She playfully shoved me out of bed and pointed to the kitchen.

I got up and did a victory strut across the room with a big smile on my face. When I came back with the ice pack, she put it on her head.

"Too much wine last night and it's all your fault!" she said. "And by the way, don't be acting like a big shot. I saw Dr. Howell slip you something last night and slap you on the back. If I had to guess, I would say it was a small blue pill." She grinned.

I'd been caught. He gave me several for the honeymoon and instructed me to take only half a pill at one time. But I'd decided that, since it was my wedding night, I would take the whole thing. As a result of that decision, it had been quite a night.

I left Aubrey with the ice pack and headed to the bathroom for a shower. I extended an invitation for her to join me, but I got no reply.

After a long shower, I ran my new bride a hot bath and squeezed in a little bit from each one of the bottles she'd lined up on the tub. I'm not sure what was in them, but it created the bubbles I was looking for. I lit a few candles she had placed around the room and turned on the radio. She loved the big-band sound from the 1950s, so I was not surprised to hear the sound of the Glenn Miller Orchestra coming through the speakers. I had to chuckle when I realized which song they were playing. It was "In the Mood."

Wearing just a towel, I danced back to the bed and scooped her up. She gave me a look and said, "You don't give up."

I carried my bride to the bathroom and gently put her down on the side of the tub. She looked around the room and rewarded me with a smile. I gave her a stately bow and left her in the care of Glenn Miller and his boys.

While Aubrey enjoyed her bath, which I hoped was repairing what was broken, I warmed some croissants and made a pot of coffee. I took them to the front porch and eased into a cane-bottomed rocking chair that had sat in the same spot as long as I could remember. The armrest had dark oil stains from years of therapeutic rocking.

Gazing at the front yard, I sipped the strong, black coffee and noticed the newly planted trees that still had the yellow tags they'd put on at the nursery. We'd lost a lot of old ones the year before when an explosion rocked the place. Yes, the chase to stop a group of madmen had been an ordeal.

It had barely been a year since Aubrey and I had spent our first night here together, looking for a place to hide from the pursuing terrorist. Of course, the circumstances then were wildly different. You could say that both our stays had been explosive, but I much preferred the fireworks in the bedroom from the night before.

Hearing the sound of paws and claws on the porch, I turned to see Hannah and Savannah, and I had no doubt about what it was they were after. Whining and working me with their best pitiful expressions, they were determined to beat me out of a croissant. They stopped begging when they heard the front door open. Upon seeing Aubrey, they began to wag their tails.

She was dressed in a colorful, very thin sundress, and I could feel the other half of that blue pill begin to take effect. I knew I had better get rid of those thoughts for now. Of course, the dogs ran to her, and she reached down and scratched their ears. They loved her. As for me, I was just a source for food.

She sat down in the rocking chair next to me and took the cup of coffee that I'd poured her. She added all the stuff that made it no longer taste like coffee. We rocked while the dogs wagged their tails.

After a minute or so, she took my hand and said, "I really love this place. I know I'll never forget all the things that happened here, but that's not such a bad thing. If it weren't for that, we might not be here now, and that would be the tragedy."

I knew she was right, and it warmed my heart to hear her say it. I squeezed her hand and asked, "Mrs. Cameron, may I offer up a toast on this first day of our marriage?" I held my cup in the air.

"Yes, Mr. Cameron, you may," she said, raising hers.

I smiled. "May our hearts always be filled with passion and joy. May we always trust each other and never let the sun set without expressing our gratitude and love."

With a touch of our coffee mugs, we both softly said, "Cheers."

—

We spent the rest of the day relaxing and catching up on much needed rest. Late in the afternoon, we took a leisurely walk with the dogs. We started down the Jeep trail, a trail my dad had cleared and named many years before, just wide enough for his old CJ-5 to fit through.

On the way to the pond, we passed an old homeplace from the early 1800s. The only visible remains were crumbled piles of brick and an old hand-dug well. To keep anyone from falling in, Dad had placed several runs of bob wire around the twenty-foot hole. As a kid (and an adult), I'd thought many times about tying a long rope to a nearby tree and rappelling to the dry bottom. I'd imagined all sorts of treasures and secrets and could almost hear the excited sound of the metal detector as it moved across some lost pieces of Confederate gold.

Scattered on the ground near the remains of the house were broken pieces of featheredged pottery. I would hold them in my hand and imagine people eating their supper by candlelight almost two hundred years before. I thought about how different the conversations must have sounded and about how isolated from society the people must have been with no electricity, phones, or TV. Back then, people were closer, I supposed, because they had no choice but to personally engage and communicate. You couldn't text your way out of a disagreement. You had to take a walk and work things out.

With the dogs well ahead of us, we arrived at the pond, removed a couple of deck cushions from a storage box, and laid them on the dock. Lying on our backs with our faces pointing west, we watched as the sun cast heavenly colors on the water and dipped below the tall pines. We could barely hear the muffled barks of Hannah and Savannah as they furiously worked to dig something from a hole beneath an old sycamore stump. We didn't talk much, just held hands and enjoyed the peaceful surroundings. For the moment, everyone was content. We stayed on the dock until the mosquitoes signaled that it was time to go home.

Hot and sticky from our walk back, I began shedding my clothes for a dip in the pool. I extended an invitation for my new bride to join me, but she headed straight for the house. After the chemical-fueled wedding-night extravaganza, it appeared that for now she wanted nothing more to do with me without my clothes on. The dogs were also feeling the heat of the summer and crawled underneath the porch, retreating to holes they had dug in the cool sand. We would not see them again until the following morning.

I swam a few lonely laps and observed the soft glow of twilight transitioning into dusk. It was that magical time of evening when the night seems to come alive. On cue, the cicadas, which had emerged after seventeen years of living dormant underground, joined in with the frogs for their nightly serenade in two-part harmony. I never tired of listening to the sounds of nature. A couple of minutes into their concert, I heard the back door open and looked up to see Aubrey standing in the doorway.

"Supper's ready," she called out. "Put some clothes on that thing and come inside."

I laughed, thinking that my *thing* must not have done too badly, being singled out like that. I grabbed a towel from the back of a lounge chair, wrapped it around my waist, and headed on inside.

Aubrey wasn't in the kitchen, nor was the table set for supper. Walking back to the bedroom, I found her lying in the bed.

Shadows from the flickering candles she'd placed around the room danced across the walls, giving the space an alluring and intimate appeal. Aubrey was leaning against the headboard with her long legs stretched out as if in invitation. She was wearing nothing but a seductive smile. On the bedside table was a tray with cheeses, fruit, and a bottle of white wine. She had already poured herself a glass, and she sipped it slowly as she watched me take in the scene.

"Are you ready for a little nourishment?" she asked, giving me a smile and a wink.

"Is that offer for me or my thing?" I asked, easing onto the bed.

"Both, if you play your cards right." She closed her eyes and, arching her back, leaned further back into the pillows. I knew what cards she wanted me to play, and I got busy dealing.

It didn't take long before she was flush with pleasure. What little wisdom I possessed said this would be a great opportunity to show a little constraint, despite how much I would have loved to escalate our fun. A little discretion might later pay off in spades, I thought.

Knowing we had big day ahead, I kissed my bride on the cheek and reached for the light switch to draw the curtains on our perfect day. Early the next morning, after checking the weather forecast and finalizing my flight plan, we were heading to the Washington County airport, loading up my new airplane and officially starting our honeymoon with a trip to Grand Cayman Island.

CHAPTER FIVE

Nathan

Nathan left the reception feeling a wide range of emotions. He was honored to have been a part of the joining together of two people he loved—although *love* was a world he seldom used, especially for people. Maybe it was an occupational hazard from dealing with people he could never trust, maybe something deeper from his childhood, but by his own design, Nathan had few close friends. That had changed with Aubrey and Colby. With everything the three of them had been through, they'd built a bond of trust and faith, which is the foundation of love.

Also on his mind was a phone call he'd received at the reception. It was from someone who meant as much to him as Aubrey and Colby did, and it had brought some sad and disturbing news.

Needing time to think things through, he decided to take the country roads back to his home in Madison. The warm and humid heat of the day had given way to cooler, refreshing temperatures as the evening hours came. He rolled down his windows as he left the Reeses' driveway and turned west on Highway 16. A waning crescent moon left just enough darkness to showcase the sky full of stars. The rise and fall of the Middle Georgia landscape reminded him how different it was from the sandy lowlands of South Florida.

Nathan Roark had been born in the orange-grove town of Vero Beach, Florida, in 1944 and unfortunately would be raised solely by his mom. He would never know his dad, Major William Roark, one of the last casualties of World War Two.

On May 7, 1945, Major Roark and his platoon had been involved in an ambush by a German battalion just a few miles across the Czechoslovakian border. While patrolling a road that was heavily wooded, his unit was attacked by mortar and small-arms fire from enemy troops in a concealed position. He and his fellow soldiers jumped into a ditch and returned fire. The fight went on for about an hour until a radio operator reported a cease-fire.

The order, however, came too late for Nathan's dad, who was giving chest compressions to a fallen soldier. The movement drew the attention of the German soldiers. Apparently, the Germans had not heard news of the cease-fire or they didn't care. Major Roark lost his life a mere nine minutes after the cease-fire had been ordered and six hours before Germany's unconditional surrender.

As Nathan grew older, he became more troubled by the fateful end of his father's final battle. He would lie in bed many nights playing the scene over in his mind. Sometimes in a dream, his father would make it back. Nathan never found a resolution to his dad's death and in his sophomore year at the University of Florida, he made a decision that he hoped would put his mind to rest. He realized he needed to experience a war.

With no notice to his friends, his family, or his girlfriend, he enlisted in the army. Right away he showed a knack for military protocol, and he did very well in basic and advanced infantry training. He applied and was accepted into officer candidates school, which was followed by airborne and Special Forces training. Upon graduation in 1968, he was commissioned as a second lieutenant and was assigned to a Special Forces unit in Viet Nam.

In the spring of 1969, Nathan almost didn't make it home. He was stationed in a Special Forces compound in Khe Sanh, located just a few miles from the demilitarized zone and the Laotian border. In the early hours of an April morning, during a violent thunderstorm, the compound was suddenly overrun by the North Vietnamese.

With no time for backup forces to attempt a rescue, his platoon fled to the perimeter of the base. Lieutenant Roark led them through the North-Vietnamese-infested jungle, taking on heavy enemy fire. Knowing they were greatly out-numbered and that returning fire would just mark their position, he told his men to hold their fire and to stay low and silent.

Nathan led the men as they crawled through the willows. His goal was to reach a flooded rice field where he could call in an air strike. Every time a bolt of lightning flashed, he could see the enemy searching for them, sometimes just a few feet away.

Against all odds, he managed to lead most of the platoon to safety. He received the Distinguished Silver Cross for his brave and courageous actions.

Surviving Viet Nam, he made peace with the past. He came to realize that the battlefield was the backdrop to a dynamic set of circumstances that changed by the second. Men were as prone to fate in the midst of war as they were in other aspects of their lives. Someone had to die and someone had to live. He felt he had the answers to the questions that bothered him about his father's death and was ready to move forward with his life.

Back home, his first course of action was to propose to and marry his childhood sweetheart. He and Laura had been "dating" since the fourth grade and he finally sealed the deal. They moved to Gainesville, where he re-enrolled at the University of Florida and received an undergraduate degree in economics and a master's in agricultural economics. While at UF, he joined the reserves of a Special Forces unit, in which he was promoted to the rank of captain.

Just after graduation, he prepared to distribute his impressive CV to prospective employers—but one found him first. It seems his military and academic accomplishments had attracted the attention of his soon-to-be employer—none other than the CIA. His first assignment was in Haiti, a place that he just so happened to know a bit about. His thesis had compared the effects of politics, culture, and economic development in Haiti, the Dominican Republic, Cuba, and Jamaica.

Despite its corruption and poverty, he and Laura quickly fell in love with the troubled island nation. They were there until 1980, when Nathan no longer agreed with his government's economic plans for Haiti and the other Caribbean nations. They moved back to the States, where Nathan enjoyed a successful career in the private sector, but just for a few years.

In 1986, the political situation in Haiti imploded and was ripe for revolution. The CIA, not having anyone in Haiti with the knowledge and skills that Nathan had, convinced him to return for a temporary assignment. His expertise was needed to engineer the departure of Haiti's President, Jean-Claude Duvalier, also known as "Baby Doc." His clandestine and political skills were also valuable in aiding in Duvalier's exile to France.

After a successful mission, Nathan's clout at the CIA headquarters in Langley grew immensely and they had big plans for him, but he respectfully turned them down. He didn't mind stepping in to help every now and then when his expertise was needed, but he wasn't interested in a full-time job with the agency. That would mean being gone for long stretches at a time, and after talking it over with Laura, he decided to return to his land development company in Florida.

He would return to Haiti in 1994 as part of an advance team to reinstate President Jean-Bertrand Aristide and then in 2004 to get rid of him. His last assignment was during the aftermath of the 2010 earthquake. It was then that he would become reacquainted with Jeanne-Marie Lamartiniere, also known as Marti—and his beloved goddaughter. She was the reason he was now taking the long way home.

—

Nathan met Charles Lamartiniere, Marti's dad, in the spring of 1974 when they both hailed the same *taxi rouge*, which was basically a beat-up car with a red scarf tied around the rearview mirror. He and Nathan shared the taxi and after a few minutes of conversation began to form a bond that would last for years.

Charles was from one of the oldest and wealthiest families on the island. His grandfather was a German engineer who had been hired as a contractor in the late nineteenth century to help design and build the island's water system. What was to only be a year in Haiti turned into a lifetime when he met Charles's grandmother. They had three children, with the oldest girl being Charles's mom. She met Charles's French father while spending a summer in Paris.

Charles had just graduated from Yale and in the fall was headed to Paris to complete his master's at his dad's alma mater, the Sorbonne. Over that summer, he spent many days and evenings with Nathan and Laura, introducing them to places around Port-au-Prince and

Petionville that were normally off limits to foreigners. Charles and Nathan would drink rum and have long debates regarding the future of Haiti; its coexistence with the Dominican Republic, its contentious neighbor to the east; and Communism in the Caribbean. Nathan always felt that Charles suspected he was more than an agricultural and economic attaché, but he never inquired, probably not wanting to know.

Charles later returned to Haiti after his time in school in Paris, but like his mother, he did not return alone. At the Sorbonne, he'd met Madeline, the girl who would become his wife.

In 1984, Nathan and Laura returned to Haiti for a short economic development assignment for the US Agency for International Development. There they found Charles deeply entrenched in Haiti's private and political societies. The two men picked up with their previous relationship as if they had never been separated. As in the old days, they spent hours drinking rum, arguing, and debating everything from politics to the best way to grow oranges.

Laura and Madeline spent their time preparing for a new arrival. Charles and Madeline were expecting their first child.

After the baby girl was born, the couple asked Nathan to serve as Jeanne-Marie's godfather. It was an honor he accepted and pledged to uphold.

Now the time had come to make good on that pledge. Charles had called him, very upset, to deliver the news that Marti was missing and presumably had drowned. There was apparently more to the situation that led Charles to believe it was not an accident. But he was at a loss over what to do—or who to trust. It was the first time in his life he'd felt so helpless, he told Nathan. With Nathan's background and the resources that he had in Haiti, could Nathan come and help?

Nathan told Charles that he'd be on the first flight out of Atlanta and instructed him not to talk to anyone until he got there.

—

Almost back to Madison and anxious to take his mind off Marti, Nathan reflected on how he and Laura had chosen Georgia as the place where they'd retire. Like many residents of Madison, they had landed in the place they now called home because of a serendipitous event.

Driving home to Florida from his last company function in DC, they had decided to make a detour through Atlanta. Laura had attended Emory University there in the 1970s and wanted to visit a few friends. So she made a few phone calls and was able to line up several of them for dinner. They agreed to meet at a restaurant in the Emory Village shopping district, and she was excited, but she never made it. About an hour east of Atlanta, something happened that would change the course of the couple's future.

Nathan, known for being overly thrifty, had resisted Laura's repeated requests for a new car one day longer than he should have. Their fifteen-year-old Oldsmobile started choking out a death cough about three miles west of the Oconee River bridge and then began spewing blue smoke, barely hanging on. Nathan turned on the flashers and pulled the car to the emergency lane, hoping it would limp to the next exit.

Just as they were closing in on exit 114, a connecting rod from somewhere deep inside the engine decided it no longer wanted to be connected and flung itself through the side of the engine block. Burnt oil seeped from the hole, filling the air with black smoke. He coasted as far up the ramp as the car would take him, then pulled off to the side.

Laura simply glared. He'd barely had time to tell her she'd been right about needing a new car when a tow truck pulled up behind them. Nathan watched in his mirror as the driver approached the car. Lowering his window in defeat, Nathan greeted him and explained their situation.

It turned out that the driver was returning from a job in the nearby town of Greensboro, and he offered to tow their newly departed Oldsmobile for a fee of a hundred dollars. Nathan wanted to negotiate the price, but he could feel Laura's icy stare and accepted the offer. He asked the driver if he could store the car at the towing company lot until he decided what to do. He also asked if the town had any car dealerships and decent places to stay.

With all the questions answered, the driver loaded up the car and headed into town. He dropped the stranded couple at the newly built James Madison Inn, a Greek Revival reproduction built to compliment Madison's antebellum homes. It was situated in front of an in-town park that had manicured green lawns, stately old trees with spreading limbs that provided shade to a row of picnic tables, and a large covered pavilion. The place made Nathan feel like he'd gone back in time.

They happened to have arrived just in time for the annual June Downtown Dance, and the park was festive and alive. Lights had been strung on the pavilion, and a band was playing beach music while a crowd danced in front of the stage. Laura immediately pointed out to Nathan that it was The Tams, a band they had heard many times over the years at beach dances and festivals.

"Maybe we could go dance a little bit later?" she asked, wrapping her arm in his, forgetting she was mad.

Nathan had never been too keen on dancing and quickly moved them inside to check in at the counter. "Possibly later," he said.

Opening the door to their room on the second floor of the inn, they were pleased to find it was a suite with a balcony that overlooked the park. They ordered supper and a bottle of wine and spent the evening on the balcony enjoying the music and excitement. Laura suggested they go down to the park and watch the band, but Nathan told her no, knowing her motive was to get him in front of a bunch of people he didn't know and make him dance.

After a few songs and a couple of glasses of chilled Chardonnay, they were standing on the balcony when Laura slipped her arms around him and began to sway to the music. He knew that she was thinking of the first days of their marriage, the parties they'd have on the beach, the dancing, and the music. Nathan knew she wanted to dance and after the episode with the car, he knew it was time.

They moved the chairs and table to the side of the balcony and made a small dance floor. Laura was smiling as the band began playing "Hey, Hey Baby," one of her favorites. For the next hour, they danced, laughed, and drank more wine.

The last song of the evening was "Be Young, Be Foolish, Be Happy." Nathan looked at Laura and said, "Why not?" He led her back into the room, and it would be a night to remember. Although they didn't know it yet, the magic that was Madison had begun to lure them in.

Early the next morning, Nathan sat at the desk in the room and began preparing notes, eager to measure his negotiating skills against those of the local car dealers. He'd studied the dealers' websites and warned Laura that it might take a day or two to get the deal done. She'd been hoping for a car, but Nathan had made his case with a thirty-minute speech about the merits of the Ford F-150 truck. Both of them understood they would probably be riding back to Florida in a truck. Nathan had made a career of communicating ideas and carefully cultivating them into reality; this time would be no different. Laura always joked that Nathan had sold her on the idea of marriage. She was still waiting, she teased, for that idea to pay off.

From an advertisement he had seen on the internet, he had set his sights on a dealership a few miles up the road in Covington. In the ad, the dealer was pictured mounted on a bull, dressed up like a cowboy and vowing to ride that bull across the parking lot if he could not get you the best deal in town. Nathan told Laura that was something he had to see and that he probably would not be back until early afternoon.

She told him to stay off of the bull and not to be late for supper. Nathan borrowed the inn's courtesy car and took off toward Covington.

Later that evening when Nathan returned, he asked about her day before telling her they were the owners of a new Ford F-150. (Although she probably could guess as much because of the silly five-gallon hat he had on his head.)

She told him she had taken a leisurely walk around Madison and been delighted by the beauty of the historic town. The park where the concert had been the night before was just as beautiful by day, with camellias in full bloom. She then had strolled along Main Street and been greeted with a smile from everyone she met. Unlike most cities, which were marked by hustle and hurry, Madison and its people seemed to enjoy a calm and comfortable rhythm, one that she was ready for herself. She confessed that she was quickly falling for the charms of the small southern town.

Nathan found himself charmed as well, not by the town as much as by the way his wife was almost giddy. When had he last seen that giggly exuberance that lit up her tired eyes? It hadn't been an easy life, living with a husband who'd sometimes disappear on secretive—and not so safe—adventures.

After her walk, she said, she stopped in the hotel lobby to look at a few brochures, and there she met Colette, the owner of the inn.

Colette invited her to the parlor for a cup of coffee, and within minutes, they found many things in common and became fast friends. She also invited Laura to lunch and afterward, gave her a tour of the numerous antique shops, museums, and art galleries. Laura met several of Colette's friends and by early afternoon, was fully taken by the town.

Things had changed over the last few years in Pembroke Pines, where they now lived, and she expressed to Nathan that it might be time for them to make a change as well. She said her last stop of the afternoon had been to see a local real estate agent. While Nathan was making a deal on a truck, she was making a deal on a house.

The next day they took their shiny new Ford F-150 to meet the agent at a house just south of town. Nathan was sporting his brand new cowboy hat when they drove up to a white house with a big front porch. Confederate jasmine was in full bloom, intertwined between the railings on the porch. It gave the house a warm, inviting feel. While walking through the home, Nathan watched his wife. Laura beamed with joy, and Nathan knew there was a good chance that Madison would soon be their new home.

After the tour, Laura uncharacteristically pulled Nathan aside and wanted to make an offer. He quickly looked at the numbers and said with a smile, "Why not? If you're happy, I'm happy. Let's buy a house."

She kissed him and gave a nod to the agent across the room. Madison had them! Within a few short months, they'd sold their house in South Florida and were comfortably settled in Madison.

Nathan loved to see his wife so content. The slower-paced life and wonderful set of new friends were exactly what she wanted, and she was happy now—with one exception. She wanted Nathan to retire completely. He had already retired from his CEO position and sold his part of his land development company, but it was the other job she was ready for him to quit. After the events of the previous year with Aubrey and Colby, she didn't think her nerves or patience could handle any more, and she let him know that in no uncertain terms. She had spent most of their life worrying about his extracurricular job, wondering if he would return home safely, or even return at all. The fact that he had to keep the details secret made it even worse.

Nathan knew it was time as well, but the urgent phone call had suddenly postponed any thoughts of retirement. Thinking about Marti, he realized he had not seen her since the earthquake in 2010, and then the contact had been brief. He had been in Haiti to help after the disaster and she had been passing through Port-au-Prince, focused on her organization's efforts to bring aid to the rural areas. They sat in the ruins of an old church and had a quick cup of coffee. He told her that she should come to Madison for a visit after things calmed down, and she happily accepted. They hugged goodbye, and he now regretted not following through on that invitation.

He thought back to her eleventh birthday, when the Lamartinieres had come to Pembroke Pines for a visit. She had been so excited about her first trip to the States and just plain ecstatic when she got the opportunity to go to Disney World. It was hard to believe that little girl, who'd insisted on wearing her Minnie Mouse outfit night and day, had grown into a smart, responsible, beautiful woman who now carried the weight of the impoverished and disadvantaged people of Haiti on her shoulders.

He had no idea what had transpired in Haiti and wouldn't know until he arrived.

If it was, in fact, a drowning, he would only need to have with him a dark suit, handkerchiefs, and a lot of love and compassion for his dear friends Charles and Madeline. If it was something else, he would probably need his professional bag that contained his weapons and technical devices. Too bad that wouldn't be an option.

In order to bring them, he would have to officially register his equipment at the airport and inform his company, who would alert the Haitian government. As he well knew, Haiti was replete with corruption, making it impossible to arrive unnoticed. They would know before he landed. His best choice was to travel as a civilian and worry about weapons after he found out more from Charles.

Thinking about the trip, he felt slightly nervous, which almost never happened to Nathan. He could be facing an unknown situation in a country where he had no backup or resources. The protocol was to always work as a team, but his instincts told him he had to take this one on alone.

The night air became a little cooler when he realized he could possibly be facing a different kind of retirement than the one he had planned—the kind that came with a casket instead of couch. He rolled up the window for the rest of the drive home. The following day, Nathan would be on an airplane bound for Haiti. Laura had at least one more trip to worry about.

CHAPTER SIX

Colby

W aking up on the morning of a flight, the first order of business for a pilot is to check the weather. I don't mean pulling it up on the computer; I mean taking a walk outside and looking up. Today I didn't have to look higher than the tops of the pines to see that the weather people had been wrong. An accumulation of thick fog hung in the limbs as a light mist filled the air.

How could the weather service so consistently blow it with the forecast? They had called for sunny weather over the next three days. There had even been an icon with a big orange ball on the weather report the day before.

I immediately found my cell phone and pulled up the weather. Sure enough, it had been changed to morning fog and light rain. Someone had probably made the change when the weatherman turned on his windshield wipers on the way to work. I had last checked it at midnight, and everything had looked fine then.

The current forecast was for a layer of fog reaching up to fifteen hundred feet. You'd have to get above that point to find that big orange ball. As in most cases, the fog would burn off by noon, and the day would turn clear and sunny. But with our tightly coordinated schedule, we needed to take off by eight thirty or delay the flight until the next day. Our flight plan had us departing that morning from Sandersville, a small town in Middle Georgia, and arriving in Key West at noon. Due to our customs appointment in Grand Cayman and possible late-afternoon thunderstorms in the Caribbean, we had a tight time frame and needed to leave Key West no later than one thirty. It was currently seven and we had to be wheels-up by eight thirty. It was time to make a decision.

I had two options: cancel the flight and reschedule it for the following morning when the weather might be better, or take off in the fog and hope for the best. After a couple of minutes, we'd break through the fog and the cloud layer, and it would be clear skies all ahead.

The problem would be … well, if we had a problem. If, for some reason, we needed to turn back, it would be impossible to find the runway in the fog. I had taken off in zero visibility before, but never with such precious cargo.

We decided to go to the airport and see if the conditions might improve by the time we had to leave.

I loaded the luggage in the truck, and we hugged the dogs and said goodbye. Not wanting us to leave without them, Hannah and Savannah jumped into the back seat. When I yelled at them to get out, they whined and refused to budge. This was not like them. A ride in the truck usually meant a trip to the vet for shots, and they both hated that. If they knew my friend Andy, who always gives them way too many treats, would be taking care of them, they would not have protested—unless they knew something we didn't know.

I could see the concern on Aubrey's face. I knew what she was thinking. Was this some kind of sign? I didn't say it, but I was wondering as well.

Sniffing a bag of venison jerky in the front console, they climbed up in the front and turned their attention from us to the food. When I tossed the jerky on the grass, they leapt out of the truck, their protest seemingly forgotten. Food always solved their worries, and hopefully, a little fog burn-off would solve ours.

As we pulled into the airport, the fog was heavy on the windshield. Things would have to greatly improve if we had any chance of leaving in the next hour. I drove the short distance to my hangar and parked the truck around back and out of view. Anyone seeing a vehicle parked in front of a hangar for more than a day would know the pilot was away, and that could be bad news. A few months earlier, a hangar belonging to a traveling pilot had been broken into and vandalized.

My own hangar held the new Cessna 310 and my prized Cessna 182P, and I'd done everything I could to keep them safe. But multiple door locks, alarms, and security cameras would have to be enough since the airport manager balked at the idea of wiring up a few pyrotechnic discouragements around the perimeter of my space.

Closing in on eight o'clock, I could see a slight break in the sky and, according to my weather app, things were beginning to clear to the south. I called flight service and the news was good based on reports from other airports in our path. If we had an emergency after takeoff, we stood a good chance of finding somewhere to land with the visibility I'd need.

Aubrey was not quite as enthusiastic about the weather outlook. I tried to explain that the new airplane had two engines, which doubled our chances of survival, but that didn't do much to impress her.

Nevertheless, while we were talking, the fog continued to burn off, opening up a partially blue sky for a safe departure.

With our luggage loaded in the Cessna 310, I did a pre-flight check and pushed the plane out of the hangar. I'd always wanted a twin-engine airplane, and after years of waiting, I finally had one. We had received a sizeable reward from the FBI for our part in the previous year's adventure, and my part was enough to buy the airplane.

I had yet to take the 310 on a long flight, and our honeymoon would be my first opportunity. After reviewing a long list of options for our trip, we had chosen the Grand Caymans for their wonderful reefs and caverns for diving and snorkeling. One of the most famous attractions is a wall dive that slowly descends to about eighty feet and then drops straight down another ten thousand. We both had our basic diving certifications and we each needed a deep dive (of more than a hundred feet) to complete our advanced training. The wall would be a perfect place to check that off our list.

—

The winds were favoring the northwest runway, so we lined up on runway thirty-one and prepared for takeoff. I did a quick scan of the navigation and engine monitoring systems, and everything checked out. As I added power, I gave Aubrey a reassuring smile. The most dangerous aspect of flying is the takeoff. The airplane is at high power, low airspeed, and low altitude. If the engine were to fail, the results could be catastrophic, especially in conditions with low visibility.

As we gained speed traveling down the foggy five-thousand-foot runway, I said a little prayer, as I always did. With my right hand full forward on the dual throttles, I eased the yoke back at 70 knots, and at 83 knots the 310 steadily lifted off the runway. I held it just above the runway to gain airspeed before climbing through the fog at a thousand feet per minute. As soon as the runway was behind us, I retracted the gear and set the throttle and props to their appropriate settings. Within a minute, we were clear of the fog and flying in sunny skies.

Technically, I should have filed a flight plan, as is the rule for any flight that might take you off a path that's always visible and clear of clouds. But I felt the risks were miniscule in not alerting the controllers of my plans. After all, I'd be in the clouds for less than a minute, and I was taking off from an uncontrolled airfield where there was not another airplane for miles.

Of course, if anything had happened, the first thing the news anchors would report was that the pilot "had not filed a flight plan." It would not have mattered if a wing or engine had fallen off. The cause of the accident would have been the failure of the negligent pilot to file a flight plan.

With three GPSs on board and a full array of maps, we didn't need navigation assistance, but it was always a good idea to contact Air Traffic Control and ask for flight following. They could inform us of any aircraft in our path. It was always nice to have an extra set of eyes.

With the cruise checklist complete, the route activated on the GPS, and the autopilot engaged, there was nothing to do but sit back and monitor the flight. Our route would take us over Southeast Georgia and down the center of Florida. The jumping-off spot for the Caymans was Key West, and if everything went according to plan, we would arrive by noon. With everything else complete, the last item on my checklist was to reach over and squeeze Aubrey's hand and give her another reassuring smile.

The trip took us just over three hours and was uneventful. I made a few offers to induct my bride into the mile-high club, but she turned me down each time. I would never admit it, but I hadn't joined the club either. I was never comfortable with the idea of taking my attention away from the controls. I always pictured FAA investigators finding nude bodies in the wreckage. I'd forever be the irresponsible pilot that they talked about in safety seminars.

Instead, Aubrey and I enjoyed the beauty of the meandering rivers as they carved their way to the coast and to the amazing expanse of the Florida Everglades.

About thirty minutes out, the Miami center informed us to begin our descent into Key West International Airport. With the airport in sight, I disengaged the autopilot and lowered the landing gear.

Aubrey jumped when the landing gear extended from the doors. "What was that?" she yelled.

I tried not to laugh, but I couldn't help it. Over the headset, I told her not to worry, that everything was fine.

While the airplane was being refueled, Aubrey and I made our way to the airport café. As we were dining, we could see towering cumulus-cloud formations building over the ocean. The worry started up again, rising in my chest. Flying across the Caribbean and Cuba was, for me, uncharted territory, and the last thing that we needed was the threat of thunderstorms.

As we were finishing lunch, which consisted of dry, over-toasted club sandwiches, we heard a loud bang near the front of the café. Jerking around toward the noise, we instinctively dived onto the floor. Before the previous year's ordeal, we wouldn't have reacted so dramatically, but being shot at multiple times by a bunch of terrorists will change one's perspective.

It turned out that it was not a terrorist storming in with a gun, but an actual storm. In the short time we'd been in the café, a thunderstorm had moved further inland from the coast. The high winds had blown the door open and slammed it against the wall.

Aubrey gave me an alarmed look, and I returned it. In the world of non-aviators, it was just a small squall moving through. In the world of a pilot preparing for his first flight over the ocean, it was quite daunting. As we left the café and walked across the tarmac, I tried not to show concern, but Aubrey knew my every emotion and could easily read my feelings.

She asked the very question I was wrestling with myself. "With the winds like this, can we still make the flight?" she asked.

Just as she spoke, the wind grabbed my lucky cap with the Aircraft Owners and Pilots Association logo, and it went tumbling across the tarmac. I ran for it and temporarily avoided her question. Catching up with the cap, I glanced at the wind sock near the end of the runway. It was sticking straight out, dancing and jumping in all directions— except down the runway.

Wind is generally not an issue if it's blowing in the direction one happens to be flying. If it's gusting and blowing across the runway and tied to thunderstorm activity, it's an issue in any situation. I caught back up with Aubrey and she was waiting for an answer.

"Well, what about the wind?" she asked.

"Did I mention that we had an extra engine?" I joked while tugging my hat on and making sure that it fit tightly.

She didn't find that funny and gave me a push. "I'm serious! Maybe we should wait until later or take one of those," she said, pointing over to the airplanes at the commercial hub.

I certainly did not want to miss the opportunity to fly my own plane to the Caymans, and looking at the sky, I could see that the thunderstorm was passing and clearing to the south. The winds would calm after the storm dissipated.

"Everything's fine, I promise. Look. the thunderstorm is passing," I reassured her, glancing at the sky.

"How do we know another one won't show up?" she asked, still not convinced.

I answered her with confidence and an authoritative tone. "Because, ma'am, the dew point in relation to the temperature is spreading, indicating an increase in barometric pressure and an abatement of moisture, lowering the convective opportunity in the direction of our flight." I had no idea if that was even close to being meteorologically correct, and I tried my hardest to suppress a smile.

She caught me and shook her head. "You're so full of it!" she said.

We crossed the tarmac and made our way back to the Landmark terminal. It was nearing one o'clock, and if we wanted to stay on schedule, we needed to be wheels-up in the next thirty minutes. While Aubrey went to the bathroom, I settled the fuel bill and found the pilots lounge to file my flight plan and manifest on the airport computer.

After filing, I double checked my flight bag for all the documents I'd need to fly over Cuba and land in the Caymans, then I made a quick trip to the bathroom. Walking back to the counter, I found Aubrey sitting on the couch, nervously shaking her leg and flipping through a magazine.

"Ready?" I asked.

She looked up, took a deep breath, and got up from the couch. "I guess," she replied with some hesitation.

I needed to lighten her mood and knew a little foolishness always did the trick. In a loud and dramatic fashion, and with an English accent, I bowed and pointed to the 310 sitting in front of the FBO (Fixed Base Operator). "My lady, your winged chariot and capable captain are at your service and ready for departure," I said. "If you will, please make your way to the aircraft."

This got me the patented headshake and eye roll, which are always good signs. She grabbed her backpack from the table and headed toward the door.

I followed right behind her and gave her a little pinch on her backside for good measure.

She jumped in surprise and turned to swat me.

The staff behind the counter got a good laugh, and I think it helped ease her nerves.

We boarded the airplane and, after securing Aubrey in her seat, I did my pre-flight inspection. Switching on the fuel pumps, I fired up each engine and saw that all the gauges were safely in the green.

Ready to taxi, I contacted ground control. On instructions from the controller, I navigated through the maze of taxiways and made my way to the hold short line for runway twenty-seven. Ground handed us over to the tower, who cleared us for immediate takeoff.

I eased the 310 onto the runway and could feel the wind buffeting over the fuselage and wings, rocking the airplane from side to side. I turned the wings into the crosswind, anticipating the sharp side force of wind that would try to push the airplane sideways as we gained speed down the runway.

I glanced at Aubrey as I was applying the brakes and running up the engines to full power. She was twisting her hands and staring straight ahead. As strong as she was in most situations, flying was her weakness. She had only been up with me a half a dozen times and never seemed very comfortable. I suspected it was her fear of not being in control. Maybe when we got back, I'd suggest she take a few flying lessons.

With the gust and 18-knot crosswind, I wanted as much speed as possible and held the brakes while applying full power to give us a little extra boost. The powerful engine rumbled and vibrated through the cockpit. I released the brakes and we shot down the runway, quickly gained speed, and launched before the halfway marker. With aileron and rudder control, the crosswind turned out to be a non-event. The 310 loved to climb and within seconds was clear of the airfield and heading for an altitude of seventy-five hundred feet.

We were headed to the Caymans! Leveling out, we could already see the white-capped ocean below. Aubrey came out of her frightened trance and leaned forward to check out the view.

No matter how long I flew, I never stopped being amazed that man had figured out how to defy the laws of gravity. I've always felt privileged to be a part of that.

Chapter Seven

Towering white cumulus clouds were building around us, and they were spectacular. The tops billowed out in a dynamic fashion as the currents pushed them from below and made them appear to be alive. My attention was focused, however, on flying over Cuba. I could see the long, narrow island on the horizon and felt a little nervous as we moved into the Cuban airspace.

Miami turned me over to Havana Center and I held my breath. I had purchased a forty-dollar permit from a broker to overfly the country and had my permit number ready. I had filed a flight plan and hoped that everything was in order. The last thing I needed was to be escorted to Havana and forced to land by a couple of Russian MiGs. I had heard that sometimes, even with a permit, the Cuban controllers would turn back aircraft inbound from the States. I was hoping that no one had pissed off any Cuban officials that day.

After a couple of minutes, Havana Center made contact and cleared us to Grand Cayman. I felt immediate relief.

After crossing over Cuba, I could see nothing but water in all directions, and it was a little disconcerting. I'd heard too many stories about pilots having to ditch into the ocean after experiencing serious mechanical problems. It seemed that more times than not, the aircraft would flip upside down after impact, leaving the people inside only seconds to disembark. I had taken every precautionary measure, including bringing life jackets and a life raft and doing a thorough inspection of the aircraft. Hopefully, with all the preparations, we wouldn't be added to the list of planes that never made it across the Caribbean.

Perched on her seat, Aubrey was taking in the spectacular views and seemed to have left her worries on the mainland. "This is awesome," she said with an ear-to-ear grin. "I'm really glad you talked me into this. Can I take this off? Is it allowed?" She pointed to her seat belt.

Again using my best deep captain's voice, I looked at her suggestively. "Ma'am, you're flying on Cameron Airlines, where you can take off anything you want."

"Anything?" she replied in a seductive voice, unbuckling her seatbelt.

I liked where this was going.

"The good captain is here to accommodate your every wish and need," I said with a wink. I was thinking I might reconsider my stance on that mile-high club.

"I'll tell you what, captain," she said. You get me to Grand Cayman safely, and *then* I'll express my appreciation."

I should have known it was too good to be true.

Aubrey pulled her camera from her backpack and started taking pictures. After a few shots of the ocean, clouds, and plane, she eased into my lap.

Again, I got my hopes up, but all she had in mind was a selfie. I smiled, and she leaned in to kiss my cheek as she snapped the picture. I could already see the photo sitting on our mantle in a palm-tree picture frame. A part of me still could not believe I was married to this woman. I glanced at my wedding ring and smiled. I'm not sure if it was her fate or mine that had brought us back together. It was almost as if I'd been given two lives, and the new one had just started. In my first life, I'd let Aubrey go; this time I got her back. I decided that it must have been her fate, not mine, because there was no way I deserved to have this second chance.

She gave me another kiss and went back to her seat. Contented, she pulled out a book and settled in to read.

Not expecting any radio communication for at least the next hour, I tuned in to the Margaritaville station on the satellite radio and heard Jimmy singing about someone who'd gone off to Paris looking for some answers. I'd been to Paris several times and agreed that it was a good place to ask questions and hopefully find some kind of peace. Thinking about the horrible things that had happened to that man in the song, I looked at Aubrey with her book and felt anxiety creep in. What if our love affair ended in tragedy like the one in the song?

It frightened me that our "second chance" might not turn out to be everything I hoped. What if this was just a glimpse of what it might have been, if I'd decided right the first time?

Then I snapped out of it. I realized that I was just indulging in irrational thoughts brought on by my subconscious guilt, but it was disconcerting nonetheless. I took a deep breath and forced myself to shove those bad thoughts aside and focus on the great gift that we'd been given.

Jimmy had moved on from Paris and was singing about trying to convince a group of Jamaicans that he was not the ganja plane when Havana radio made final contact. They advised me to contact Cayman Approach, who welcomed us to their airspace. About thirty minutes out from Georgetown, I could see the island on the horizon and announced to the controller that I had it in sight.

Soon I was lined up for runway twenty-six and we were glancing out the window at a turquoise sea. Several boats hovered near the coral reefs, and from our altitude of a thousand feet, I could watch people swim and snorkel. I couldn't wait to get in that water and explore.

"See the dolphins?" Aubrey said with excitement in her voice. "There are four of them right under us." She pointed out the side window.

I tried to lean over, but they were directly below by then and out of view. I had begun tilting the wing to see further underneath the airplane when a loud buzzer started going off.

"What's that?" Aubrey asked, snapping her head toward me.

With all the warning devices on the airplane, it took a second to identify where the noise was coming from. But seeing the red flashing lights near the landing-gear indicator, I quickly identified the problem. I had forgotten to lower the landing gear and, thankfully, the "idiot light" and the "idiot buzzer" had been there to remind me.

With the runway directly in front of us, I immediately lowered the gear and the buzzer sound was silenced. Another few seconds and it could have been a costly and dangerous mistake.

We landed safely, and I was thrilled to have officially joined the ranks of international pilots. So many of my pilot friends had already flown outside the States, to the Bahamas mostly, and I was now part of the group.

We taxied to a row of brightly colored buildings. The FBO was painted a very loud yellow, and located next to it was an equally bright blue building with a *Customs and Immigration* sign. I shut down the engines and was happy to be on the ground. It had been a long, adventurous day of flying, and I was ready to enjoy the sun and sand.

Aubrey touched me on the shoulder. "I think you've earned your reward," she said with a smile.

A few minutes later, we were at the customs office, where it took just a few minutes to complete the paperwork, which was good news for Aubrey. I noticed that she had her legs twisted up and was doing some kind of weird dance beside the counter.

"What's wrong with you?" I asked, giving her a strange look.

"I've got to pee," she said in a low voice, but not low enough for the man behind the desk not to overhear. He laughed and pointed toward the bathroom down the hall. After a few minutes, she returned and we walked back to the airplane and removed our luggage.

—

Our domicile for the week was to be the Turtle Nest Inn resort. It had been enthusiastically suggested by a few friends and had been rated number one by Trip Advisor. According to the website, it was situated on a secluded beach, miles away from the commercial Seven Mile Beach area. It sounded like the perfect place for our honeymoon. Included in our fee was a car for the week.

So far, everything was great.

While I filled out the paperwork to get our rental car, Aubrey had a thousand questions for the woman behind the counter about where to go and what to do.

By the time I finished, Aubrey and her new Avis friend had our whole week planned and were discussing the best places to eat and shop.

Anxious to get the party moving, I pointed them toward the lot. They never stopped talking as the agent escorted us to a lot full of cars. There were rows of brightly colored convertibles, Jeeps, Lexuses, BMWs, and Mercedes. I had my eye on the Jeeps and it appeared that's where we were headed. We could explore the island with the top off, enjoying the sun and tropic breezes.

Unfortunately, the agent kept on walking and turned a corner toward what I presumed to be the economy lot. She walked up to a Suzuki that was just slightly bigger than my ATV at home, and she handed me the keys.

I'm sure my disappointment showed. I could have put that car in the back of my truck and had room to spare.

Aubrey giggled and said, "You'll sure look cute in that one." I was not amused, but what could I expect from an extra that came with the hotel? I considered upgrading to one of the Jeeps, but we were anxious to get our honeymoon started and decided it might not be that bad. We thanked the agent, raised the back hatch, threw in our luggage, and jumped into the car to head to our hotel.

Aubrey let out a laugh as soon as we were seated. Beside her, I reached out for the steering wheel, but grabbed only air instead.

"Looking for this?" she asked, pointing at the wheel, which was on her side of the car.

"Stop fooling around and put that thing back over here," I said, quoting an old line from *Caddyshack*.

We both had a laugh and traded sides.

Driving on the left went against my intuition, and I was constantly confused. To make matters worse, the island used roundabouts instead of traffic signals. The Avis agent had given us a handout on how to negotiate entering and exiting the the things.

Aubrey frowned down at a chart with about fifteen diagrams of cars going in all directions. She turned it upside down and sideways a few times and then tossed it into my lap in defeat. "I'm glad you're driving," she said.

Somehow, we managed to make it out of Owen Roberts International Airport on the correct side of the road and negotiated without incident the first roundabout. The drive would at least be brief. Our hotel was about ten minutes from the airport, located in the old colonial area known as Bodden Town.

About three miles from the airport, we came to a stop sign at a busy intersection, and Aubrey pointed to a sign that told us to go left. Seeing that it was clear, I pulled the miniature Suzuki onto the road. It took only a split second to realize I had made the first—and sometimes the last and fatal—mistake that American drivers and pedestrians make in these kinds of situations. I'd looked left instead of right.

I had no time to react; instead, I simply froze. All I could see was the massive front of a cargo truck bearing down on us. I'd always heard that time slows down and the brain goes into hyperactivity in life-threatening situations. I can now attest it's true.

In the split second before an almost-certain impact, my thoughts raced back through recent scenes with Aubrey. We'd dodged bullets and explosions. We'd done battle with assassins. We'd foiled a madman's evil plot. But it appeared that a truck filled with green bananas would finally do us in.

As the truck's huge tires screamed, I knew the outcome would be left to fate and physics. I kept my eyes tightly closed.

Thanks be to God and to the weight-and-drag coefficient, the truck lurched to a grinding halt just inches from my door. I still cannot explain how the truck had the time or space to stop. I only know it did. Other than it not being our time to go, I can only believe that the truck driver had learned to be on a constant lookout for tourists in little white Suzuki rentals and that he was constantly on guard for little stunts like ours.

I looked at the driver and made a thankful, prayer-like gesture. I repeated "Thank you" several times, and he smiled and nodded. It was one of those rare moments when strangers suddenly make a deep and powerful connection. We both knew the magnitude of what had just occurred: the man had saved our lives.

The moment was broken by the sound of horns. The drivers lined up behind us were anxious to get moving. With the truck blocking the road, I crossed into the eastbound lane and pointed the little car toward the hotel.

After we'd driven in silence for a while, Aubrey reached over to rest her hand in my lap. I think she just needed to feel me, to acknowledge what had happened, and that it had passed.

The panic hadn't left me. While the moment might be over, I had a sinking feeling that it be might have been an omen; there might be more to come.

—

When we finally arrived, I was glad to unfold myself from the tiny car. There was a row of white Suzukis in the parking lot, confirming my idea that our little rental was like a warning badge: *Caution! Clueless Tourist.*

We popped open the back hatch and unloaded our luggage. The muggy heat hit us hard and it felt just like home.

Not for the first time that day, Aubrey shook her head at my long cargo pants and blue fishing shirt. Aubrey didn't like my collection of expensive fishing shirts, saying that they were for middle-aged men with Rolexes who wouldn't know a fishing pole from a selfie stick. Now she'd started up again with her playful teasing.

My rebuttal, after glancing down at my Submariner Rolex, was to point at the twelve-hundred-dollar Louis Vuitton on her arm. That was a bag for wannabe divas, I said, and probably cost less than twenty dollars to make.

She punched me in the arm and gave me a big smile.

We left the parking lot and walked down a small stone path beneath a canopy of palm trees. The ocean and beach were just beyond the hotel, and the sight, smell, and noise coming from the surf made me want to shed my traveling clothes for swimming trunks and not waste another minute. Now that we were closer to the beach, the breeze had dropped the temperature by ten degrees at least.

We entered the lobby of the Mediterranean-style hotel through a set of French doors and made our way down a tiled hallway to the front desk. The friendly staff welcomed us and explained how things operated then handed us our keys and gave us directions to our room.

We walked down a sandy path to our room and upon opening the door, I knew that we had made the perfect choice. It was a two-story condo with a rear patio just steps away from a pool and only a few more to the ocean. The view from the room was framed by a pair of trees, their branches heavy with coconuts. Just feet into the water, a coral reef stretched along a private beach where the sounds of crashing waves immediately soothed and intoxicated this tired traveler.

According to the inn's host, the sea life lived between the breakers and the beach, creating an encapsulated outdoor aquarium. The turquoise water blended with the pink-tinted sand as if painted by an artist. The scene was even better than we had imagined.

We ditched our luggage and had a quick look around. There were two bedrooms upstairs, one of which would just be used for luggage unless I did something stupid. There was a full kitchen downstairs and a cozy den with a full view of the ocean.

Eager to get into the warm sea, we changed into our bathing suits. I was about to suggest some honeymoon time before our swim, but Aubrey had already grabbed the snorkeling gear provided by the inn and was headed down the steps, calling for me to follow.

I caught up with her at the shoreline and, after adjusting and putting on our snorkeling gear, we eased into the water. Talking through the breathing tube, I tried to tell her that it felt like we were in bathwater, but she had already submerged her head and was kicking her fins toward the coral reefs.

The world under the surface was just as the staff had described: full of exotic fish and colorful coral. We spent the next thirty minutes making muffled exclamations to each other as we came across new wonders.

Seeing that we were near an old anchor line, I swam toward it to explore. I had a goal in mind. While checking in, I'd noticed that the attendant wore a striking silver bracelet, and I'd told him that I liked it. He said he used to have a gold one—until the day before. He'd lost it while out snorkeling with some guests near an old anchor line. I had smiled and told him not to worry, that I would find it for him. He laughed—but I didn't. He didn't know my history with such things. I was always the person called when someone lost something.

Now, I dove to the bottom of a steep outcrop of coral and swam to a spot about thirty feet from the rusty chain and buckle. Feeling drawn to an odd-colored rocky ledge, I grabbed it to hold myself down and looked around.

As I knew it would be, the shiny bracelet was lying under the ledge. It was between two pieces of coral and slightly buried in the white sand. I had just enough air to swim the additional few feet and grab it. I stuck it in my pocket, which was secured with Velcro, and swam back to the surface. I found Aubrey, tugged on her leg, and motioned for her to swim back toward the shore. We had neglected to put on any sunscreen and I could feel my arms and shoulders beginning to burn.

Back on the beach, I didn't have a chance to ask her what she'd thought about the dive. We were barely out of the water before she burst out with a string of words. "That was absolutely awesome! Could you believe all those amazing fish? And the coral! I could have stayed out there all afternoon! I can't wait to do this all week. I think we have found a very special place. What did you think?"

"The same. I'm as happy as a clam. I just wish that we could talk while we're underwater. I had so many things I wanted to show you, but I sounded like a sea lion, trying to talk through that tube. Maybe we can come up with some hand signals for tomorrow."

We walked back to the condo and changed into dry clothes. We needed to make a run into town to pick up our week's supply of wine, rum, and groceries.

On the way to the car, I told her I wanted to run by the office for a second.

"Why? What do we need?" she asked.

"Nothing," I replied. "It will only take a second."

We walked into the office, and the owner of the bracelet was standing at the counter, typing on a computer. He greeted us as we walked up. "So far, so good?" he asked with a big smile. I think Aubrey thought he was talking about the room and the trip in general, but I could see the twinkle in his eye. He knew we were on our honeymoon.

"Everything is great, and I'm anticipating they'll get even better," I told him with a wink.

He laughed and asked what he could do for us.

"Well, we did a little snorkeling after we got squared away, and I told you I was going to do a little something for you. Do you remember that?"

He and Aubrey both wore puzzled looks.

"Ah, no, I don't think I do," he said.

"Hold out your hand," I told him.

When he did, I dropped the gold bracelet into his palm.

His opened his mouth in surprise.

Aubrey's expression mirrored his.

"You found it!" he said. "I can't believe you found it! Wow. How in the world did you do that?"

"I have no idea." I shrugged. "I just knew that I would. Guess I'm just a lucky guy." I put my arm tightly around Aubrey.

They both beamed at me. I was the man of the moment. "Have a great afternoon and try not to lose that thing again!" I said as I grabbed Aubrey's hand and walked toward the door.

"I don't even know what to say about all that," she said. "You never cease to amaze me."

I stopped to answer with a kiss and said, "I hope I never do."

CHAPTER EIGHT

After cautiously driving the pint-sized car to the grocery store, we returned to the condo and settled on a quick supper of warmed brie and hummus. It was an easy meal to prepare and one we frequently had at home. From our selection of wines, we chose a bottle of chardonnay and took the cheese, hummus, and crackers and walked to the beach.

Nestled between the two coconut trees were a table and two chairs that faced the sea. Aubrey laid a towel over the table and and set out the food and wine along with a candle. As we sipped our wine in the warm Caribbean breeze, I felt that ours most likely beat any table at any restaurant on the island. We talked about what we were going to do that week and laughed about the antics of our friends at the wedding. We also wondered what Nathan might be up too.

After supper, with a little wine buzz, we changed into our swimsuits so we could go exploring. While Aubrey finished getting ready, I packed a bag with towels, a couple of plastic wine glasses, and a bottle of chardonnay. It looked like it would be a perfect night for a walk on the beach.

Out by the sea, the sun was sliding down between a couple of building thunderstorms, casting brilliant colors as it made its way toward the horizon. The fresh, briny smell coming from the ocean breeze mixed with the scent of Aubrey's perfume. Her thin white cover-up gave me a tantalizing peek at the low-cut bikini underneath. I was thinking about the plans I had for later, but little did I know that Aubrey had plans of her own.

We left the comfort of our little island paradise and began walking west along the shoreline. Sections of dark coral stretched out from the water against a backdrop of dense vegetation and palm trees. It was hard to believe no one else was out enjoying the spectacular evening. We seemed to have the whole place to ourselves.

Exploring the beach, we found large conch shells among other treasures. Rubbed and polished from years of rolling in the surf, shards of antique green and blue glass were scattered on the beach and among the coral. We also spotted pieces of blue featheredged china with faded Victorian designs. I had found similar pieces back home and knew they dated from the early colonial days. I imagined the dishes spilling out with the cargo of ancient ships that had crashed into the coral reefs. I filled my pockets, thinking I would display them on our mantle at home in a small mason jar. It would be a unique reminder of the trip.

About a quarter of a mile from the inn, we found ourselves in a recessed cove, blocked from view in either direction. It had the pinkest sand, and Aubrey decided it would be a good place to set out our towels and watch the ocean. I poured two generous glasses of chardonnay and handed one to her.

She raised her glass and made a toast. "Here's to an interesting evening," she said, looking deep into my eyes as she tapped my plastic wine glass. Something in her smile told me I was going to like what she had in mind. I was ready then and there to grab our stuff and head back to the condo, but that was not her plan.

We sipped the semi-cool wine and watched a group of thunderstorms put on a show about ten miles offshore. As we sat in silence, she moved closer and gently placed her hand high up on my thigh and slowly started rubbing. I quickly realized that what I had hoped would happen at the condo was about to happen on the beach.

She kissed my neck and whispered, "Let's go for a swim, okay?" It was more of a directive than a question. She stood up and slowly slipped out of her cover-up and took off her bikini. Never once did she look to see if anyone was watching.

Quickly taking off my swimming trunks, I got with the program. We moved into a small pool the surf had carved into the coral. I noticed two oversized indentations that would be the perfect place to lie back and enjoy what I was almost sure was about to happen.

With her eyes locked on mine, she pushed me further into the shallow turquoise water. She backed me into the carved-out resting spot that I could almost imagine the universe had created for our pleasure. She pressed hard into me and began rocking slowly back and forth. With her eyes still fixed intensely on me, she increased her rhythm. She had me where she wanted me, and I was more than willing to play my role in the Aubrey show.

Electrical charges flashed from the distant thunderstorms, their potency and power matching Aubrey's passion. It felt like the energy of the storm was surging through my body as I felt her move. With a wild and primal sense of urgency, she arched her back and pressed hard against me one last time. It was at that very moment that a bolt of lightning exploded right above us.

The evening was surreal.

Maybe it was the freedom that came from being on the beach. Maybe we were feeling the electric energy that was lighting up the skies. Whatever the inspiration, the night was magical. If I ever created a bucket list, I would put this first, and then with satisfaction, immediately check it off.

We left the pool with shaky legs and collapsed back on the towels. I poured us some more wine.

She gazed at me, contented, then kissed me and said, "If you keep that up, we will definitely have a successful and fulfilling marriage."

"Keep what up?" I laughed. "The only thing I did was to just ... be there."

She stretched back on the towel, sighed, and said, "Sometimes that's all you have to do."

I had to smile at that. I decided that I just might turn out to be a decent husband after all.

After a few minutes she fell asleep. The fading light had turned from dusk to dark. Then another show began. A meteor shower was putting on a stellar display just above us. I wanted to wake Aubrey, but she'd already had her fireworks and was fast asleep.

I guess it would have been much simpler to sit back, watch the display of lights, and just accept and appreciate the majesty of the heavens and leave it at that—but that had never been my nature. I could never look up at the canvas of creation and not think about the more complex questions surrounding our infinitesimal existence. Many times I've contemplated the origin and destination of space and time and have always come up empty.

I don't think we are on this earth waiting for eternity, but could we be riding on the edge of time, traveling between this eternity and the next one?

Watching Aubrey peacefully sleeping a few feet away, I realized that the only thing that truly mattered was the here and now—and that the route of infinity and the unfolding of the universe were happening just the way they should.

Staring up into the complex layers of distant stars and galaxies, many of which had been extinguished for millions or billions of years, I made the decision to leave things in the hands of God. Maybe, I thought, our purpose in this life was not to understand it, but simply to enjoy—and I certainly had enjoyed that evening.

CHAPTER NINE

The next morning, I tried to keep the party going with some moves of my own to show Aubrey I was still the man. Unfortunately, the room's beige walls and lackluster artwork didn't compare to the majestic scenery of the night before. It wasn't a bad attempt, but it would take something very special to match the little show she'd put on at the beach.

We ate some quick bowls of cereal and packed a bag with towels and a few snacks and drinks along with our snorkeling gear. Then we jumped into the little shoebox of a car for a day on the beach. According to Aubrey's friend from Avis and the large stack of travel brochures in the condo, Cemetery Beach was the number one place to snorkel on the island. It was supposed to be about a twenty-minute drive from the hotel, but with our heightened fear of roundabouts, it took us an attentive forty minutes.

When we arrived at the address on the map, there was no mistaking that we were at the right place. The whole block was filled with tall tombstones that were bleached white and had dark, mildewed lettering. Most of the tombs were above ground, which I found a little spooky. As are most Southerners, I'm a bit superstitious. It just didn't feel right—laughing, playing, and having a great time in the beautiful water while just a few feet away, dead people were lying in their cramped, dark boxes.

Aubrey told me I was being morbid—and ridiculous—and shot off toward the beach. I gathered up our gear and, even though I'm not Catholic, crossed myself and said a prayer.

As soon as I caught up with Aubrey, I was once again in a beach state of mind. The beauty of the surf, the warm tropical breeze, the coral reefs, and azure water made me forget about the tombs.

Ahead of us was white sand with a line of dark coral reefs extending out into the sea. Wading into the water, we put on our gear and agreed to stay together.

I was still adjusting my mask when Aubrey dove in and made a beeline to the nearby reefs. The plan of staying together had lasted ... what, two seconds?

I caught up with my eager bride and we hung around a small patch of coral for a while, but the larger, more alluring reefs soon tempted us to venture further. The depth was about fifty feet, and the current had shifted, moving parallel to the beach instead of toward of it like before. For the moment all was good, but I worried about later.

Aubrey was ahead of me, and I swam out to join her. She had found a fascinating reef that held dozens of species of marine life. Some grouper that were slightly bigger than our car were swimming beneath a ledge along with thousands of multi-colored fish, the kind I had only seen in the saltwater tank in Dr. Howell's office.

We swam a little further around the reef, and a moray eel stuck its head out and startled Aubrey. She yelled something that I'm sure wasn't ladylike and grabbed me. As we swam away from the eel, I couldn't resist sneaking up and pinching her leg. That got me a swat and led to more unladylike expressions.

We were having an exciting time looking at all the interesting fish and coral until I stuck my head above the water and became immediately concerned. I couldn't see the shore. Aubrey was just a few feet away and I don't think she had any idea we were that far from land. The tide had pushed us out so far that I could barely see the houses sitting above the beach. I knew we were in trouble—well, I knew *I* was in trouble. Because I had begun to panic, which I knew could be the downfall of a swimmer swept out too far to sea.

All my training in handling highly stressful situations seemed to go right out the window. I was beginning to get tired and wondered if I'd have the strength to make the long swim back to shore. The panic began to affect my breathing. I knew that if I were to hyper-ventilate, I would surely drown right there in the warm waters of the beautiful Caribbean Sea.

My mind went back to a friend from college who had tragically drowned in the Caymans on his honeymoon. I had not thought about that in years, and now I wondered if he'd panicked at how far out the tides had swept him. I'd never understood how a strong young man could have perished in such civil waters, but now I thought I knew. My breathing became more rapid, and I had a horrible thought that I could leave Aubrey a widow on our honeymoon. An image of the tombs flashed back across my mind.

I glanced at Aubrey, who had her eye on a school of parrot fish. She had no idea that I was struggling. Gasping, I took in a mouthful of water and began to sink. I cannot accurately describe what I was feeling.

At that very moment, I had to make a choice—get myself together or continue in panic mode and die. I knew it was purely a mental issue, that I did, in fact, have what it took to make it to the beach. We had too much of life ahead of us for things to end right then. We'd already defied the odds. I got angry and decided I was not going to drown on my honeymoon. I rose to the surface and flipped over on my back. With only my face out of the water, I inhaled and exhaled as deeply as I could and tried to calm myself.

There was no one around to save me, and I knew I had to save myself. The last thing I wanted to do was let Aubrey know I was in trouble. I'd read about people who panic and cling to their rescuers only to drown them both. I had enough of my senses in place to know I could not put her in jeopardy. I tried to swim a few feet toward the shore, but the waves were getting stronger and moving us further out to sea.

Heaving and trying to get more air, I sucked in a mouthful of water when a wave hit me unexpectedly, causing me to choke. I was out of air, and my energy was spent. I could feel myself begin to sink and knew I wouldn't make it. This time was totally unlike the split-second, life-flashing-before-me moment with the cargo truck. I was living my impending death second by desperate second, and I was terrified.

All of a sudden, Aubrey popped up from the water and saw what was going on. She flipped off her mask and snorkel. "Colby, you all right?" she yelled, a sense of panic in her voice.

"I don't think I can breathe," I said in a trembling voice that didn't sound like me at all.

She appeared to be on higher ground, where the water came only to her waist. "Quick! Swim over here," she said. "I'm standing on a ledge of coral."

Hope immediately replaced despair. I could not believe that in this vast, deep part of the ocean, there was one elongated piece of coral reef just a few feet from the surface—and right in front of me. We had been swimming in those waters for an hour, and nowhere else did a coral reef come anywhere near the surface.

I found the energy to swim to the lifesaving reef and set my feet down on the most precious piece of real estate I would ever encounter in my life. It was then that I felt safe.

"Are you all right? What happened?" Aubrey asked, taking my arm to hold me steady.

"I'll explain later, but we need to get back to shore. Look how far out we are," I said.

She put her hand over her eyes to block the light and looked out in the distance. "I can barely see the shore," she said in a hushed voice.

"I know," I said. "We're out too far as it is, and I think we're in some kind of riptide that's pushing us out further."

"What should we do?" she asked. There was no stress in Aubrey's voice, and she didn't look tired at all; she looked like she could swim all day if she needed to.

I caught my breath and calmed down. "Let's swim slowly back, and what we need to do is swim at an angle of forty-five degrees," I said. "If the current tries to take us out, don't fight it. I don't think these riptides are very wide or long. I think we should be able to just swim around them." I had read that somewhere. Now I'd find out if it was right.

"I'm following you," she said.

In all reality, it should be the other way around, I thought.

We kicked and swam with the current for a hundred yards or so, staying parallel to the beach until the current changed and began to move us back toward shore. It took us a good thirty minutes to swim back to the beach, and toward the end, I was running out of energy. In fact, I barely made it.

When we finally got to shore, I heaved salt water for a few seconds and collapsed onto my back. I think it was then that Aubrey realized how close I'd really come to drowning. She was kneeling next to me when a small child walked up and stood beside her. With her hand gripping mine, Aubrey was whispering to me that everything would be all right.

The little girl leaned over and propped her hands on her knees. Her long brown curls and white cotton dress were blowing in the breeze as she smiled warmly at me. She echoed Aubrey's words. "Everything will be all right."

Who was she and where had she come from? I closed my eyes for only seconds, and when I opened them, she was gone.

I quickly sat up and saw that Aubrey and I were by ourselves on the beach. I could feel the hair on my arms and neck stand up when I asked Aubrey where the child had gone.

"What child?" She looked at me, confused.

Lying back down on the sand, I shut my eyes. Maybe it was a lack of oxygen causing visions in my head. Or it might have been a little angel with sand caught up in her curls. I'll probably never know, but I'm betting on the angel.

We walked back to the car, and Aubrey got in while I threw our bag in the rear hatch. We had parked only a few feet from the graveyard, and as I opened the door, I noticed a small tombstone in a row of taller ones. It seemed out of place and I stepped closer to read the inscription.

It belonged to a young girl by the name of Elisha Kirkconnell. She'd lived from November 6, 1958 to June 24, 1966. She was only seven and a half years old and had died exactly fifty years before—to the very day. The inscription read "Our little Angel."

This time, the cold chills came with a few tears. I thought about telling Aubrey about the child and about the marker, but for some reason I decided to keep it to myself.

We began the drive back in silence, like our time of quiet reflection after our near collision. I felt like there was something ominous that was on its way; it was becoming more apparent. We had been in the Caymans for less than twenty-four hours and had been involved in two almost-tragedies.

I reached over and squeezed Aubrey's hand two times, which was a signal between us that all was fine.

She didn't return the squeeze.

We made it back to the Turtle Nest Inn and entered the condo in silence. Aubrey walked up to the bedroom and shut the door. I think it all had been too much for her and she needed time alone to process. There were no signs of friction, just the seriousness of what had happened, or almost happened.

I went to the guest room and took our suitcases off the bed. I laughed, thinking that I had ended up in the guest room after all. I climbed into the bed for a nap and quickly fell asleep.

When I woke, Aubrey was curled up asleep beside me. In her sleep, she seemed tranquil and shielded from any of life's concerns. Our minds can only handle so much stress, I thought. Sometimes sleep is the only place we can renew our strength and find the peace we need.

I ran my fingers through her hair, and my thoughts wandered to a memory that always made me smile. When we were in our teens I could never keep my hands out of her hair, and it often irritated her. One Friday night I went to pick her up and found her waiting on the front porch with what looked like a wrapped gift. With a giggle, she instructed me to sit down and open it.

I was quite pleased, being that she was not the type for gifts unless it was Christmas or your birthday. But when I pulled the item from the box, I knew right away it was not a proper gift. It turned out that she had been visiting a friend who worked at a consignment shop, and she'd found an old wig that was about the same color and length as her own hair. She'd told her friend about my obsession and I'm sure they'd had a good laugh while wrapping up the gift.

"What the heck is this?" I remembered asking. I'd been so confused.

"It's your own wig!" she said. "You can rub it and twist it and yank it all you want. My poor hair needs a break. Go ahead. Try it out." She was having a good time.

But if she thought she had me, she had grossly miscalculated. *Awesome* was not a word we used back then, but I said something to that effect. "I think I will!" I told her.

I headed to the drive, and using my reflection in my car window, I pulled the wig over my head. I made a scene out of tugging and adjusting it until it fit just right. Of course, it looked ridiculous, but that made it all the better.

"It fits great. I love it. Let's go!" I said, opening the passenger door and motioning for her to get inside.

She folded her arms and, with an expression that could kill, walked to the car and somehow got settled in with her arms still folded into place.

I got in beside her and fussed in the mirror for a moment, read-justing my long locks and trying not to smile.

She looked straight ahead and didn't say a word.

We drove to Thomson for dinner and a movie, and I wore that horrible wig all night. She was so embarrassed but had too much pride to say so. I told her I kind of liked the new look and might consider growing my hair long.

The next day when I showed up at her house with the wig in place, she immediately snatched it off my head and threw it in the trash. I started laughing and she stormed out of the room.

About the same time, Mr. Reese passed her in the hallway and gave me a puzzled look. "What's wrong with her?" he asked.

To answer him, I opened the trash can and pulled out the wig.

"Oh, I heard about that," he said. "It didn't go over quite the way she planned."

We started laughing and couldn't stop. It was quite a moment.

—

Now, Aubrey stirred while I was rubbing her hair, and with a sleepy voice, she asked, "What are you smiling about?"

"Remember the wig?" I asked with an even bigger smile.

"How could I forget that? I was so mad, hearing you and my dad laughing in the hall. That backfired on me for sure."

"Yeah, but you accomplished what you wanted. After that, I left your hair alone."

I took my hands out of her hair, and she gently put them back.

"No," she said. "I was young and stupid, and I should have known that it was a nice thing to have you touching me like that. Over the years, when I would run my hands through my hair, I would sometimes think about you. You have my permission to run your hands through my hair as much as you want to now. For the rest of our lives, you can." She leaned up to kiss me.

We got out of bed and wandered down to the back patio and sat in the chairs overlooking the ocean. It was late afternoon and the sun was making its daily trip toward the horizon. I handed her a beer I'd pulled out of the fridge, and we sat in silence, watching and listening to the ocean. I was thinking about the right words to start the conversation about what had happened at Cemetery Beach. I assumed Aubrey was doing the same thing. I was still partly in shock.

She was the first to break the silence. "I'm hungry. We haven't eaten since this morning. Want to go out or cook here?" It appeared my compassionate wife's hunger had trumped the almost-drowning conversation we had yet to have.

I decided that I and my bruised feelings would give her one more chance. "Let's eat out," I said. "I'm not up for cooking after the day that we've been through." I sighed as I said that last part, hoping to remind her that I'd almost drowned . . . and might want to talk about it.

"I don't think I want to cook either," she replied. "How about that restaurant at Rum Point, the one the waiter at the Royal Palms suggested? What was the name of that one?"

"Lure." I answered in defeat.

"Great." She smiled. "Let's get dressed and go."

We showered and it felt good to wash away the remnants of Cemetery Beach. I waited on the porch as she finished getting ready.

As I was watching the sun set, I heard the door slide open, and out walked Aubrey in a blue sundress with just a hint of tan. I thought about how beautiful she looked and what a lucky man I was. She leaned down and gave me a kiss. That was all it ever took to change my mood.

—

For the trip to Rum Point, I'd prepared a couple of *travelers*, as we Southerners called them—white wine in Dixie cups. We had yet to venture to the north side of the island and were looking forward to seeing Rum Point, even in the darkness. Our destination, the Lure restaurant, was in an old colonial hotel that, according to the waiter, had great ocean views and some of the best food on the island.

A few miles into our drive and after passing it twice, we finally found the north interior road that led to our destination. The road was dark and desolate and appeared to have been cut through the middle of a large swamp. I was thinking how bad it would be to break down there when something very strange and creepy ran across the road.

"What was that?" Aubrey sat up straighter in her seat.

"I have no idea," I said.

After seeing a few more of them dart across the road, we came to one that had not made it past the white center line before getting hit.

Aubrey grabbed my hand. "Pull over, pull over," she said. "Let's see what it is."

I backed up the car and opened my door over the carcass. Aubrey unbuckled her seatbelt and leaned over to see as well. Using the flashlight on my phone, we could see it was a large blue crab, still wiggling and looking at us with beady eyes.

Aubrey sucked in her breath. "Aww, look. It's not dead. We need to save it."

"Save it? It's a crab. You don't save a crab. It's not like it's a cat!" I said with a heavy emphasis on "cat." Because of some unfortunate encounters, Aubrey would save a roach before she saved a cat. She gave me the glare I was expecting.

"Come on. We can't just leave it," she replied.

"I'm not having this conversation about a crab," I said, closing the door and driving off. It was not a minute before another unfortunate, underestimating crab attempted to make an ill-fated crossing, and our car smashed him flat.

"You did that on purpose!" Aubrey said, hitting me on the arm.

"I did not. They're on a suicide quest like the possums are back home. They wait until you're right on them and run underneath your tires," I said with a chuckle. We hit several more in the fifteen minutes it took us to get to Rum Point.

Aubrey was upset and a nervous wreck by the time that we got close. "You'd think they could do something about it, like put up signs or something," she told me.

"I don't think crabs can read," I said with a laugh. That earned me another punch on the arm.

"Stop it! I'm serious," she said.

My arm was gonna be very sore by the end of the night, but I couldn't let it go. "Maybe somebody should start an emergency clinic for crabs ... or better yet, an emergency restaurant," I said, still laughing.

"You're so mean. How would *you* like to be a crab squashed up on the road?"

What could I say to that?

Arriving at the restaurant, we followed a path that led to the rear of the hotel. It was a two-story structure that would fit in well with the antebellum homes back in Madison. Large white columns held up a second-story veranda laced with strings of white lights.

Along the beach were candlelit tables that stretched toward the shore of the calm bay. We could hear music that sounded like Count Basie or something from the fifties. It felt like we were in another era. We were greeted by the hostess and had the choice of dining on the veranda or the beach. Aubrey chose the beach. There was a slight wind coming from the bay, and it cooled our lightly sunburned skin.

The waiter arrived and barely had a chance to introduce himself before Aubrey fired off a question about the crabs we'd seen on the road.

I caught his eye and winked and gave him a small nod. "She's upset about them getting hit and thinks something should be done. I'd say you probably serve some of them right here, right?" I winked at him again.

"Oh yes, sir. If you order the blue crab tonight, there is a good chance it was a casualty of the road. We have runners that scoop those crabs up while they're fresh." This guy made it believable. I was duly impressed with his acting skills. Aubrey was aghast. It was one of the few times I had seen her speechless.

"See, my emergency restaurant idea is not so far-fetched after all," I said, opening my arms expansively to emphasize my point.

"That's sick," was all she said, and she began to tap her foot the way she did when something was heavy on her mind.

A few minutes later, the waiter came back for our order. He asked Aubrey if she was ready and, still put out and tapping her foot, she told me to order first.

"Yes, my man. I think I'll have the blue crab with the motor-oil glaze, served over a bed of ground tire rubber." I closed my menu and handed it back to him. We were both dying, trying to hold in our laughter. He was holding his breath, and I had to turn my head.

"Sir, would you like that glazed with a 10W-30? Or maybe topped with the new synthetic motor oil the chef has just perfected?"

He tried, but he couldn't hold it together. I couldn't either. I was laughing so hard I had to get up and walk. We finally caught our breath, and I sat back down. Aubrey's tapping foot was about to break the sound barrier. She still was not amused.

In a weak, cracking voice, the waiter spoke to Aubrey. "Ma'am, will you be having the same?" He barely got it out.

I let out a snort and had to put my hand over my mouth. Everyone was looking at us, trying to figure out what was so funny. I knew I would soon be paying dearly for my fun.

To her credit, Aubrey answered in a pleasant voice. "No, I think I'll have the *frigid* sea bass, served over its *own bed* of rice." She smiled. "I would also like to order ahead for dessert. Bring me a piece of your garlic cheesecake."

The waiter looked at me, confused.

"Ma'am we don't have ... garlic ... cheesecake," he said, not quite knowing what to say. "I can bring you a regular piece of cheesecake."

"That'll be fine. Just bring a cup of warm minced garlic on the side."

The dinner was wonderful and our conversation pleasant with the exception of the few times I made tire-screeching sounds when taking a bite of crab.

After the meal, the waiter brought Aubrey her cheesecake with a small bowl of warmed garlic butter. He looked at me and grinned. I returned the gesture. We both watched as she picked up the bowl of garlic and poured it over her dessert. I was thinking that she'd just ruined a good piece of cheesecake until she cut it in half, moved it to the middle of the table, and handed me a fork.

I must say, I didn't see that coming. I was trapped and knew I'd have to take a bite.

The waiter was still grinning like a mule until Aubrey handed him a fork. His grin quickly disappeared. He held the utensil indecisively.

"If you want a tip, hoss, you better take a bite," I instructed him.

He looked around and seemed uncertain. The staff was watching from the kitchen as we sliced off pieces of the cake and reluctantly put them in our mouths.

Our horrified expressions caused Aubrey and the staff to burst into laughter.

The waiter tried to swallow and gagged. I chewed mine a few times and then spit it into my napkin. It's hard to describe the nastiness. I doubt either of us will ever eat cheesecake again.

The poor boy ran back to the kitchen with his hand over his mouth. I downed my whole glass of water, but it didn't help.

He returned a few minutes later, grinning, and handed me the check. In the end, we all enjoyed the joke. Leaving him a sizeable tip and a story that he would probably tell forever, I shook his hand and thanked him for being a good sport.

We left the restaurant and, driving back to Bodden Town, we didn't see any more crabs trying to cross the road, nor did we see the roadkill from earlier in the evening. Maybe the waiter wasn't joking, I told Aubrey. She laughed and said that it would serve me right.

A few minutes later, she reached out for my hand and said tenderly, "I love you, and what happened today scared me so badly that I just can't talk about it. I hope you understand."

I squeezed her hand twice to tell her that I did.

CHAPTER TEN

When I heard a loud buzzing on the final approach, I quickly realized my mistake and reached down for the landing gear. Damn! I had forgotten again. I kept reaching for the lever, but it was just beyond my grasp. The runway was rapidly approaching, and I could not take my eyes off the instruments to find the landing gear in the darkened cockpit. I was desperate to find the lever and extend the gear. In a hurry to get home, I had broken the cardinal rule of flying and dismissed the weather forecast, thinking I could make it back before things could get too bad.

Unfortunately, I had miscalculated, and the storm was quickly rolling in. I was a half mile out, following the instrument landing system that guided pilots to the runway during bad weather, and could just begin to intermittently make out the fuzzy runway lights. They would be visible one second and then disappear. If I missed this approach, it was doubtful that I'd have another chance. I was low on fuel, and from the weather reports, most airports within my fuel range were socked in as well. I had to get the airplane on the ground. After groping for the lever, I finally got my hand on it and yanked—except it wasn't the gear lever that I had in my hand.

"Why are you tugging on my boob?" Aubrey asked, sitting up in bed. She pulled my hand away. In a very calm but deliberate voice, she asked what I was doing.

"Huh?" I asked, half awake. Thank goodness I was safe, still in the gorgeous Caymans.

It was too dark to make out Aubrey's face, but I knew exactly what her expression must be like.

"I thought that it was buzzing … I mean, I was trying to extend it … I don't know what it was that I was doing," I answered in complete confusion.

"Buzzing? My boob was buzzing? These dreams of yours are getting a little out of hand. Maybe you should lay off on the sleeping pills."

I guessed she had a point. As I lay back on the pillow, thinking it might be time to go back to Benadryl, we both heard a buzzing, and this time it was real. Not able to help myself, I reached up and tugged her boob.

"Stop!" she yelled, and knocked my hand away. "Where is that coming from?" She got up from bed and turned on a lamp. After a few seconds, we heard it again. It seemed to be coming from the chair near the sliding-glass door.

Aubrey walked over toward the noise and reached into the pocket of the jacket she had worn to dinner. She pulled out her cell phone. It was blinking red, indicating a missed call. She'd put it on vibrate while we ate.

"Who could possibly be calling at this time of night?" she asked, a little frightened as she checked the number. The Cayman Islands were only an hour behind the time at home, so it was the middle of the night back in the States as well. Someone had an emergency if they were calling at this hour—and on our honeymoon. I jumped up and quickly put on my pajama pants. It somehow didn't seem right to get tragic news while I was in the nude.

"It's Nathan," Aubrey said.

We were immediately concerned. Nathan would be the last one who would call unless it was an emergency, and even then he would have waited until morning.

"Did he leave a message?" I asked.

She nodded that he had. I pulled two chairs out from underneath the table and we sat down to listen. We looked at the phone with dread.

"Go ahead and play it," I said as I grabbed the hotel stationery and a pen. She tapped the button, and we heard his voice.

"Hey, I know it's early in the morning, and I'm sorry to interrupt your honeymoon, but I'm in Haiti and I've found myself in a tight situation. Something tragic happened here on the night before you got married. It's someone that I care for deeply, and I flew down right away. I thought I was only coming to console my friends, but I'm afraid that it's turned into an investigation.

"Aubrey, this is personal and I'm here unsanctioned. I thought about reaching out to our employer, but I can tell you right now what their response would be. They wouldn't touch this thing, and I wouldn't blame them.

"This may be going way beyond the bounds of our friendship but, Colby, if you and Aubrey are willing, I'm asking you to fly to Ile-a-Vache as soon as possible. It's an island just off the southwestern coast, near the city of Les Cayes. I think it would be about a four-hour flight.

"Once you arrive, someone will meet you at the airport, and they'll tell you more. You know I wouldn't ask if I had other options, but, unfortunately, I don't. I'm not sure when you'll get this message, but please call me back or text me if you can. And if this something you can't do, guys, I will understand."

The voicemail ended, and we stared at each other in silence and disbelief.

"Call him back. Hurry!" I instructed.

She did, but there was no answer. My mind raced with questions—not only about the danger Nathan might be in, but about what it would take to fly from the Caymans to Haiti. As an international pilot, I was as green as they get and didn't even know if it was something I could do. Nervous was an understatement in describing how I felt, and I needed answers. "Does this have anything to do with the trip you and Nathan took a few weeks ago?" I asked.

"Colby, you know I can't divulge that information. It's ... "

But I wouldn't let her finish. My adrenaline was flowing from the call and from the anticipation of what might happen next. Things had become too serious to allow her to pull out the same old line. "Stop it!" I yelled, holding up a palm. "I don't care if I'm cleared or not. What was supposed to be a little sideline consulting job has gone way too far. Do you realize what it is he just asked us to do? We'd have to make it through the airspace of some countries that aren't exactly stable. They could shoot us down, thinking we're drug smugglers—or maybe just for fun. Then we'd still face who knows what kind of unknown dangers in a situation that we don't know a single thing about. Or at least one of us doesn't know a single thing about it. There's no way I'm going to even consider doing anything until you tell me exactly what's going on." I was completely out of breath by the time I'd finished.

Aubrey was silent as she stared down at the table. We'd been through a lot over the last year, and her new job had been at the center of much of the stress. She looked up with a pained expression. "The trip Nathan and I took was to Quebec City to work on a joint task force that was dealing with international financial fraud. Most of what we did was sit in meetings and discuss how to prosecute the Canadian suspects, who were breaking the law in both countries. I have no idea why I was even there. All I could think about sitting in that conference room, looking over the St. Lawrence River, was how much I wanted me and you to go back to that breathtaking place for a romantic weekend. It had nothing to do with Haiti. I have no idea what Nathan's gotten himself into now, and I promise to never keep anything from you. You're more important to me than that job will ever be. You're more important than anything." She got up and embraced me tightly.

Immediately, I softened. "I'm sorry for yelling. I guess I'm a little overwhelmed at what he's asking us to do. We overcame some incredible odds last year, and I think God got us through it because he wanted us to have a second chance. I'm not so sure about his policy on third chances. What are you thinking we should do?"

She sat back down and looked around the room, trying to come up with the right words. I already knew what she was thinking and what she would say. I closed my eyes and thought back to another conversation we'd had about a year before on the tarmac of the Barrow County airport.

Along with Nathan, we had managed to pinpoint the location of some suspects in a murder-terror plot. At the moment that we stood on the tarmac, the suspects were in a mountain house a few miles from the airport. With the FBI and CIA preparing an assault on the house, I thought we were finally out of danger and had completed our part of the mission—but not Aubrey. Some dear friends had been victims, and she felt she owed it to her loved ones to see the job through to the end.

In those few short days, she and Nathan had formed a bond that in some ways had grown to be equal to ours: a bond solidified by trust and faith. I knew that there was a feeling between them that, no matter what, they would always be there for each other. They both had a drive to do the right thing, no matter the consequences.

I left her at the table and slipped out the sliding-glass door to the balcony. I thought that I could think more clearly when peering into the black infinity of night, knowing that whatever decision I made, it most likely would have no relevance in a hundred or a thousand or a million years. Not that it made it any less important, just less relevant in the grand scheme of things. Sometimes it took feeling small to overcome the fear of things so large and overwhelming.

I decided then that we were all a part of destiny, and ours seemed to have just arrived with a late-night call. Looking up one last time, I took a deep breath of the warm, salty Caribbean air and went back into the room. Fate awaited us, and we would prove to it once more that we were worthy allies.

I looked at my wife and nodded. "I guess we need to pack," I said.

We quickly packed our bags and in thirty minutes had them stationed by the door. It was three o'clock in the morning, leaving the rest of the night to try to sleep. With the rush of emotions over Nathan's phone call, we were both very much awake. But we knew we had a long day coming up and that we needed rest.

We climbed back into bed, and Aubrey was asleep in less than five minutes. She had the unique ability to fall asleep any place and at any time. I didn't have that talent, and I lay there wide awake.

Staring at the ceiling, I decided to put my insomnia to good use and grabbed my iPad off the bedside table. I did a search on *flying private aircraft to Haiti*, hoping for some info that would help me with the challenge I'd just agreed to take. The internet was loaded with reports from pilots blogging about flights they'd made to places all across the world. I'd used those blogs many times to take the guesswork out of the planning process.

After ten minutes of searching, I'd found nothing. Frustrated, I logged into the Aircraft Owners and Pilots Association website. It always had the information that I needed—until then. There were countless pages on flying everywhere in the Caribbean except for troubled Haiti, where no one (other than, apparently, yours truly) would pick as a travel destination. Why couldn't Nathan have had an emergency in Dallas, Jacksonville, or Paducah?

My eyes were beginning to burn, so I gave up on my search and set the iPad on the table. Trying to be quiet, I knocked over a glass, which hit the lamp and made a noise that was loud enough to wake Aubrey up.

She turned over in the bed. "What are you doing?" she asked with a long emphasis on "doing."

"I was trying to find some information on how to fly in to God-forsaken Haiti," I replied with an equal emphasis on "Haiti."

"Any luck?"

"Nope. It's a *placez pas accueillir* or *persona non grata* or something like that. I've checked every site I can think of and can't find one example of anyone who's gone there. It appears that no one does it," I said, growing even more frustrated.

Aubrey raised a hand to stifle a yawn and asked "What about missionaries or those doctors without borders? Don't they fly down there?"

I had not thought in that direction. I guess I'd found out who the brains were in our operation.

"Great idea, and you're pretty too," I said, reaching out to grab my iPad. I did another search and found all kinds of information on doctors, missionaries, and relief workers who routinely flew from the States to Port-au-Prince. The processes for obtaining permits, customs and immigration forms, and permits needed to fly to Haiti were all well documented. Fortunately, much of what was required I had already done for the Caymans trip. It appeared that most of the Caribbean countries followed the same processes. It was good information, and I began feeling better about the flight. If I could fly over Cuba with no problems, surely I could make it to Haiti.

I leaned over to tell Aubrey she was brilliant, but she had already fallen back asleep. Carefully putting the iPad back onto the table, I willed myself to try to do the same. At the most, I could get three hours of sleep and would need every single second of that allotment.

After what seemed like only minutes, we were startled awake at six o'clock by an overzealous rooster crowing just outside our room. Whether trying to woo a girl or just liking to hear himself, the foul thing crowed for a solid ten minutes. At least the roosters back home in Georgia had the decency to announce the morning briefly and shut up.

I was thinking, *if only I had my shotgun*... when Aubrey threw back the covers and jumped out of the bed in a rage. She shot across the room, flung open the sliding door, and walked onto the balcony. I sat up to watch, knowing things were about to get very interesting. The bird was perched in a palm tree just a few feet from the door.

"Shut the fuck up!" Aubrey yelled with her hands placed firmly on her hips. No one or nothing messed up Aubrey's sleep and got away with it. I watched as she picked up a heavy glass candleholder from a table on the balcony and reared back with it. There was no mistaking her motive. The bird must have realized he was dealing with a sleep-deprived crazy woman and quickly acquiesced. He was gone from the palm tree in seconds, flying toward the beach.

I laughed, thinking how the scene might have appeared to the casual observer on a peaceful, early-morning stroll. Of course I didn't laugh out loud.

Still gripping the candleholder, Aubrey stomped back into the room and collapsed onto the bed.

For a very brief second, I considered letting go with a few loud crows of my own. But staring at the candleholder still in her hand, I acquiesced as well.

She was back to sleep in seconds. I carefully removed the weapon from her hand and shut the door to the balcony. I left her in bed and eased into the bathroom for a long, hot shower. Staying until the water began to run cold, I felt sufficiently awake and ready for the day. I quietly dressed and walked down the stairs to the kitchen.

Needing caffeine, I doubled up on the scoops and made the coffee extra strong. The digital clock on the microwave said six forty-five.

In the shower I'd been thinking about the flight and had begun to feel less confident about taking on the job with just a few internet reports to give me any guidance. Then it occurred to me that there was someone who could help. Being a cantankerous old bastard, he would certainly be displeased with an early-morning call. Despite my nervousness about the day ahead, I had to smile a little, thinking about the pleasure I would take in waking the guy up.

He was a pilot friend and had spent his career flying military jets in the Royal Air Force. Having been all over the world, flying missions in several wars and conflicts, he eventually became the pilot for the Queen of England and the Prince of Wales. He had many stories and would promptly pin you in the corner of a room and tell you one or two, whether you asked him to or not. After retirement he relocated to the US and took a job ferrying airplanes from the States to South America and the Caribbean.

I dialed his number and it rang continuously. I was starting to become afraid that it would go to voicemail when a sleepy voice answered with a thick British accent. "Hello?"

"Hey, Mike. It's Colby."

He didn't immediately respond and it sounded like he dropped the phone and was scuffling to find it. "Bloody Hell, mate. What time is it?" he asked.

I jumped right in. "Six-fifteen and You're not up?" I asked, knowing he would sleep to noon if given the chance. We'd enjoyed a satirical banter since the day we'd met.

"Hell, no, I'm not up. What are you calling me for? I thought you were on your honeymoon. Don't tell me you need advice on shagging, you bugger." He was laughing and having a coughing fit all at the same time.

"If I did, you'd be the last person I'd ask. I'm guessing you haven't had any this century," I said.

"Don't rub it in, you bastard. What do you bloody want?"

I'd never understood why the Brits used the word "bloody" so much. I'm sure there's some historical reference, but an explanation would have to wait. "I need to fly the 310 from the Caymans to a small airport on the southeast coast of Haiti. Have you ever flown to Haiti?" I asked.

"Why the hell would you want to do that? No one flies to Haiti," he said.

"Yeah, I've gathered that, and it's not by choice. Can you help me or not?" I heard more shuffling around at the other end of the line.

"Okay, give me a minute to get out of bed and get to my office," he said.

I waited a couple of minutes until I heard a familiar sound. "Are you peeing?" I asked, laughing.

"Yes, I am, and how rude of you to mention it. A Brit would never be so crass."

"Well, hurry up, okay? And if there's any other bodily business you need to take care of, I'd rather not have to hear it," I said, laughing even harder.

"Shut up, you little shit. I'm walking over to my office. Give me a second to turn on this damn computer." I could hear him humming, and after a minute, he came back on the line. "I don't see any problems flying to Haiti, no particular flight restrictions that are any different from the other Caribbean countries," he said. "It would be basically the same as your flight to the Caymans except it's mostly over water. I suggest you file IFR and stay in close contact with the controllers. Of course, you know you'll have to complete an eAPIS manifest electronically and print three copies of the immigration and customs forms. Just like flying to the Bahamas or the Caymans. And that's about it, mate." I was relieved to hear that Mike's account matched the pilots' reports from the internet.

"Thanks, my friend. I really appreciate your help, and I'm sorry for calling so early," I replied in a more serious and thankful tone.

"You know I'm always glad to help. But listen, you need to be very cautious. Haiti's not a place where you want to get in trouble. Take a lot of cash and be ready to have to use it. It's a poor country, and corruption is rampant over there. If you do get into anything over your head, you give me a call. I'm not sure that I'd be any help, but I could be down there in the 350 in less than five hours and bail you out of jail at least. Of course, it would cost you dearly and you would never hear the end of it." Mike had a Beechcraft King Air that could easily make Haiti with only one fuel stop. I had no doubt he would do as he said.

"Thanks for the offer, but I can't imagine it would come to that. I'll buy you a beer when I get back."

"Cheers, mate, and have a safe voyage."

We ended our conversation about the time Aubrey dragged into the kitchen.

"Who was that?" she asked while pouring a cup of the strong coffee.

"Mike Moseley. I called him for some pointers on the flight."

She took a sip of coffee and made a face like she had bitten into a sour persimmon. "Was he any help?" she asked.

"He was." I said, laughing at her expression. "He basically confirmed what I'd read on the internet, that it shouldn't be a problem. I guess we haven't heard back from Nathan?"

I watched while she adulterated her coffee with cream and sugar. She shook her head, indicating that we hadn't.

We took our coffee and sat on the back porch. The ocean stared back at us, gray and unforgiving. After a few minutes, the sun began peering over the horizon, turning the water a warm blue. Birds were fishing in the shallow surf, putting up a fuss about something or the other.

Closing my eyes, I let myself enjoy the fresh breeze and the sounds and smells of the coastal morning. Aubrey took my hand and squeezed it twice. I wanted to sit there all morning, holding her hand and feeling the warmth of the sun, but something else was waiting. "I guess it's time to get ready and head off to the airport," I said, reluctantly breaking the silence. I opened my eyes to find her staring out into the now-blue ocean. I could only imagine what was on her mind. "I'll need at least thirty minutes to file a flight plan, check the weather, and prepare the plane," I said. "We'll also need to drop by Avis and return the shoe. What do you think we need to do about checking out? The office doesn't open until nine."

"We can leave the key in the mail slot with a note. I'll send them an email when we get home. Give me fifteen minutes to get ready. Can you put the big luggage in the car?" she asked, getting up from the chair.

"I can do that," I said. "And I'll also drop off the key."

Aubrey went upstairs to get ready, and I searched the credenza for some stationery. I found a little note pad and wondered what to write. We were leaving three days early and I was sure they would wonder why. I thought about writing something mysterious or scandalous but settled on putting down that we'd been called back home for an emergency. We'd already paid in full for the week, so there was no issue with the payment. Hopefully, we could return in a few months and the bracelet guy might give us credit for the days we missed. I'm sure Aubrey could handle that once we were safely home.

It took two trips to the car to load my one bag and The Princess's three. Aubrey only wore two or three outfits when we traveled, so I had no idea what she packed in the other bags. Being the good husband, I never asked.

On my way back from the second trip to load the car, I slipped the envelope with the note and key through a gold slot located on the front door of the hotel. I did one last loop around the condo to see if we'd missed anything, then I poured us two cups of coffee and filled a thermos to go. Aubrey met me in the foyer, and together we walked to the car.

Before we left, I paused to feel the ocean breeze and smell the salty air one last time. I told Aubrey that I'd miss it, and she laughed.

"Don't worry," she said. "You'll get all the ocean air that you want in Haiti, but I have a feeling the circumstances will be different." She had a point, I guessed.

Opening the car door, I realized for the umpteenth time that I was on the wrong side. I cursed the little car and I cursed the British, then I slammed the door. I'd had enough of all this opposite-side stuff and was beginning to feel the stress and anxiety of our possibly dangerous trip to Haiti.

We left the Turtle Nest Inn and made it through the roundabouts without incident. About a mile from the airport, we passed a white cargo truck carrying a load of bananas, and I wondered if it was my friend. I would never eat another banana without thinking about the day I was almost killed.

After making a quick stop to refuel, we drove straight to the rental place and turned in the car. They did a quick inspection and sent us on our way.

Pulling our luggage down the sidewalk, we crossed the street at the terminal and entered the aviation office. I informed the attendant we would be departing in an hour and requested they pull the airplane to the flight line. I looked out the tarmac window and down the long row of airplanes, hoping not to see mine. I didn't see it, and that was a good thing. I'd paid a fee to the FBO to have it stored in a hangar, but I knew if a larger jet were to need the space, it would easily get bumped to the ramp. I'd also given the hangar attendant a hundred-dollar bill to pay special attention to the 310. Sometimes an airplane would incur damage known as "hangar rash" after being carelessly handled by an attendant. Hopefully, money talked in the Caymans, as I hoped it would in Haiti.

Leaving Aubrey in the main terminal, I found the pilots lounge down a long hallway. I walked in and sat at one of the many computers used for flight planning. Logging into a paid subscription site that had all the information and performance data for my airplane, I put in the destination, current weather, weight, and fuel requirements for the flight. The program created a flight plan with the route, communication and navigation frequencies, time in flight, etc. With a push of a button, I had my flight plan printed and was ready to go.

Unfortunately, after checking on how to handle customs and immigration, I found the airport on the island did not have a customs office. It appeared I would have to make a stop in Les Cayes to clear customs. I printed an alternative flight plan, adding the stop in Les Cayes, left the pilots lounge and went back to the FBO counter to settle my bill.

On a whim, I asked the attendant if he knew anything about customs and immigration procedures in Haiti. He said they had a customer who flew there at least twice a week and never seemed to have any problems. I asked where he flew into and, as luck would have it, it was Ile-a-Vache, where we were flying into as well.

Knowing there wasn't a customs hub on the airfield, I asked how he handled getting an inspection. According to the attendant, there was an inspection office at the marina to handle the large number of boats traveling through the area. With a preset appointment, the Haitian inspector would usually meet you at the airfield. The attendant volunteered to phone the inspector and see if he or she would be available to meet us there when we arrived.

After a minute or two on the phone, the attendant asked us what time we'd be arriving. This was working out better than expected.

"Tell them ten-thirty," I said.

He gave the inspector our names, airplane type, tail number, and the time of our arrival. The attendant hung up and said the inspector would meet us on the airfield at ten-thirty. He was all smiles, knowing he'd just saved the day. He was smiling even more when I handed him a hundred dollars.

According to the attendant, it was now customary for the customs and immigration agent to meet inbound airplanes by appointment at non-customs airports. Since the earthquake in 2010, there had been a large increase of missionary and relief flights into remote areas of Haiti. Back then, it had taken hours and sometimes a whole day to clear customs at the main airport in Port-au-Prince. It was solidly in the top ten of the world's worst commercial airports. It was so bad that many medical and relief organizations threatened to abandon their efforts to help. Thankfully, the Haitian equivalent to the FAA changed the customs and immigration requirements to allow off-site inspections. The premium for this perk, as well as the indubitable cost that would come on the side, had me a bit concerned. This was my first time operating in the world of corruption and bribery (other than the little hangar payola in the Caymans).

With everything in order, it was time to board the aircraft and go see what Nathan had gotten himself into. Over dramatizing was definitely not part of his character, so whatever it was, there was probably some kind of conspiracy involved as well as lots of intrigue. It was seven now, and the plan was to be wheels-up by seven thirty. The flight time was about four hours. My honeymoon was over.

Chapter Eleven

We left the terminal and walked the fifty feet to the airplane. The ramp personnel had placed our bags under the cargo door and opened both doors to the cabin. With the hot Cayman sun, it hadn't taken long for the interior to heat up. The 310 was not equipped with air conditioning, meaning it was now a hot aluminum box until we could get airborne and cool air could begin to move through the vents.

After loading the bags, I situated Aubrey into the copilot's seat and did one last walk around before climbing in. She already had fastened her seat belt, which was a complex puzzle of a metal clasp that still took me a couple attempts to get right myself. She had her headset plugged in as well. This was her third flight in the new airplane, and she was quickly becoming familiar with the protocol. She was just finishing a text as I fastened my own seatbelt and put on my headset.

"Check, check, check," I said to see if the two of us had communication.

"Check, check," she replied. "I just texted Nathan to say we're on our way and should arrive around ten thirty. Let the adventure begin."

"Check, check," I said as I fired up the two Continental engines. The oil pressure gauges shot into the green arc, signaling all was good.

With everything registering normal, I called the tower and informed them we were ready to taxi. The controller instructed us to taxi to runway twenty-six. Usually we would hold short of the runway, waiting on traffic, but with no aircraft in the pattern or on final, we were cleared for immediate takeoff.

Lining up on runway twenty-six, I shoved both throttles full forward, and the thrust of the 310 pushed us back into our seats. I never got tired of that feeling. We quickly gained speed down the runway, and Aubrey sat calmly in her seat, not twisting her hands or shaking her legs. Instead of looking out the window, she was actually paying attention to what was going on at the controls. Maybe after the little scare we'd had on landing, she thought it might be prudent to be more observant.

We lifted off the runway with plenty of room to spare and began the climb to our cruising altitude of 5,500 feet. Climbing at a rate of 1,500 feet per minute, it took no time at all. Reporting to the tower that we were at altitude, we then turned east toward Haiti. I then set the engines for cruise and engaged the autopilot for the four-hour flight to the island of Ile-a-Vache.

The small island, located about twenty miles off the southwest coast, had just built an airport in the last few months. According to the website, it was uncontrolled and had a shorter-than-comfortable 3,000-foot runway. But it did have aviation fuel and twenty-four-hour security.

An hour into the flight, the Cayman air traffic controller informed us we were leaving her airspace and to contact Jamaican control on the published frequency. I found the frequency on the GPS and called in our position. Aubrey's laughter came over the intercom when the voice on the other end sounded like Bob Marley. She made the international gesture for smoking a joint. I could picture the controller sitting in the tower with dreadlocks and a knitted multi-colored sock hat.

He was very friendly, instructing us to change our heading about ten degrees toward the south, reported the current wind direction, and gave us the updated barometric pressure reading. I was a little disappointed that while bidding us a good day, he didn't call me "Mon."

Secured in the Jamaican airspace and knowing we had a while before we entered the Haitian airspace, we settled in for the flight. Aubrey was reading, and I stared out the cockpit window, finding it hard to tell where the blue sky ended and the turquoise water began. With the harmonic, hypnotic drone of the engines and the early-morning caffeine from the coffee wearing off, I was also trying hard to keep my eyes open. Not wanting to fall asleep, I reached behind me and pulled out the thermos of coffee I'd brought from the condo.

Yes, I'd stolen a thermos from the inn, but I had full intentions of one day returning it. After pouring a cup, I offered it to Aubrey.

Without looking up from her book, she held up her hand and said "No, thanks."

I laughed, knowing why she'd turned it down (other than not having all the stuff she puts in it). She went to the bathroom more than anyone I knew and was afraid she would have to go on the airplane. She refused to use the anatomically correct "Ms. Johnnie" container I'd purchased for the flight. I had a "Mr. Johnny" and didn't hesitate to use it. She would pinch up her face with disgust when I'd try to hand her the container after I'd filled it up. It tickled me to think about it.

I drank the coffee and monitored the instruments while Aubrey pulled a few magazines and a Blow Pop from her backpack. She unwrapped the candy and stuck it in her mouth and flipped, uninterested, through the pages. Watching her, I realized it was sometimes the simplest of things that could be the most endearing.

Looking toward the horizon, I could see land to the southeast. It was the tip of Jamaica and, according to the GPS, the city in our view was Montego Bay. I pointed it out to Aubrey and sang out a familiar chorus that it brought to mind. "Oh, oh, oh, oh. Oh, oh, oh, oh."

She laughed and together we sang a few verses about the city of Montego Bay, made famous in the 1970s by Bobby Bloom.

With a smile, she went back to her magazine and I thought about how happy we were at that moment and how fast things could change. We were leaving Grand Cayman and the near misses with the truck and the sweeping tide at Cemetery Beach. Now we were heading toward Haiti and the unknown.

I always try not to dwell on the negative and end up stuck somewhere in the middle, between thinking liking a fatalist and being optimistic. I had no idea what we were about to get ourselves involved in, but I knew it was likely dangerous. Of course, it might be possible that Nathan would have the whole thing solved before we even got there. Then Aubrey and I could continue with our honeymoon. But being a realist at heart, I didn't think that would be the case.

Gazing out the side window, I saw nothing but an empty ocean. Jamaica was about fifty miles behind us and, according to the moving map on the mounted GPS, Ile-a-Vache was a hundred and three miles ahead. Our estimated time of arrival was in a short thirty-two minutes, and I was thinking about making a call to the Haitian air traffic control when a voice broke through the silence on the radio.

"Cessna 7571Q, Les Cayes Approach." Approach Control, or Approach for short, was the controller who guided inbound airplanes to the airport. Once the pilot landed, he or she would be turned over to Ground Control, or Ground for short.

"Les Cayes Approach, Cessna 7571Q level at fifty-five hundred," I replied.

"71Q, radar contact confirmed. We have your current position at ninety-five miles east of Ile-a-Vache. Your flight plan has you terminating at Ile-a-Vache. Is that still correct?" I never understood why pilot vernacular came with such ominous connotations: *terminal, terminating flight, final approach ...*

"Roger. Our arrival is still Ile-a-Vache. ETA is thirty minutes," I replied, refusing to use the dire terms.

"71Q, you are cleared for Ile-a-Vache. Expect runway twenty-seven, winds calm, and no reported traffic. Please note construction activity and equipment around the taxiways and ramp. Pressure altitude is 29.92, report airport in sight."

Following protocol, I read back the instructions.

About fifteen minutes later, Ile-a-Vache came into view and a few minutes after that, the airport appeared on the horizon. I could see several large yellow pieces of equipment that appeared to be moving but, thankfully, none were near the runway. From what I'd read online, Ile-a-Vache was a popular destination for vessels cruising through the Caribbean and had several hotels to accommodate the mariners. Previously, the only way to get to the island had been via private boat or a commercial ferry but, with the increasing demand, the government had built an airport. I informed Les Cayes control that I had it in sight.

"71Q, would you like to terminate your flight plan at this time?"

There was that term again. I decided to take them up on their offer and cancel my flight plan while still in the air. The approach controller is usually at a regional facility, far from where the pilot is landing. Due to the radio reception breaking up as the airplane gets closer to the ground, sometimes a pilot is unable to make radio contact and cancel their flight plan at that point.

Cancelling a flight plan was a big deal in the United States, and I assumed it was the same everywhere. An unclosed flight plan after the scheduled arrival time technically meant the aircraft had never made it to its destination. Usually the pilot had just forgotten to take the steps to close it, but the air traffic controllers had to assume the worse—that somewhere a plane was down.

Most pilots forget once early in their careers—but they only do it once.

In the US, the FAA will make every effort to make contact with the pilot by phone or to confirm with the airport or FBO that the aircraft is on the ground and safe. If they are unable to confirm, they track the radar history of the flight and possibly mount a search. Nobody wants to be the pilot who forgets and sets off a search and rescue. At best, the pilot would be "invited" to participate in a serious phone conversation with a representative of the FAA. If an actual search takes place, it could lead to a possible suspension or mandatory retraining.

I had once forgotten to close my plan as a student pilot. After landing and securing the airplane, I drove the twenty minutes home and walked into the house to a ringing telephone. (This was in the days before cell phones.) It was the airport manager telling me the FAA had called to inquire about my whereabouts. He'd informed them that the airplane was safe on the ramp.

"They want you to call them," he said, a serious tone creeping into his voice.

I did, and was thoroughly chewed out and instructed to never again let a flight plan go unclosed.

"Roger, Les Cayes," I said. "I would like to cancel my IFR flight plan at this time."

"71Q, IFR flight plan terminated. Customs and Immigration will contact you at the field. Good day."

"Thanks for your help. Good day," I replied.

Preparing to land, I removed the checklist from the pouch next to the seat and handed it to Aubrey.

Her eyes became large and she held up her hands in protest. "What? Why are you giving that to me?" she asked.

I laughed and told her that her free ride was over. It was time to start performing her copilot duties.

She continued to protest, so I put the checklist in her lap.

"Just start from the top and read the items out in order. I'll complete the task and then I'll tell you 'check.' Okay?" I directed more than asked.

"Okay," she replied with some hesitation.

We went through the checks—for descent, pre-landing, and landing—without a hitch.

She gave me a big smile as she instructed "landing gear down, locked, and three in the green." She watched as, with the push of a lever, the gear retracted and three green lights lit up on the panel. She gave me a thumbs up and seemed to be warming up to the job.

Lining up on runway twenty-seven, I gripped the yoke more tightly than I usually did. I had yet to land the twin-engine airplane on a runway shorter than five thousand feet, and the narrow strip of pavement here was just three thousand. It also ended abruptly at the water's edge.

The issue was not the airplane. The 310 was very durable and could easily handle the short runway. I'd read several accounts of 310s making successful road landings in emergencies. The concern was the inexperienced multi-engine pilot. The large land movers and bulldozers were closer to the runway than I'd anticipated, and they were producing clouds of dust that were moving across the runway. I had to remind myself to pay attention and not let them distract me.

As we descended toward the runway, everything was on the mark. Using only three-quarters of the twenty-five hundred feet, I pulled the power back to idle as the wheels touched the rough aggregate surface, and I was pleased with the outcome. My newly enthusiastic copilot began reading the after-landing portion of the checklist as we turned off the runway and taxied toward the ramp.

With all the construction traffic moving around in clouds of dust on the runway and taxiway, I was a bit nervous about proceeding to the ramp. I could see there weren't any mirrors on the machinery, and airplanes don't have horns. I was hoping they knew to look for planes before crossing the taxiways and runway.

After a few turns, we made it safely to the ramp. The only completed building on site was a newly constructed fuel shed with three pumps underneath a canopy of blue, shiny tin. It was located about a hundred feet from the currently-under-construction FBO.

I was wondering if the new fuel pumps were in service when the driver of a military-style truck wheeled around the corner and came to a stop. Aubrey was still looking at the checklist when I nudged her and pointed.

"Oh, shit," was her reaction, which is the appropriate response when one sees the military approaching unexpectedly in a foreign country. I was hoping it was the customs and immigration agent.

As we rolled to a stop, the door of the truck opened and a short, stocky man stepped out and approached the plane. He had a bushy moustache and wore a sweat-stained uniform of light blue with gold epaulettes. With his arms folded in front of him, he stopped about twenty feet away and waited for the engines to shut down. I noticed his uniform was complete with a thick black belt that held a line of bullets and holstered a semi-automatic pistol. When the propellers stilled, he walked toward the airplane.

I waved and gave him a big smile, trying to look friendly. It then dawned on me that someone who was trying to hide something would probably do ... what? Wave and give the officer a big smile, trying to look friendly.

To my relief, he returned my wave with a big grin of his own. With passports and customs documents in hand, we exited the airplane and approached the man who, according to his name badge, was Agent Pierre-Toussaint.

He reached out and with a firm handshake, welcomed us to Haiti.

Agent Pierre-Toussaint took our passports and travel documents and fixed them to a worn clipboard. He studied them for a minute and then asked permission to board the aircraft to do an inspection.

"Certainly," I replied, and waved him toward the door. He climbed aboard and did a cursory inspection of the cockpit then moved on to the cabin. Aubrey and I were standing by the door watching as something behind the seat caught his attention. He leaned down and picked it up. He was about to open the lid when I saw Aubrey wince and turn away.

I was not about to let the agent subject himself to the souring contents of the jug, and so I quickly spoke up.

"Agent, ah, I really don't think you want to open that," I said, pointing at the jug with a pained expression on my face.

He looked a little closer at the jug and shook it.

"Is this what I think it is?" he asked, holding the jug at arm's length.

I pointed an accusing finger at Aubrey and said, "I'm afraid it is."

She let out a loud gasp and pushed me. "That's not mine!" she cried.

Agent Pierre-Toussaint and I both laughed. Holding the jug carefully with two fingers, he attempted to hand it off to Aubrey.

She held her hands up in the air, appalled, and took a big step back. The agent and I laughed even harder then.

He put the jug back behind the seat and quickly completed his inspection. Exiting the airplane, he apologized to Aubrey. Smiling, he pointed to me and told her to watch out; the guy she was hanging out with might be a bad influence.

"You don't know the half of it," she said, smiling. "Maybe you could lock him up for a few days and give me a little peace."

The agent seemed to be a great guy, and I was already feeling that things were going to be fine.

We walked over to the fuel shed to complete the paperwork. Just a few feet away, construction workers were putting the finishing touches on a beautiful FBO. It would've been nice to have had the amenities ready for our use on the brutally hot day. While the agent reviewed the forms, I trotted to the airplane and grabbed three cold Cokes from the cooler (my first official act of bribery). We drank them while the agent asked the perfunctory questions from his list.

"Where do you plan to stay and what is the nature of your visit to Ile-a-Vache?" he asked with his pen ready on the page.

"We have reservations at Colline Sacrée, and we're visiting our friend from the States. He's coordinating some sort of agricultural-economic project with the Haitian farmers," I replied, having previously come up with our excuse for being there. I told him we'd been on our honeymoon on Grand Cayman and decided to leave a few days early and check out what our friend had going on in Haiti.

He stopped writing and looked at me, surprised. "You left the amazing island of Grand Cayman to spend part of your honeymoon in Haiti to see an *agricultural-economic project*?" He looked at Aubrey and shrugged. "Maybe I *should* lock him up for a few days."

We all had a laugh at that.

While he completed the paperwork, I noticed some movement in the agent's truck. The tinted windows kept me from seeing in, but something was causing quite a ruckus in the back seat.

Agent Pierre-Toussaint saw what had caught my eye. "That's my boys," he told me. "They love airplanes and being that most of my inspections are in Les Cayes and during the week, they never get an opportunity to see them. I'm sure they're all balled up with energy, wanting to get out."

I saw a chance to be accommodating and offered to give them a tour of the 310.

Another big smile appeared on the agent's face. "You really don't mind?" he asked. "I hate to hold up you and Mrs. Cameron."

"Of course I don't mind," I said. "In fact, I'd enjoy it, and it's every pilot's duty to encourage kids to take an interest in the world of aviation. Bring those boys right over."

The agent raised his fingers to his mouth but didn't get a chance to whistle before the door burst open and two identical twins piled out. They were standing next to us in seconds. They looked to be ten years old or so and were miniature images of their dad, sans, of course, the moustache.

"Simon, Sandley, say hello to Mr. and Mrs. Cameron," he instructed.

The two little boys, with ear-to-ear smiles, spoke out in unison. "Hey!"

Beaming at our new friends, Aubrey tousled their hair and asked if they wanted to see the airplane. They replied with an exuberant "yes" and latched onto her.

With Aubrey in the middle and one boy on each side holding onto her hands, they climbed into the airplane. I was quite surprised, as I had assumed that I would be the one to give the tour. I glanced at the agent to acknowledge the moment, and I saw that his expression had turned solemn. I was wondering if maybe we had overstepped our bounds.

We climbed aboard behind them and watched as Aubrey put them in the pilot and copilot seats and positioned the headsets on them. She then pulled out a spare headset and plugged it into the auxiliary audio panel so they all three could talk and listen. I didn't know she even knew what the auxiliary panel was.

Squeezing into the space between the two seats, she looked back at me and asked if she could turn on the master switch to activate the audio panel. I gave her two thumbs up. "Impressed" was an understatement. My bride had been paying attention for sure.

She showed the boys how to move the dual yokes, then pointed out the window to show them what they'd just made happen. She also pointed out the dials and instruments and did an impressive job of describing what they did.

After a few minutes of playing flight instructor, she took off her headset and turned toward me and the agent. "They want to hear and see the engines running. Can you do that for us?" She was smiling just as big as her young students were. It was clear that she was taken by them.

"I sure can, if it's all right with their dad," I said.

He said it would be fine.

Agent Pierre-Toussaint and I switched out with the boys and got into the pilot and copilot seats. They stood behind us eagerly like two little birds.

I had several extra headsets, so everyone listened as I went through the checklist. When the engines fired up, the boys were so excited that they could not stand still. To their delight, I taxied down a ramp where there was no construction and, of course, they wanted me to take off. I told them, to the relief of their dad, that we'd save that for next time.

We taxied back to the ramp and when we disembarked, the boys again latched onto Aubrey with seemingly no plans to ever let her go. She was fully engrossed with them as well and seemed to have momentarily forgotten the reason we were there. It was amazing to watch her interaction with them. I'd never seen that side of her and realized what a great mom she would have been.

Agent Pierre-Toussaint walked over and stood next to me silently, watching his boys play with Aubrey. After a few moments, he lowered his head and stared down at the ground. Tears were trickling down his face.

He saw that I had noticed. "The boys lost their mother in the earthquake. It's been five years since it happened, and they still miss her just as much as the first day she was gone. I thought time would make it better, but it hasn't. Mr. Cameron, this is the first time Sandley and Simon have shown the least bit of affection to any female who wasn't family since the tragedy." He turned his gaze toward Aubrey. "I can't thank you and Mrs. Cameron enough. This has been a special day for all of us," he said, wiping away the tears, which by now were flowing.

I thought about how God puts us in the places where he needs us, and I truly believed that this was where he needed us that day. I now understood why we were spared the tragedies on Grand Cayman. He had a job for us, or at least he did for Aubrey.

As Aubrey and the boys walked back toward us arm in arm, she playfully told their dad that she would like to keep them. Both of the boys agreed and gazed at Aubrey with the wonder of rediscovering something lost and precious. The agent and I traded troubled looks.

"Boys, Mr. and Mrs. Cameron are here to visit friends, and its time for us to go. Maybe before they leave, they can come for supper. What would you think of that?"

With sad faces, they let go of Aubrey's hands. She leaned down and gave both of them a long hug. Then, not wanting to leave, they moved slowly toward the truck.

She put her arm in mine and watched them wistfully. I imagined she was thinking about things that might have been—while they dreamed of things that used to be. I knew she would be devastated when she heard what had happened to their mother.

With swollen eyes, Agent Pierre-Toussaint told us goodbye. "Thank you both for what you've done today. I will always be indebted." He shook my hand and gave Aubrey a gentle hug.

I walked him to his truck because it just seemed the thing to do. The boys had already climbed into the back seat and closed the door.

"If there is anything you need or anything I can help you with while you two are in Haiti, please don't hesitate to ask," he said, opening his door. "Also, if the two of you can find the time, we'd love to get together." He glanced toward the back seat. I'm sure his heart yearned for more comfort for his boys.

"Agent Pierre-Toussaint ..." I began.

But he stopped me before I could continue. "Please call me Jules," he said.

I reciprocated and told him I thought the boys had had an equal effect on Aubrey. I told him I would do my best to get them together before leaving Haiti. I shook Jules' hand once more and walked back to Aubrey.

Watching them drive away, she asked in a frightened voice, "Colby, what's going on?" She'd noticed the tears on the father's face, and she knew that his effusive thanks were centered on something more than a simple airplane tour.

I tried not to get emotional, but I got choked up when I told her what had happened. "They lost their mom during the earthquake. He said it's been a rough five years, and you're the first person they've connected with since the day it happened."

I could tell it stabbed her heart, and her silent tears began to flow.

"Those poor boys," she said. She gently lay her head on my shoulder and stared in the direction of the truck. I knew at some point we would have a serious discussion about what had happened and what it meant, but for now we had to focus on why we'd come to Haiti (or at least why I *thought* that we were there).

Chapter Twelve

Nathan

With a loud mechanical whine, the landing gear of the big Boeing 737 rotated and disappeared into the bays underneath the wings. The aircraft climbed into the clouds above Atlanta and headed southeast toward Port-au-Prince. Just hours earlier, Nathan had been able to secure a seat on the Sunday morning flight, the only one scheduled to Haiti for that day. Being the middle of summer and the height of vacation season, he thought he'd been fortunate to get it.

After boarding, he saw that very few seats were taken. Since the earthquake in 2010, Haiti was not high on the vacation list, if on the list at all. Most people were trying to get out instead of in.

Finding he had the choice of pretty much any seat on the airplane, he chose one on an empty row next to a window. The fifty or sixty other passengers appeared to be expatriates or mission workers. (Mission workers always seemed to wear the same color t-shirts with their church's name and city printed on the back.) He was glad he wouldn't be bothered by an overly talkative seatmate or, even worse, someone with poor hygiene. Being a seasoned traveler, he had many horror stories.

As the jet ascended into the clouds, he closed the window shade and settled in for the three-hour flight. He began thinking about Marti's disappearance. (He refused to believe she'd drowned.) He had a strong feeling it was related to her growing popularity with the Haitian people, making her a possible threat to the corrupt political establishment.

Nathan remembered the day she was born and how honored he'd felt to accept his role as godfather. He thought about how proud he was of the person she'd become.

Jeanne-Marie Lamartine, born in 1981, was precocious, polite, and the child that every parent dreamed of having. Nathan never tired of hearing reports from Charles about his beloved little girl. It was clear very early on that Marti was destined for big things.

Growing up in a walled and gated estate in Petionville, the family lived high above the poverty that permeated Port-au-Prince, separated from the masses in almost every way: geographically and socially and economically as well. For the most part, Marti lived a sheltered life, unaware of the poor living conditions that plagued the vast majority of her fellow countrymen. That changed the day she accompanied her father to a conference as part of a school project.

The conference was on the current status and outlook for the country's education system. According to Charles, the slides and photographs of the deplorable conditions of the inner-city schools instantly broke his daughter's heart. She'd known there were differences between her own private school and the public schools, but until that day, she had no idea how huge they were.

The outlook for the underprivileged was bleak and, at only twelve years old, she announced to her parents that she had to fix it.

Over the next several months, Marti educated herself on the issues surrounding the problems that she'd seen. She wrote a paper for her sixth-grade class on the lack of educational opportunities for the children of Simon Pele in the nearby community of Delmas.

She found the teachers were grossly under-qualified, concerned more with discipline than with teaching. The high-school graduation rate was only 35 percent, compared to 90 percent in Petionville, just a few miles away. The children had basically been tossed out of a system that seemed to only cater to the middle and upper classes.

As she began attending lectures, always the youngest in the crowd, her new passion for helping bloomed. Charles kept Nathan informed about his daughter's newfound determination to bring more fairness to the world. She felt those who were born without privilege deserved as many opportunities to succeed as anybody else. She decided that it would be her calling to work toward that change.

She petitioned her father for permission to help the children of Simon Pele, which had the most crowded living quarters in the city along with the lowest incomes. It was a crime-riddled area and no place for the daughter of a high-profile, wealthy businessman. When he emphatically said no, she refused to accept his answer, and he eventually conceded.

But he did insist on some conditions. She was allowed to visit schools and community centers only and had to be back before dark. He also required that she make all As, which wasn't hard for Marti. She had yet to make anything less in all her years at school. He also assigned two of his best armed bodyguards to stay with her at all times. She agreed, and it wasn't long before she began to make things change for the children of Simon Pele.

Still, Charles often worried—as did Nathan from afar.

By the time she graduated high school, Marti had brought much attention and awareness to the plight of Simon Pele. Collaboration between the business community and the government was producing visible improvements in the inner-city schools. With her successes, she had become a minor celebrity in Simon Pele and Delmas.

Upon graduation, she reluctantly left Haiti to attend college in the United States. She received her bachelor's degree in sociology at the University of Virginia and her master's in political science from NYU. When she returned to Haiti in 2005, it was her father's wish for her to join him and her brother in running the family real estate business, but she respectfully declined.

She expanded her work from the inner city and committed to making sure that every Haitian had the opportunity for success through an academic or technical education. After college, she was keen on understanding even more the issues and roadblocks that kept so many of her countrymen from realizing their dreams.

Farming was one of the largest industries in the country and almost the only way for the average Haitian to escape from poverty. The government and private banks for the most part refused to make agricultural loans and, on the rare occasions that they did, the loans came with a rate of 20 percent or more. It was clear that no one at the top wanted change to come. But through her foundation and with the support of members of the private sector who saw things as she did, Marti worked to make things happen. She found investors willing to take a chance on Haiti with low-interest agricultural loans.

In just three years, they had made over ten thousand loans, and the program was an overwhelming success. She was putting improvements in place that the inept government could not or, more correctly, wouldn't.

In 2009, she became the sweetheart of the country when she was crowned Miss Haiti after entering the pageant with much encouragement from her peers. To Marti, it was an opportunity to put her foundation in the spotlight. When she came home with the crown, all the eyes of Haiti were focused on the young reformer, but not everybody liked what they were seeing.

In the summer of the same year, Marti married her longtime boyfriend, Dominique Roumain. They'd met in Petionville as children and dated all through high school. They continued their romance through the college years when, instead of joining Marti in the States, Dominique remained in Haiti to study journalism at Quisqueya University. At the same time, he interned with *Le Nouvelliste*, the oldest newspaper in the country. After graduation, the newspaper hired him as an investigative journalist. He excelled at the job and became well known for uncovering fraud and corruption within the government.

Tragically, just shy of their first anniversary, Dominique was mysteriously gunned down in a parking lot after a dinner meeting at a restaurant in Port-au-Prince. He had been investigating the violence and corruption wrought upon the country by Jean-Claude Duvalier and Jean-Bertrand Aristide during their times in office. The murder was never solved, with supporters of Duvalier and Aristide blaming each other for the killing.

A devastated Marti threw herself into her work. She continued to expand her foundation's efforts toward educational and economic development in rural areas. As a hands-on CEO, she traveled across the country, sometimes hiking miles to remote locations to learn and understand the hardships and needs of the people. She also traveled the world to raise funds for the foundation.

Immediately after the earthquake in 2010, while the government was focusing on relief for Port-au-Prince, Marti and her foundation worked to provide assistance to the rural areas. She and her team were responsible for saving countless lives, and she became even more of a heroine in Haiti. Over the next few years, as her influence and successes continued to expand, so did the whispers about a possible run for the presidency in 2016.

With her rising popularity, the passionate advocate for the poor had become a threat to the stability of the corrupt political infrastructure. If they had killed her husband for investigating the old regime, what lengths would they go to in order to protect the one that was now in place?

—

Lost in his thoughts of Marti, Nathan felt the bay door of the landing gear disengage and could not believe they had arrived already. As the 737 broke through the gray and misting clouds, he was saddened to see that the landscape of Port-au-Prince hadn't changed. With the vast influx of relief funds from the international community, he had hoped the city would have received a much-needed facelift.

What he saw instead were ragged palm trees surrounded by a sea of decaying concrete. Colorless hovels with tired, rusted tin roofs covered the city like a plague. The country he had put his heart into for so many years was continuing to spiral down into the pit of corruption and neglect. A sense of despair washed over him for the country that he loved.

The flight attendant announced their arrival into Port-au-Prince, welcomed the Haitians home, and wished visitors a safe trip. Usually at this point in a flight, there were instructions for making connections at the airport, but no one connected through Haiti.

For better or worse, Nathan had arrived, and his focus was on finding Marti—and finding her alive.

Having packed lightly, he grabbed his overnight bag from the overhead and waited patiently for his turn to disembark. The Haitian passengers were busy unloading bags full of products only available in the US. Nathan didn't mind putting off a little longer his reunion with his old friend. For years he and Charles had greeted each other with smiles and big hugs and talked excitedly about their plans for the visit. This time would be different.

As he exited through the jetway and entered the terminal, things appeared much brighter than the depressing view he'd seen from the plane. Hearing traditional Haitian music, Nathan turned the corner to find a five-piece band made up of elderly, toothless men. It made him smile. It was the one thing he could always count on. For as many years as he'd been traveling to Haiti, there had been a band to welcome new arrivals.

These men exemplified the warm and friendly spirit of the people. He was reminded of an old Creole proverb: "Bel Cheve Pa Laja" (You can't judge a book by its cover). They may be living in a dirty, stained, and polluted environment just a few rungs up the ladder from abject poverty, but there was no question they embraced a wonderful wealth of spirit. Nathan pulled out a five-dollar bill and dropped it in the Duvalier-styled top hat sitting on a worn guitar case.

Walking toward the long customs line, he was pulled aside by a tall, muscular Haitian in a fine tailored black suit. The man had the kind of communications device in his ear that Nathan was all too familiar with.

"Mr. Roark?" the man asked.

"Yes?" Nathan was suddenly afraid that his employer must have somehow learned about his trip. He had not told anyone, but whenever anyone in the company used their passport, someone at Langley would take note.

"Please follow me," the man said.

Nathan followed the official-looking figure and took notice of the disconcerting stares from fellow passengers. It must have looked like Nathan was in some kind of trouble, being detained perhaps—and possibly he was.

The man escorted Nathan to a private office, where he was cleared by Customs. Wordlessly, the stranger then led him through the airport and outside to the passenger pick-up area.

The first thing Nathan noticed was the presence of the UN. About ten Brazilian soldiers dressed in camouflage stood guard with automatic weapons. They wore serious expressions as they studied the departing passengers.

Just a few yards into the parking area were several military trucks with gun turrets mounted over the beds. MINUSTAH (Mission des Nations Unies pour la stabilization en Haiti) was a United Nations peacekeeping mission that had been in operation since 2004. They had never been received well by the people. The mandate from the UN had been to provide a stable presence during the electoral period. The mission had been set to terminate in 2010, but when the earthquake ravaged Haiti, the deployment was extended.

From what Nathan had been reading, MINUSTAH was building up troop levels in anticipation of the fall elections. With the distrust of the electoral process and with 138 presidential candidates on the slate for the primary, Haiti was primed for mass demonstrations and chaos. It was not a place Nathan would want to be during the month of October.

They walked past the troops toward a black Chevrolet Suburban that was parked at a curb. The man in the suit stared at the soldiers with distaste, and they returned the glare.

The Suburban reminded Nathan of the last time he had been in the back of one. It had been with Colby and Aubrey in the mountains of North Georgia. That perilous night had ended with the death of the men they'd been pursuing. It had also rekindled a relationship between two people who were meant to be together. Thinking of Colby and Aubrey now, he wondered how things were going on their honeymoon in the Caymans. He also thought about the coldness with which Laura had sent him off. It might be time to plan a second honeymoon for the two of them to smooth things out a bit.

The night before while he was packing, she'd walked into the room and caught him in his fabrication about the reason for the trip. Spread out on the bed were all the items that he took on company assignments, and it was then that Laura figured out exactly what was up. Nathan had convinced her to let him go ahead of her and spend a few days with Charles—in the role of friend as opposed to investigator. If it happened later that the drowning was confirmed, she could fly down for the funeral. But seeing what was set out on the bed, Laura wasn't happy.

"You're not going down to console Charles! You're getting involved in the investigation," she said, leaning against the door-frame with her arms folded across her chest. "Does the company know you're doing this?"

"No, and I'm not getting myself involved in anything. I'm just going to take a look around," he said.

"Nathan, we agreed you wouldn't do this anymore. You're supposed to be retired. What do you expect to accomplish down there anyway? You don't do this anymore and haven't in a long time. Please leave it to Charles and the authorities."

Nathan just looked down at his feet and tried to find a way to tell her that he'd made up his mind. "It will just be for a few days and I'm not going to get into any trouble. I promise." He walked toward her with his arms held out for a hug, but she turned away and walked out of the room.

A few seconds later, she returned. "Think about your boys, your family, and how much we mean to each other. You know that none of us could stand the thought of losing you. So many times I've cried myself to sleep when it was days past the time you were supposed to be back from some assignment. Please," she pleaded. "Don't do that to me again." She turned and left the room once more.

Nathan thought about her comment about family, and it made him even more sure about what he had to do. Charles, Madeline, and Jean-Jaques had possibly lost a daughter and a sister. They loved each other just as much as he loved Laura and their boys. He had to go to Haiti and do whatever he could to help his friend.

He left the bedroom and found Laura in the kitchen chopping lettuce for a salad. Slipping up behind his wife, he put his arms around her and told her how much he loved her.

She didn't comment, but paused what she was doing. With his arms still around her, he gently explained his case: that he had the skills that Charles needed, that he was doing this for love—the kind of love a father feels for a daughter or a son. Then Nathan felt some of the tension loosen from her shoulders, and he knew she understood.

She turned and pointed the knife at him. "This better be the last *last time*," she said.

—

Nathan was instructed to climb in the back of the big black SUV and was surprised to find Charles waiting.

"How are you, my old friend?" Charles asked, patting him on the back and sticking his hand out to shake. It was another glimpse of the heart and loving nature of the Haitian people. With all of the heartache he must be feeling, the man could still manage a smile to welcome his good friend back to Haiti.

Nathan took his hand and gave it a firm shake. "I'm fine, but I've been worried. How are you and Madeleine and Jean-Jaques? Have you heard anything?"

Charles instructed the driver to take them to his office, which was just a few miles away, then he answered Nathan. "We are doing as well as possible. Madeleine is taking it very hard, and she's with my sister. As for Jean-Jaques, he doesn't know what to do. He's retreated to his house and has barely said a word to anyone since we received the news. I think he's in shock. We can talk more at the office."

After they left the airport, they traveled up the hill toward Petionville until they reached Charles's office. It was a four-story building next to the Hotel de Ville, which housed the mayor's office. Exiting the Suburban, they were met by another man in a black suit, this one carrying a shotgun. He escorted them into the building. Kidnappings in Haiti had become rampant, and Charles would be a windfall if someone were to snatch him.

No one spoke as they took the elevator to the top floor. When they entered Charles's office, Charles pointed Nathan to a chair and then sat behind his desk. He sat quietly and watched his friend, seemingly trying to figure out the right way to begin.

Finally, he started. "I have my doubts that Marti drowned. The reason I wanted you to come was to get your take on everything that happened on the night that she went missing—and possibly to help with an investigation." He paused. "I also have some information that this might be a part of something very complicated. It might also lead us to the reason that she disappeared." He paused again, and Nathan nodded for him to continue.

Charles continued with his story. "I'm sure that you've kept up with all the things that Marti's been doing for our country. She has far surpassed the goals I'd hoped to see our nation reach forty years ago when I began my own work, and I could not be more proud. The people here love and support our Marti, and it's starting to appear that Haiti might finally have a chance to pull out of the poverty that's hung over us for the last fifty years. Her programs for agricultural education and loans have been a huge success, and Haiti is exporting more coffee and sugarcane than it has in years. Farmers can finally make a profit, and things are expanding at a rate we've never seen before.

"Marti has been able to do all this through her foundation, but she's been feeling pressure recently to step things up and run for president. You are well aware of the legacy of the elite in Haiti. They've prospered for many generations by keeping down the poor. Finally, we're starting to see some change, but it's come with a price."

Nathan had been reading the political blogs and knew there was some sort of political underground movement working to bring positive change to the country, but until the phone call last Saturday night, he had no idea his goddaughter was involved. "So I have been reading," he said to his friend. "Things are about as politically charged as I've ever seen. Tell me everything you know."

Charles got up and headed to the bar. Nathan understood. His friend would need more than water to get through a story that had ended with his daughter missing. Charles poured himself a rum on the rocks and tossed Nathan a bottle of water. Sitting back down at his desk, he continued with the story.

"Marti was having a fundraiser at her cottage on Ile-a-Vache last Friday night for her Haiti foundation. She had spent weeks putting everything together, and she was so excited. There was a caterer and a great band from the mainland, and big tents were set up on the patio next to the beach. There was also a ceremony to recognize her benefactors and celebrate the successes of the year. Madeleine and I were supposed to be there that night, but I had a board retreat that I couldn't miss." Charles picked up his glass and downed two fingers of rum, then leaned back in his chair and stared up at the ceiling. "If only I had been there, it might have never happened."

With a deep breath, he continued. "Marti's party wrapped up around two thirty in the morning and, according to her bodyguard, Marti left the house and walked out to the beach to take a swim. He was a little concerned about the swim because she had been drinking, which was unusual for Marti. While she was in the water, the bodyguard went off to do a check around the perimeter of the cottage. And then when he got back, Marti's clothes were still there, hanging on the tree. But my girl was gone. He said he ran up and down the shore, yelling out her name, but there was no sign of Marti." Charles tipped his glass back and finished off his drink.

Nathan had a sinking feeling. Could Marti have misjudged the amount of alcohol in her system and gone too far out into the ocean? He'd heard stories of that happening. A sense of sadness overtook him until Charles came to the next part of his story.

Charles leaned back in his chair. "Then the guard—his name is Hector—pulled out his phone to call for help, and that was the last thing he remembered."

Surprised, Nathan rose up in his chair and asked, "What happened to the guard?"

"This is where the story takes a crazy turn. And this is why I asked you to come to Haiti. The next morning, Marti's maid came to clean up from the party, and she found Hector passed out in a chaise lounge on the patio. When she couldn't locate Marti, she called the police.

"When they got there, they found Hector half dressed with an empty bottle of rum in his hand and a ... " Charles paused, struggling to continue. "They found a syringe with drugs next to Hector's arm.

After the police got him to the station, that's when I got the call, and I immediately took a helicopter to the island. When I got there, I found the police had roughed him up pretty good. Everyone loved Marti, and they, of course, believed it was his fault that she'd drowned."

Nathan leaned forward toward his friend. "And you don't think it was?"

"Nathan, he swore up and down he hadn't been drinking or doing drugs. But up and down his left arm, he had the classic track marks that you see on someone who does heroin. He said he'd been set up, but the police think he was lying. Nathan, I've known the guy for thirty-five years. He's been nothing but loyal and reliable to Marti and the family. I know his kids, his wife, and they're all upstanding people. He would give his life for us. I just don't know how this could have happened." He got up from his chair and paced around the room.

"Where is Hector now?" Nathan asked.

"He's here in the building," replied Charles. "I was afraid to leave him on Ile-a-Vache. As upset as the police were, I'm not so sure he would have been able to stay alive if I hadn't brought him here. They agreed to turn him over to me if I kept him under house arrest. I wanted you to talk to him. If we find that what the police believe he did is true, the police will be the least of that man's worries." A dark look crossed Charles's eyes, then he walked to the door and turned to look at Nathan. "Come with me. I'll take you to him."

Nathan followed Charles down a series of halls that led to a room with an armed guard posted at the door. Charles motioned for the guard to unlock it, and the two men walked in.

Nathan found himself in a conference room with a long table in the center. The man who must be Hector was sitting in the end chair with his head buried in his hands. He looked up when they entered. What Nathan saw before him was a defeated man. He had seen many suspects in his time and usually knew if they were guilty within seconds.

Charles spoke coldly to the man. "Hector, I'm sure you remember Marti's godfather, Nathan Roark." At the mention of his daughter's name, Charles paused and stared at Hector with a look just shy of disgust. "He's going to ask you some questions about last Friday night. I expect you to fully cooperate."

Hector nodded that he understood. Charles left the room and Nathan heard the door lock behind him.

There were many forms of interrogation that Nathan had used or observed. It was up to the investigator to choose wisely. The wrong technique could result in a lot of wasted time, leaving you with nothing but useless information. Sizing up Hector, Nathan felt he knew just the tactic he should take. In a calm manner without accusation or aggression, he asked him a question that the guard most likely had not yet been asked. "Hector, please tell me what you think happened on that night."

He could immediately see the tension drain from the man across from him. The question seemed to instill a new energy in Hector, who sat up straighter in his chair.

"Mr. Roark, I first want you to know that I love Marti like my own child," he said insistently. "For thirty years, I've protected and watched over her. The only reason I haven't already retired is because I've been afraid for Marti's safety. She is a national figure now and, as you probably know, has made a few people very uncomfortable. I promise you with my life that I had nothing to do with her disappearance."

Nathan noted that Hector did not refer to a supposed drowning. "So you don't think she drowned?" he asked.

"No, sir. I do not. She was an excellent swimmer, and the ocean was calm and clear that night. She'd had a bit to drink, but she was not intoxicated enough that it wasn't safe for her to swim. Somebody took Marti that night, and it was the same person—or people—who knocked me out and put me in that lounge chair. Mr. Roark, I don't drink or do drugs. Please. You must believe me. You can ask anyone who knows me," Hector pleaded.

"You say they knocked you out. Did you feel someone strike you?"

"No, sir. I was in a panic and so focused on finding Marti that I didn't feel a thing." Nathan felt that things were not quite adding up, and he had an idea what might have happened.

"Hector, do you mind removing your shirt and letting me examine you?" he asked, moving toward him.

Hector had his jacket and shirt off before Nathan could get to him.

Nathan asked him to sit up on the table directly underneath the florescent light. He first examined the track lines on his arm and immediately found what he'd been expecting. There were about ten small pricks in and around the bend of his arm. They were pink and irritated, a few of them possibly infected. It appeared they'd all been made at the same time. He didn't see any signs of scarring from past needle use.

"Hector," he asked, "did a doctor examine you on Ile-a-Vache?"

"No, sir. There's not a doctor on the island," replied Hector.

Nathan on a hunch pulled out his wallet and took out a random business card. He placed it on the table with a pen. "Write your wife's name and number on the card," he said. "I may need to call her later."

Hector picked up the pen and did as he was told. It was just as Nathan thought: Hector was right-handed. If he had been a drug user, he would have put the needle in his left arm, yet the needle marks were on the right. Nathan now had a good idea about what had happened on that night.

He had Hector bend his head over so he could examine the back of his neck. Once again, his suspicions proved to be correct. He found a pink, slightly irritated needle prick. Things were about to get interesting.

"Thank you, Hector, for your cooperation," he said. "I want you to know that I believe you, and I'll let Charles know as well." Nathan gave him back his shirt and jacket.

Hector reached out to grab Nathan's hand. "Thank you, my friend, for believing me. And please don't stop stop looking for the answers. I hope and pray you find our Marti."

Nathan gave him a smile and knocked on the door to signal to the guard that he was ready. When the guard let him out, he walked back to Charles's office, a whirlwind of thoughts swirling through his head. Since the culprits hadn't murdered Hector, Nathan didn't think that they'd killed Marti either. This was beginning to look like an elaborate kidnapping, and it was the best news of the day. It meant that she was likely still alive.

He hurried down the hall to tell Charles the good news.

Chapter Thirteen

Nathan found Charles sitting at his desk staring at the open door, anxious for his return. He relayed to Charles what he had discovered. "The bodyguard is exactly who you thought he was: a loyal employee and friend who loves Marti like we do and wouldn't even think about hurting one hair on her head," he said. "Charles, it's my professional and personal opinion that Marti did not drown. I think she was kidnapped."

Charles leaned forward eagerly and said something in French Creole that Nathan didn't understand. "What? What do you mean?" he asked.

Nathan explained about his examination of Hector's arm and what he found and did not find. He told Charles about the needle mark behind Hector's head. It all made perfect sense. Hector had been set up.

Charles sat back in his chair and eyed the rum bottle on the bar. Nathan knew that Charles never took a drink during the day; he hardly drank at all, but this day was tailor-made to be the exception to the rule. Charles poured himself a second drink and this time made one for Nathan. "Here," he told his friend. "I think you're going to need this. What I'm about to tell you is information that only a few people in this country have—and I'm not supposed to be one of them."

Nathan looked at him, confused.

The person that gave me this put his life at risk and his family's too," said Charles. "Nobody can ever know who that person is." He leaned back in his chair to begin the long explanation. "Four years ago, the second wealthiest man in the country held a meeting in the mountains. There were only three people invited to the meeting. One was a senior colonel in the national police. Another was a university president, and the third a successful banker. The reason for the meeting was to organize a cabal. The new president, just elected a few hours earlier, was not prepared to run the country. His naïve ideas and sensationalism were a recipe for even more disaster. If the country was going to recover from decades of abuse, the host of the party felt that something drastic must be done.

"The cabal had no plans to remove the newly elected president. They would need time to create their coalition. Their plan was to publicly build a council of twenty high-powered businessmen, environmentalists, educators, farmers, and tourism professionals who over the next four years would create a powerful political party. They planned to have this all in place for the next election. Of course, the council would unknowingly be controlled by the cabal. The original four would choose and convert eight of the twenty and have the majority vote. They would then select the future president and prime minister. These candidates would appear to win the offices in a fair election, but in reality, the government would be controlled by the cabal.

"Once this was set in motion, the four would slowly begin to implement laws, regulations, and policies to shape the future of the country as it suited them. The way my friend explained it, the plan seemed to be going smoothly. The current president, unable to run for re-election, endorsed his party's nominee, but that candidate was weak and performed poorly in the polls. The cabal's candidate, on the other hand, was positioned well in front and primed to win the office. All that changed, however, in these last few months. Something totally unexpected popped up to spoil their plan. Would you like to guess what it might have been, the fly in their ointment?"

"Marti, of course," said Nathan.

"I'm afraid that you're correct. A new party was created, mostly from the agricultural community. They didn't feel that any of the current candidates could change the direction of the country. And, as you have guessed, my friend, they asked Marti to run with their backing. Now, mind you, she has not officially accepted, but there's a huge outcry from the public for her to be a candidate. It appears that if she were to run, there's a pretty good chance that she could win this thing." He gave Nathan a sad smile. "That would make my little girl our first female president."

Nathan could hardly catch his breath.

Charles nodded to acknowledge the immense nature of his revelations. "As you can imagine, this has not gone over well with the cabal. My friend is not one of the original four, but he is one of the eight who was later brought into the inner group. When they chose him and took him into their confidence, saying no was not an option. And now he curses the day he ever got involved. He had no idea—and others didn't either—that the true goal of the council was to subvert the government. He's afraid—he's terrified—for himself and for his family and, of course, for the future of our country."

Charles went on to say that his friend had grown to fear that the cabal had been planning to do something drastic to make sure that Marti did not disrupt their plans. It now appeared they had. Charles sipped his drink and asked, "What do you think we should do?"

Nathan already had a plan. "First of all, you publicly stick with the story that you're still looking into things. That should buy us a couple days until we can sort things out. I believe you are correct that the cabal abducted Marti. I think they're holding her to see if people buy that she has drowned. If not, they'll contact you for ransom, making it look like she was kidnapped. The last thing they want is to have anyone believe this is political. Of course, they'd structure it to look like it was a kidnapping by a gang."

Nathan hesitated. He owed it to his friend to be absolutely honest. "They could kill her, Charles, after you pay out. I'm sure their candidate would use the country-in-mourning angle to the cabal's benefit. They'd promise that once elected, he would put an end to the lawlessness that brought about her murder. We should keep Hector briefed and keep him here at the estate so he'll be out of view. Knowing he's a key piece to the drowning story, the cabal will be watching him.

"You make a statement to the press that Marti's body hasn't tuned up, but you say a person of interest is being interviewed and will hopefully provide answers about her disappearance. That should be ambiguous enough to keep the cabal questioning what's going on—and enough to keep our girl alive. Also, as much as I hate the idea, we can't tell Madeline or Jean-Jaques any of what you've told me."

Charles nodded in agreement. "They know that Hector was present when it happened, but they don't know any other details. As far as they know, he was just a witness and Marti simply went out for a swim and never made it back to shore. No one knows about the real investigation into Hector except the police on Ile-a-Vache and whoever they might have told. And, of course, the maid. I still can't believe this all is happening." He drained the last of his drink, leaned back in his chair, and stared wearily at Nathan. "You have to find Marti. Please."

"I'll do whatever it takes," said Nathan. "I promise you that, my friend."

He would search until he found her.

—

Nathan left Charles's office with a roughly sketched out plan. In his semi-career with the State Department and the CIA, he'd solved many problems and was well versed in strategic planning. He usually had dozens of analysts backing him up with real-time data, and his job would be sitting in an office, ten floors underground, analyzing scenarios and their possible outcomes. With the exception of his early days with the company, he'd rarely ventured into the field.

The latest exception had been a situation about ten years ago in western Sudan. The UN Security Council had issued a warrant for the president's arrest on charges of genocide and crimes against humanity. Nathan coordinated the mission from a comfortable mobile command unit about fifty miles from the operation.

The current case would be different. He would be the analyst, strategic planner, and field operative, but he knew that wouldn't be enough to get the job done. If he hoped to find any useful information about Marti, he would need some help. His thoughts went back to a young man he'd hired on his first assignment in Haiti. Like himself, the man was no longer young or quite as capable as he once had been. But he was the only one Nathan could trust to help him with the investigation. He needed to find Reagan Flexion.

He'd first discovered Reagan early on in his career when he needed some help on the job in Haiti. As a young agent, Nathan had quickly learned that Haitians barely trusted one another, let alone *the blanc*. The language barrier was another issue. So he needed to find one of Haiti's own to work as his assistant. He needed someone reasonably trained and educated in the complexity of the country's unstable political and economic structure.

In the Haiti of the 1970s, that was a tall order. The country was lacking a military, and the police were ill-trained, barely more than security guards. But in the stack of resumes on his desk, he did manage to find one that stood out above the rest.

Reagan Flexion had been born on the southeast coast of Haiti in the coastal town of Jeremie and was just a few months younger than Nathan.

When he was six, Reagan's parents, unable to find work, left Haiti and moved to the Dominican Republic. Educated in Santo Domingo, the capital city of the DR, he spoke fluent Spanish, English, French, and, most importantly, Creole.

The year he turned eighteen, his mom and dad returned to Haiti to care for their aging parents. Not being a citizen of the DR or having a work visa, Reagan was forced to return as well. From the Universite d'Etat d'Haiti, he earned a bachelor's degree in political science with a minor in economics. It was this education that caught Nathan's eye.

Most of Nathan's responsibilities in Haiti involved monitoring and reporting on the changing political climate. Reagan had the right education and, if the interview went well, Nathan could teach him the rest of what he'd need to know.

When the two met in person, Nathan was impressed. The pair worked together for the next four years until Nathan left the company and returned to the United States.

After Nathan's departure, Reagan accepted a job with the International Economic Development Council. After just five years, he was promoted to director, and he spent the next thirty years in that job—well, mostly in that job. He and Nathan remained close friends, and in 1994, when Nathan returned to Haiti to assist in the removal of Aristide, Reagan was once again commissioned to be his assistant. Now, twenty-two years later, Nathan would need to commission him once more.

So far, he felt things were stacking up rather nicely. Just a few hours into his time in Haiti, he had learned more about the situation surrounding the disappearance than he could ever have imagined. His examination of Hector had been like winning the lottery—an investigator's dream. During the ten-minute interview, he'd found that the bodyguard was not involved and that Marti had probably been kidnapped. He'd also found out from Charles about an underlying criminal conspiracy against her.

Leaving the office and walking to the Kinam Hotel, where Charles had arranged for him to stay, he thought about how he would get to Ile-a-Vache. Charles had offered to have a driver take him there the next morning, but Nathan had declined. A shiny new Suburban would stick out in the rural part of the country, and he wanted to remain anonymous as long as possible. He knew that when he got to the island and started asking questions, his presence would be quickly known, and he thought it would be best to take the bus. He had traveled the country many times by bus, packed in with a crowd of locals and as many goats, chickens, and pigs as they could squeeze on board. Fortunately, the bus business had improved, and he would be on a large charter type of vehicle and without the animals. The bus would take him to Les Cayes, a port city on the southwest side of the island, where he would catch the noon ferry for Ile-a-Vache.

Almost to the Kinam Hotel, which was adjacent to the park and all the street-front markets, he prepared to be accosted. He could already hear the "two for one, special deal for the American" sales pitches. He could speak enough Creole to fend the vendors off, but he knew that one small purchase might be a vendor's only sale that day to feed his family. That's the way it was in the poverty-stricken nation. There was no welfare or government assistance, and there were no food stamps. It was like that before the earthquake and, even with all the money that had been pumped into the country, it was like that still. The poor people were still poor. Everyone had to do what they could to survive.

He took a deep breath, knowing it was time for the negotiations. He had done it many, many times. He would ask about a particular painting in one of the booths, and it would be on. All the vendors who had the same painting would fight each other to prove who could sell it for less money. For Nathan, escape was not an option. He would be leaving with a painting. After listening to the vendors haggle aggressively with each other, he chose a meek little guy standing behind the crowd and paid him twenty-five dollars for a painting of an old fishing boat.

After buying the painting, he held up his hands and told them in Creole that he was done and not buying any more. It was a useless statement. There was blood in the water, and they weren't giving up. A group followed him to the hotel, trying to sell him another painting with the discount getting deeper the closer he got to the gate.

A guard with a shotgun opened the gate and let Nathan in. Not nearly as politely as Nathan had, he informed the vendors that Mr. Roark was finished with his shopping.

As he entered the historic Kinam Hotel, he looked forward to shucking off his tired clothes after a day of traveling. The hotel had been recently remodeled and had a new modern wing, but Nathan preferred the older section. Feeling nostalgic as he reached the desk, he requested room number 415. He and Laura had spent a wonderful week in that room in the late seventies.

Opening the door ten minutes later, he discovered that the room was just as he remembered. He settled in, then set out for the open-air dining room after a hot shower. Well, since the knobs were put on backwards (to his American eyes, at least), it was an ice-cold shower that suddenly turned into a very, very hot one.

Sitting at a table above the pool, he saw a friend from the old days approaching with a big smile. Jean-Luc was a mountain of a man who had been a bartender and waiter at the Kinam for at least thirty years. Nathan stuck out his hand and it disappeared into a much larger one when the big man gave it a hardy shake.

They talked about family and how long it had been since they'd seen each other. Since Jean-Luc spoke very little English, it was a chance for Nathan to practice the hundred or so Creole words he knew. He knew just what to say when Jean-Luc returned from the bar with a chilled glass and asked, "Ou toujou bwe chardoney?"

Nathan was able to gratefully reply, "Mwen toujou fe."

It was good to come to a place that was so foreign to his daily life and culture and yet, within a few minutes, feel the friendliness and comfort of home. It was one of the reasons he loved Haiti.

He ordered the traditional black beans and rice with a side of shrimp. It didn't take him long to finish, and after saying, "Bon nuit" to Jean-Luc, he made his way back to the room. The bus would depart at seven fifteen, and it would be a four-hour ride to Les Cayes.

Before he got in bed and brought to a close a very successful and interesting day, he had one last thing to accomplish. At dinner, he'd thought about what to say. Now he made the call to Reagan.

Chapter Fourteen

The cab pulled into the bus station, and although it was only six thirty in the morning, the city was alive, bustling with street vendors peddling food, candy, and cheap souvenirs. The stream of vendors always greatly outnumbered the customers, and Nathan rarely saw anyone buy a thing. There were no tourists within a hundred miles, and a local who could barely feed his family was not about to shell out money for a cheap souvenir.

As the only American in sight, Nathan was a magnet for the merchants. As a swarm of them approached, he picked up his pace and avoided eye contact as he waved them off with a few words.

Arriving at Transport Chic, where he would catch the bus, he walked into a small office in a back courtyard with a mass of others buying tickets to Les Cayes. He knew most had spent the weekend in the city, stocking up on things they could only get in Port-au-Prince. Fifteen minutes later, he had his ten-dollar one-way ticket.

For the average Haitian, this ticket was the same thing as shelling out to fly first class. Most natives opted for the still available chicken-and-goat bus. It only cost about two bucks. But Nathan wasn't on a budget and was not quite as adventurous as in the early days. Of course, the cheap bus had been the scene of some of his more memorable experiences and conversations (with people, not with goats.)

After he sat down to wait, he watched as the courtyard filled with passengers laden down with packages, appliances, and bags stuffed full with everything from pillows to electric hot plates. It reminded him of the flight from Atlanta, which had been packed with treasures from the States as people came home to a country without the convenience of a Walmart.

Around seven, the driver announced that it was time to board. Somehow, he'd managed to stuff most of the cargo and luggage into the storage area underneath the bus.

Nathan was already standing near the door, ready to jump on and claim the first seat. Sitting up front, he would have great views of the towns and communities along the route. As one left Port-au-Prince, the cleanliness of one's surroundings improved exponentially. The large piles of putrid trash, the burnt cars, and crumbling buildings vanished as the greener countryside appeared. It was a marked change from the decaying city, but the green space had not gone untouched by the decades of abuse that had ravished Haiti.

Mountains and valleys once flush with tropical trees lay useless and barren now. With charcoal as the primary source of fuel for cooking and heating, about ninety percent of the country had been deforested. Propane and solar power had been recently introduced to the island, but unfortunately, these innovations had come too late to save the trees. Reforestation, in fact, was one of the newest goals of the foundation Marti ran. It was one of the reasons the agricultural community, whose numbers were large, had chosen her as their candidate. It was likely an added reason the cabal would want her gone.

With only a few hours until he got to Les Cayes, Nathan began thinking about how he could best disclose what he knew to Reagan. If the cabal had indeed been involved in Marti's disappearance, as he felt sure they had, Nathan could be putting Reagan into danger—and his family too. When it was over, Nathan would be leaving the island to go home. Any repercussions, if their mission was unsuccessful, could be disastrous for Reagan.

If he had more time, Nathan could have gone through the proper channels and solicited help from his employer. But with only a couple of days to act, the window of opportunity was closing too quickly. He decided to just lay it all out to Reagan and let him decide.

Pulling into the town of Petit Goave, his thoughts and concerns for Reagan were suddenly sidetracked. The police had set up a roadblock in the middle of the town with military-type vehicles and police cars with blue flashing lights. Nathan had been traveling in Haiti for forty years and had only been caught in one other road block that whole time.

His heart rate sped up a little. He wondered if it was just a coincidental encounter or maybe something else. If the cabal was indeed capable of the things Charles's confidant had described, it was possible they had found out that he was there already, and his investigation would end before it had begun.

He thought about all the things he should have done. He should have hired a car and not made himself so visible by taking the bus. And he could have gotten his own transportation from the airport. If he had done a better job of gathering information before he left Atlanta, he might have been more prepared and made better decisions.

It had been a while since he'd worked in the field, but that was no excuse. Maybe Laura's assessment had been right.

As he got closer, the large white letters on the side of some of the camouflage-colored trucks gave him a start. BOID stood for the Brigade of Operations and Departmental Intervention, which was the new specialized force of the national police. It was the equivalent of the SWAT team in the United States and, according to Charles's friend, had been recently created by the top police official in the country—one of the cabal's original four. Nathan imagined this new force had complete control of law enforcement across Haiti.

Nathan watched as stern-faced men in grey military uniforms walked slowly from the trucks and circled the bus. Everyone was silent. With the hiss of the air brakes, the driver opened the door and shot Nathan a furtive glance. Two policemen, armed with automatic rifles, got on board. They said something to the driver and then turned their attention to the passengers. One of them moved down the aisle and began asking questions while the other stood rigidly in place with his hand on his weapon. He held his gaze on Nathan.

Sliding a book out of his bag and pretending to read, Nathan tried to make out the questions the policeman was asking passengers, but he couldn't understand the rapidly spoken Creole. Unarmed and with the police surrounding the bus, he felt— and was— defenseless.

The policeman made his way back to the front and leaned down to speak to the driver. Nathan heard the word *blanc*, not necessarily a derogatory term but it concerned him, being he was the only blanc on the bus.

The driver said something and shrugged.

Raising his eyes slightly from his book, Nathan could see that both of them had their eyes on him. He thought about the interrogation that was likely just ahead and about what would happen when they found out who he was. He also thought of the trouble he would be in when his employer found out he had been arrested—assuming they or anyone else ever found out.

Just when he expected the policemen to approach him and haul him off, they got what sounded like an emergency call over their radios, and suddenly they were off. Quickly, they loaded into the trucks and sped away. A last-minute save, he thought. Just like in the movies.

With a sigh of relief, he felt the swarm of bees settle in his gut. Maybe the roadblock had been completely random. It was possible they were just curious about the blanc on the bus. Or maybe for now, this was just a message to show that they were watching. Either way, when he started asking questions on Ile-a-Vache, everyone would probably know that he was there, including BOID and the national police. He would have to be very careful how he handled the investigation.

When the drama of the roadblock had passed, the rhythm of the bus returned to normal with people laughing and talking like nothing had ever happened. Nathan thought about asking the driver a few questions, but the policemen may have warned him not to talk or instructed him to report any conversations he had with the blanc. They may have also told him to report who Nathan met when he got off the bus.

With this in mind, he pulled out his iPhone and sent Reagan a text telling him not to meet him at the station but at a bar and restaurant that was just up from the pier. He remembered it from his last visit to Les Cayes and hoped it was still there.

About an hour later, the bus began slowing down. Nathan knew they must be on the outskirts of Les Cayes. There were no road signs in Haiti, and the only way to know where you were was to hopefully find it written somewhere on a building. There were no buildings outside his window, but with the throng of people waiting with bags and luggage, he knew they'd arrived at the bus terminal.

When the bus came to a stop, there was a frenzy of activity behind him. People were already opening the overhead bins and lining up to disembark. When the driver opened the door, Nathan grabbed the travel bag stowed below his seat and quickly jumped off.

The "station" was just a pull-off on the side of the road near a canal, surrounded by street vendors. He waved them off, in search of transportation. There were several tap-taps parked along the street near the bus, already loading up with passengers, but Nathan wanted to avoid them if he could. They were small, brightly colored vehicles that were both dangerous and highly visible. If Nathan jumped on one, he would surely draw attention. Also, the drop-off point was probably somewhere in the middle of town, and although it was probably too late for trying to take a clandestine approach, he wanted to stay out of sight as much as possible.

Lined up next to the bus were a few cars that were Haiti's version of taxis, but they were quickly claimed by others wanting rides. Reconsidering the tap-taps, Nathan saw that they too had filled up.

Noticing a lone taxi on the other side of the road, he was about to cross the street to inquire about a ride when he suddenly thought twice. He eased back out of view and surveyed the situation. With the flurry of passengers trying frantically to secure a ride into town, no one had approached that taxi. The driver was standing by the door and was easily accessible. Of course, maybe Nathan was mistaken in assuming that it was a ride for hire. There were no official taxis in the rural parts of Haiti, just entrepreneurs with cars.

Inspecting the driver closely, Nathan noticed that he was dressed like everyone else, with one exception—shiny, patent leather black shoes. Just like in the States, it was the mark of a policeman. If he was law enforcement, it would make sense that the locals would know and stay clear.

A few feet away, sitting on a motorcycle that was spewing blue smoke was a skinny, leathery old man who had to be close to a hundred years old. The shirtless, toothless man saw Nathan looking at him. With an empty grin, he motioned for him to get onto the back of the bike. It wasn't a great or safe option, but it seemed to be his only one. Nathan climbed on back and pointed in the general direction of town and the pier. Then he held on tightly.

As they pulled away, Nathan looked back to see if the "taxi driver" had noticed them leaving, but he was already gone. Nathan had a feeling he would probably be seeing him again.

The ride into town took only a few minutes, but they were frightful minutes. If the old man had a driver's license, someone needed to take it away. After a few close calls, Nathan had the driver drop him off a couple of blocks from the pier. He paid him a few American dollars and watched as he pulled back into traffic without looking.

Walking toward the pier and seeing that no one was following him, he snuck up a narrow dirt pathway where he had a clear view of the parking area as well as a partial view of the restaurant where he was meeting Reagan. As suspected, the taxi from the bus stop was parked by the pier. The driver was standing by the car, causally smoking a cigarette.

Nathan thought of the reasons the police might be watching him. They ranged from the possibility that the cabal had their eyes on Charles—and was now watching him in turn—to something as simple as wanting to know what his business was in Haiti. It was not uncommon for the police to keep tabs on a foreigner, especially a blanc.

Not taking any chances, he continued on his back way to his destination. He slipped back down the path and followed it behind a row of two-story buildings that had partially collapsed and were covered up in vines. He approached the rear of the restaurant, edged his way through a partially opened back door and, to the great surprise of the young cook, walked through the kitchen and peeked out the service door into the dining room.

Reagan was sitting alone and drinking a beer while two policemen a couple of tables over did the same. The bar was near the National Maritime Police station, so hopefully it was just another coincidence.

Nathan motioned for the cook to join him at the door. Then, putting a hand on the young man's shoulder, he pointed a finger at Reagan. He then attempted in Creole to ask the cook to bring Reagan to the kitchen without alerting the police. When the cook didn't understand, Nathan pointed to Reagan again and then to the policemen while shaking his head to communicate an emphatic *no*. The cook seemed even more confused until Nathan pulled a twenty from his wallet.

The cook then sprung to action. He gave Nathan a thumbs-up and headed out the kitchen door. Nathan watched as he bumped Reagan's chair, accidentally spilling a small bowl of salsa on his shirt. Reagan leaped up from his chair and began wiping off the salsa with a napkin. The apologetic cook tried to lead him to the kitchen to wash off his shirt, but Reagan shook his head to decline the help. The cook, wanting his twenty dollars, literally pulled him into the kitchen. It was not quite an Academy-Award-winning performance, but it seemed to have fooled the policemen, who chuckled quietly at the show.

When Reagan came through the door, Nathan put a finger to his lips. Then he put the twenty into the hand of the smiling cook and hurried Reagan out the back door. They made it to Reagan's car and got out of town, hopefully unnoticed.

CHAPTER FIFTEEN

"So I take it this is not a social call?" Reagan asked with a crooked grin. When Nathan had called the previous night and asked to meet in Les Cayes, the conversation had been brief. Reagan had most likely guessed that the subject was too sensitive for discussing on the phone. Likewise, he probably hadn't been surprised by the scene at the bar.

Looking out the back window to see if they were being followed, Nathan let out a quick laugh and said, "No, not a social call exactly. Take us somewhere we can talk."

Knowing the drill, Reagan took several turns down side streets and waited after each turn to see if anyone was following. After a few miles and many turns, it appeared that no one was. He pulled the car down a narrow dirt driveway that led to a run-down, vacant building. He parked the car behind it and shut off the engine. Then he extended a hand toward Nathan and said with a smile, "Great to see you. Just like old times."

Nathan shook his friend's hand and repeated, "Yep, just like old times."

He spent the next thirty minutes explaining Marti's disappearance and, reluctantly, telling Reagan about the cabal and their probable involvement. He realized that once he exposed the cabal to Reagan, there was no going back.

When he finished, both were silent. Reagan tapped the steering wheel and stared out the window. Nathan sat and waited.

About thirty seconds later, Reagan turned toward Nathan. "When you called last night, knowing you're Marti's godfather, I suspected that her drowning might be the reason for your visit. Rumors from the island are that things about the drowning just aren't adding up. I'm not surprised to hear that there's more to the story, and I'm also not surprised to hear about the cabal. This country has suffered from corruption and instability so long that something like the cabal was just bound to happen.

"When the word got out that the Lavi party wanted Marti as their nominee, people were really hoping that she would accept. We are all so sick and tired of the same old politicians pulling the country further into the abyss. With her integrity, honesty, and financial accomplishments, she seemed like just the person to give us a brand new start. The whole nation was absolutely crushed when we heard she was dead." He paused for a second, choosing his words carefully. "Nathan, I'm old and I'm certainly not the man I once was, but if you think Marti's still alive, it would be my duty— and my honor— to help you find her," he said proudly.

Nathan knew that this was about much more than helping a friend in need. The future of the nation, Reagan's nation, was in jeopardy; this was his patriotic duty. The thought loosened the guilt that Nathan felt over putting his friend in danger. If it were Nathan's country, he would do the same. "I'm old as well," he said, "but we have years of experience and wisdom on our side, and we can play our geriatric status to our advantage. Some of that *Art-of-War* strategy," he added, referring to the famous combat book. He was half kidding and half serious.

"Last time I checked, wisdom, experience, and old age couldn't stop a bullet. Tell me you have a better plan than that," Reagan told him, laughing.

"I do, and here's what I've been thinking. Stop me if you see any problems or have any better thoughts."

Reagan nodded, and Nathan continued. "As I said, the bodyguard was set up and they made it look like he was drunk and high. The cops could get him on the illegal drugs, but other than that, they've got no crime to pin on him. He just looks guilty of being irresponsible in letting Marti go swimming when she'd had too much to drink.

"No one except Charles, the bodyguard, and now you knows that Marti in fact didn't drown. The plan is to keep it that way. Our trip to the island will be as personal friends helping Charles and Madeline deal with Marti's things and close down the house. In a few days, Charles will make a statement that Marti's body hasn't been recovered and that new evidence supports a possible abduction rather than a drowning.

"He will also make a statement that he believes it was politically motivated and that he plans to petition the UN to bring in a team of investigators to take over the case. Hopefully, it will force the cabal into what I think is their plan B—disguising it as a kidnapping by a gang and demanding ransom money. That would give us more time to find her as Charles would need time to set up the logistics for making the exchange." Nathan paused before continuing.

"In my professional opinion, they will never turn her over for ransom. They will make it look like a kidnapping exchange gone bad and kill her rather than take a chance on getting caught. The last thing they need is to involve more people, making things more complex. My guess is we just have a few days left to find her. The first thing I want to do is to check out Marti's house. I want to get a good look at the crime scene and see if we can figure out how she was taken from the beach. Since her house is on a dead-end road, someone might have seen them if they took her away by car.

"We also need to know what else was happening on the island on that night. I know her house is a bit isolated, but if I remember right, it's just down the beach from a small village. Maybe someone there saw something that can help. Also, we need to get the guest list from Charles and see who was at that party." He took a breath. "Okay, what do you think?"

Reagan tapped the steering wheel some more while he thought about it. "Sounds like a solid plan," he said, "We'll have to watch our backs and be very careful who we talk to," he said, looking at his watch. "Look, it's almost noon, and the ferry to Ile-a-Vache leaves at twelve thirty. We could take a private boat, but I think we should take the ferry with the rest of the islanders. If we want to look like we're just here to help the family, we should just act normal, play the part. Sound good?"

Nathan nodded. "I do have one concern," he said. "Do you think the cook will tell the police about our theatrics back there and how we sneaked out the back door? And I'm sure those policemen had to notice that you never came back from the kitchen."

Reagan laughed and said, "I can promise you that kid's not gonna say a word. That twenty you gave him is more than he makes in a whole week. And as for the policemen, they'd just gotten off of work and were relaxing with some beers. I don't think they paid me the least attention." He started up the car and with no room to turn around, backed down the driveway and wheeled onto the road. They traveled the few blocks back to the new marina and made a slow pass first to check things out before turning in. Thankfully, the taxi from earlier was nowhere to be seen.

Seeing that the ferry had just docked, they parked the car in the back lot and got out. Reagan opened the rear door and removed two bags.

"So, you always pack a bag when you meet a friend to have a beer?" Nathan asked sarcastically.

"When I'm meeting you, I do. I never know what to expect and I don't care to share your toothbrush." Reagan locked the car, and they walked the hundred yards across the gravel parking lot to the pier.

The ferry to Ile-a-Vache wasn't much of a ferry. Looking years past retirement, it was a long, narrow wooden boat covered with a thin coat of flaking fiberglass. For seating, it had five rows of benches. Each bench was meant for two, but they all were filling up three and four across.

The captain motioned for Nathan and Reagan to climb aboard and pointed them to the front bench. Nathan laughed, thinking it might have been for first-class passengers. As more people boarded, the top edge of the boat began creeping closer to the water. In back was an engine that looked like it belonged in an antique museum or, more appropriately, a salvage yard. It was coughing blue smoke and sputtering while the first mate was busy adjusting something, coaxing it to run.

It was ten miles to the island, and Nathan had doubts about whether the sick engine would even make it out of the harbor. He was glad to see the captain pass out life vests. He normally used his as a seat cushion, but, with the overloaded boat, he put in on and pulled the straps till it was snug.

Reagan gave Nathan an uneasy look and tightened his as well.

Nathan was thinking the private boat might have been the better idea.

The boat, submerged to the point of almost sinking, pulled out from the dock and began its journey to the distant island. Looking back at the shoreline, Nathan thought about how beautiful the coastal region was compared to the depressed and stricken mainland. The mountains, still abundant with trees, extended to the water, where white sandy beaches lay in the protected coves.

It took a while, but, amazingly, the boat made it across the bay. As they were nearing the island, it felt like they were arriving in another country—and to some extent, they were. Some inhabitants of the island, either because of economics or by choice, had never stepped off of its shores.

The captain cut back the engine and navigated into a small harbor. They passed several sailboats moored tightly together. Nathan and Reagan were the only passengers disembarking at this stop. The others, Nathan knew, were either day workers who commuted to Les Cayes or residents who lived on the island and would get off at the public pier.

—

Colline Sacrée was one of three inns on the island and was Nathan's favorite. It sat high on a bluff, affording 360-degree views and a picturesque landscape, complete with scenery that encompassed both the mountains and the ocean. Its presence was one of times long past and always reminded Nathan of a place where Hemingway would have come to write.

Carrying their bags, they climbed the serpentine-rock staircase that led to the inn. After checking in, they took thirty minutes to get settled in their rooms and then met back at the bar to make a plan. They still had a good part of the afternoon left and needed to begin their investigation.

With only a few days to find Marti, time was of the essence.

It was close to two when Nathan arrived. After a few pleasantries with the hotel owner, he ordered a Prestige for him and one for Reagan too. Prestige was Haiti's most popular lager, and Nathan ordered it not so much to drink it but more to place the ice-cold bottle on his neck. The heat reminded him of home. Hot and muggy.

Just as the beer arrived, Nathan looked up to see Reagan. He handed his friend one of the drinks. "Here's to finding what we're looking for," he said holding up the now-dripping bottle.

Reagan clinked his drink to Nathan's and seconded the toast.

With several guests sitting near them at the bar, Nathan tilted his head to suggest a move to a table by the pool. It would certainly be hotter out there in the sun, but they couldn't risk someone overhearing.

Anticipating the warm air outside, Nathan took a pull from his beer, then held the cold bottle against his neck.

Reagan laughed. "What's the matter, man? It's no hotter here than in Atlanta. I think you're getting soft!"

Nathan couldn't argue. "Yeah, but we rarely get out of the air-conditioning when it's hot like this, and I'm ashamed to say that, yes, I've gotten soft. I might just jump in that pool and pull you in with me."

"No way," Reagan said, holding his hands up. "You know that I don't swim."

"How is it that a guy who was born on an island and grew up around the water does not know how to swim? I've never understood that. Maybe it's time I give you some swimming lessons," Nathan told him mockingly as he reached over and grabbed his arm and pulled him toward the pool.

"No way. You stay back," Reagan protested loudly. Everyone from the bar noticed the exchange and turned to watch. Reagan laughingly told the small crowd, "Te chale a vinn blanc a," which meant, "The heat has gotten to the blanc." They all laughed before returning to their drinks.

Sitting at the table, Nathan took another long draw from the now-warming beer. "On a more serious note," he said, "let's discuss a plan. It's been a while since I've been to Marti's house, but I think it's just about a twenty-minute walk from here. We can either walk or catch a tap-tap. I don't think it really matters. We will be just as visible either way. Do you have a preference?"

"Let's walk. We have to pass a few communities, and maybe we can learn something on the way," said Reagan.

"Sounds good. Let's go."

They finished their beers and stood up from the table. With his eye warily on Nathan, Reagan cautiously put some distance between himself and the pool. "Not today, you old fox," he warned his friend.

Walking back down the long stone staircase, they encountered two guards waiting at the bottom. Both were wearing military-style uniforms and held government-model Colt AR-15s. With a flick of a lever, one of those automatic rifles was capable of letting loose a burst of bullets in just a couple of seconds. Nathan knew because he had several in a gun safe locked behind a false door in his condo back in Madison.

Both guards smiled and wished Nathan and Reagan a good day. The owners of the inn, like those at other upscale resorts in Haiti, were serious about security. Rarely were there any reports of crime at the resorts.

Leaving the property, the men took a narrow, sandy path that skirted the harbor and followed the shoreline heading west. It intersected with a road that led to the villages and eventually Marti's house. Along the way, Nathan was subjected to stares from curious islanders. Foreigners on the island were a rare sight, especially one as white as Nathan. If word of his arrival hadn't spread yet, it certainly would soon.

With the heat, it took a little more than twenty minutes to reach Marti's house, a single-story stucco that was beige with large green shutters. The roof was made of terracotta tiles, giving the cottage a Spanish feel. It was nestled between the road and beach, surrounded by flowing bougainvillea with brilliant blooms of crimson and magenta. Layers of palm trees towered over the house and grew in rows that led out toward the beach.

Nathan had been there a few times years earlier when the cottage had belonged to Charles and Madeline. They'd only used it for vacations, and when Marti began spending more time on the island, she had purchased it from them. Of course, they'd wanted her to have it as a gift, but in typical Marti fashion, she'd refused their offer.

Nathan and Reagan walked up the driveway and followed a limestone path that led to the backyard with an incredible view of the sea. Nathan recalled the times he and Laura had sat out on the patio with Charles and Madeline, having drinks and great conversation and watching the waves wash gently against the rock-lined beach. With the island protected by the mainland and because the inlet to the bay was narrow, the currents rarely produced waves much larger than a foot. It was an idyllic and peaceful setting that held fond memories. Unfortunately, with the crime scene tape surrounding the patio, those memories gave way to the reality of Marti's disappearance.

Surveying the patio and backyard, Nathan was surprised to see that the large white catering tents were still up. Chairs, tables, strings of lights, and full trash cans appeared to have been untouched since the night of the party. Technically, it was still a crime scene, and Nathan was glad that everything had been left just the way it was. Silently, he and Reagan moved about the patio, trying to connect with what might have taken place the previous Friday night. They walked toward the beach, passing the old tree where the bodyguard said Marti had hung her clothes.

Nathan could picture Marti cautiously scanning the shoreline in the moonlight to see if she was alone. Being the daughter of a wealthy businessman, she was trained to always take notice of her surroundings. He glanced toward the edge of the patio to a group of smaller palm trees and dense foliage where the bodyguard said he had stood and watched her.

Other than the rocky outcrops and trees that stood at the top of the beach, the area was flat and clear in both directions for at least half a mile. If anyone had been approaching from the beach, Nathan felt sure that either Marti or Hector would have seen them.

It could have been that the abductors had been hiding in the trees, waiting for the bodyguard to make his rounds. It was plausible, Nathan thought, but if Marti had spotted them before they reached her in the water, she could easily have evaded them. She was that strong of a swimmer.

And even if they had surprised her in the water, they would have had to drug her like they'd done the bodyguard or dealt with a screaming woman in the middle of a silent night. If they had somehow managed that, they would still have needed to exit through the villages. Since there was not a car ferry servicing the island, they would have had to have stolen a car or hired a car and driver to remove her to the pier. That would not have been possible without everyone on the island knowing. Word of strangers or new arrivals traveled fast.

Standing there looking out over the ocean, Nathan realized it would be almost impossible to kidnap a person from the beach and escape unseen. That left only one other way it could be done. Apparently, it occurred to him about the same time that it did to Reagan.

"Nathan," said his friend, "the road borders the ocean on one side, and on the other is nothing but jungle and swamp. There is no way they could have gotten her out of here by car without anybody seeing. It only leaves one possible way."

Nathan, with his back to Reagan, was still staring out over the ocean. Without a word, he pointed to the empty sea. "It's the only way. I think we've figured out how; now we need to find out who— and where they've taken her."

They walked back down the road to a small village that sat on the edge of the sea near Marti's house. Consisting of a few rudimentary buildings made of misshapen concrete blocks and thatch, it was one of the few communities that had outdoor lighting. Powered by solar panels, it was the central area for parties and festivities.

Nathan and Reagan walked to the beach to see what kind of view there was to Marti's house. They were unable to see the house tucked back near the road, but could easily spot the old tree where she had hung her clothes.

Next to where they were standing was a community center where anyone would have the same view. Actually, with the pavilion elevated about three feet above the beach, the view was even better. Thinking that there could have been an event held there the Friday before, the two men paid a visit to a small open-air shop wedged between a couple of coconut trees. Noticing the dozens of coconuts about thirty feet above him, Nathan decided the shopkeeper could have likely found a safer place to set up her business.

On the table before him was everything from plastic-wrapped food to plumbing supplies to household cleaners and handcrafted jewelry. And of course there were the ubiquitous cheap plastic toys with "Haiti" emblazoned on almost every spot that it could be stamped. If people here would put as much effort into industrialization and agriculture as they did trying to sell cheap souvenirs, Nathan thought that Haiti could be a country to be reckoned with.

Behind the counter, an old lady wearing a University of Alabama Alumni t-shirt sat half-asleep in a rusted rocking chair.

"I wonder what year she graduated," Nathan said quietly to Reagan. They both laughed, and it was enough to stir the woman from her sleep. She didn't look too happy.

Nathan pointed to Reagan. "You're on," he told his friend.

Reagan approached the table and picked up a few candy bars, a pack of gum, and two Cokes. It instantly brightened the clerk's mood. As Reagan was paying, he asked her if anything had taken place in the community center the Friday night before.

Her speech was quick and her Creole accent so thick that Nathan couldn't understand. She pointed to a thatched house just down from the ocean-side community center. He could tell by Reagan's reaction that whatever it was she'd told him might be something they could use.

Reagan motioned for Nathan to follow him to a picnic table, where he handed him a coke and candy bar. "Nathan, my friend," he said, "I think we just got our first lead. According to the lady, last Friday night there was a year-and-day vodoun ceremony celebrating the death and life of a local mambo, which is the term for a female high priest. She said it lasted into Sunday morning and that the priestess who held the ceremony lives in that house right there." He pointed to the house that had been indicated by the vendor. "You sit here and enjoy your Coke. I'll go see if the woman's home and if she'll talk with us."

"I'll go with you. Maybe I can help." Nathan stood.

But his friend held up his hand. "No offense, my brother, but all your whiteness might be a problem for us. She might think that you're some kind of *bokor*." Reagan laughed.

Knowing that a bokor was a kind of sorcerer known for casting dark spells, Nathan sat back down. "You're being a bit dramatic, but I'll wait here in all my whiteness," he said. "If she gives you any problems, tell her to cooperate or I'll unleash a spell."

He watched Reagan knock, and the door was opened by the priestess right away as if she'd been expecting him. There was no doubt she'd been watching them since they came into the village. She cautiously waved Reagan in and abruptly closed the door.

Nathan finished his Coke and candy and walked back to the market, where he paid way too much money for a wind-up toy and a small stuffed green lizard that was apparently named 'Haiti." The vendor responded with a smile big enough to show off all four teeth. She placed the prizes in a bag.

The University of Alabama school of business would have been proud to watch, he thought. He'd hand out the toys to the first kids he ran into.

About fifteen minutes had passed when he saw Reagan and the priestess step out of her door. Reagan gave a half bow and shook the mambo's hand. Both were all smiles and nods. Nathan took that to be a good sign, until she looked over at him and the smile left her face.

Nathan, sitting on top of the picnic table, smiled and waved, but she scowled at him and made her way back into the house.

Reagan met Nathan back at the picnic table.

"I don't think she likes me," said Nathan, still looking over toward the house.

"It's not that," said Reagan. "She just doesn't trust you is all. Sometimes evil spirits, zombies, and bokors are portrayed in the vodoun culture as being ashen white. As you can imagine, it all goes back to the people's not-so-pleasant treatment by the French. It's not everyday they see a blanc walk into their village. So even with your charming personality, wit, and cleverness, your skin, I'm afraid, is still the color of death. That's kind of hard to overcome." Reagan smiled and shrugged.

Trying not to show how irritated he was by that kind of nonsense, Nathan got straight to the point. "Did you find out something that could help us?"

"I did. Last Friday night, the village held a ceremony at the community center and, according to the priestess, it went on almost until dawn. A local mambo died a year ago, and the ceremony was to welcome her spirit back into the physical world. The priestess said she'd seen something early on the morning of the ceremony. But she didn't know what it meant until the following day—when they heard that Marti disappeared. She says she knows what happened to Marti."

Nathan jumped off the picnic table in a flash. "What?" he yelled. "Reagan, what did she say?"

Before Reagan could reply, the door to the house opened and out walked the priestess, dressed in a wildly colorful ceremonial suit. She carried a matching bag. With a look of determination on her face, she walked toward the beach without paying them the least bit of attention.

The men caught up with her, cautiously following a few steps behind her. They watched as the priestess entered the thatched hut that served as the community center. As opposed to the other buildings, it was soundly constructed of weathered beams, the stubs of ancient limbs protruding out in certain spots. The ceiling joist consisted of hundreds of narrow bamboo poles tied together and covered with thatch, reeds, and palm leaves. It was a design that was timeless and most likely brought over from Africa.

Still not acknowledging Nathan and Reagan's presence or that they were observing her, the priestess lowered herself to the concrete floor, where she sat silently and began pulling objects from her bag. In front of her she lined up strands of incense held in small cylinders of wood, several clear jars containing what appeared to be colored powder, and a pot made from clay.

She placed the incense holders in front of her in a circle and said a few words for every one she lit. Nathan recognized the sweet, smoky, and earthy essence of vetiver. One of Haiti's most valuable natural resources, vetiver was made from distilling the roots of the grass of the same name. It could be found worldwide in expensive perfumes, colognes, and massage oils.

Chanting in Creole, the priestess pulled the smoke from the incense toward her.

Nathan leaned closer to Reagan and very softly asked, "What is it that she's doing?"

Reagan, not taking his eyes from the priestess, said, "Mambo Djeyma is praying to a *loa*. I think it's Lasiren, who's the wife of Agwe, the most powerful aquatic loa."

After a few minutes, the priestess stopped her prayers and, using the contents of the jar, began drawing an image on the floor.

Before Nathan could even ask, Reagan explained in a whisper, "There's a reason for the *vèvè*. The African slaves were prohibited from worshiping their gods or possessing any religious objects, such as carvings or pictures of the deities. They were reprimanded harshly if they didn't adopt the Christian ways. Their way of appeasing the masters and also staying true to their beliefs was to draw symbolic images of African loa spirits in the disguised form of Catholic saints. Let's see what she draws."

Lost in her own spiritual world, the priestess quietly sung prayers while, with long, fluid, ritualistic strokes, she outlined in sky blue a woman's heart-shaped face. She added flowing locks of hair, which were the color of the clouds. The face was blue-green like the sea.

"Lasiren," whispered Reagan. "That is the loa known as Lasiren, and I think I know where this is going. Lasiren is a mermaid who's described as a long-haired mulatto. The legend is that this mermaid attracts women to the shore, then takes them into the ocean and transforms them into her image. But she doesn't hold on to them forever. After a period of time, she lets the women go. At first, no one recognizes who the women are, but after a while, they welcome their loved ones back and understand the new power they possess: the power of healing and unity, a gift from Lasiren."

After finishing the drawing, the priestess turned to the men and with a soft voice said, "Lasiren te pran Marti, men li ap retounen li y oak le sa, li pral deliver nou ak peyi nou an."

Nathan understood enough Creole to know what she had said.

"Tell her there are evil people who want to stop Marti from fulfilling her purpose of bringing the country together," he said to Reagan. "Tell her I'm her godfather and that I'm here to find and protect her."

Before Reagan could answer him, the priestess herself replied. "Mr. Roark, I know who you are and I know why you are here. It is the only reason you were allowed to witness this sacred ceremony."

With a smile she added, "Papa Legba, who holds the key and is the keeper of the gates, has given you permission to enter and assist us with protecting our Marti. We will help in any way we can."

Nathan replied, "Di ou mesi pou konfyans nou." Thank you for your trust.

The three of them left the community center and walked the short distance to the picnic table. Nathan and Reagan sat on one side and the priestess on the other. With her hands clasped together on top of the table, she was ready for their questions.

Nathan knew, or at least he thought he did, that Larsiren did not actually take Marti from the ocean, but he needed to be careful in how he formed his questions. "Mambo Djeyma, can you take us back to last Friday night and tell us what you saw?" It was as basic and to the point as he could get. Normally, he would ease into an interview with questions having to do with background and credibility before pressing the witness for information on the main event, but this was not an interrogation.

She took a few seconds before she answered. "It was late in the morning, around three a.m. We had been with the spirit for hours in song and celebration and were physically exhausted. All at once, as they usually do, the spirits left us, and a cool breeze blew through the ceremony space. We all collapsed in silence. Wanting to be alone, I walked away from the others and sat down by that tree next to the hut." She pointed to a palm tree that was about ten feet up the beach in the direction of Marti's house.

"I was staring into the ocean, thinking about my friend and where her spirit would find its resting place when a kind of buzzing broke the silence. With the full moon, I could make out something moving across the water toward the shore in front of Marti's house. The buzzing stopped way before the shore and then it silently moved in toward the beach. About thirty minutes later, the buzzing noise came back, and I could see the dark object moving at a much faster pace, away from the beach and toward the mainland. I didn't think anything more about it until the next day when I heard the sad news of Marti." She looked Nathan in the eye. "Mr. Roark, she did not drown. Something took your goddaughter, and I pray it was Larsiren and not an evil *baka* from the sea."

Nathan knew it was not Lasiren who took Marti from the sea, but more probably a baka by the name of "The Cabal." Mambo Djeyma's account helped confirm what he suspected, and he thanked her once more for her trust. He also asked that she and the community continue to pray for Marti's safe return.

She nodded that she would and left the table to go back to the hut to gather her supplies.

Reagan and Nathan sat in silence, thinking about their next move.

CHAPTER SIXTEEN

They walked back to Colline Sacrée, both lost in their own thoughts about how to proceed with the new information. It was clear the synopsis Nathan had laid out to Charles at his office was becoming very real. The cabal had captured Marti and was holding her to see if the family and the public bought the drowning story. If the drowning was publicly confirmed, then the cabal would kill her. If not, they would make it look like a kidnapping by gang and then kill her at the ransom transfer.

Passing the guards as they walked back up the steep staircase at the resort, they could hear music coming from the bar and restaurant. It was almost five, and most of the guests would have returned from a day of beaching and boating and would be settling in for cocktails and dinner.

They walked into the bar to find it full. On the small stage, an older man with a long gray ponytail was setting up a karaoke system for later, when everyone would have consumed enough of their fancy tropical drinks to lose their inhibitions. It would be nice to enjoy the evening at the bar and watch the karaoke show, but Nathan knew that would have to wait until another time. Not wanting their conversation to be overheard, he motioned Reagan over to a vacant table by the pool. "Have you unpacked?" he asked.

"No, and I agree with what you're thinking. There's no reason to hang around here when what we need is over there." Reagan nodded in the direction of Les Cayes, across a ten-mile stretch of ocean. "I'll run to my room and grab my bag and head down to the pier to secure a boat. Why don't you check us out?" He stood up to leave.

"I'll see you in thirty at the pier," said Nathan.

After gathering his bags, he hesitantly made his way to the office—hesitantly because he and the French proprietor, Monsieur Duplechain, had been friends for many years and Nathan knew he would be disappointed with their early departure. But Nathan would explain that a family emergency required his immediate attention. And, in fact, it did.

Fortunately, the clerk at the front desk said Monsieur Duplechain was taking an afternoon nap, anticipating a long night at the bar with the karaoke crowd. Nathan scribbled him a note explaining why he had to leave and said he would email him when he got back to the States.

He had great memories of sitting at the bar until early morning, talking politics and drinking too much wine with his old friend, the hotel owner. Handing the note to the clerk, he wondered if he would ever see his friend again. They were both getting older, and Nathan had heard a rumor that Monsieur Duplechain might be selling Colline Sacrée and retiring to France. Maybe he would visit him there. He and Laura traveled to Western Europe at least once a year.

Leaving the inn, Nathan took one last look up the hill at the place he had been visiting for the past thirty years and would possibly never visit again. "C'est la vie," he thought as he reverently closed a chapter of his life that held a collection of colorful tales. With a quick wave to the guards at the base of the steps, he disappeared into the foliage and hurried down the shoreline path. He made the twenty-minute walk in fifteen minutes.

At the pier, Reagan was having a discussion with a man next to a long red and blue boat with the name "Clarita" written across the side. Watching Reagan shake the guy's hand, Nathan assumed the Clarita would be their private transportation to Les Cayes. It was much smaller than the craft they'd come over on, and, unlike their previous ride, this one appeared to be dry, sitting high up out of the water, and without other passengers to crowd them.

The captain stowed their bags under a ripped-up blue tarp that would be only slightly better at keeping them dry than leaving them in the open. He then pulled the rope of a two-stroke engine that instantly came to life. It sounded much better than the one from the earlier trip.

Ready to depart, the captain made a wide arc around the pier and pointed the Clarita toward Les Cayes. With the rhythmic noise from the engine, the warm sun, and the boat bouncing lightly on the clam sea, Nathan's eyes grew heavy, and about halfway across the bay, he began to doze.

Asleep but still faintly aware of his surroundings, he floated in and out of a dream. He was just a kid and was playing in an orange grove when his peaceful reveries were interrupted by a noise. The sound had taken over the drone of the Clarita's engine and finally woke him up.

When he opened his eyes, they fell on a site that immediately gave him the answer he'd been searching for. Suddenly, Nathan knew exactly how the perpetrators had taken Marti from the beach. In the time he had fallen asleep, the Clarita had made it to within a mile of the pier at Les Cayes. Just out from the maritime police pier was a small six-man inflatable military raft known as a Zodiac. Standing at the helm was a tall figure in a military uniform. And, yes, the Zodiac was buzzing.

Nathan tapped Reagan on the shoulder and pointed to the raft. The look in Reagan's eyes showed that he understood. With the information from Charles that one of the top officers in the national police was one of the cabal's original four, it made perfect sense that the maritime police would have been infiltrated and used to kidnap Marti.

While the Zodiac continued to move further offshore, the Clarita pulled to the public pier and, to their good fortune, it was empty. Usually a few opportunistic kids were hanging around to assist with luggage and supplies, but since the afternoon ferry had already departed, there was no one there. Nathan grabbed their bags from under the tarp, and Reagan paid the captain.

Within a minute, the boat was headed back toward the island, and Nathan and Reagan were walking through the parking lot, heading to the car. Once they had arrived, Nathan was about to reach for the passenger door when Reagan stopped him. Nathan watched as Reagan walked to the driver's side and carefully inspected the car. He explained what he was doing. He'd placed a few small sticks under and over the tires and stuck a few blades of grass on the driver's window and door. If anyone had tried to move or mess with the car, he would have known.

"I didn't notice you doing that before we left, but I guess that's the point. Anything been moved?" Nathan asked.

"No, it all looks good."

Satisfied, they hopped in and Reagan cranked the car and turned the air conditioning on full blast. They waited a few minutes to cool down and then, seemingly for no particular reason, Reagan drove toward the airport. Checking his mirror, he asked Nathan about their next move.

"It's probably not standard procedure to be doing maneuvers or patrolling in the early hours of a Sunday morning, like the time when she was taken," said Nathan, "and anyone up at that hour would have certainly noticed or heard the Zodiac traveling across the bay. I can think of only one place that would have been open at that time, and I think we have a friend that works there." Nathan raised an eyebrow as he glanced at Reagan. "Maybe he would like another American twenty to go with the one I gave him earlier? How about we head back to the pier and get ourselves some supper? We can see if he is working."

"Sounds good," Reagan replied as he turned the car around. "We also need to decide where we're staying tonight. I talked to Tamara earlier and told her we'd be working together on an agriculture project for a few days, and unless you want to stay at my house—where there will be a lot of questions about this so-called project—I suggest we find a hotel."

Nathan gave him a quick glance. "I think we should stay in a hotel. I'm afraid if we stay at your house, we might get on the subject of the old days and I don't want to have to lie to your sweet wife about your actions from back then or now," he said with a sly smile.

"Lie about what actions?" Reagan shouted.

"Have you forgotten the 'assignment' in Jacmel?" Nathan asked, making air quotes around the word. "If I recall, I played gin rummy with my subject all night, and I think we know what you did with yours." In the late seventies, they had been assigned to stake out the girlfriends of two Columbian drug smugglers. It was a joint operation with the national police, set up to intercept the smugglers as they met their girlfriends at a hotel in Jacmel, a small town on the southeast side of Haiti. While fellow agents were watching the hotel from the outside, Nathan and Reagan were inside, keeping an eye on the girls.

"You know I did not do anything with that girl!" Reagan shouted.

"All I remember is you with a big smile and that beautiful girl in a low-cut dress walking up the steps to her room. Also, if I recall correctly, I didn't see you until late the next morning, hours after the stakeout had been called off. Would you like to finally come clean with the truth?" Nathan asked with a smirk.

"I told you the truth back then, and I don't feel the need to repeat myself thirty years later," Reagan said sternly.

Mockingly, Nathan turned toward Reagan, tapping his finger on his chin. "Oh, I think I remember. She wanted to confess about her role smuggling drugs and conveniently wanted to do it in her room. She was upset and didn't want the other girl to see her crying, so you comforted her privately, and you were also kind enough to do it all night long. You have such a tender heart. Did we ever tell Tamara that story? We should, in case she doesn't know what a tender heart you have." Nathan laughed.

With his hands clenched tightly on the wheel, Reagan just stared forward.

Nathan had him and was not about to let go. He pressed on in the accented English of a seductive Haitian girl. "Oh, Monsieur Reagan, if you could just touch me right here, it might make me feel better and help me get through this terrible night. Yes, that's it. A little lower."

Unable to suppress a smile, Reagan shook his head. "Okay, stop it. That's enough. You know it didn't happen that way, but I'm sure Tamara would love to hear your fabricated story instead of the truth. You're one lowlife rascal to threaten me with that!"

"Things are not so funny now like they were at Mambo Djeyma's?" Nathan asked him, laughing.

Again, Reagan just shook his head.

After a ten-minute ride back to the pier, they pulled in and checked the parking lot for the suspicious taxi, but it wasn't there. Walking to the restaurant, Nathan asked, "You think the cook is still working?"

"I doubt it, but you go case the rear and I'll walk around the front and see who's in the restaurant."

Nathan looked through the back door and saw several young men wearing dirty white aprons and hairnets, but not the cook from earlier. Disappointed, he walked to the front porch and joined Reagan. "He's not back there. You ready to get a bite to eat?"

Reagan nodded that he was.

The restaurant was crowded for a Monday night, but thankfully none of the others around the tables were policemen. A host met them at the door and suggested a booth up front, but Nathan shook his head and pointed to a table near the back exit facing the front. He always placed himself near the exit and sat facing toward the entrance. It drove Laura crazy to have to wait for a table that suited his criteria. As embarrassing as it was, she'd learned to call ahead and request a specific table to accommodate the strategic maneuvers that she called *paranoia*.

At their table in the back, they ordered a Prestige and asked the waiter for a few minutes to check out the food selections. Peering above the menu, Nathan scanned the room for anyone he might recognize or who might look out of place. Nudging Reagan, he nodded toward a corner table in the front.

The young man was dressed in a pair of black shorts, an Atlanta Hawks jersey, and a matching NBA hat that still had the 3-D promotional tag hanging from the side. He was sitting by himself and had his head down, texting or playing a game on his phone.

"Looks like someone didn't get enough of this place today. How would you like to handle it?" Reagan asked.

Nathan studied the young cook. "How about we go over and offer to buy him a beer for helping us earlier?" he asked. "We can tell him we suspected that one of the policemen at the table this morning was getting it on with your wife and I wanted to get you out of the restaurant before he saw you. Tell him I'm an attorney friend from Petionville who's come here to help you." Nathan paused to think. "Also tell him you think your wife and one of the policemen snuck over to a hotel on Ile-a-Vache last Friday night. So tell him we were wondering if he might have seen or heard a boat leaving the harbor sometime late Friday night or early Saturday morning.

"Let him know that it's a private matter and that you will not need him to make a statement or go public. You just want proof before you leave her. And last but not least, tell him there's an American hundred if he has information that is useful. What do you think?" Nathan asked.

"Sounds like a perfect plan. Haitian people have a general distrust of the police, especially ones who cheat. For that reason and, more particularly, the American *hondo*, he'll probably tell us if he saw anything," Reagan replied.

Before they could get up to approach the cook, the waiter returned with their beers and to take their order. They quickly ordered and, as subtly as possible, walked over and sat down at the table with the cook.

The man looked up from his phone. It took him a couple of seconds to recognize them, but then he flashed a big smile while reaching out to shake their hands. Nathan knew immediately that if the guy knew anything, that information could be theirs if the price was right.

Reagan took the lead and with a hushed tone began to tell the story they'd come up with. When Reagan started with the questions, the cook pulled a pack of cigarettes from his shirt, grabbed his beer, and motioned for Reagan to step outside with him.

Nathan quietly slipped Reagan the hundred-dollar bill.

They had been gone about ten minutes when the waiter came back with the food. He gave Nathan an inquisitive look. Nathan pointed outside and gestured with his hand that the two were smoking. The waiter set down their plates and Nathan quickly dug into his stuffed flounder. He was just finishing when Reagan returned.

"Couldn't wait, I see?" Reagan asked, looking at Nathan's empty plate.

"Nope, and I was about to start on yours. Where's the cook?"

Reagan sat and took a bite of his fish before he answered.

"I don't know, but thanks to the blanc, he's happy and a hundred dollars richer. Let me finish and I'll fill you in outside. I don't want to have the conversation in here."

Nathan sipped his beer while Reagan finished his meal.

Leaving the restaurant, they walked to a small public park a few feet from the pier. They sat down on a bench. From the faint scent of cigarette smoke that lingered in the air, Nathan assumed it was the same spot where Reagan and the cook had had their conversation.

"So, I think our friend has unknowingly solved part of our case." Reagan tried to hold back his excitement.

"What did he say?" Nathan quickly asked.

"Last Sunday morning around two, after they'd closed down the restaurant, the cook and his girlfriend came to this park to, as he put it, 'smoke a little weed and wind down.' We talked some more about the affair and, as I figured, he had a few not-so-pleasant things to say about the police. So then I asked the guy if he'd noticed any boats leaving the harbor at the time we talked about. Right on cue, he told me that he hadn't—but that he'd seen a Zodiac leave the maritime police pier. He actually called it that—a Zodiac.

"What caught his attention, he said, was that it was out so late and that it was heading across the bay. He said the Zodiacs mainly patrol along the shoreline and in the daylight hours. It was the first time he'd ever seen one out at night. And then he said the Zodiac came back about an hour later and docked at the maritime pier." Reagan paused. "But that's not the best part even.

"A few minutes after the boat docked, this guy and his girlfriend started walking home. As they were passing the entrance to the police station, the gate opened and a military truck pulled out. In the front seat he saw two men, and in between them was a girl who had dark hair. He said it must have been my wife."

"No shit!" Nathan said, jumping to his feet. "Do you think they saw him and his girlfriend walking by?"

"I asked him that. He said they'd already walked past the gate and were in the shadows of the building when they saw the truck. He said the entrance was well lit, so he had no problem seeing inside the truck. He also said he thought he knew where they were going." By that point, the excitement showed on Reagan's face.

"Where?" Nathan whispered loudly.

"He'd overheard the police talking at the restaurant about a camp or training facility up near Pic Macaya. He told me that he bet that's where the cheating bastard took my wife."

Nathan could no longer sit. "I think this confirms Charles's theory about Marti being abducted by the cabal. They're probably holding her in that camp until they see if the drowning story holds up. We need to call Charles and tell him what we've found."

CHAPTER SEVENTEEN

They walked back toward the car, marveling over the bizarre turns that the day had taken. Just twelve hours earlier, Nathan had been on a bus with no plans other than meeting Reagan and hopefully catching a boat to Ile-a-Vache. His only goal had been to get settled at Colline Sacrée and start working on a plan. He never imagined that in the course of the morning and afternoon, they would piece together a complete picture of what had happened on the fateful evening his goddaughter disappeared.

Needing to find a hotel room, Nathan asked if the historic Hotel Les Cayes was still in business, and Reagan told him it was. After driving the short distance up Highway 7, they pulled into the parking lot, and the sight of the hotel brought a flood of memories.

Built in the 1950s, it would have taken weeks in the early days to get a reservation. Back then, trees still covered the mountains and valleys, and exports to the United States made for a thriving economy that made Haiti a tourist destination. Now, with a depleted economy and zero tourism, one just needed to show up.

Walking into the hotel, Nathan noticed that little had changed since his last stay during the 1970s. The lobby was still richly adorned in mahogany trim, and hanging proudly from the ceiling was the same crystal chandelier. Even the old man who checked them in was smartly dressed in his antique uniform, appearing to be clinging to an era that had long since past. Nathan wondered if Monsieur Duplechain from Colline Sacrée and the old man might know each other since they were contemporaries. It would be interesting to spend an afternoon with the two and listen to tales of Haiti from the days when she was burgeoning and alive.

With their keys in hand, they headed down the hallway to their rooms. They came first to Nathan's room and he told Reagan to give him a few minutes, then they could meet back in his room.

Reagan nodded and replied, "See you in a few."

Ten minutes later, hearing a quiet tap on his door, Nathan opened it and motioned Reagan in. He directed him toward a desk with two chairs placed around it.

"Have a seat," said Nathan. Grabbing two bottles of water from the small refrigerator, he tossed one to Reagan and joined him at the table. After their long day in the sun, they both emptied the bottles in a few gulps.

Reagan propelled his over the table and into the trash. "What's the plan?" he asked.

"I have about fifty running through my head, but first let's talk about our friend, the cook. I know I'm probably being overly paranoid, but running into him at the restaurant seems a little too coincidental. If he was caught this morning by the taxi driver or anyone else who might have been watching us, they could have either paid him or threatened him into cooperating. I think it's a little odd that after working all day, he would hang around the restaurant, playing games on his phone. Why wouldn't he spend his night off with his girlfriend? Also, he didn't seem all that surprised when we sat down at his table, and don't you think he was just a little too forthcoming with his information? I think this could be a setup to lure us to Pic Macaya. What are your thoughts on that?" Nathan tapped a pencil on the desk.

Reagan thought about it. "I hear what you're saying, but I don't think they got to him. Let's go over the facts. No one could have known the information we got from the mambo. They take their religion very seriously here, and there is just no way she would ever betray Papa Legba, the gatekeeper of the spirit world, who gave her permission to talk with us about it. Even if she did, they would only have had an hour or so to find the cook, feed him the information, and place him in the restaurant. Nothing works that fast in Haiti, I can promise you. The only logical explanation is that it happened just exactly like the cook said."

Nathan nodded slowly. "I agree. There wouldn't have been enough time unless they were following us, and I'm fairly sure they weren't. Why don't we make a reconnoitering trip up to Pic Macaya tomorrow and see if we can locate the training facility there. Any idea where it might be?"

"You know, I think I might," said Reagan. "About six months ago, there was a bad accident near the town of Duchity involving a military truck and a tap-tap full of people. There were several fatalities, and it caused a huge uproar in the community. A few days after the accident, about a hundred people traveled down from Duchity and the neighboring town of Mouline and protested in front of the government office in Les Cayes. They shut down the street for hours. I remember because I got stuck in all the traffic. My bet is that the road to the training facility is somewhere up there between Duchity and Mouline, and we can probably find out by asking questions in either or both."

"You don't think people will be a little suspicious about us snooping around, asking questions about the government?" Nathan asked.

"Not if they are a little bit farsighted," Reagan replied with a mischievous grin.

"I'll take the bait. Explain."

"Although it may be a little tight around the middle, I still have my uniform from my days as the Director of Internal Development. And although it's been expired almost for a decade, I still have my government ID. No one ever inspected it during my thirty years, and if they did, with the print so small, I doubt that they would notice that it's no longer valid. I know what we'll do. I'll say I'm there to get some information about the accident. I'll say I'm from Port-au-Prince and having trouble locating the government facility. Does that sound like it will work?" Reagan asked.

"I think that's a great idea. If we can find the road that will take us to the compound, then maybe I can find a way to slip in—and find some sign of Marti. Let's sleep on it and meet at 0700 for some breakfast." Nathan grabbed his cell. "I still have one more thing I need to do before I hit the sack. I need to make a call to Charles."

"Good luck with that," said Reagan.

Taking a deep breath, Nathan punched in his friend's number and hit *send*. Then he listened to the phone ring and thought about what to say. He didn't have long to think, as Charles answered on the first ring.

"Nathan?" Charles asked, caution creeping into his voice.

"Hi, Charles. How are you?" Immediately he realized it was a stupid thing to ask.

"What did you find?" asked Charles, and Nathan got straight to the point.

"We have good information that Marti is alive, and we also have a good lead on where it is that she might be."

There was a pause, followed by a long sigh. "Thank God. Thank you, God," Charles whispered into the phone.

Nathan spent the next twenty minutes explaining what had taken place on Ile-a-Vache and what the cook had told them. He then informed Charles about the call to the national police he wanted him to arrange for the next day. He spent a few minutes coaching his friend on what he wanted him to say. He instructed him to be firm and direct, reporting that the investigation had been completed and that it had been determined that Marti had, in fact, not drowned and had presumably been kidnapped. Charles was to tell the media that he had come forward to report that there was evidence that the disappearance might have been politically motivated—and that his team had a few leads that they were preparing to discuss with the UN investigators.

Nathan felt this would throw a bit of chaos into the workings of the cabal and give him a day or two before the abductors of his goddaughter decided what to do.

"I'll call the national police first thing in the morning. What's your plan for tomorrow?" Charles asked his friend.

"Reagan and I will drive up to Duchity, where we think they might have taken her. If we find it, I'll have Reagan drop me off and I'll see if I can get close enough to see it. If it appears that she might be there, we'll head back to Les Cayes and make plans to get her out," Nathan replied.

"Do you think going in alone is a good idea? The cabal and BOID will be on maximum alert once I've talked to the press. Maybe I should send over a few of my best security men to help you with the job," Charles said.

"I appreciate the offer, but I think it's best if I work alone. They'll probably have video cameras, motion detectors, trip wires, and guards all over the property. It will be much less difficult for one person to avoid detection. Plus, if we get caught and they connect your men to you, I doubt that any of us, including Marti, would be heard from ever again."

After a slight pause, Charles spoke. "If you think that's best, then I'll trust your decision. Call me as soon as you get back. If you don't come back for any reason, you can be assured that I'll have the UN bearing down on that place full force. I've had enough of this devil, the cabal." The anger in his voice came through loud and clear.

They ended the conversation and Nathan quickly undressed and got in bed. As he lay there in the quiet and the dark, he thought about the conversation that he'd had with Charles. Everything he'd said about security was probably true. More than likely, he was in over his head, but Charles's men could be a tipoff to the cabal that Charles had found them out. And there was no time to call for anyone else to help; there was no other choice but to move forward as he'd planned.

Shutting his eyes, he did something he rarely did—he prayed.

Chapter Eighteen

Morning came after a sleepless night full of nervous anticipation. The night before a mission Nathan usually slept well, but this mission was far from usual. He typically went in with an organized team in addition to a well-coordinated plan. But as unorthodox as it was to take on such a dangerous assignment with nobody at his side, he reassured himself that he had made the correct decision.

This way if he were caught, he could play the role of an unassuming older man who'd just been out hiking and had gotten lost, accidentally wandering away from the trails on Pic Macaya. He'd act the part of someone who was scared, thirsty, and, most of all, very thankful that he had at last been rescued. If he were to be detained, all anyone would ever find inside his backpack would be a few snacks, some water bottles, binoculars, and a map.

With the edges of a plan in place, he felt a little better, but he still had no clue how he'd get in or out. He gathered his backpack from the desk and left to meet Reagan in the restaurant.

Just as he entered the restaurant, the rest of the plan hit him like a right hook. Reagan was sitting alone at a table in the back, but it was a man sitting in front of the restaurant who caught Nathan's eye.

The man had several books and what looked like journals stacked on the table. He was absorbed in studying one of them and was unaware that he was the object of Nathan's scrutiny. As Nathan eased closer to get a better look, something in the back of the room suddenly caught his attention; it was Reagan waving his arm. It also caught the attention of the man, who looked up from his book. Nathan was able to turn and walk toward Reagan before the man could look at him too closely.

Rolling his eyes and shaking his head, Nathan sat down at the table and said in a calm voice, "Thirty-something years in the CIA, countless undercover missions, and you didn't think I saw you sitting at a table in a room with just ten people?"

"Hey, I'm sorry. It was just a reflex. I could be the only person in the room and Tamara couldn't find me. I always have to wave her down. Did I blow our cover? And who *is* that guy?"

"I have no idea." Nathan shrugged his shoulders, toying with Reagan.

"Well, what exactly is the deal? You locked onto him as soon as you walked in."

"Oh, it's nothing much, other than the fact that he has the plan to get me into the compound." By then Nathan was all smiles.

He'd known the second that he saw him. It would be quite simple in implementation, but complex in design.

"Well, I can't wait to hear his plan to snatch away Ms. Marti from underneath the nose of BOID and whomever else they have protecting her. Should I go ask him to join us? Won't he need to give you the key to a time machine or something?" Reagan asked sarcastically.

Just then the waiter approached with a large plate of fried eggs, hash browns, bacon, sausage, and toast. He sat the plate in front of Reagan and asked Nathan if he would like to order.

"Just coffee," Nathan answered, plucking some bacon from Reagan's plate.

"It looks like your man with the plan is leaving." Reagan nodded his head toward the man, who had risen from his seat.

"I have all the information that I need to get from him. I'll fill you in later on all that. Right now, I'll tell you what I have in mind for today." Nathan took a slice of toast to help Reagan with his breakfast.

They talked about what would happen next. Duchity was only about fifty kilometers from Les Cayes and sat at the base of the national park. The first part of the plan was to get close to town and pull to the side of the road so Reagan could change into his old uniform. He didn't want to take the chance of wearing it out of the hotel and getting stopped for a road block.

Once they got to town, they'd park a few blocks from the main road. Reagan would visit the gas station and a few of the markets while Nathan waited in the car. Just like in Ile-a-Vache, the locals might be much less likely to give up information if Reagan was in the company of a fearsome blanc.

Once they found the camp, Reagan would drop Nathan off a kilometer or so from the entrance, then either drive north toward Jeremie or head back to Les Cayes. They'd decided it would look suspicious if Reagan hung around too long in the small village. After the drop-off, Reagan would wait eight hours and then check back at the pickup point at the top of every hour. If Nathan had not shown up after twelve hours, Reagan was to let Charles know and let him decide what was to happen next.

With the plan in place, Nathan grabbed the last piece of toast, sopped up the last of Reagan's eggs, and laid a ten-dollar bill down on the table. "Let's go," he said. "I'm full."

Reagan shook his head and called Nathan a Creole name that he didn't understand.

Walking through the lobby, they saw the old man behind the front desk, dressed just as sharply that day as the day before. As they were leaving, the old man told them, "Please be careful out there. I hope to see you back this evening."

Walking out the front door, Reagan turned to Nathan. "What did he mean by that?" he asked.

Smirking, Nathan replied, "Maybe he knows we're taking on the cabal in an undercover mission and feels there's a chance we won't make it back. It's really very simple."

Reagan shoved him as they continued on their way. "You know," he said, "there's a part of me that hopes the cabal catches you, my friend, and hangs you up by your toenails."

They jumped into the car, left the parking lot, and turned on to a side street that led to Highway 7. As they approached town, Nathan noticed the street vendors lined up by the road. Not much could break the resolve of a Haitian who needed to feed his family. Even after the worst earthquake in the country's history, the street vendors had been back at work the next day, selling water and supplies to the relief workers. Nathan had to smile as one of the vendors approached the vehicle, waving one of the patented, cheap souvenirs.

Crossing the highway, they headed north, climbing from sea level through the landscape of the treeless hills. About thirty minutes from Les Cayes, traffic came to an abrupt stop. A few hundred yards ahead, Nathan could see several police cars parked on the side of the road with their lights flashing. Anticipating another road block, he shot Reagan a nervous look.

"Roadwork," explained Reagan, the frustration showing on his face. "Our hour drive to Duchity could take up half our day. They've been working on this road for years. About the time they start making progress, the government pulls them off the project and the heavy rains end up eroding months of work. It's just another example of the corruption that's destroying our country and our culture—and another reason why we need to find Marti. When she is president, she can finally finish paving this damn road!"

It took about an hour before they made it through the work-related roadblocks and hit the outskirts of Duchity. Looking for a remote spot to change into his uniform, Reagan found a small, overgrown, unused driveway and pulled down far enough to make sure they were hidden from the highway. They both got out, and Reagan opened the trunk and took out his uniform.

While Reagan was changing, Nathan walked down the drive and found a small stream that paralleled the driveway. A little further down, next to the stream, he found the remains of a camp, including what appeared to be an abandoned charcoal production pit. With hardly any trees around, he could see why it was no longer being used. It was common in the lower elevations to see land stripped of trees and, unfortunately, the practice was beginning to spread toward the mountains. With the advent of solar power on the island, he hoped it was not too late to save the trees that were left.

He headed back up the drive to find Reagan dressed in his old uniform. "Is it supposed to bulge like that between the buttons and ride up over your stomach?" He tried to keep a straight face.

"It does look a little ridiculous. I feel like an overstuffed pillow-case. Needless to say, it's been years since I've had this on."

"Well, don't exhale too hard, or you might pop one of those buttons and put out someone's eye," Nathan said, laughing as Reagan waddled toward the car.

"Let me get out of here and get this over with," said Reagan. "I think you need to stay put. I was planning on parking on a side street and letting you out there, then walking to the gas station. But now I'm not sure that would work. I'm afraid I'd split my pants."

"No problem," Nathan replied, chuckling. "I'll wait here. Good luck."

"When this is over, I'm going to have a long talk with Tamara about our eating habits," Reagan said, easing slowly into the driver's seat. He turned the car around and disappeared down the driveway.

Nathan returned to the old camp and did some exploring. Mostly he found remnants of broken bottles and half-burnt plastic containers, but one thing caught his attention. Someone had dammed the creek, and a long, black plastic pipe was diverting water somewhere. Following the pipe, Nathan came upon another camp with a fire pit that was definitely being used for something other than producing charcoal.

Being from the South, it was something he had heard about but had never seen. It was a moonshine still—and one that looked like it was still in use.

The five-gallon copper pot and thumper keg were in good shape, and the trail leading away from the site was worn and appeared to be well used. If the Haitian moonshiners were anything like the ones back home, they would not be very happy to find a stranger at their site. Nathan figured it was time to get out of there.

Quickly walking back toward the highway, he found a secluded section of trees that had somehow escaped the machete of the charcoal harvesters. He sat down, leaning against the largest one. Having gotten little sleep the night before, and expecting Reagan to be gone at least an hour, he shut his eyes for a quick nap.

He had only been asleep for a few minutes when an explosion ripped through the air. He felt something like wood and dirt fly into his face. He rolled over as he heard the sound of gunshots all around him. A crackling filled the air, as if someone had set off a string of firecrackers.

His company was chasing about two dozen Viet Cong through the jungle of Cu Chi. The enemy was putting up one hell of a fight to keep the Americans from finding the succession of tunnels that spread for miles underneath the jungle floor. Unfortunately for the VC, the tunnels were no longer secret.

Nathan's company had orders to blow up the entrance and infiltrate the tunnels. They knew the VC were packed inside, waiting for them to enter. They also knew the plan would mean almost certain death for the first man to go in.

As the platoon leader, Nathan could have easily ordered a subordinate to take on that task, but that's not how he operated. He grabbed a handful of tall grass and gripped it in his hand. Everyone drew straws, and Nathan drew the shortest.

On his belly, armed with his flashlight and a Colt .45 semi-automatic, he was just about to enter the tunnel when the crunch of gravel woke him up. He opened his eyes to find that he was soaked in sweat.

He welcomed the sight of Reagan's return. Compared to the horrors of Vietnam, the day's mission no longer seemed as daunting. He met Reagan at the car. "Have any luck?" he asked. He noticed that Reagan had unbuttoned his uniform, both the shirt and pants.

"I did. The owner of the gas station was eager to talk after I explained that I was there to investigate the accident and the problem with the speeding trucks. He said they fly through town about twice a day and then turn up on a road about a mile from the station. After I left, I did a satellite-map search on my phone, and I found the road." Reagan tapped some keys on his phone then handed it to Nathan.

"As you can see," he said, "there's a gate about a quarter of a mile up this private road. It's located at the end of a long stretch, presumably so they can easily see any vehicles that approach. If you zoom in, you can also see the partially concealed roofs of several buildings sitting below the bluff. I'm not sure why they would place them in a valley, giving up the high ground."

"Well, they probably never considered having to defend the place," said Nathan. "There is no military in Haiti and they *are* the national police. Their only concern would be the UN snooping around, but I bet the police keep pretty good tabs on their whereabouts. Also, the trees and the dense canopy keep them hidden from view and sheltered from the heat.

"Looking at the satellite image, it appears the best way to approach the compound is to enter the jungle above the road and make my way to the bluff. And that would work well with my cover as some poor lost hiker since it's on the same side as Pic Macaya. What do you estimate the distance is from here to the compound?" Nathan asked Reagan as he zoomed in on the map and used a small twig to point to the spot where they'd set out on the highway.

"My guess is about four to five kilometers," said Reagan. "Since you're coming in from high ground, it's mostly downhill and flattens as you get near the bluff. I do see a few dark areas that are probably valleys, but they don't look like they're very wide and shouldn't slow you down."

"That's what I was thinking," Nathan said. "Normally, it would take several hours to carefully work through the area, stopping for surveillance and security checks. Being that I'm taking on the role of a lost hiker, I can make better time, not having to worry about hidden cameras or detection. Once I get to the bluff, I'll need to be more cautious. If they do have cameras or guards, that's where they'd likely be."

Nathan handed the phone back and laughed as he looked Reagan up and down. "Why don't you get out of that severely stressed uniform and let's head up and find a drop-off point. It's almost eleven now and if I get in by noon, I should be at the bluff by two thirty or three. If I can find a vantage point near the bluff, I can monitor the camp and hopefully find some signs of Marti. I also want to see how they transition the guard detail and what happens after dark. Since they really have no outside threats, they're probably only guarding the road and the perimeter of the compound. It gets dark around nine o'clock, so start cruising the drop-off point sometime around ten. If I have service on my cell, I'll try to text you when I get back to the road. You okay with everything?"

"Yep. I think it will work," Reagan said as he changed his clothes.

"Good. Now, I'll wait in the car. I don't think I can witness any more of your nakedness. You really need to get Tamara to back off on the portions."

They left the cover of the driveway and headed north. Just as they reached Duchity and were in sight of the gas station, Reagan suddenly told Nathan to get down in the seat.

"Why?"

"Because I can see the owner of the gas station up ahead, and he doesn't need to see a blanc in the car. Hurry!"

"Get down where? There's no room." Nathan glanced around. He had placed his backpack on the floor board, and there was no room to slump down out of sight. He didn't have enough time to pick it up and throw it in the back. As they got closer to the station, he reluctantly leaned over onto Reagan's lap.

With a mischievous grin, Reagan started rubbing Nathan's hair.

"Stop it!" Nathan yelled, reaching up to push his hand away.

Reagan couldn't hold it in, and just after passing the station, his laughter filled the car. "Unless you're enjoying yourself down there, you can sit up now," he said.

Nathan quickly sat up and fixed his hair. Then he laughed as well, knowing he would have pulled the same prank. "That was a good one, I'll admit, but I'll get you back," he said to his friend.

A few miles out of town, just as the station owner had said, they found the private road. Reagan slowed the car enough to look, but not enough to attract attention. Near the entrance to the road, dual tire ruts were set deep into the gravel, signs that lots of trucks passed in and out on the road. The men couldn't see the gate, but according to the map, it was just around the curve. Nathan scanned the area for poles or trees that might have video cameras attached, but he didn't see any signs that they were being watched.

They thought about driving by the entrance a few times to get a better look, but didn't want to take a chance on meeting a truck that might be entering or leaving the compound. Plus, they'd risk getting caught on any cameras that were hidden in the bushes or behind the large boulders that bordered the road. Continuing up the highway about a mile, they found a pull-over as they crested a hill. It was the last stop before the eight-degree descent to the bottom of the mountain, and it was a common place for drivers to make a final stop before the steep downhill ride toward Jeremie. There were no cars or trucks there, but not being able to see over the crest of the hill, that could immediately change. They had to be cautious. It would certainly cause suspicion if someone saw a blanc exiting the car and entering the woods.

Reagan pulled over and shut off the car. "Okay. You've got everything you need, right?"

Nathan nodded that he did.

"Set your watch with mine." Reagan glanced down at his wrist. "It's eleven forty-eight."

"Eleven forty-eight. Roger that. Get out and raise the hood and pretend to check the engine. When everything is all clear, tap the hood to let me know. I'll lay low in the seat until your signal. I should be back between 2200 and 0000," said Nathan, lowering himself onto the seat.

Reagan exited the car and Nathan could feel the car shake as Reagan raised the hood and began his "inspection." Just as he was expecting to hear the tap that signaled him to get out, Nathan heard instead the sound of a truck driver laying on the brakes. He waited for the truck to pass, but it never did. Apparently, it had stopped in the middle of the road. The hiss of the hydraulic parking brake meant the driver was planning to get out. Nathan craned his head to see, and, just as he had feared, they were in the company of one of the giant two-and-a-half-ton trucks the government liked to use.

Irrationally, he thought about making a run for the woods. But they were at least a hundred feet from the clearing, and he knew he would never make it without being seen by whoever was driving the duce and a half.

Taking a deep breath, he realized it was probably just a coincidence that the truck had stopped. If someone were pursuing them, they would have certainly arrived in something smaller and faster than a slow, behemoth truck. He decided to lay low. If he were to be discovered, he'd act like a sick hiker hitching a ride to the hospital. It wasn't much of a plan, but without his gun, he was out of options.

He could hear Reagan talking to someone, and after a few minutes, he felt the car door open. Fearing the worst, he looked up, but, thankfully, it was Reagan.

Reagan spoke to him in a whisper. "The driver forgot to pack any water for the trip to Jeremie, and he asked if I have a couple bottles to spare. I've only got the one, so give me one of yours. I would tell him no, but we need to get him out of here."

Nathan reached into his bag and pulled out one of the two bottles he had to last him ten hours in the hot sun. "I can't believe we're supplying the enemy with water." He was careful to keep his voice low as he passed the bottle to Reagan.

After a few more minutes, he heard the doors to the truck shut and listened as the driver released the brakes and headed down the hill. Then, finally, he heard the two taps on the hood that meant all was clear.

He unfolded himself from the car, and with one quick glance at Reagan, he disappeared into a wall of weeds and bushes.

The mission had begun.

Chapter Nineteen

Hidden from view, Nathan watched as Reagan disappeared down the hill to head back to Les Cayes. Thinking the big truck could possibly be a decoy, he had to wait a good ten minutes before he felt confident that it had indeed been been a coincidence. Spotting no activity on the road, he pulled his compass from his backpack and set it to lead him southwest, the direction he thought would take him to the compound.

Moving out of the thick overgrowth and searching the horizon, he spied a large tree about a kilometer away that could serve as a reckoning point. He knew that focusing on a marker in the distance could keep a traveler from fixating on his compass. Pilots used the same form of navigation—called *dead reckoning*.

Noting that the time was three minutes until noon, he began the trek down the hill and through the low-lying scrubs and waist-high grass. Not being able to see below his knees, he was thankful that, of the twenty-seven species of snakes that inhabited the island, none of them were highly venomous to humans.

Making good time with a quick pace, it took less than an hour for Nathan to get to the tree. From there, he could see the bluff above the compound and knew he needed to slow down and start paying more attention—but not too much attention, remembering his guise as a lost hiker.

Entering the valley, he decided to stop for a water break and check his map. He knew exactly where he was, but if anyone was watching, it would be a good chance to showcase his lost-hiker routine. Reaching into his backpack, he pulled out his only bottle of water, and took a small sip. Being that he had given away half his supply, he would have to limit his consumption.

From the valley, it took another hour of pretending to be lost before he reached the bluff. When he arrived, he found what he'd expected. About fifteen feet from the crescent-shaped edge was a well-worn path about four feet wide—the proper width for soldiers walking side by side. This was a patrol route.

Standing on the edge of the path, he was trying to decide if he should take a chance and follow it when he suddenly heard shouting. He quickly scrambled back into the woods, barely escaping a small patrol marching down the trail. When they got to the place where he had ducked down, they abruptly stopped.

He froze, hidden behind a cluster of scarlet milkweed. He watched as about a dozen soldiers dressed in camouflage, carrying rifles and small backpacks, sat down in the middle of the trail no more than twenty feet from him.

Being well concealed, he wasn't too worried about detection—unless one of them walked into the woods to take a bathroom break.

What worried him was the thought of dogs. Earlier he had heard a few of them barking in the distance, and if they were with the patrol, they would surely smell him.

Luckily, he didn't see or hear any signs of dogs nearby.

Listening to the men, he determined they were on a training patrol, which they absolutely loathed just like the troops back home. There was zero excitement to be found in trudging count-less miles with heavy backpacks and firearms in what always seemed to be extreme heat—if not miserable cold. He smiled, thinking that if the men smoking cigarettes just a few feet away knew that he was there, their patrol that day would go very quickly from boring to exciting.

After a few minutes, as the slow-moving and complaining patrol got back up on their feet, Nathan had an idea. Assuming they were at the end of their hike and heading back to the camp, he might use them to his advantage. Staying inside the woods and following about a hundred feet behind, he would have his own escort to his destina-tion. With the clanking of equipment and the trainer occasionally speaking up to berate his soldiers, it would be easy to keep up, and there would be little risk of Nathan being seen.

Cautiously, he followed, and after about thirty minutes, he began to hear the sounds of vehicles, generators, and, to his dismay, barking dogs. He knew all soldiers had their weaknesses, like sleep deprivation, boredom, distracting personal issues, impatience, and bad judgment. But that was not the case with dogs. Dogs were always alert.

As they got closer, he could make out the rooftops of the buildings he and Reagan had seen on the satellite map and could hear voices coming from the compound.

Easing forward, he watched the soldiers gather around a guard shack and casually talk with the soldier manning the post. Looking beyond the shack, he could see that the yard of the compound was fairly clear and open under a canopy of trees.

Lined up in a row were three rectangular buildings of white-washed concrete block with metal roofs that matched the color of the trees. Toward the rear and to the left of the main structures were several smaller buildings. The larger ones were probably the barracks. He figured the smaller ones were used to hold supplies; one was possibly the mess hall. But one building caught his eye. It had a solid metal door facing the main buildings, and on the side, placed high up near the top, just below the eaves, was a single window covered with metal bars. The building was clearly designed to keep someone or something locked in—or out.

On the right side of the main buildings was the parking area. Nathan could see a duce and a half truck like the one that had stopped at the top of the hill and left with his water. He also saw several black SUVs with dark, tinted windows. The compound was surrounded by a ten-foot-high fence, which was topped with several strands of concertina wire positioned at a forty-five-degree angle. That would certainly discourage any would-be climbers.

The camp appeared to be tightly secured, set up in a square grid. Nathan couldn't tell how far it extended, but just beyond the main gate was a common area with a collection of benches, chairs, and tables.

After a quick stop at the front gate, the soldiers staggered to the tables, dropped their gear and weapons, and collapsed. Nathan thought about how easy it would be to sneak in if these undisciplined soldiers were the only troops on the compound, but he was sure they were just the new recruits and that the elite members of the BOID were somewhere out of sight.

He was watching the soldiers and thinking about his next move when the silence was broken by an outburst from the dogs. They were going crazy, and he wondered if they were reacting to the returning soldiers or if they'd caught his scent. Not wanting to find out, he worked his way back up the bluff and found a small patch of trees that were out of sight—and smell—to anyone at the camp.

Settled in, he reached into his pack for a protein bar, his binoculars, and what was left of his water. Then he started his surveillance.

Systematically, as he'd been trained to operate, he worked up a mental grid of the compound and began to scan the area, looking for any signs of Marti. He found himself focusing on the smaller building with the metal door and barred window. He felt sure that if they had her in the camp, that's where she would be.

After thirty minutes of watching, he was lowering his binoculars for a rest when he caught a glimpse of movement at the main building. It was a soldier walking toward the smaller building, carrying a tray with what looked like food and a jug of water. He was dressed in a different uniform than the training patrol had worn; it was a uniform that Nathan had seen before. It was the uniform of the BOID unit that had boarded the bus from Port-au-Prince.

The soldier set the tray on a table next to the building, fumbled with a set of keys, and unlocked the door. He disappeared inside, only to reappear seconds later with an empty tray. He relocked the door and walked back to the main building. It was obvious he was taking food to someone being held there. Nathan was confident it was Marti, but he needed proof.

He watched the compound for a few more hours, and as evening and dark approached, a heavy smell of smoke rose above the camp. Someone was cooking dinner, and it gave him an idea. With the troops about to be occupied with supper and with the smoke covering his scent from the dogs, it would be a perfect opportunity to sneak into the camp.

Carefully, he snuck down the hill under the cover of the woods and worked his way along the edge and towards the fence. With the aid of a full moon and an unobstructed view of the guard shack and the compound, he kept careful watch. After waiting almost an hour, he crawled down the fence line until he found a washed-out drainage area with a small depression at the bottom of the fence. It seemed they had become complacent about securing the perimeter, not expecting anyone to penetrate the compound. Without incident, he made it under the fence and waited a few seconds until the clouds moved in front of the moon. He then crossed the open ground to the side of the building with the bars across the window.

Standing under the window and out of sight, his first challenge was to figure out how to communicate with whoever was inside. With the thick block walls and the small window all the way under the eaves, whispering wouldn't work. He would have to find another way, but he had an idea. He took a pen and notepad from his shirt pocket, and he wrote a message: *Godchild, is that you? If so, make a tear in this note for each sibling you have and toss it back.* He then wrapped the note tightly around a small rock and, standing on the tip of his toes, flicked it up and through the window.

He knew there were several problems to this approach. First of all, it might be too dark for her to read what he had written. Secondly, she might be asleep and never hear the rock hit the floor or whatever it might land on. For all Nathan knew, it could be a recalcitrant soldier inside instead of Marti.

He waited about ten minutes, and no stone came back. He repeated the process with a new note: *If you find these notes in the morning, I'll be gone. Destroy them right away.* After another ten minutes with no response, he silently made his way back to the drainage ditch and under the fence. He exited the compound the same way he had entered.

Back at his observation point, he watched the compound for the next hour and saw no movement. It was going on ten o'clock, and his eyes were getting heavy and his arms were tired from holding up the binoculars. Also, his water had long been gone, as had his stash of protein bars. Since he needed to be back at the pickup point by midnight, he knew it was time to leave, but he was not quite ready. He decided to take a quick ten-minute nap then do one final check.

—

About five minutes into his nap, he was startled awake by the sound of screaming. Someone was mad as hell, and it sounded like a woman. He quickly grabbed the binoculars and, with the help of the moon and several lights mounted on poles close to the buildings, he could see a solider struggling with someone at the building where he suspected his goddaughter was a prisoner. With a loud reprimand, the solider snatched the screaming figure and pulled him or her toward the larger buildings. As they passed underneath the lights, Nathan could see that it was indeed a woman. It was Marti; he was sure. Wide awake by then, he followed them with the binoculars as they disappeared into the building.

With renewed strength, his first thought was to sneak back into the compound, overtake the guard, and make a daring rescue. It was an illogical thought and one he quickly dismissed. Glued to the binoculars, he watched for another fifteen minutes, but nothing happened after that. He struggled with the decision of whether or not to leave, but he knew he must get back to the pickup point by midnight.

After checking for any evidence of his presence, he headed up the hill and over the bluff. A strong surge of adrenaline had him moving through the moonlit woods with a feeling of youthful invincibility. Thinking of tomorrow's mission, he hoped the feeling would stay with him for one more day at least.

CHAPTER TWENTY

With the aid of a hooded flashlight and full moon, Nathan found his way back to the pickup point shortly before midnight. Waiting in the bushes by the road, he could feel the short-lived surge of youthful energy slowly give way to stiffened joints and sore muscles. Thinking about having to do it all again the next day, he made a mental note to start a regiment of Ibuprofen.

Glancing at his watch, he saw that it was straight-up midnight and time for Reagan to make his final pass. Not wanting to miss him, Nathan pulled out his cell. "The eagle has landed," he texted.

It was, of course, an overused spy cliché and one that any professional in his business would never dream of using, but it gave him a laugh to think of the eye roll it would draw from Reagan.

"10-4, Bald Eagle, will be there in five," was Reagan's quick response.

In less than five minutes, Nathan could hear a car coming up the hill in low gear. When it crested, the driver flashed the headlights twice. Nathan returned the signal with two clicks of his flashlight. As soon as Reagan pulled over, Nathan emerged from the bushes and jumped into the car.

"Eagle, huh? Old buzzard is more like it." Reagan slapped his friend on the back, smiling at his safe return. "How did it go?" he asked, turning the car around and pointing it back down the hill.

"She's there and not too happy about the situation." Nathan recounted the events.

"You really followed a training patrol and snuck in under the fence?"

"Yep. When you're given lemons, you make lemonade," Nathan casually replied.

"What?" Reagan asked, confused.

Nathan laughed. "In a nation that has proverbs and idioms for everything, I can't believe you haven't heard that. It means when given an opportunity, you take it. That's exactly what I did, and that's what I plan to do again when I get to work tomorrow."

"You can have all the lemonade you want, but I'm going to need something a little stronger. Let's get back to the hotel and have a drink and talk about tomorrow. I picked us up some sandwiches. Oh, and you might want this." Reagan reached into the back seat and handed over a large bottle of water.

"Thanks. I was just about to ask." Nathan almost drained the bottle in a single gulp.

They arrived back at the hotel with plans to meet in Nathan's room after taking time to quickly shower.

It was a little past one o'clock when Reagan tapped on the door and let himself in. Nathan was resting on the bed with his arms folded behind his head and his eyes closed. Hearing his friend come in, he straightened up and eased his sore body from the bed. He moved toward the table and chairs.

"Moving kind of slow?" Reagan asked as he took a seat.

"Yeah. We're not quite the assets to law and order that we used to be," said Nathan.

"Speak for yourself." Reagan leaned back in his chair and touched his protruding belly. "I preformed *my* task exceptionally well and—after an afternoon nap—I've been feeling great."

With a quick movement, Nathan reached over and shook one of the legs on Reagan's chair. Reagan fought quickly to regain his balance, raising his voice in protest.

"Never mock the asset," said Nathan. He grinned as Reagan lowered the chair safely to the floor.

After grumbling a few chosen words, Reagan reached into a brown paper bag and tossed a sandwich Nathan's way. He pulled out a small bottle of Scotch and began fixing drinks. "One finger or two?" he asked.

"Better make it two," Nathan replied as he turned on the TV.

They sat at the table and mindlessly watched a reality survival show from the States. The "survivor" was some city-boy celebrity who was carrying on as if he were on the verge of dying any moment from hunger or from thirst. The producers had him crawling through a remote and desolate desert somewhere in the US.

Nathan shook his head. "This is the kind of crap we have to watch back home. I can count at least five camera angles from five different cameramen, who I can guarantee you are not starving or dying from thirst. Why can't they give the guy some water or food? I'll bet his air-conditioned, fully-stocked trailer is within a hundred yards of where he is currently 'on the brink of death.' " Nathan picked up the remote and turned the TV off.

"Speaking of survival, what's tomorrow's plan?" Reagan asked. Nathan took a taste of the Scotch and then replied, "Remember the guy I noticed at breakfast yesterday?"

Reagan nodded that he did.

"Well, seeing him gave me an idea. It was inspired by the philosopher William of Ockham and the principles of Sun Tzu, the military strategist who was also a philosopher. The idea is very basic. I'm going to walk right into the camp and introduce myself."

Reagan gave him an incredulous stare. "Really, Nathan? Just walk right into the camp? I think you've watched too much of that crap that was just on the TV. You can't just walk in and introduce yourself at a BOID camp that's holding captive the daughter of the wealthiest man in Haiti and the leading presidential candidate. Who exactly do you plan to morph into in the morning, Indiana Jones?"

"Actually, one can follow the exact course of action that I just described, and you're not too far off the mark with your reference. But *Doctor* Jones would be more exact rather than *Indiana*. My plan is to take on the cover of a history professor, much like Indiana Jones himself. It seems, you see, that the retired 'Dr. Roark' has lost his way while searching for old ruins from the days of the revolution and the years right after that. He is in the area doing research on a book he's planning to write on the aftermath of the revolution, concentrating primarily on the southern peninsula as most of the previous work has focused on Port-au-Prince and the north." Confidence bled through in Nathan's voice.

"So, just where did the esteemed Dr. Roark teach, and how many articles and publications would our friends find if they did an internet search and plugged in his name?" Reagan smugly asked.

"My good sir, I'll have you know that Dr. Roark did not teach at one of the attention-seeking 'publish or perish' universities. He taught in the international studies program, with a concentration in the Caribbean basin, at the more esoteric Flagler College in St. Augustine, Florida. He retired fifteen years ago to take care of his elderly mother, whose wealth was such that he did not have to return to work after she died. With proof from stamps on his passport, he will show that he has traveled the world and is now working on the book he always wanted to write."

"Okay, so let's say you fool them temporarily, assuming they don't already know that Nathan Roark the CIA agent is in the country and snooping around. Once you're in the camp, how do you plan to get Marti out? Tell them you need a research assistant and that you were thinking the girl they have locked up in a cell would be the perfect choice?" Reagan had gotten into the rhythm of the challenging banter the men had long enjoyed.

"You know, that might be a good idea. I'll be sure and give them your full name and address so you can get the credit," Nathan fired back with a grin.

Nathan spent the next thirty minutes explaining the details and nuances of his plan.

Reagan agreed that it might actually work. "How long do you think you have before they notice that a guard is missing and they launch a search?" he asked.

"I'm not sure. I'm hoping to buy about thirty to forty-five minutes. My plan is to slip back under the fence, skirt the guard shack, and haul ass down the gravel road to the main one. We won't have time to go back through the woods. If all goes well, Marti and I will meet you near the entrance of the compound. Then we can head back to Les Cayes and make our escape via the airport."

They spent a few more minutes fine-tuning the plan, then, with nothing more to discuss, it was time to call Charles with an update. Grabbing the bottle of Scotch, Reagan told Nathan that he'd meet him in the hotel's restaurant at 0800 for breakfast, and then he slipped out the door.

—

Charles answered on the first ring and skipped the pleasantries. "What did you find?" he asked.

"She's there," Nathan immediately responded.

His reply was followed by brief silence then a long sigh of relief.

"Just as we thought," said Nathan, "they're holding her in a national police compound just north of Duchity. I spent most of the day and evening monitoring the camp. I even found a way to breach the security fence and found the building where they're holding her. Around nine I saw them take her to a larger building that I believe to be the HQ. She was putting up a struggle. I was already outside the camp and was watching through the binoculars. I wanted to stay and see what happened but had to meet Reagan by our cutoff time of midnight. Assuming they haven't moved her, my plan is to enter the compound tomorrow afternoon." Nathan was about to give the Charles the details of his diversion plan when he was interrupted.

"Nathan, I appreciate you more than I could ever put into words," said Charles. "Madeleine and I couldn't have chosen a better godfather for our Marti, and you've proved to be the most trusted friend I've ever had."

Nathan sensed a "but" was coming.

"I'm extremely grateful that you found her, and I'm not sure anyone else could have done that and gone undetected. But now that she's been found, my men and I will take the reigns from here with the rescue mission."

This time it was Nathan who paused before he spoke. He had heard and seen this reaction many times in his career, but mostly from governments, not fathers. As irrational as it was, he understood the need that Charles had to take control and do as any father would—rush in to save his child. Charles felt that with the trained and skilled security force that he had in place, he had what he needed to secure his daughter's rescue—but he was wrong. Charles was out of his league. His security force would be no match for the special op's unit. Nathan had to change Charles's mind.

"Charles," he said, "you called me last Saturday night, desperate. You realized after weighing all your options that I was the only person you could completely trust, the only one who had the skills to find out what really happened on the night Marti disappeared." He paused.

"You need to continue to trust me, Charles. If you attempt to move your team into the compound, they will kill your men and they'll kill Marti—on the spot. There is no way that they're going to let her leave that place alive. I spent all day and half the evening reconnoitering the camp. I know when they change the guards, when the lights come on, and when they eat. I even figured out what the dogs are barking at. I've been in and out of their camp undetected, and I have an escape route planned for tomorrow evening. Listen to the details of my plan and I believe that you'll agree—it's the best option that we've got." Nathan took a deep breath and waited for the answer.

"Okay. Let's hear your plan."

Nathan explained how he would enter the compound and how he planned to extract Marti. Charles remained silent as he listened. To get his friend's approval, Nathan knew he would have to somehow include Charles in the mission. Actually, he'd give Charles an important part to play. "Charles, there is indeed something you can help us with," he said. "You can have your airplane waiting at the Les Cayes airport. We'll need to get out of the country as soon as possible."

Charles hesitated. Then when he replied, the answer was unexpected. "I think your plan is good, and after your explanation, I agree it's the best option for getting Marti out, but unfortunately I won't be able to assist you with my airplane." Nathan could hear the dejection in his voice. "You see," continued Charles, "I can't trust my pilots. They both were trained and previously employed by the national police, and they still spend a great deal of their off time at the academy. I have no doubt their allegiance is with them, and they may have already been alerted to watch for any activity that might interest the police. If your plan is to leave the country, you will have to figure out another way. I'm very sorry, Nathan."

Nathan felt a flash of anger. If Charles couldn't trust his pilots, how did he think he could trust his security force who had probably been trained at the national police Academy as well? But since he was suddenly preoccupied with finding an alternative solution to getting out of Haiti, he let it go and didn't ask. He knew that with the unlimited resources of the police and BOID, staying in country was simply not an option.

"I wish I knew someone from Haiti or one of the local islands with an airplane—someone I could trust—but I'm afraid I don't," said Charles. "I hope that you will be able to figure something out. You've done so much for me."

That made Nathan think of something. "Charles, it's a long shot, but I might know a way. But let's not talk about it; the less you know, the better. Just say a prayer that I can arrange it. If I can't, I'll call you back and we can discuss some other options. If I can, you won't hear from me until all this is over."

Nathan ended the call and glanced at the time on the old digital analog clock by the bed. It was after two and he had one more call to make, one that could determine the success or failure of the mission.

CHAPTER TWENTY-ONE

Nathan woke and saw the time was seven thirty. Not trusting the old clock, he had set the alarm on his cell phone to wake him up at six. Now he wondered if he had been so tired that he'd slept right through it.

Picking up the phone, he noticed that he had two missed calls. They were both from Aubrey. According to the time stamp, the first call had come in just a few minutes after he'd called them at two thirty and the other just five minutes before he'd woken up. He couldn't understand how he could have missed both the alarm *and* the calls, and then he remembered: he had silenced the ringer the previous day before leaving on his mission.

Unfortunately, there were no messages, but there was a text. He tapped the message icon.

Nathan, we got your message and tried to call back. 0730. In the air, headed your way. ETA at Ile-a- Vache is around 11:30.

Nathan checked the clock. It was 0736. He quickly called her back, hoping to catch them before they lost their cell signal.

To his dismay, the phone went straight to voicemail. He left them a quick message that he had received their text and hoped they had a safe flight. He also left them a heartfelt thanks.

Lying back on the bed, he was relieved that he now had an exit plan with two people he could trust. But he was also worried, knowing that he was drawing them into something dangerous. Staring at the ceiling, he wondered if Laura might have been right after all. Taking on the cabal and the national police would be an arduous task for even an experienced team, and here he was attempting it with an old retired co-worker and two friends recruited from their honeymoon.

Rubbing his temples, trying to discourage the beginnings of a headache, he thought about Aubrey, Colby, and Reagan. Reagan had convinced him that his reason for helping find and hopefully rescue Marti was to work toward a better future for his country. He had said that it was a risk worth taking.

Turning his thoughts to Aubrey and Colby, Nathan tried to justify his actions in involving them. Their role would, after all, be limited to providing a ride out of the country, and they wouldn't be anywhere near the more dangerous part of the mission. Of course, they still needed to know the seriousness of the operation, but being in Les Cayes, miles away from the compound, he felt they would be safe. He smiled, thinking that Colby would never let him forget that he'd had to leave his honeymoon to come rescue Nathan. Nathan knew that he'd be hearing that story for years to come.

With his conscious semi-clear, he eased out of bed, feeling the soreness in his back and legs. Shuffling to the bathroom, he looked into the mirror at his tired reflection. He rubbed his gray two-day-old beard and told himself, "The asset is definitely too old."

After a long, hot shower and a couple of aspirin, he began feeling better. Dressed in a lightweight khaki safari shirt with cargo shorts and a floppy bush hat that might be worn by a history professor, he left the room to meet Reagan.

He found him in the restaurant sitting at the same table as the day before, reading a paper. Nathan pulled out a chair and sat.

Reagan lowered the newspaper, smiled, and shook his head. "Ah. If it isn't Dr. Roark. What brings the esteemed professor to Les Cayes? Shouldn't you be in a nursing home somewhere, writing that elusive article now that you're retired from that non-publishing college?"

"Sir, you must have me confused with someone else," Nathan replied. "I'm a private investigator hired by your wife to investigate a case of infidelity from back in the 1970s. It seems you had a one-night stand with a girlfriend of a drug smuggler. Do you have a few minutes to answer some questions?"

Reagan dropped the newspaper in a dramatic fashion. "Here, I'm trying to have a little fun and you bring that up. Why can't you just let it go?"

"So you confirm it happened. Will you speak a little louder and repeat that statement, please?" Nathan pretended to hold the button of his collar closer to Reagan's lips.

Reagan picked up his newspaper and was about to swat him when the waiter appeared beside their table. They ordered their breakfast and turned the conversation to the matter of the day ahead.

"How do you feel? We have a big day ahead of us," Reagan said.

"Sore, but I took a few aspirin and have the bottle in my backpack. Hopefully, that adrenaline from yesterday will show back up." Nathan adjusted his position in the hard wooden chair. "There has been a change in our exit plan," he said. "Aubrey and Colby are flying into Ile-a-Vache from the Caymans and will arrive around eleven thirty. You're going to need to meet them at the airport."

"I thought they were on their honeymoon? Why are they coming here?" Reagan asked, looking confused and troubled.

Nathan explained his conversation with Charles and how Aubrey and Colby now fit into the plan. "I don't know any other way. This all just happened so fast, and I had just assumed that Charles would have a way to get us out of here. All they will be doing is picking us up at the airport. Once we're in the air, we will be fine," Nathan said, trying to convince himself that he had made the correct decision.

Reagan starred at him, noncommittal.

After a few seconds of silence, Nathan spoke. "Right after you drop me at the top of the hill, head back to Les Cayes and catch a boat over to the island. Call ahead and see if you can use one of the trucks that Colline Sacrée keeps at the marina. I'm sure Monsieur Duplechain won't mind you borrowing one, especially since you'll be checking Aubrey and Colby into his hotel. Then they can wait there and be comfortable until it's time for us to go. Have Colby re-fuel the airplane and get familiar with the Les Cayes airport and airspace. Also have him look at a route from Les Cayes to Puerto Rico. I'm thinking that will be the best place for us to go." Nathan paused. "There is one other thing I need for you to do," he said. "They don't have any of the details about why they're coming here. I just told them on the message that I'm in a bit of a jam and need their help. You'll need to fill them in on what it is that we're involved in."

Then he knew exactly what was coming.

Reagan leaned forward as he spoke. "Nathan, you pulled them from their honeymoon and they *have no idea what they're getting into?*" His voice was low and stressed. "And by the way, it's not just 'a bit of a jam.'" He rubbed his hand through his hair. "You should have called me last night before making that decision."

Nathan shot him a defensive look. "Well, what would you have done? What other options do you think we have? I've explained why Charles can't fly us out, and you know we can't stay in the country. We can't steal an airplane. Do you know how to fly? I don't! Give me an alternative, because it's not too late. Then Aubrey and Colby can stay out of this mess and have a nice extended honeymoon at Colline Sacrée," Nathan said in a hushed, frustrated tone.

After a few seconds, in a softer voice, he said, "I know they should never have been brought into this, and you know I hated asking them, but I just don't see any other options."

Reagan looked as dejected as Nathan felt. Nathan could tell that Reagan felt bad about laying into him.

"Maybe our friend the cook knows how to fly?" Reagan asked with a small grin.

Nathan returned his smile, and in an instant he knew that everything was fine between them.

Then, with perfect timing, the waiter returned with their coffee and their breakfast.

—

After breakfast, Nathan went to his room, grabbed his backpack, and met Reagan at the car. It was eight fifteen, and Reagan had just enough time to drop him at the top of the hill, return to Les Cayes, and catch a boat to Ile-a-Vache.

Soon they were at the drop-off point, where the scene became surprisingly emotional. Maybe it was because of the intensity of the talk they'd had at breakfast—or the reality of the perils that lay just ahead.

Whatever the case, as Nathan rose from his seat to exit the car, Reagan gently grabbed his shoulder. Nathan turned and saw the seriousness of his expression, and he sat back down.

Reagan spoke to him from his heart. "So many years ago, you had faith in a young man who was trying to make a better life for himself and his family. With your help and guidance, I've had a wonderful career and a life that most people here could only dream of. No matter what happens today, know that you've done a great service for our country and that I'm proud to have been a part of it." His voice cracked a little, and his eyes were misty as he added, "I'm also proud to be your friend and brother."

No more words were needed. Nathan gave him a warm smile and a nod of affirmation. Reagan returned the gesture.

Nathan climbed out of the car and, without looking back, he disappeared into the woods.

Chapter Twenty-Two

Just off the trail, Nathan settled in the same spot as the day before, behind a clump of bushes, blocking him from the view of anyone who might be looking up the hill. Retracing his route from the day before, it had taken just at three hours to reach the bluff. Knowing the layout of the land, he could have made better time by entering the woods from lower down the hill, but he didn't want any surprises. There weren't any cameras on the valley approach; it was possible they had them closer to the compound road.

Watching the camp, he saw that the gate was being guarded by a single soldier. The rest of the compound was eerily quiet. Being that it was almost noon, most of the troops were probably in the mess hall, but Nathan had still expected to see more than the one guard. He hoped this complacency would work to his advantage.

Moving his binoculars to the building where Marti was being held, he saw an armed, alert guard by the door. He had not been there the day before. Maybe they'd found the notes, or maybe it was

Charles's call to the police that had gotten their attention. Whatever the reason, they were paying more attention to their prisoner—so much for complacency.

He watched the compound for another few hours and around 1600, he began to see troop activity around the common area. Since these men were wearing the same uniforms and packs as the soldiers from the day before, Nathan assumed they were preparing for another training patrol. He quickly gathered his gear and silently moved through the woods toward the compound road. In order for his ruse as the lost, weary professor needing rescue to be believable, he needed to make contact with the soldiers first. If the troops found him in the woods, the rescue he had planned could turn into a capture.

It took thirty minutes to skirt the bluff and make it to a place along the road just above the gate. He did one last check of his backpack to make sure he had everything he needed to back up his story: a reference book, notepads (with notes on his "research"), maps, pens, a compass, a multipurpose knife, food, a mini-stove, water bottles with Aquatabs, and binoculars. The one item he hadn't packed was his cell phone. Instead, he'd hidden it behind a tree and marked the spot with a large rock that he could see clearly from the road. He hated leaving it since it was his only way to contact Reagan, but if confiscated, it would reveal too much compromising information.

Taking a deep breath, he stepped out of the cover of the woods onto the road, where he was now exposed. This was the first time in his career he had entered a dangerous situation without the backing of a team. But he felt it was the right decision and in a few short hours, he would know for sure.

As he walked around a curve in the middle of the road, the gate came into view, and a startled guard flew out of the shack. He ran toward Nathan with his gun leveled, yelling into a radio.

With a friendly smile planted on his face, Nathan stopped and raised his arms. It was time to play his role.

"Jwenn sou te a, jwenn sou te a!" the guard screamed at him.

Nathan knew that meant, "Get on the ground," but he remained upright. Raising his arms higher and shrugging his shoulders, he gave the man his best look of confusion.

The guard then pointed the rifle at the ground. He yelled the command again. This time, Nathan followed his directions and moved down to the ground.

It didn't take long before two trucks full of soldiers appeared on the scene. Nathan could feel an excitement among the troops over the idea of an intruder being caught. He imagined that it could get pretty boring at the camp with just the one prisoner to watch. He found the idea amusing; they would be disappointed when they found it was just an old, lost retired professor who'd wandered into their midst.

But if all went to plan, later in the evening he would give them a little something to whet their taste for excitement.

Stepping out of one of the trucks was a man in an officer's uniform, and he didn't seem to be as filled with enthusiasm about Nathan's presence as the others were. Walking slowly and not taking his eyes from Nathan, he approached. "What do we have here?" he asked in perfect English.

Nathan frowned apologetically. "Hi. I'm sorry to have caused such a disruption, but I seem to be a little lost, and I would appreciate it if you could please tell me where I am."

A smile spread across the man's face. He'd surely never expected anyone to show up at a BOID camp and ask where they were. "Who are you and where are you supposed to be?" he asked, not answering Nathan's question.

Good tactic, Nathan thought. "May I stand?" he asked, knowing he could be more convincing if he was standing up.

"You may," the officer replied.

Nathan, in no need of exaggeration, slowly pulled his still-sore body up off the ground and promptly stuck his hand out. "Professor Nathan Roark," he said.

The officer accepted his hand but did not return the introduction or reply to Nathan. Nathan knew his kind and how his mind would work. The officer was waiting for this wanderer to explain why a lost professor had turned up at his compound. If it had been anyone else other than an old, arthritic professor, Nathan knew that the man would have been suspicious about the timing of it all: the sudden appearance of a stranger while the female presidential candidate was being held captive in the camp.

Nathan continued with his act. "Please allow me to again apologize for disrupting you. I started this morning at Pic Macaya, studying the ruins of Camp Gerard. I made the acquaintance there of a fellow historian who told me about another fort—just recently discovered. It's supposedly from the Saint-Domingue revolution. This man pointed the way that I should go and said it was only about a mile south of Camp Gerard, where we were. I took a compass bearing and walked at least a mile, but I never found it. Then, when I was trying to make my way back, I somehow got turned around, and I'm afraid that I've been lost almost the entire day. I'm so thankful I stumbled upon this road and found someone to ask. I don't know what I would've done if it had gotten dark. I could have gotten myself into some real trouble!"

The officer studied Nathan. Nathan knew that officials here must be aware that Camp Gerard was only a few miles over the mountain, giving credence to his story.

"May I see your passport and examine the contents of your backpack?" the officer asked Nathan, holding out his hand.

Nathan lowered his backpack, removed his passport from the front pouch, and then handed both to the officer he believed to be a lieutenant. He suddenly worried that he might have done too good of a job convincing the officer who he was, which could result in an escort off the property before he could make it into the camp. He needed to distract the officer and the troops.

As the man examined his document and backpack, Nathan began to sway, appearing to have suddenly grown weak in the knees. He kneeled and put his hands to his face.

The lieutenant immediately reacted. "Are you okay? What's wrong?"

Nathan responded, "I'm not sure, just became dizzy all of a sudden. I've been out of water for a long time and haven't eaten since this morning. I do have a few medical issues. But thinking I'd be back to my hotel by noon, I didn't bring my medication. If you'd be so gracious as to allow me to replenish my water and rest for a little while, I would be most grateful. I will, of course, pay you for your trouble. I will also need to call my taxi driver and tell him to pick me up here instead of Pic Macaya." Nathan said this knowing that the lieutenant would never allow a taxi to enter the compound.

The lieutenant continued to examine Nathan's passport and the contents of his backpack; he didn't answer Nathan's question. After a few minutes, he spoke in Creole to the men, telling them to take the professor to the common area and to give him water. He also told them to keep him in their sight. Returning the backpack but keeping the passport, he looked at Nathan with a disingenuous smile. "We welcome you as our guest," he said. "My men will show you where to get water and show you a place where you can rest. I have a few things to do and will check in with you later about transportation to Les Cayes."

Nathan was pointed to the passenger door of one of the trucks and got in as the soldiers climbed into the back. He was about to enter the compound—for the second time.

The driver pulled into the common area that he had seen the previous day from the bluff. He dropped Nathan and one of the soldiers off beside a couple of picnic tables surrounding a few large trees. The other truck disappeared with the lieutenant further into the compound. Nathan could only imagine the conversation he was about to have with his superiors.

The main concern was what might pop up if they checked the internet. He knew they wouldn't find anything linking him with Flagler College, which he had mentioned as his past employer. That he could explain, but he wasn't sure what might turn up that could hurt him. He should have done an extensive online search of his own name, but with the plan coming together so quickly, he hadn't thought about it earlier. Another example of why it takes a team to fully execute a mission.

All of the soldiers sans one left the area and entered the surrounding buildings. The remaining soldier asked in broken English if he could get Nathan some water. Nathan removed the two water bottles from his pack and handed them to the guard. Knowing he was being watched, he did what any aging professor who had been walking all day would do—pulled off his boots and socks and began to rub his feet. He also emptied the contents of his pack onto the ground.

While waiting on the guard to return, he opened a can of beans and leaned back against a tree and ate. With his belongings spread out in disarray, a floppy hat on his head, and his pants rolled up to his knees, he looked like anything but a spy. He hoped his disguise would hold up for a few more hours, long enough for him to break Marti out of there and make his escape under the cover of the night.

CHAPTER TWENTY-THREE

Colby

Aubrey and Colby watched as a vehicle approached the airfield in a cloud of dust. Just before turning onto the airport road, the driver stopped alongside the inspector's truck as Pierre-Toussaint braked on his way out. The inspector rolled his window down and talked for about five minutes with the other driver.

Looking at his watch, Colby saw it was one thirty. This was their contact, he assumed. He hoped there would not be any trouble, and as he would later find out, there was no need for worry on that front. It turned out that Reagan and Jules Pierre-Toussaint had known each other all their lives. But in that moment no one knew how that brief meeting—two old friends catching up on the airport road—would profoundly affect the future of so many.

Then the light green SUV was stopped beside them on the tarmac. A banner on the door advertised the Colline Sacrée hotel. The door opened and a tall, older Haitian man emerged. His warm smile was somehow made friendlier by the slight gap between two of his front teeth. Walking up to them, he held out his hand. "Good afternoon. I presume you are Aubrey and Colby?"

Colby took his hand and said that indeed they were.

"I'm Reagan, or I might say your *contact*, as labeled by our mutual friend Nathan." The man had a hint of sarcasm in his voice. He then offered his hand to Aubrey. "I've heard a lot about *you*, young lady. Nathan told me about all the things that went on last year. What an amazing story. You were quite the hero."

She smiled and pulled her hand away, embarrassed by the praise.

Colby came quickly to the rescue. "So, how do you know Nathan?" he asked.

Reagan shifted his feet and leaned against the truck. He looked uncomfortable—and Colby understood. The question in the air would surely lead to the bigger question—*What has Nathan gotten himself into, and why exactly are we here?*

"We met about thirty years ago," said Reagan. "He was on assignment here in Haiti, and I was just starting my career in government. My original job was to translate for him, but after getting himself into a couple of sticky situations that I had to bail him out of, the job began to change. Nathan liked my instincts, and we made a good team. With permission from our governments, he hired me. We worked together until he was assigned to a job back in the US. Over the years we've stayed in touch, and a couple of days ago he called to get my help with, as he called it, *a personal matter.*"

Colby noticed the way that Reagan stretched out the last three words. "Let me guess," he said. "This personal matter turned out to be much more than personal."

"You know Nathan," Reagan said. "Never a dull moment."

"What's he involved in now? Why are we here?" asked Aubrey, giving Reagan a hard stare.

But she didn't get an answer.

"Let's get to the hotel. Then I'll tell you everything and answer all your questions," said Reagan. "Colby, Nathan requested that you fill up both tanks and have the airplane ready for immediate departure."

"No problem. I was getting ready to do exactly that," said Colby.

They were already at the fuel station, and as Colby filled the tanks, Aubrey began pulling their bags from the plane.

Reagan quickly stopped her. "Ah, I don't think you'll need all those," he said. "What Nathan is planning will take place in the next twelve hours, so all we'll be doing at the hotel is waiting on his call. Just grab what you think you'll need."

She returned the big bags, picked out their smaller carry-ons, and handed them to him.

Finished with the fueling, Colby climbed into the 310. "I'm going to move the airplane to the transient ramp," he told them as he closed the door.

He wasn't liking this. Like most pilots, he was not spontaneous. Pilots need to know things ahead of time so they can plan, check the weather forecast, and think about the flight. Pilots don't like being told to wait for instructions for immediate departure.

As Colby taxied to the far end of the field, Reagan and Aubrey followed in the SUV. Aubrey was in the back seat, leaving the front for Colby.

With the 310 secure, Colby opened the passenger door and got into the SUV. "We're fueled and ready for some unknown, probably dangerous, immediate departure," he said. He knew that his displeasure was likely showing in his voice.

Speaking over Reagan's shoulder, Aubrey ventured a question in a low voice. "How bad is this situation?"

Reagan took a deep breath. "Pretty bad if things go wrong. It could possibly turn into an international incident. Hopefully, that won't happen."

"Could this matter have been handled by our company?" she asked. "And *should* it have gone through them?"

"The answer's yes and no. Yes—most definitely, at this point—but not initially. When you hear the story, you'll know what I mean."

As Reagan pulled away from the airfield, he tried to lighten up the mood. He glanced at them with a playful smile. "When this is over, we're going to stuff Nathan in a burlap sack and take turns beating that guy with a rubber hose," he said. He smiled and waved one hand in the air as if he were beating an imaginary version of the friend who'd brought them together for this crisis. Everybody laughed.

"That sounds good as long as I get to go first," Colby said.

The drive took about thirty minutes on a bumpy, gravel road. Then Reagan parked the SUV and welcomed them to Colline Sacrée. They grabbed their bags and walked past some armed guards at the gate, then headed up the hill toward the resort.

Once inside, they walked down a long, arched, open-air hallway. The floors and walls were decorated in mosaic tile and led to the check-in counter, where they were greeted by a gentleman Reagan introduced as Monsieur Duplechain.

"Bonjour, comment allez vous," the man said enthusiastically, his comments directed primarily towards Aubrey. "Monsieur Duplechain at your service."

"Monsieur, these are friends of Nathan's, Aubrey and Colby Cameron," Reagan said.

Duplechain immediately stepped out from behind the counter to give Aubrey a big hug and a kiss on each cheek. "Ah, welcome to my hotel," he said, ignoring Colby altogether. "I have rooms ready by the pool if you would like to swim." Clearly smitten, he continued to focus on Aubrey.

Colby couldn't help but have a little fun. "Thanks. Aubrey loves to swim. Maybe you could join us and tell us more about the island and the hotel." He offered his hand for a shake.

"Excellent! I would love to," the man replied, shaking Colby's hand with vigor. "Let me get your key so you can change into your bathing suits. Of course, we are French, so if you prefer to go bathing au naturel, that would be okay too."

"No, no! Bathing suits are fine. Thank you," Aubrey replied, turning three shades of red.

As they walked out of the lobby, Colby and Reagan traded amused glances.

Aubrey turned and swatted Colby when they were out of view from the check-in desk. "I can't believe you said that!" she exclaimed.

The two men burst into fits of laughter.

"Maybe you prefer to go au naturel, Madame?" Colby asked, putting his best French accent to good use.

That earned him another swat, and the men laughed even harder.

Aubrey folded her arms and chewed on her lip. Colby knew that she was laughing on the inside.

When he finally caught his breath, Reagan got back to business. "Let's meet in an hour by the pool," he said, "and I'll fill you in on what our friend Nathan has been up to. I need to head back to the desk. In all of the excitement, I forgot to get my key from the love-struck monsieur."

A quick hour passed and Aubrey and Colby were ready to hear about whatever dire situation had pulled them from their honeymoon.

Reagan began his story.

He started on the night of Marti's disappearance, then he told them about the investigation on the beach and the eventual understanding that the cabal was involved. When he had finished speaking, both Aubrey and Colby sat in silence, processing all that they'd been told.

With her eyes on Colby, Aubrey was the first to speak. "So that must have been the phone call he got at our reception. Remember how he left abruptly and didn't tell us why?" Then she turned to Reagan. "This is unbelievable. I mean no disrespect, but you and Nathan are in way over your heads. He should have consulted our boss, and I've got half a mind to call him now. I'm sure you're well aware how bad this thing could turn out?"

Colby nodded in agreement.

Reagan shook his head and threw his hands up in the air. "Oh, I know. Believe me! When things first started getting crazy, I tried to convince him that it was just too risky to proceed without any help. But he wouldn't listen. He wants to keep control of the situation. And I know that he means well, but this time I think he's gone too far."

He took a deep breath. "But for better or for worse, I'm afraid it's too late now. He's probably near the compound if he's not inside already. Sometime after dark, I expect to get a call to pick them up from a nearby road. We will just have to wait and see what happens then." He looked each of them in the eye. "And this is important: If you choose not to take the risk, Nathan and I both will understand. This is not your battle. It was unfair to drag you from your honeymoon. We can find another way."

Another long silence followed. To Colby, the moment felt familiar. He thought about a time a year or so before when he'd stood on the tarmac of the Barrow County airport in Northeast Georgia. On that day, he'd tried to stop Aubrey from hurling herself even further into something very dangerous; he'd told her they should leave the final resolution to Nathan and his team.

He would never forget the look she gave him then. It was a look that reflected something between disappointment and betrayal. He had always regretted his decision to question her motives then, and now here was his chance for redemption. He wasn't sure where Aubrey was on joining Nathan and Reagan's plan, but he assumed she would probably go along. He needed to speak first and finally broke the silence. "I'll go along with it if Aubrey is comfortable, but with a few conditions."

The others looked at him and waited.

"When we wallop Nathan, I'm going to need a longer, thicker hose. And on my turn, I want double time." He got up from the table. "Now, if you will excuse me, I have to plan a flight to Les Cayes and Puerto Rico."

As Colby stood to make his exit, Monsieur Duplechain was making his entrance. Dressed in a Speedo, he was all smiles as he walked toward the table where Aubrey and Reagan still sat. His eyes were focused on Aubrey. Colby had to look down to hide his laugh. He glanced back at Aubrey and her expression of shock was priceless.

CHAPTER TWENTY-FOUR

Nathan

Nathan was just finishing his can of beans when a truck appeared.

The driver pulled up to the clearing, and two officers got out of the back seat. One was the lieutenant, still holding Nathan's passport, and the other, moving with an air of confidence, was likely his superior. The lieutenant nervously tapped his fingers against the passport as the men approached. Both wore serious expressions.

Nathan thought of the soldiers searching the bus and the person who had followed him from the bus stop in Les Cayes. Had it just been a coincidence, or did they know why he was here? He was fairly certain he was about to find out.

Nathan slowly stood to greet the soldiers. He imagined he looked ridiculous, holding an empty can of beans with his pants rolled up past his old, knobby knees and with gear, boots, and socks strung out all around him. He hoped he looked ridiculous; it was the look he was going for.

With a smile, he put the can down and stuck a sticky hand out toward the men. They shook then frowned down at their hands, now coated with bean juice. They discreetly tried to wipe them on their shirts.

So far, so good, thought Nathan.

"From what the lieutenant has told me, it sounds like you've had a rough day," said the man Nathan was meeting for the first time. "This is not a good place to be lost. A person could easily disappear for good. But that, fortunately, didn't happen, and to demonstrate our good will to the traveling professor, we would like to make you our guest tonight." Nathan could hear a touch of sarcastic humor in his tone.

He had met military officers like this man before: intelligent, confident, and seemingly in possession of some kind of sixth sense. Telling Nathan that he wanted to *make* him a guest was not just a figure of speech; it meant Nathan had no choice.

"If you're sure it won't be too much trouble, Captain. It *is* captain, right?" Nathan could determine the man's rank from his uniform, but he was hoping to get his name.

"Yes, captain is correct. The lieutenant, will show you to your quarters. I'll send someone for you around 2000. You'll have dinner with us tonight."

The captain returned to the truck, and the lieutenant addressed Nathan. "I'll give you a couple of minutes to get your gear together and then show you to your room. I need to make a quick call." He pulled out his phone and walked away.

Things were going well, thought Nathan as he gathered up his gear. He was in the compound now by invitation and hopefully would be staying somewhere close to Marti. But he also knew the realities of the situation. Military men, especially ranking officers, were suspicious by nature and didn't believe in coincidences. Nathan knew the captain was keeping him there until he found out exactly who he was—a retired professor or maybe someone else?

"Dr. Roark." The lieutenant was returning. "Follow me, please," he said.

Nathan grabbed his pack and walked behind the officer—unfortunately in the opposite direction of where they were holding Marti.

They arrived at a building about fifty yards from the clearing. With small, open slits for windows and a solid metal door with a large lock, it was similar to the place where he knew Marti was being kept. The lieutenant unlocked the door and motioned for him to enter.

The room had a wall of bunk beds, and in the corner was a small bathroom with no door. There was a table with four chairs in the center of the room. This was most likely a prison cell. The lieutenant told him that if he needed anything, there would be a soldier stationed by the door.

As his escort left, Nathan knew that he would soon find out if he was truly a prisoner in that place. He waited to see if would hear the lock click. Thankfully, he didn't.

Ten minutes later, he opened the door and looked outside. A few feet away to his left, just like at Marti's building, was a soldier sitting in a chair. He had a weapon holstered on his side, and a rifle was leaning against the wall. With a look of indifference, the man glanced up at Nathan.

Nathan went back inside and shut the door. He noticed that he couldn't lock the door from the inside. Having nothing else to do, and knowing that he had a long night coming up, he crawled into one of the bottom bunks and tried to take a nap.

He woke to what sounded like metal pressing and scraping against the side of the concrete wall. He climbed out of the bunk and walked to the door, easing it open to inspect.

It had been the guard's chair. Paying no attention to Nathan, the soldier was watching two black SUVs approaching from the front gate. Judging by the anxious look on the guard's face, someone important had arrived.

Nathan slowly slipped out of the building and walked a few feet toward the courtyard for a better view.

The drivers of the SUVs parked in front of the HQ building. In addition to the two drivers, six people climbed out of the vehicles. One was wearing a military style uniform and appeared to be in charge. Nathan couldn't hear what the man was saying, but he appeared to be giving instructions to the other five.

Nathan was certain that these guests were members of the cabal. Post Charles's phone call, they had probably called an emergency meeting to decide the next course of action.

He tried to ease closer to see if he recognized any of them, but he hadn't gotten any further than a nearby tree when the guard tapped him on the shoulder with his weapon and motioned him back into his quarters.

Lying on his bunk, he thought about the new arrivals and how their presence would affect his plans. So far, things had gone well. After dinner with the staff and captain, he had planned on waiting a few hours for the camp to quiet down and get settled for the night. Then he'd get the guard's attention (assuming the door was still unlocked), overtake the soldier, make his move to grab Marti, and get out undetected—the last thing they would expect from an almost septuagenarian academic.

But this changed everything. The compound would now be very busy and on high alert.

Stuck in the room with nothing to do, he took another nap to pass the time, then woke to find moonlight shining through the slit of a window, casting a rectangular shadow on the floor.

He suddenly felt hungry. It had been a while since he'd scarfed down the beans. He was just thinking about dinner when he heard the doorknob being turned.

A dark figure filled the space behind the open door. "Dr. Roark, please come with me." The lieutenant's tone was not unpleasant, but it wasn't cordial either.

Nathan followed, assuming they were going to meet the captain at the mess hall, but that was not their destination. Walking past the SUVs, the lieutenant led him to a door at the end of the HQ building. He knocked and was told to enter. As they did, a man in uniform stared at Nathan from behind a large desk.

"Colonel, Dr. Roark." The lieutenant made the introduction, saluted, and departed.

Dressed in a freshly pressed uniform covered with medals, service ribbons, and colorful decorations, the man stood and shook Nathan's hand. It appeared to Nathan that the national police was more military than police. He pointed him to a chair across from his desk, and both men sat down.

"Dr. Roark," the man began, "I understand that you're well versed in the history of our country but not so good at navigation." He smiled slyly and spoke in perfect English. "Like you, I was not supposed to be here either," he continued as he opened a drawer and pulled out a bottle of Clan Campbell Scotch. He found two glasses and poured about a finger and a half in each. He handed one to Nathan. "Here's hoping that we both find what we're looking for." He raised his glass and stared at Nathan. "*Santé.*"

"Everyone's looking for something," Nathan replied, raising his glass and meeting the colonel's stare. This was clearly a game of double talk. They both downed the Scotch.

"Please tell me about your project," said the officer. "I've always been interested in the revolution and its aftermath, especially the forts, which are mostly gone, and, of course, the military leaders."

Luckily, Nathan had done a lot of reading on the subject years before, curious about the history of the country. He began his story, and the colonel seemed to be genuinely interested. He asked informed questions, which led to a rather thorough discussion of military history. Nathan forgot for a few moments that it was, in fact, an interrogation.

The colonel also asked quite a few questions about Nathan's background. After close to an hour of conversation, the man seemed satisfied. With a smile, he rose from his chair. "Dr. Roark, it's been a pleasure. You have a great knowledge of our country's history, and I would like to have another drink and hear more about your research, but I have a dinner that I must attend. Perhaps we can discuss this at another time." He escorted Nathan out the door, and they found the lieutenant waiting.

Nathan thought the interview had gone well, but it was always hard to tell. He had played the part of interrogator many times and had been just as convincing. It was as likely as not that the colonel knew who Nathan really was and that the subject of his dinner meeting was to determine Nathan's fate—and Marti's. Only time would tell.

The lieutenant led him back across the courtyard and into the crowded mess hall. Nathan saw about forty soldiers having dinner on long rows of picnic tables. They were all talking and laughing and paid no notice to the newcomers in the room. None of them were wearing the BOID uniforms, and Nathan presumed these were the men from the training patrol.

He followed the lieutenant to a dining room located in the back corner of the mess hall. There were about twenty-five soldiers dining there, all wearing the BOID uniform. They stopped talking and watched Nathan as he walked into the room. It was obvious these men were well trained and well disciplined. After a few moments of silence, he heard someone call his name.

"Dr. Roark, please join us." It was the captain speaking. He and a few other men were sitting at a table in the back.

Nathan and the lieutenant walked over to join the group.

"Have a seat." The captain smiled, pulling out a chair next to him.

Nathan sat, ready for a good, hot meal. That was until he looked up and came eye to eye with the person across from him. Nathan was simply stunned.

CHAPTER TWENTY-FIVE

It was Alex Manning. Nathan quickly regained his composure before anyone noticed the look of shock that must have spread across his face. That is, no one noticed except Alex. Alex knew exactly how much he'd just blindsided Nathan.

The hope of setting Marti free and saving Haiti from a future of desolation was about to disappear. The man across from Nathan was someone he never thought he'd see again. But they once had been a team.

Nathan first met Alex in Kosovo in late April of 1999. The CIA had been called in to work with the KLA (Kosovo Liberation Army) when peace talks with Serbia stalled and ended ultimately in failure. The US-led NATO alliance began bombing Serbia in March, and the CIA, along with US Special Forces, began working on the ground. Nathan was there as a liaison, Alex as a CIA contractor. They'd been assigned to coordinate a NATO undercover operation in the town of Kukës, Albania near the border of Kosovo.

A rouge element of the KLA was smuggling drugs and selling weapons, and it was Nathan's and Alex's job to catch them. They were just days from making a raid when, after seventy-eight days of bombing, Serbia agreed to a withdrawal. One conflict was over, but another had begun. Nathan and Alex were pulled from their assignment and ordered back to the US. But Alex, ever the opportunist, wasn't ready to go just yet.

During the undercover operation, Alex had formed a relationship with one of the soldiers of the KLA, and he'd decided to turn the canceled raid into a cash deal for arms. The NATO arms that were to be used in the sting operation were still located in the warehouse, and Alex found out that the soldier from the KLA still had the cash, and still wanted the arms. He decided to make a transaction before anyone inventoried the arms in the warehouse.

Nathan had become suspicious about what his partner might be planning. Alex had begun to miss their usual suppers together, and, on the night before Nathan was to return back to the States, he had not heard from his partner or seen him for the past two days. It was inconsistent. Nathan knew from his PSYOP (psychological operations) training—and years of experience—that when someone's behavior is inconsistent, it's best to find out why. And so on that evening he decided to follow Alex, and just as he expected, Alex was heading directly to the warehouse.

Nathan had an idea about what was going on, and it troubled him. Although the arms didn't belong to the US, and even though he was officially off the assignment, he couldn't allow Alex to sell them to the rebels. What Alex was up to was illegal, and that meant Nathan had a choice to make. He and Alex had been a team once, so the decision wasn't easy.

Taking a shortcut, Nathan arrived at the warehouse just ahead of Alex. He saw three men he recognized from the illegal arms investigation. They were waiting by a truck next to the cargo door. He knew that if he allowed Alex to make contact with the men, he would have to call for backup and arrest him. But he had another thought.

Slipping around the building, he hid behind a dumpster and pulled his .45 service weapon from his shoulder holster. Taking careful aim, he squeezed off several well-placed shots into the rear of the truck bed. Startled, the men quickly drew their weapons, firing indiscriminately all around them, having no idea where Nathan was or how many others might be with him. Then they jumped into the truck and quickly sped off.

Nathan left the area before Alex could arrive. He could hear sirens as he made his way back to the base.

Later that evening, at the restaurant where they always had their meals, he saw Alex sitting at the bar, looking disheveled and stressed. Nathan approached and sat down next to him. With both of them looking straight ahead, neither said a word.

After a few minutes, their eyes met. Alex, like Nathan, was well trained in reading people. Nathan knew that he couldn't hide from Alex what he knew and what he'd done. It was all too fresh. Without saying a word, he stood up and left.

And they never came face to face again—until that night at the compound.

Seventeen years had passed, but Nathan clearly remembered the hardened look that was once again planted on the familiar face across the table. His fate was now in the hands of Alex.

"Dr. Roark," said Alex with a smile. "What a pleasant surprise this is. You can't imagine how pleased I was when the captain told me you were staying at the camp and would be joining us for dinner. It's not often I get the company of a fellow American."

Nathan held it together enough to continue to play his part. "Well, it's a pleasure to be here," he said. "I almost found myself spending the night out in the jungle. Thankfully, I found the camp, and the captain was gracious enough to extend an invitation." He had no idea where things were going.

"So, what kind of doctor are you?" asked Alex. "I saw your passport and it didn't refer to you as a doctor."

"I'm a history professor," said Nathan. "I didn't complete my doctorate until later in life and never included it on any of my documents. I'm here doing research on a book about the revolution."

"So, you write about revolutions. I was present during the revolution in Kosovo. I could give you some information on that one." He shot Nathan a meaningful look. "Unless you happened to have been there yourself?"

His heart was racing. "No, never been to Kosovo, but thanks for the offer."

"So, this book—is it non-fiction? Or maybe it's a thriller. You know the kind I mean? Where the good spy stops the rogue, misguided agent who's gone bad and set off down the wrong path?" He folded his arms onto the table and leaned forward.

"No, it's just about Haitian history. It will probably end up as a few chapters in some college history book," Nathan replied, wondering what might be coming next.

"I see," Alex said. "Have you *always* been a professor? You don't quite seem the type. Any other careers in your esteemed background?"

Nathan was about to volley back when the captain spoke. "Mr. Manning, I think we've asked the professor enough questions. Let him enjoy his meal."

Nathan could sense some animosity between Alex and the captain. The captain probably didn't like that an American, especially a blanc, was there helping with his mission.

Nathan kept his head down and ate as quickly as he could. He wanted to get out of there before Alex could start back with the questions.

Just as he was finishing, some BOID soldiers opened the door and motioned the captain outside. A few minutes later, another soldier came for Alex.

The two men were gone for quite a while and, finished with his meal, Nathan was not sure what to do. The lieutenant and a couple of soldiers were still eating and the lieutenant was talking on his phone. Nathan didn't know if he was free to go or if he should wait. Deciding he was not yet a prisoner, he stood and took his plate to the wash station and walked out. He was relieved to see there were no guards waiting for him outside, but his relief turned out to be short lived.

In the dark, as he approached his room, four armed Special Forces soldiers fell in around him along with the lieutenant. Silently, they escorted him to the last place he expected. They took him to Marti's room.

They opened the door and shoved him in. This time, they turned the lock. After he'd gotten his bearings, he heard a soft voice.

"Nathan, is that you?" She'd been sleeping on the bunk and woken up when they tossed him in. Looking thinner and worn, she rose from the bunk and crossed the room to embrace him. "I got your notes," she whispered. "I destroyed them like you asked. Why are you here? How did you find me?" she asked him, breathless.

Nathan was not surprised to hear the amazement in her voice. He knew that he was the last person she'd expect to see. Maybe UN forces or a Special Forces team, but not her geriatric godfather.

"I got a call from your dad the night after you went missing," he said in a low voice. "Marti, he was frantic and felt there was no one he could trust to tell him the truth. I came down the next day and started an investigation. It's been very interesting, to say the least." He was about to tell her about his talk with Hector and about his discovery of the compound—about so many things—when he heard the lock turning on the door.

Alex walked into the room and turned on the light. He was carrying a small duffel bag and yelling out harsh orders to the guard outside by the door. The soldier quickly left.

Alex threw the bag onto the table and kicked the door shut behind him. Both Marti and Nathan froze. The yellow light above them shone down on the crazed look in Alex's eyes; things were about to get bad. He slowly walked around the room, never taking his eyes off them, like he was trying to decide what torture tactic he would take.

In a flash, he picked up a chair and hurled it against the wall, smashing it into pieces. He picked up a leg that had three sharp nails protruding from the side and walked over to Nathan with it. Before Nathan could catch his breath, the chair leg was up in his face with the nails just inches from his cheek. In one swift motion, Alex slammed it down onto a nearby table. It made a terrible sound.

Whispering in Nathan's ear, he said, "You're slipping. You are one dumb son of a bitch to think you could walk into this camp in some nutty-professor disguise and get away with it. I know they taught you better. We never go into a situation like this without a team along to help." He threw the table upside down and kicked it across the room.

"I was shocked to see you," Nathan said.

"Of course you were. Who expects shit like this? Always expect the unexpected, and always be prepared. Isn't that what you hammered into our heads? You were always on us about going in with a full team and being prepared for the unexpected," he sneered at Nathan. "Now you're up to your ass in Special Forces soldiers. You're locked up in a jail cell, about to be interrogated, and about to have your ass beat by your old teammate from Kosovo. Should have taken your own advice, *Dr. Roark*." He sneered as he drew out the assumed name that Nathan had taken on.

"Oh, and just so you know, it wasn't me who ratted you out. You did that all yourself. This isn't the third-world country you worked in a hundred years ago. You underestimate these guys. I'm not sure when they first suspected, but it was when you were getting cozy with the colonel that they figured out who you are. Fingerprints on the Scotch glass, oldest trick in the book. It took them only minutes to connect you and your prints to the CIA. If by some miracle you make it out of here, you need to retire, old man." Alex glared, then slung a metal chair against the concrete wall.

He continued to fill Nathan in. "My job, as I've just been informed, is to interrogate the two of you and use whatever means I have to to get the information that they need." His voice rose to a loud and angry pitch. "When I get it, which I will, I've been told to kill you both—and that's what I plan to do."

Filled with remorse, Nathan glanced at Marti. He was not skilled enough to take out Alex in a fight. And if he did, the guard who was probably still outside the door would surely intervene. He had failed. He should have listened to Laura after all. Thinking of her and the boys, he sunk down onto the only chair left standing and buried his head in his hands. He was at a dead end. No way out.

Marti knew it too. She slumped down to the floor.

"I have a job to do," yelled Alex. "So both of you get up, and let's do it." When no one moved, he lifted Marti up and held her against the wall.

Nathan jumped up to do what he could to intervene.

Alex put an arm out and stopped him easily. "Whoa right there," he said. "Your turn is coming next."

All Nathan could do was watch Alex's hand on Marti as he cursed himself for the decisions that he'd made.

"Marti, this is how it's going to happen," said Alex. "I'm going to backhand you hard and bust your lips. We have to have some blood, and you'd better scream like I'm killing you." In a flash, he grabbed her by her hair and slapped her hard, one time and then another.

She let out a scream as blood splattered across the wall.

At the top of his lungs, Alex yelled. Everybody in the camp could surely hear him screaming. "Answer my questions, or I'll slit your throat! Do you understand!" He slapped her again and shoved her to the ground. Then he motioned for Nathan to come toward him and threw him against the wall.

"I didn't like doing that," he said with his eyes on Marti. Then he turned to Nathan. "But this part I *will* enjoy." He punched Nathan in the gut, and Nathan instantly lost his supper. Alex then pulled him up and punched him in the nose. Blood went everywhere.

After a few more minutes of insults, threats, and yelling, Alex pulled the two of them over to the bunk. He picked up the one unbroken chair and sat in front of them. They were swollen, bleeding messes, just like Alex surely wanted.

Alex watched Nathan for a while before he spoke. "I was mad as hell at you for a long time after Kosovo. I was about to become very rich in just a few short hours—and you had to go and screw up the whole deal. I'm glad you left that night because I had some very evil thoughts on how to deal with what you did.

"It wasn't until a long time after that, when I found myself on your end of the same kind of situation, that I thought about what I would have done if I'd been in your shoes. If the roles had been reversed, I would have been super pissed at your betrayal; I'd have had your ass arrested. Nathan, I broke your trust, and that's the worst thing a man can do when you work the jobs we do. You should have arrested me that night. You risked your career—and maybe jail time too— by letting me get away. Over time, I came to respect that, and I never thought I'd get a chance to ever pay you back for what you did. But now I do cause here you are." He paused. "That doesn't mean that if you're still here when morning comes, I won't kill you both. I'm chief of security over this camp and will have to follow through on their decision. And that's their decision. So ... " He looked each of them in the eye. "I would not be here in the morning if I were either one of you."

Nathan couldn't quite say that he was proud of Alex, but he admired the risk that he was taking. Somewhere along the line, he had found the meaning of trust, loyalty, and the code.

"I'm sorry I had to rough you up," said Alex, "but if the captain or the colonel comes in here to inspect, it needs to look authentic. I think your best chance is to get out just before midnight. There will be a change of soldiers around then and the new patrol may be fresher and more alert. With all that's happened, there will also be more guards patrolling and, more than likely, the dogs will be with them. When you make your escape, you will need to move fast and be very quiet. There are two guards in the tower, but one of them is usually asleep—although I doubt that will be the case tonight. You'll have to figure out what to do when you get there.

"As for the guard outside your door, I'll tell him you are hurt real bad and to check on you periodically. I'll also tell him that I'll kill him if he lets you die on his watch. When he checks on you, it will give you the chance to overpower him and get out of the cell.

Here. This may also help." He handed Nathan a steak knife that he'd brought from dinner.

"I won't be able to control what's gonna happen when they find out that the guard is dead or missing. And all hell is going to break loose when they see that you're gone. I hope you have a solid plan for getting out of here. If they catch you and Marti, I can't protect you. It's quite possible I might find myself in the same situation that you're in. Good luck, man, and I hope that this is the last time I'll ever see you." Alex's smile was genuine. He gave Nathan a pat on the back and left, locking the door behind him.

CHAPTER TWENTY-SIX

They waited until just before midnight to make their move and alert the guard. Nathan had told Reagan to be somewhere in the vicinity of Duchity around midnight and wait for his call. If they could make it to the car, they could be in Les Cayes in less than an hour and in the air almost immediately.

The plan was for Nathan to moan and pretend that he was sick. Marti would yell for the guard that he was throwing up blood and dying. Since the guard had been warned, they were sure he would respond.

And respond he did. When Marti started yelling in Creole, it was not ten seconds before the guard flew into the room. When Nathan laid the knife against his throat, the guard knew he was a dead man. Nathan knew what he was thinking: if the prisoner didn't kill him, the crazy American would do the job. He waited without protest.

But Nathan decided not to kill him. He had taken a life more times than he cared to remember but always during war, and those times he didn't have a choice. This time he could choose. With a leg from one of the chairs, he gave the man a hard blow to the head, and the guard went limp.

Then he and Marti tied him up with the laces of his boots, stuffed a gag into his mouth, and after checking to see that no one was around, quickly carried him outside and propped him up in his chair. He was far enough away from the main building that it would look like he was just sitting in the chair. It was taking a hell of a chance, he knew, but what choice did they have? Nathan grabbed the guard's key, locked the door, and took his sidearm and rifle. It wasn't much, but hopefully he wouldn't need them.

By the light of the moon, they slipped back to the tree line and worked their way to the place where Nathan had snuck in under the fence. Looking toward the tower near the gate, they could see the two guards. Unfortunately, there were no clouds in the sky to offer any cover. The moon flooded the area with light, meaning that any attempt to move across the clearing could be clearly seen.

But ten minutes had passed since they'd left the camp, and they had to get across. There was no other way that he could think of. Nathan was fairly certain the guards paid the most attention to the entrance of the compound. There would be less reason to monitor the inside since Nathan and Marti had a guard. So he decided to take the chance.

He whispered instructions to Marti. "Crawl very slowly and keep your movements short. Hopefully, they won't see. If they do, I'll have to shoot. If that happens, run like hell. Get to the entrance quickly and find Reagan." He'd already filled her in about Reagan and their plan. "If you find him, don't wait for me," he told her. "Do you understand?"

She nodded she did.

He took a deep breath. "I'll cross right after you," he said. "Now—go."

He watched Marti crouch low until she got to the fence. She eased her body underneath and began slowly crawling up the gully. Nathan could barely see her and hoped the guards' view was even worse. After pulling herself up from the ditch, she had to run a few feet to make it to the woods. She got to a point that was mostly out of sight and seemed to have made it undetected.

Now it was Nathan's turn.

In the tower he could see the glow of two cigarettes. That meant the guards were facing him. He waited till they turned, then carefully and slowly made his way to the woods.

Their next destination was a quarter of a mile up the road where Nathan had stashed his cell. It would be a ten-minute walk through the woods along the entrance road. They had been gone about twenty-five minutes when they stopped to listen for any activity that might be coming from the compound. All was quiet there; even the dogs were silent.

Soon he was able to grab his phone from behind the big rock. He pressed the power button and it lit up with a full battery and signal. He breathed in hard, but what he felt was not relief. Instead, he was filled with dread; things weren't supposed to go this smoothly.

They walked back in the woods about twenty yards, out of the sight of anyone passing along the road. He put in the call to Reagan, who answered on the first ring. Nathan told him they were just around the curve from the compound gate. Could he meet them in five minutes at the agreed-upon location?

Reagan reported that all was good on his end. Aubrey and Colby were waiting at the airport. Everything was right on schedule.

CHAPTER TWENTY-SEVEN

The Captain

B ut someone else had a carefully ordered schedule as well. And for him, things were also falling into place.

Captain Henri Ostavien had suspected from the second he saw Nathan that the man was not the person who he claimed to be. Things like that only happened in the movies. He knew a professor would not just happen to find a compound, which just happened to be where they were holding the most important prisoner in the country.

He had heard about the blanc traveling alone on the bus and then received a report about him traveling to Il-a-Vache in the company of a Haitian. He had not thought much about it until the professor showed up at his camp. He spoke with the BOID soldiers who'd seen the white man on the bus and they confirmed that the blanc had indeed fit the description of the professor. But he still did not have proof until the fingerprint analysis came back. The cabal had contacts with computer hackers with access to the US intelligence network. During dinner, he'd gotten confirmation.

Captain Ostavien now had the opportunity to complete not just one job but two. He'd always hated the cabal's choice of Alex Manning to take charge of security. The blanc acted so superior, so much better than the Haitians; he was full of criticism about their operations. He was always bragging that American enlisted men were better trained, more disciplined than *the so-called elite special forces*, as he called them, that were in place in Haiti. It infuriated him each time Manning boasted about his stupid Americans.

He'd never trusted Manning. His instincts had been correct.

After hearing their conversation at dinner and subsequently finding out who Dr. Roark really was, he realized that Manning and Roark had known each other from the days before the "professor" showed up at the compound. On a hunch, he sent Manning in to do the interrogations. And the hidden camera that no one knew about would hopefully prove that his suspicions were correct.

But the video didn't tell the story that the captain knew was true. What the camera showed was the cunning Manning doing the exact things that he'd been told to do. As Manning left the room, he appeared to pass something off to Roark, but the captain couldn't tell for sure. The camera angle wasn't right. Also, the audio wasn't working and the captain had no idea what was being said.

The captain knew that Manning was helping the American, but he had to prove it. The video would not be enough. And with Manning being the cabal's man, they would likely take the traitor's side.

So the captain had an idea. He would catch them in the act.

The prisoners had escaped. The tower guards had reported that they'd crawled underneath the fence and were heading toward the entrance of the compound and Highway 7. The captain had figured as much and he'd planned a little surprise that would be waiting for them.

He smiled, thinking that soon he would be rid of Alex Manning and trading in his rank as captain. A major—at least a major. Maybe even higher.

CHAPTER TWENTY-EIGHT

Nathan

Working their way through the woods, Nathan and Marti reached the curve on the compound road and needed to cross over. They couldn't be seen from the tower, but they were still out in the open in full moonlight. Quickly, they shot across the road and ran along the edge of the woods until they reached the entrance to the compound. They hid behind a big rock and watched for any sign of soldiers. Everything was still and silent.

Moving to the edge of the highway, and with the aid of moonlight, they could see Reagan's car parked about a hundred yards away. With no one in sight, they ran toward the car.

Reagan had the door open when they got there. "Jump in!" he called out, softly but urgently.

They piled in the back seat.

"Any problems?" Reagan asked as they got on their way.

"None yet," Nathan answered.

They had only gone a quarter of a mile when blinding lights lit up the road. Reagan moved one hand up to shield his eyes. Then lights equally as bright hit them from the rear. Two large military trucks had moved in to block the road, and they were trapped. There was no way around. They had to get out of the car—and now. Nathan yelled for them to move.

They rolled out of the car as bullets exploded against the windshield and the headlights. It was obvious they weren't supposed to be brought back alive.

Nathan led them down the side of the steep embankment into thick underbrush. The foliage would give them a temporary place to hide while Nathan's mind went a million miles an hour, calculating and recalculating any way they might escape.

"Follow me and stay close," he told them in a low voice. He was trying to get them to the other side of the southbound military truck while the soldiers were steadily firing into the brush. Nathan could hear and see the bullets moving through the trees. They were shooting high, but that soon would be corrected. Every fourth or fifth round was a tracer bullet. Tracer rounds are incendiary ammunition that are very bright and allow the shooter to track the direction of their bullets.

And that gave Nathan an idea. "Reagan, please tell me you grabbed the flashlight," he said.

They were far enough down the embankment to be hidden from the road. But it would just be a matter of seconds before the soldiers moved down the hill.

"I did," Reagan answered.

Nathan instructed him to cover the lens and shine a small stream of light onto the rifle. Then he popped out the clip and began removing the shells from the magazine. Just as he figured, every fifth round had a red dot on the shell. These were tracer rounds. He took them and placed them at the top of the magazine.

"Let's go," he instructed. As silently as possible, they moved up the hill until they had a good view of the truck. With his borrowed rifle, Nathan took careful aim.

Just like in Kosovo, he found himself shooting at a truck. This time he was aiming at the fuel tanks. The lower tank was diesel, which would be used to fuel the truck and hard to explode. Above the diesel tank was a portable auxiliary tank that hopefully had regular fuel that would indeed explode. He fired a couple of the tracer rounds into the diesel tank to open it up, and then he sent one well-placed shot into the auxiliary tank. It exploded like a bomb and immediately set the diesel fuel on fire. The entire truck was blazing within seconds. To add to the confusion, a couple of the soldiers had been too close and were running around on fire.

For Nathan and Marti and Reagan, this was their chance to escape—but escape to where? They were still miles from any town and they were on foot. Nathan figured they had no more than ten or fifteen minutes before the burning truck was moved and reinforcements brought in.

They needed to get out of there and fast, and he could think of just one way. He pulled out his phone and made the call.

CHAPTER TWENTY-NINE

Colby

I waited with Aubrey in the cockpit of the 310. Earlier in the afternoon, Reagan had arranged a car to take us to the airport and then left Ile-a-Vache by boat. He told us he would be picking up Nathan and Marti sometime after midnight and for us to be in Les Cayes around 2300. He didn't want us there too early, which might look suspicious. But he wanted us to have a little time to spare in case there was a problem.

We'd been waiting at the airport for almost two hours now. I had already gone over my charts and set up the GPS for the flight to Puerto Rico. Aubrey was dozing, and I was trying to find something to do when my cell went off. The sound made Aubrey jump.

I looked down and saw that it was Nathan. "Hey, we're at the airport," I said. "Are you going to make us wait all night?" I didn't bother with a greeting.

"Listen carefully, okay?" Nathan's tone was serious.

"I'm listening." I put the phone on speaker.

"We're in some real trouble here, and I'm gonna need for you to take off right this minute. Listen carefully. Head north about twelve miles. Stay low and keep your gear down and your landing lights turned on. You'll come to a town that's called Duchity. There will be a stretch of road about two miles long. That's where we need you to land, okay? Just stay on center, Colby. You'll have plenty of room to do it, and there are no overhead power cables to get in your way. Your locater will be a large fire directly in the middle of the road. Set up and land well short of it. Then quickly turn around and taxi back to where you touched down. That's where we'll get on. Colby, have you got that?"

I was too stunned to answer.

"Colby this is just like when we escaped your house in Warthen under fire. Don't think, man. Just take off. You got it?" Nathan asked again.

There wasn't time to ponder; there was only time to act. "I got it," I told him.

"And Colby—hurry, please. We can only keep them back for so long."

I shut off the phone and quickly started flipping switches and brought the starboard engine to life. I followed with the port engine and began taxiing to the southern end of the runway. Normally the pilot would announce he was departing, but not tonight. I rolled onto the runway and poured full fuel into the engines.

I didn't say a word, and Aubrey didn't either. There was nothing to say and no time to say it.

The 310 shot into the air, and I leveled it on course at five hundred feet. Flying in the valley down Highway 7, at least I didn't have to worry about the terrain below.

Within a few minutes I could see a glow on the horizon. A little while later, the few lights from the town of Duchity were below us. Keeping myself calm and focused, I started my descent.

My heart rate was fine, even low, I noticed in surprise. This must be what military pilots feel like on a mission, I supposed. Focused on the immediate objective, there was no time for anxiousness.

I pointed the 310 at the road and, with the help of the moon and dual landing lights, I centered the plane over the narrow band of asphalt.

Knowing I couldn't afford for the airplane to float just above the road from too shallow of a descent, I took a steeper than normal angle of approach. Just before contact, I flared up the nose of the 310 and pulled the power. The airplane sat down hard, and I stood on the brakes. I stopped well before the fire and immediately turned around, taxiing back to where I'd touched down. A light flashed in my lap: my cell. I picked it up and it was Nathan, out of breath and firing out commands. "Fifty meters, approaching you from the north, enemy behind us pursuing, open the doors right now," he said.

Just as Aubrey began opening the rear door, they appeared. Nathan shoved Marti in, then Reagan. I could hear gunfire over the sound of the engines; they were that close. Nathan slammed the door shut and bumped his fist on the side of the airplane, which meant, *Go!* There was no time for me to question why he wasn't getting on.

But it was soon apparent. Preparing for the short-field takeoff, or in this case, short-road takeoff, I applied heavy pressure to the brakes and applied full power. The airplane began vibrating, and the wings shook from the turbulence created by the powerful engines. My plan was to get the engines to maximum power and hold the aircraft stationary as long as possible, but hearing the sound of rapid gunfire, I changed that plan real fast. I released the brakes, and the 310 shot forward.

A few feet into the roll, I caught sight of someone in the flash of the starboard strobe light. It was Nathan, kneeling by the road. I could see the repeated flash coming from the muzzle of his rifle. Nathan was giving us ground cover. He was in the wide-open and exposed. I thought it was probably the last time I would ever see my friend.

—

I kept my eyes glued to the airspeed indicator, willing it to hit the 70 knots that would have us airborne and gone. I wasn't sure where we were on the road and wanted to get in the air before I dropped a wheel off the edge of the pavement. If that happened, we could collapse the landing gear or—worse—slide sideways off of the embankment.

It finally hit 70 knots, and I yanked the yoke to my chest. Sluggishly, the plane lifted off the ground, and it slowly gained altitude. Instant relief washed over me. We were leaving behind the dangers below and after a few minutes we could ask each other, *What the hell just happened?* We could figure out where we should go from there—but that chance never came.

We were not two hundred feet from the ground when a quick series of bullets shattered the passenger windows in the rear. One bullet grazed my right shoulder and then buried itself into the left side of the instrument panel.

Everything went dark, and I completely froze.

I was totally overwhelmed. A bullet had just hit me, and I was staring at a dark panel flying at two hundred feet between two mountains in the jungle. Any similarity I imagined I might have with fearless military pilots evaporated in that moment.

There was immediate chaos in the airplane. I'd trained for countless emergency situations, but this wasn't one of them. I did know it was imperative to control the airplane. "Aviate, navigate, communicate" were what we were taught to focus on in an emergency.

I was running over the emergency checklist in my mind when I heard a strange voice yelling desperately over the headset. "Reagan's been shot! What do I do?" It took me a second to realize it was Marti.

"I don't know. Give me a second." I banked the 310 hard left. It had been less than a minute since we'd been hit and, not knowing what kind of weapons might still be pointed at us, I needed to get us as far away from the road as possible. If we could survive the next thirty seconds, we would be around the side of the mountain and out of sight from the soldiers who were firing.

It was a long thirty seconds—but we made it.

I finally had a chance to catch a breath and glanced at Aubrey. She'd unbuckled her seatbelt and was climbing into the back to help Marti tend to Reagan. She'd taken off her headset and I handed it back to her.

"What's it look like?" I asked.

"I can't tell. He's unconscious, and there's blood everywhere!"

"Is he breathing?" I waited a few seconds as she checked.

"Yes, he is, but barely. What should I do?" she asked.

I had no idea how to treat a gunshot wound. I had one myself. I had to come up with something. "Find where he's been shot and stop the bleeding," I told her. "If it's a limb, apply a tourniquet. If it's anywhere else, grab some towels or clothes and apply pressure."

I was about to start searching for the flashlight when I saw a beam of light coming from the back. I guessed Marti had a flashlight. Waiting, all I could hear was the rushing wind coming through the shot-out windows.

Suddenly, a grave voice came over the headset. It was Aubrey. "The bullet went through his chest."

"Apply pressure— it's all that we can do," I said, knowing right then his chance of survival was slim. We were at least two hours from Puerto Rico and would be arriving in the middle of the night.

As we moved through the mountain pass and climbed toward the northwest, it appeared we were out of immediate danger, giving me time to inspect the damage to the instrument panel. Most of the primary instruments, showing airspeed, altitude, and direction, were inoperative, but the Garmin 430 GPS was still working. It had a large color screen that displayed enough information to let me fly the airplane. It also had dual coms (communication radios) that would allow us to contact Puerto Rico flight center.

As bad as the situation was, it would be much worse if we couldn't navigate or communicate—especially at night. Thinking about Puerto Rico and the uncertainty of arriving in the middle of the night without a flight plan in an airplane full of bullet holes and most likely—I hated to even think it—a deceased passenger on board, I considered other options. We could fly an extra hour and be back in the Caymans. It was much smaller, less congested. We were in their system and that might mean something, but it might not be the best place to take Marti. It might be that the cabal had contacts in Cayman.

We would be on American soil in Puerto Rico, and we would have due process. I wasn't sure why Nathan had picked PR in the first place, but that wasn't important now. There were too many other concerns, like the landing gear. If the tires and hydraulic lines were damaged from the bullets, we could be faced with a very dangerous nighttime wheels-up landing. One wrong input could cause the airplane to turn sideways and cartwheel down the runway. I began thinking through the emergency checklist for a wheels-up landing, but I never got to finish.

That's when a huge explosion rocked the plane, and I no longer had to figure out how to get us to the ground.

CHAPTER THIRTY

A fireball flew across the windscreen as the airplane shook. The starboard engine had exploded and was engulfed in flames.

For the second or third time that night, I was shocked and panicked at the same time. I'd never had an engine failure and hadn't even realized that engines could explode. I immediately pulled the fuel mixture lever and shut off the fuel pump to the starboard tank. If the fire were to reach the tank, it would all be over. Within seconds, the fire was out.

As I was desperately trying to control the airplane, I could hear Aubrey and Marti screaming. I would have screamed with them if I'd had the time. We were now flying at low altitude on a single engine. Counterintuitively, I reduced the power to the port engine. At full power, the asymmetrical thrust side slips the airplane drastically to the side of the inoperative engine, making it extremely hard to control. We would basically be flying sideways.

Pressing hard on the left rudder peddle and reducing the power, I did my best to keep the airplane level and to maintain a speed that would keep the airplane flying. The GPS showed we were losing about two hundred feet per minute. We were already at a thousand feet. I'd always heard the old saying that when a pilot lost an engine in a twin-engine aircraft, the working engine was good for one thing—taking him to the scene of the crash. We had about five minutes before we would arrive.

The screaming stopped, and all I could hear was the sound of the struggling engine and the rush of wind blowing through the cabin. I quickly turned my attention to preparing the airplane for what the manual referred to as a *non-airport emergency landing*. Aubrey dashed up to the front and strapped herself in.

From the GPS, I could see we were still headed northwest. The overlay showed mostly mountainous terrain with the coast and the small town of Pestel about ten miles away. Had we gained another thousand feet of altitude, we could have possibly made it out of the mountains and closer to the flat land of the coast. With our current altitude and rate of descent, our only option was to turn back to the stretch of road we'd taken off from or fly straight ahead.

The landscape in front of us was dark. In flight school, we had learned that usually meant a planted field or a canopy of trees. Since there were no fields in the mountains, that meant we were heading into the trees. The chance of a surviving a night landing in trees was slim, but it was better than returning to the gunfire that had gotten us into this situation.

I'd have to reduce the airspeed to just above stalling and keep the plane as level as I could when we breached the trees. Theoretically, the treetops would absorb most of the energy and keep the airplane from crashing to the ground. I had no idea what kind of trees were below us, how close they were together, or if they would support the weight of our plane.

As we lost another three hundred feet, the GPS started blinking red, warning of low terrain and flashing instructions to immediately climb and take avoidance. I wished that were an option.

I flipped the switch to turn on the landing lights. Thankfully, it worked. Illuminated before us and drawing closer was a dense canopy of trees. At about two hundred feet, I shut down the remaining engine and turned the fuel selector to the off position. To keep sparks from igniting the fuel, I would shut off the electrical power just before we hit the trees. It would be tragic to initially survive the crash only to die a fiery death trapped inside the burning airplane.

With both hands firmly on the yoke, I pressed back into the seat. We'd arrived at the scene of the crash. I eased up the nose, reducing the airspeed and situating the tail to take most of the force of the impact.

Then I closed my eyes and waited.

Until a few days earlier, I'd never faced death before. It was an odd feeling, waiting for the inevitable. I won't say I felt peace, but I accepted what was coming. It was different from the panic I'd felt when I'd been on the brink of drowning. The water was not my environment, but the air was the place where I felt at home. Maybe this was what the captain of a ship felt like before going under.

Just before we hit, I heard Aubrey's soft voice come through on my headset.

"Colby, I love you."

If this was it, I thought, those three words had made my life complete.

The airplane crashed into the trees with a force so strong it knocked the air from my lungs. If I had wanted to scream, there would have been no way. As the plane pitched forward, I could feel the safety belts dig deeply into my shoulders and waist. I waited the millisecond that I knew it would take for us to slam into the ground—but it didn't happen.

The airplane came to an abrupt stop. I opened my eyes, not believing we'd defied the odds. But the reprieve didn't last for long.

With the trees unable to support the aircraft, we dropped like a rock. The sudden weightlessness felt like a ride at an amusement park. Terrified, I again waited for the impact. The plane slammed into the forest floor and, for a few surreal moments, the world went silent and black. I wondered if I was dead.

But when I reached for Aubrey, I knew for sure I was very much alive. The pain from the gunshot wound shot through my shoulder. She grabbed hold of my arm, and it hurt like hell, but it was much-welcomed pain.

"Are you okay?" I asked. Her first response was a moan, but then she said that yes, she was. I didn't hear any noise or sense any movement from the back seat, and I feared the worst. From the description of Reagan's wound and the blood loss, I had doubts he was still with us. I could not help feeling that if Marti hadn't made it, this situation that Nathan had put us in would have been for nothing.

I was about to ask Aubrey to grab the flashlight when I smelled the strong odor of aviation fuel. We were sitting in a potential bomb.

"We have to get out now!" I yelled. It would only take one spark to turn the 310 into a raging inferno. "Get the flashlight from the glove box and let's move," I yelled.

Aubrey grabbed the light and pointed it at the back seat. Then I heard her gasp.

I turned and saw Reagan on the floor with his eyes wide open. His shirt was off and his upper chest was covered in blood with a huge hole in the middle.

As I feared, he had left us. He had been sitting behind Aubrey in the direct line of the gunfire that had come through the side door and the window. Had he not been there, the bullet that had killed him would have come through my seat and into my back. Reagan might well have saved my life.

Marti was still strapped into her seat and leaning against the window. I didn't see any apparent wounds. Hopefully, she was just unconscious. Needing to get us out, I pushed my door open and motioned for Aubrey to follow. Before exiting, I asked for the flashlight to make sure we were, in fact, on the ground. Once I had confirmed that, both of us jumped out.

My shoulder had stopped bleeding, and the bullet didn't appear to have hit anything critical, so I decided not to mention it. We didn't need any more distractions.

But that all changed when I reached into the back seat to try to unbuckle Marti. I let out a yell as the pain dropped me to my knees.

Aubrey grabbed the flashlight and pointed it at my shoulder. "You're bleeding! What happened?" she yelled while reaching for my shirt.

I pushed her hand away. "It's fine. Just an injury from the crash. We need to get Marti out."

She reluctantly turned the flashlight toward the rear seat. It took both of us, but we managed to pull Marti from the back seat and carry her to a clearing about fifty feet away. I wanted to pull Reagan from the wreckage, but there was no time. We had to get away from the fuel-soaked airplane, and I knew he would understand. As much as it pained me to do it, I left him inside.

Other than a large goose egg on her head, Marti didn't seem to have any other injuries—that we could see, at least. Since her pulse and breathing seemed normal, we hoped she had just been knocked out and would come around in the next few minutes.

While we waited, we decided it was worth the risk to do a quick search of the airplane and salvaged anything that we might need. I found my flight bag with all the maps of the area, and Aubrey located the first-aid kit and a few blankets in the rear baggage compartment. We returned to the clearing and placed the blankets around the still unconscious Marti.

Aubrey then turned her attention to my shoulder. She removed my shirt and shone the flashlight on the injury. "This is a gunshot wound, Colby," she said. "It's not from the crash."

"I know," I said in a low voice.

We both were silent for a moment. Then, with tears streaming down her face, she cleaned and dressed the wound. I sat and stared at the twisted heap that had been my new airplane. The irony of how I'd come to own it had not escaped me. I had bought it with money the CIA had given us for helping to close the case the year before.

I found it surreal that so much had happened after lifetimes of nothing more exciting than a few close calls on the racetrack for me, and for Aubrey, a few run-ins with a jigsaw. Now, we'd been involved in two murder-terroristic-political plots—or whatever one wants to call them—in less than two years. They say things come in threes. I certainly hoped not!

Aubrey finished with the dressing and then took something out of the first-aid kit and leaned over toward Marti.

"It's time to wake her up," she said. She snapped a small cartridge and placed it under Marti's nose. With a loud moan, Marti opened her eyes and tried to sit up.

Aubrey gently eased her back onto the blankets. "Marti, you're fine," she said. "Just lay down for a couple of minutes, okay?"

"Okay," Marti answered in a weak voice. Then she asked, "Where are we?"

Aubrey gave me a look. "Do you remember us picking you up in the airplane?" she asked Marti.

"I do, but where is Nathan? Where is Reagan?" Marti asked, leaning up and only seeing us.

Aubrey gave me a look. I nodded for her to go ahead.

"Nathan didn't get on the airplane. It was just you and Reagan," Aubrey began. "The people on the ground shot at the plane, and we crashed here in the jungle. Do you remember that?" Sometimes with head trauma, a person is unable to remember the most recent of events.

"Yes, of course … " She stopped. "Oh God, Reagan was shot! Is he okay?" Panicked, she tried to get up. She barely made it to her knees before grabbing her head and lying back down.

Aubrey put a hand on her shoulder and gently consoled her.

When Marti asked about Reagan again, it was my turn to answer her. "Marti … " I didn't know how to say it. I tried to look at her but couldn't. "Reagan didn't make it. I'm so very sorry." I lowered my head.

Marti let out a whimper and put her hands over her face. "It's my fault. I never meant to put any of you in danger," she said, continuing to cry.

I didn't know what to say.

It had been about thirty minutes since the crash and I was sure the cabal and soldiers were desperately trying to find us. We needed a plan.

I retrieved my flight bag and pulled out a few aviation maps showing the towns and roads of Haiti. I figured we were about five to six miles north of the road we had landed on. Since it was apparent that our escape would have to be on foot, it looked like our best option was to continue north and try to make it to the coastal town of Roseaux. Hurriedly, I studied the map. From Roseaux, we could follow the coast a few miles to the town of Jeremie. It had a commercial port and an airport, both of them potential avenues for escape.

There were only four inches on the map from where we were to our new destination. Looking into the dark jungle, I figured it might as well have been a million miles. If we'd still had Reagan with us, he might have been able to make contact with someone who could help.

That gave me an idea. Maybe Reagan could still help us.

I carefully climbed back into the airplane and leaned over the compartment in the rear seat. I said a little prayer over Reagan's body and gently closed his eyes; it seemed the decent thing to do.

Then I grabbed his cell phone from his pocket. Because I could still smell fuel, I scrambled out of the plane before I tried the phone.

At the press of a button, it lit up with two bars in a top corner, giving us a ray of hope. Thankfully, it was fully charged and not password protected. I navigated his applications until I found the icon for Google Maps. Then I touched the screen.

After a few seconds, the map appeared with a red dot marking our location. It was within half a mile of where I had determined us to be from the aviation maps. I typed in *Roseaux*, and the GPS calculated a direct route from our location.

If we could maintain cell service, the digital map would be our guide. It would give us the best and quickest route out of the jungle, but I also knew that it could be the same route the soldiers might use to find us. We would have to be observant and very, very careful.

While Aubrey tended to Marti, I slipped away and opened up Reagan's phone. On a hunch that he might be in there, I typed in the first letter of his last name. The name and number of the person who could be the key to our survival glowed brightly in the darkness.

I tapped the number and within a few seconds the phone began to ring.

Chapter Thirty-One

Even as the phone was ringing, it occurred to me that I had no idea what I was supposed to say. I'd dialed the number on an impulse; I hadn't thought it through.

It could go one of two ways.

Jules Saint-Toussaint could be upset that we broke the law by not informing him of our unscheduled departure. Or he could be empathic. That moment at the airport had touched something deep inside us all.

If my instincts were correct, he wouldn't be involved with the kind of murdering scum who'd taken Marti and killed Reagan.

If I was wrong, the enemy would know we were alive—and exactly where we were. Our slim chances at survival would be gone.

The phone continued to ring, and I was about to hang up when I heard him say, "Hello."

In the silence that followed, I froze.

"Hello ... Reagan, is that you?" he asked. He must have had Reagan's name and number programmed in his phone.

I breathed in deep. "No, Jules. It's Colby Cameron."

That was followed by more silence.

"Jules, something bad has happened and we could really use your help."

"What's going on?" His voice was calm.

There was no easy way to say it. "Jules, we've crashed the airplane in the mountains above Les Cayes." I could only imagine what he was thinking, especially at two thirty in the morning.

"Mr. Cameron, let me talk to Reagan." His voice had had turned official. And he was ignoring our agreement to address each other by our first names. There was no way that was good.

My heart was pounding in my chest. "I really wish I could, but I'm afraid that Reagan has been killed. He was shot while we were taking off from Highway 7," I solemnly replied.

"Mr. Cameron, I'm not sure who you are or what it is you're up to, but this is way out of my area of responsibility. I'm going to have to report this right away."

I had to think of something fast. "Jules, I promise—we're good people. We're not up to anything. What we told you at the airport is all true. I had no idea then *why* our friend wanted us to come here, and now Aubrey and I badly need your help. Please let me explain."

I'd made a calculated move when I'd thrown out Aubrey's name. He might hear me out for her sake.

"Is Aubrey okay?" he asked in a soft voice.

That was a good sign, and I ran with it. "She is, but she's scared and she's upset. It was her idea to call you. She has talked so much about your boys since we left the airport, and she thought that you might help." It was a lie and pretty low down to bring the children into it, but I needed an advantage.

"Okay, Colby." He sighed. "Tell me what has happened."

I wanted to tell him the whole story but wasn't quite ready to take the chance. If he was loyal to the government or connected to the cabal, the link we had to his boys wouldn't be enough; he still could turn us in.

"Jules, before I start, I need you to know that this involves the government—a very corrupt part of the government—and the national police are involved as well. In my heart I believe that you're a good man and wouldn't be involved with those kinds of people, but I need to hear you say it."

His reply was quick. "Colby, I assure you I am just a border and customs agent and not involved in anything like you have just described. But if you and Aubrey have crossed paths with those kinds of people, there may not be much that I can do. Tell me exactly what has happened, and maybe I can help."

"Do you know a young lady by the name of Marti Lamartiniere?" I asked.

"Well, of course I do. Everyone knows who she was." His tone implied that the question was preposterous. "She was the most generous, compassionate person. If it had not been for the search and rescue teams that she put together after the earthquake, those little boys who took so fast to Aubrey wouldn't be alive. The government was so overwhelmed with their efforts in Port-au-Prince that they couldn't get to everyone. My wife and boys had been missing two days already when Ms. Lamartiniere's team made it to Les Cayes. And they didn't give up until they found them. They had been trapped in a collapsed school building. Their mom didn't make it." He paused, caught up in the emotions and the memory.

"By the time they got to them, my wife was gone, and the boys were barely hanging on. It was that team who saved their lives. My family will always be indebted to Ms. Lamartiniere. When we heard that she had drowned ... well, that broke our hearts. She wasn't just an angel; she was the hope and future of our country."

"Jules, my friend, she didn't drown. She's right here—sitting a few feet away from me in the middle of a forest in the mountains above Camp Perrin."

"She's alive?" he whispered into the phone.

"She is, Jules. Reagan gave his life to save her, and now we really need your help."

"I'll help you, Colby, any way I can. Tell me what I can do."

I told him my plan was to reach Roseaux—and then Jeremie—and that if I could reach my pilot friend from the States (an idea I had yet to discuss with Aubrey or Marti), I'd have him fly in and get us out. I explained to Jules that we would need him to monitor the Jeremie airport and clear my buddy as a fishing tourist when he got there.

"When do you think that this will happen?" he asked. "How are you getting to Roseaux?"

"It's only about five miles, and we have a phone with GPS. I think we can get there in three hours, maybe four. How we get to Jeremie, I haven't figured out. I'm hoping Marti—Ms. Lamartiniere—can help us figure that part out. We should be leaving here in fifteen minutes."

"Okay. I'll get dressed and head to Jeremie right now. I have business at the port and at the airport, so it won't seem unusual for people to see me there. If I see anything suspicious, I'll give you a call or text. You call me from Roseaux if Ms. Lamartiniere has any trouble getting you to Jeremie. Maybe I can help." He paused. "Colby, on behalf of myself and the people of Haiti, I want to thank you for everything you're doing. And please—please be very careful."

"You're very welcome, Jules. See you in Jeremie."

I hung up and turned to see Aubrey and Marti had walked over from the clearing and were staring at me.

"Who were you talking to?" Aubrey asked, surprised.

"It was Jules Pierre-Toussaint. I called him on Reagan's phone." She paused. "They knew each other? And how did you know that?"

"I didn't, but I had an idea that they might. Reagan's office was right there at the port, and he dealt with lots of customers who came in by boat. Also, when Jules was leaving the airport at Ile-a-Vache, he stopped and spoke to Reagan. So it just made sense. I checked Reagan's phone and found Jules' name."

"So you told Jules what was going on? How did that go?" she asked.

"I believe that we can trust him. He told me it was Marti's team who saved his boys during the earthquake. Because of the people she brought in, his boys are alive." I turned to look at Marti.

"I remember them," she said. "They were trapped in a school building in Les Cayes. That was such a sad time. So much death, so much destruction. If I recall correctly, their mother was there too, but their mother didn't make it." She stood up, looking stronger now.

"Yeah. That's what he said, and he wants to help," I said.

Looking at my watch, I saw it was nearing three fifteen. We'd been at the crash site way too long. It could be just a matter of minutes before we saw the glow of flashlights coming through the jungle. I quickly told them what I was thinking we should do next, and I asked their opinion.

"What about Nathan?" Aubrey asked, ignoring the urgency in my voice and the question that I'd asked.

I felt a flash of anger. With the most elite forces in the country about to be breathing down our necks, we had to concentrate on getting out of there. *Fuck Nathan*, I thought. If it wasn't for him we'd be snorkeling in the Caymans and not in some Haitian jungle running for our lives. Of course, I didn't say that, and I really didn't feel it. I was just stressed out to the max and my controlling nature had gone into overdrive. "If Nathan survived last night—which, knowing him, I'm sure he did—we can try to reach him from Roseaux," I said, hoping to get back to the subject of planning our escape.

"Why don't we try to call him now?" she asked, and I took a deep breath.

"Because they could have captured him, and if they did, they might have his phone. Reagan's name would come up if we called. And then those guys could track us since we're using the GPS on Reagan's phone."

That wasn't enough for Aubrey. "But how do they know that Reagan's with us?" she asked, still determined.

I'd had about enough. "Aubrey, think about it!" I said in a raised voice. "If a Haitian—who I'm sure has been seen with Nathan all over this godforsaken country—calls *in the middle of the night* and *after a botched escape,* what would you expect for them to think?"

In the moonlight I could see and feel her icy stare.

It was Marti who replied. "I think I know a way to get from Roseaux to Jeremie. My cousin lives in Roseaux, and he has some fishing boats. It might be safer if we go in one of them—and try to hide as best we can—instead of getting caught up in a roadblock. Does that sound good to you?"

I wanted to hug her for bringing the discussion back to what mattered most.

Now, I had to make peace with Aubrey. "I think it's a great idea," I said. Then I turned to my wife and asked in a gentle voice, "What do you think, Aubrey?"

"That sounds good to me," she said. "Once they figure out that we survived the crash, I'm sure that they'll assume we'll try to make it to an airport. They know we have a pilot. Les Cayes and Jeremie are the closest ones, and I'm sure they'll be out in force to block the roads." She bent down to start packing up the blankets and getting our stuff together.

Something Aubrey said gave me an idea. I looked at the airplane and then back at the others. I wasn't sure exactly how to say what I was thinking.

I hesitated; this part would not be easy. "If we survive to tell our story," I began, "Reagan will be remembered as a hero here among his people. His efforts—and the sacrifice that he made to save Marti—will be taught in all the schools; it will be a major part of Haitian history. Reagan loved his country, and I think that our good friend has one more act of love to give."

Aubrey stopped packing, and they both stared at me, confused.

I continued. "I think there's a way to divert their focus from the airports, and Reagan is the key. What I'm thinking is that we can strap him in to the pilot's seat and set the plane on fire. Then, when they find the airplane, they'll think we lost our pilot. And it might buy us extra time while they sift through the wreckage to look for other bodies." I paused to see what they were thinking.

"And when we get to Jeremie, I think I know a way to get us out. Aubrey, I'm going to call Mike Moseley. When we talked in the Caymans, he told me he'd be around Mitchell for the next few days and that I should feel free to call him if I needed something more. I don't think this is exactly what he had in mind, but I'm sure that he'd be willing to fly down and pick us up. I've told Jules to watch for him and to clear him as a 'fishing tourist.' Hopefully, I can get in touch with him.

"Also, with Jules being at the airport as a government official, the national police might have him on the lookout for suspicious flights, inbound and outbound. I know that it's a long shot. But I think it could work. What do you think?" I asked.

They both nodded to signal their approval.

"Then let's get started," I said.

First, we gently took Reagan from the rear and placed him in the pilot's seat. It felt strange to strap him in and place the headset over his ears. The whole thing was eerie; he looked like he was about to fly that torn wreckage out of the jungle at any minute. But he had already made his final flight, and I think he would have been okay with what we were about to do.

After securing him in the seat, we threw in all the blankets and anything else we weren't taking with us. I took the tie-down ropes from the baggage compartment and soaked them in fuel. They totaled about twenty feet, and they would be our fuse.

With our packs on and all the evidence removed, I struck the two ends of an emergency flare and lit the rope. As soon as the airplane caught fire, it would be visible for miles around, a beacon for the enemy to track.

The rope immediately caught fire and slowly began to burn. I timed how long it took for the first foot of the rope to burn, and it took two minutes. As another six to eight inches burned, we watched to make sure the fire took hold and wouldn't burn out. At the present rate, we had about thirty minutes before the flame reached the aircraft.

After Marti said a sweet prayer for Reagan, it was time to go. I took a compass reading from the phone's GPS, and we headed into the night. Since barely any sun ever penetrated the jungle canopy, there was little underbrush, making our trek fast and unencumbered.

We had had been gone about thirty minutes when we heard a slight explosion, which was probably the tires, and saw a bright light appear to the south. The airplane had caught fire. Hopefully, the ruse would give us enough time before they realized we were gone.

Now that we were safely away from the crash scene, it was time to call Mike Moseley. It would be the second time in two days I had called and woken him up in the middle of the night. I said a little prayer that he was home again for me to waken.

CHAPTER THIRTY-TWO

Mike

In the great room of the large house, the grandfather clock struck four. Hearing the last chime, Mike pulled his arm from under the covers to read the luminous radium dial on his vintage Omega pilot's watch. Odd. The chimes never woke him up.

The old grandfather clock had kept perfect time for as long as Mike could remember. It had been in his family since Thomas Wright built it in Warwickshire, England, in 1710. Again and again, it had been passed down from grandfather to grandson. Mike's grandfather had given it to him and, unfortunately, the tradition would stop there. It was one of the few possessions he'd brought from England when he moved to the United States.

Mike had spent his career flying with the Royal Air Force and had never found himself in one place long enough to settle down and start a family. After retiring and wanting a fresh start, he relocated to the US to take a contract position ferrying Beechcraft King Air aircraft from the States to South America and the Caribbean. It was a low-stress job that let him continue to indulge his love of flying.

Now that he was awake, he decided he might as well take care of his mid-morning trip to the bathroom. At his age, his bladder would not allow him an uninterrupted night's sleep.

Rolling over on his back and pointing his feet off the bed, he began the long three-foot slide to the floor. He felt ridiculous every time he got out of the bed and cursed himself for buying one that was so high off the floor.

It hadn't been his choice, though. The pretty little interior decorator with the blonde hair and captivating blue eyes had pushed him to buy the insanely expensive monstrosity of a bed. All it had taken was a wink and a suggestive comment about how comfortable she thought the bed would be. And he'd bought into it, thinking he might get her to try out the bed with him. As it turned out, all he got was a huge bill and an occasional twisted ankle.

Making it to the bathroom injury free, he was trying to locate the toilet without turning on the light when his cell phone began ringing. It was sitting on the vanity and lit up the room.

Grabbing the phone and squinting at the bright display, he didn't recognize the number but recognized the country code—Haiti. He immediately felt uneasy, thinking about his and Colby's conversation. Something must have gone wrong. Having flown that region for several years, Mike had heard many stories of corruption and kidnapping and had actually been involved in one case himself.

Several years earlier, while preparing to depart the Dominican Republic for the States, he had been doing a final check on his airplane when he was approached from behind by two armed men. Forcing him into the airplane at gunpoint, they instructed him to fly to a small central-coast airstrip in Ponce, Puerto Rico.

He was sure that drugs were somehow involved, and he knew that upon arrival they would steal the King Air and that they almost certainly would shoot him and toss his body in a ditch. Thinking quickly, he made up a story: he was just doing a check after someone had reported mechanical problems; the plane was not airworthy.

They laughed. Holding the gun against his temple, one of them told him to *fly or die*.

Mike shrugged his shoulders with indifference. He said he guessed they all would die.

Spooling up the turbo chargers and adding fuel to the engines, he began rolling down the taxiway to the five-thousand-foot runway up ahead. Indiscernibly, he set the left engine throttle position just a few hundred RPMs lower than the right. The aircraft vibrated slightly and made an out-of-sync kind of whine. As the hijackers closely watched, Mike pointed to the engine instrument gauge on the left and then to the one on the right, showing them the difference. Apprehensively. they glanced at each other; it was the reaction Mike was hoping for.

He'd just committed a huge infraction by not announcing to the tower that he was entering an active runway and preparing for takeoff. The controllers were yelling at him over his headset that he was not cleared for takeoff and to return immediately to the terminal. He clicked the mic button several times to let them know he'd heard them.

With both men hovering over him with their guns pointed at his head, he jammed both the throttles forward and about halfway down the runway, snapped the King Air off the ground at a sharp angle. With the steep ascent, the men lost their grips on the back of the pilot seat and were temporarily distracted. It was the opportunity Mike was looking for. He quickly reached down and shut off the fuel to the port engine. With the loss of fuel, it only took a few seconds for the engine to start sputtering, and a few more before it shut down. The airplane yawed drastically to the left and, with a little help from Mike, who was pushing the yoke forward, it tilted toward the ground.

Panicked, the hijackers yelled for Mike to set it right.

In truth, he had complete control of the airplane, having trained many times for an engine-out scenario. The King Air was designed to fly with just one engine, and they weren't, in fact, in any danger. But he had the crooks fooled.

In a dramatic fashion, Mike held up his hands, controlling the airplane with his feet on the rudder pedals, and screamed that it was too late, that they all were going to die. As they begged him to try anything, he turned the airplane back toward the runway. Knowing exactly what he was doing, he made the worst landing of his life. He had already alerted the authorities by dialing his radio transponder to the hijacker code, 7500. By the time they came to a stop, the police were waiting.

—

Now, with nervous anticipation, he answered the phone.

And, yes, it was Colby. "Mike, I can't talk for long," he said, "and I need to tell you what has happened. I've crashed the 310 in a jungle. I'm in Haiti and . . . "

Incredulous, Mike interrupted. "You've done *what*?" he asked.

"We were shot down by some corrupt people Nathan got involved with. And now we're on foot, trying to get out of here before they get to the wreckage and find out we're still alive. Our plan is to get to the airport in a town called Jeremie and get out of Haiti. I know it's an enormous favor, but can you possibly come get us?"

"Of course I can come and get you. When you said that your friend Nathan was involved in something, I half expected trouble, but not anything like this! Tell me what to do," said Mike.

"Load up any offshore fishing gear you have, and list your flight as a fishing-trip vacation," said Colby. "Also, go online and try to find a hotel in Jeremie. Make a reservation. It needs to look like you've planned the trip. If all goes well, a customs agent by the name of Jules Saint-Toussaint will meet you on arrival, and he will get you cleared. Jules is a friend of mine. Have the airplane ready for immediate departure. You may or may not be able to refuel. Hopefully, when you make your landing in Miami or wherever you jump off, you can fill up on fuel and have enough to make it back."

"I'll have plenty of fuel to make it back to Miami or wherever it is we're going," Mike replied. "Without checking the route, I think it will take about three hours for the flight and about an hour for customs and refueling when I get to Miami. I can be airborne within an hour. I should be there by ten fifteen. Anything else I need to bring?"

"Maybe some clean clothes and a first-aid kit. Keep your phone close by. I'll try to call you on this phone or possibly my own, but it could be from another number. We should also be in Jeremie in about five or six hours, I believe." Colby paused. "Mike I know I have a lot of explaining to do, and I hope I get the chance. If we don't make it to Jeremie by tomorrow evening, call the American embassy and tell them what has happened. Then, leave the island right away. I can't tell you how much Aubrey and I appreciate you doing this. You are a true friend."

"You just get your ass to Jeremie, and I'll be there to get you. You can count on that." Mike's career in the military had always been based on loyalty, trust, and commitment. A soldier never left another soldier in danger, and neither did a friend.

He ended the call, used the bathroom, and then went to the kitchen to set a kettle of water to boil. He had a long flight ahead of him and would need a large thermos of tea to keep him alert and awake.

While waiting, he got dressed and removed a couple of handguns from a safe in his closet. They were left over from his days in the military. He carried one or both on every mission that he flew. He had never needed them and hoped he wouldn't this time.

CHAPTER THIRTY-THREE

Colby

After talking to Mike Moseley, I was feeling much better about our prospects of survival. If we continued at our current pace and managed to get a few hours ahead of the enemy before they found out we'd survived the crash, we just might make it after all. I was certain they'd be able to track our route through the jungle, but with luck, we could lose them once we made it to Roseaux—and hopefully met up with Marti's cousin.

Following the directions on the GPS, we walked a little more than an hour before coming to a place I'd seen on the map and anticipated. I'd figured the blue line was either a creek or a river and it turned out to be, unfortunately, the latter. It appeared to be about twenty-five feet wide, and it looked pretty deep. We removed our packs and shone the flashlight up the sides of the banks. They were steep and looked like they'd be tough to negotiate.

"What do you suggest?" Aubrey asked.

"Let's see if we can find a tree that's fallen over the river and maybe we can walk across it," I replied as we sat down to take a quick break.

Marti leaned back on her pack and closed her eyes. She had not said much since we'd left the crash site. I was sure her head was still hurting—as well as her heart.

Aubrey sat down next to me. She put her arm in mine and leaned against my shoulder. "Will you please do me a favor?" she asked, giving my arm a double squeeze. That basically meant there was just one answer: yes.

"Sure," I replied.

"Will you try to call Nathan? Please? I have a feeling he survived, and he's probably worried sick about all of us. I really don't see how it could hurt. They're going to know real soon that we survived, and maybe Nathan has some info that can help us. Even if they're holding him, he'll give us the information, whether they're threatening him or not. Also, you can turn off the location service on the phone so they can't see our position."

I was just about to make an argument for waiting when she asked Marti what she thought.

"I agree," said Marti. "I'm also worried sick about him and would greatly appreciate you trying."

They both stared at me and waited for my answer.

"All right, we'll call him," I said, "but let's not tell him about Reagan. You both know he'd insist on finding us if he knew Reagan wasn't with us. We've made it this far on our own, and I feel confident we can make it to Roseaux. We don't need the complications of trying to coordinate a place to meet. Plus, if he's not in captivity, we're probably miles south of where he is. Is that okay?" I asked. And they agreed.

I went to settings and turned the location service off. Then I made the call.

CHAPTER THIRTY-FOUR

Nathan

After shoving Marti and Reagan onto the plane, Nathan thought of Laura. Most likely, he would not be keeping his promise to her; he hoped she would understand.

The last thing he'd said to Reagan was to please protect the others. An impossible request, he guessed, but if anyone could pull it off, he was somehow certain that Reagan was the man.

With the soldiers fast approaching and rapidly firing at the airplane, Nathan took an infantryman's stance on the side of the road. He returned fire as Colby shot forward and quickly became airborne.

Exposed, Nathan jumped up from the road and rolled into the ditch. Within a minute he could hear the soldiers yelling on the road above him and was certain they had seen him.

Surrender was not an option. The interrogation would be brutal, and Nathan knew they would ultimately get the info that they needed and then kill him. According to Alex, he should already be dead. He would not allow that. The mission and his friends were too important. Lying prone and facing up the hill, he aimed the rifle, waiting on the soldiers to breach the hill—but then it all changed in a terrifying flash.

To the south, the sky lit up with a loud explosion. And something in Nathan exploded as well. Of the very small number of people that he truly loved, he had just lost four. His mission had failed. Rising to his feet, he charged up the hill toward the road. He was not going to wait for the soldiers to reach him. He would take out as many as he could—but they were gone.

He then realized that in the glare of the plane's bright landing lights, the soldiers had never seen him. They probably had assumed he was firing from the plane.

Overwhelmed by emotion, Nathan dropped to his knees and wept. He looked up toward heaven and said a prayer that he knew was hopeless, but he said it anyway.

His first thought was to rush to find the crash site, but he'd be moving through a dense jungle area at night; he knew that the soldiers would beat him there, so what good would that do?

In the distance he could see that the truck on the road was still in full blaze. With all the rubber tires, they would burn for hours. He could also see a string of smeared lights that were the towns along the coast: Roseaux, Pestal, and the last and brightest, which was Jeremie.

He figured his best option was to reach Jeremie and try to find a way out of the country. His other option was calling Charles, and he just couldn't do it. Charles would insist on coming to get him, and that was too dangerous. Also, he wasn't prepared just yet to tell Charles about Marti. The news would be the same when the morning came, and the news could wait till then.

Walking toward the camp, he saw a flood of lights coming from the compound road. He slipped into the woods and watched as several trucks filled with soldiers passed. It appeared they were sending the entire force to the crash site, which gave him an idea—as well as a dilemma.

He was sure the colonel and the members of the cabal would still be in the compound. It would be Alex's job, and possibly the captain's, to confirm and secure the crash site. With most of the soldiers gone, he could easily sneak back into the camp to exact revenge. His dilemma was this: He was the only person who knew the entire story of the kidnapping and murder. If he did not succeed, the truth would die with him. Charles could try to get the word out, but he wouldn't have the proof to back up his claim.

It took him about ten minutes to run up Highway 7 to the entrance of the compound. He stood at a crossroads. He looked north toward the lights of Jeremie and then into the darkness of the compound. Thinking about the loss of his friends, he felt the heat of anger rise, and he made his decision.

Skirting the edge of the compound road, he reached the guard tower and saw only one guard at the post. The lone guard was smoking, like they always did. Nathan could easily take him out with one shot, but he didn't want to alert the others who were still there. He was after bigger prey. So he slipped under the fence like he'd done before.

Just as he was moving toward the clearing, he heard the crack of the guard's radio. He watched as the guard climbed down the ladder from the tower and hurried into the camp.

At a short distance, Nathan followed. When the guard veered toward the HQ building, Nathan made his way through the shadows, passed the old tree, and carefully made his way to the colonel's quarters. From about twenty feet away, he could see through the window. The colonel and the cabal members were in the midst of a heated discussion. Nathan felt sure he knew the topic.

A few of the BOID soldiers moved in and out of the headquarters building. If Nathan were to rush in and shoot the colonel and the murderous cabal, he might not make it out alive. He waited until the soldiers were gone.

Moving back to the shadows of the tree, he reached for the pistol, then the rifle, and checked the magazines. Both had cartridges in the barrels, and the clips held three rounds apiece.

Nathan took a deep breath and, with the pistol leveled and the rifle on his shoulder, he began walking toward the door. He had only taken a few steps when he felt his phone vibrate in his pocket. He wanted to ignore it, but with everything going on, the call could be urgent. He was stunned when he pulled the phone out of his pocket and saw Reagan's name.

Reagan. Or at least someone calling from his phone. He took a deep breath before he answered.

"You owe me a new airplane." It was Colby's voice.

Nathan rushed back to the cover of the tree. It took him a couple of seconds before he could respond. "How are you alive? I saw the plane explode." Despite his excitement, he kept his voice to a whisper.

"It did. Well, one of the engines exploded, but I was able to land it in some trees."

"Where are you now? Is everyone okay?"

"We're all beat up, and trying to get out of here before anyone shows up. Are you okay?"

"I'm fine. Where's Reagan? Let me talk to Reagan."

There was some hesitation. Then the next voice he heard was Aubrey's. "Hey, Nathan."

"Aubrey," he whispered as relief washed over him.

"We were worried about you," she said. "And thank God that you're alive. We're trying to find a way to get across a river, and I need to go and help the others. Colby will give you details on where we all can meet. So—we'll see you soon."

Then it was Colby on the line. "Nathan, Reagan's phone has GPS and we're headed to Roseaux. Marti has a cousin there who will get us get to Jeremie by boat, we hope. Where are you? Can you meet us in Roseaux? Or can you get to Jeremie?"

"I'm back in the compound, but I'll leave right away. From the area where the airplane went down, I think it's about a mile or two back to the main road. Taking into account that you will have to navigate the dark forest and rough terrain, I'm probably two to three hours ahead of you. And I'll see what I can figure out about getting to Roseaux. Keep me posted on your progress, and tell Reagan to call or text me when he can."

"Will do. Be careful, Nathan. And we'll see you soon," said Colby.

Nathan ended the call and made his way toward the gate. Taking out the colonel and the cabal would have to wait for now. Improbably, his prayer had been answered, and he was headed to Roseaux.

Chapter Thirty-Five

Colby

Filled with relief that Nathan was alive and would be joining us in Roseaux, Aubrey and Marti were now in a hurry to find a way to cross the river. With me carrying the flashlight, we worked our way up the bank, but we couldn't find a tree to walk across. We were beginning to think we would have to slide down the steep, long bank and wade across the wide, fast-moving river. Then we stumbled upon an old footbridge: an ancient pedestrian rope bridge about three-feet wide. Every other board was missing. With its frayed ropes and heavy coat of green moss, it looked like it might have been around since the Revolution.

I eased down the bank and tried out the first couple of boards. The bridge was shaky, but seemed strong enough to hold my weight. I climbed back up the bank to find the girls in the midst of a discussion.

"We think you should go first," Aubrey told me.

For some reason, I thought that was funny. I started laughing, and they joined in. It felt good to laugh.

"Oh, you do?" I asked her. "Might I please hear the logic behind that plan?"

"Well, you're a lot a lot bigger than we are, and if it supports you, then we know we can get across it too," she replied.

"Are you calling me fat?" I asked with a mock accusatory tone.

"Of course not; you're just a big, strong, brave man," she said, snickering.

It was true that I was the largest and it made sense that I'd go first.

With Marti holding the flashlight, I carefully took the first step. Keeping my feet on the more solid-looking boards near the edge of the rope and slowly shuttling across, I was doing well until I got about halfway. I'd gotten a little too confident and picked up my pace by moving to the center of the bridge. As could have been predicted, one of the old boards suddenly buckled with the weight, sending my right leg through the bridge.

Aubrey and Marti screamed.

I mentally cursed myself for my carelessness. It was only about twelve feet to the water, and I probably would have been just fine, but a tumble into the river would have taken up time we didn't have. I grabbed the side ropes and pulled myself up. Keeping this time to the side of the bridge, I carefully made my way across. With me having shown them the way *not* to do it, Aubrey and Marti followed and made it safely across as well.

The whole river crossing cost us thirty minutes. By that time, we had to assume the enemy had made it to the crash site and discovered that we were on the run. Most likely, they were on the hunt for us, and when they got to the river, they wouldn't take the time to cross the bridge. They were probably trained for river crossings and would jump in and be across in a matter of only minutes. Now we had to hurry to make up the time.

With the GPS guiding us, we continued toward Roseaux. It was now four thirty and, according to the GPS, we were a couple of miles away. If all went well, we would make it out of the jungle a little before dawn.

But all did not go well.

We had been stopping every ten to fifteen minutes to check for movement to our rear. Since crossing the river, we'd steadily been moving up a hill and had a good view of the valley. If anyone was tracking us and using lights, we'd be able to spot them easily. As we neared the crest of the hill, I kept looking back, expecting to see something. But there was nothing but silence and the pitch-black night.

Then, when we made it to the top, something finally appeared, but it wasn't coming at us from behind. In a scenario that had never crossed our minds, they were approaching from in front of us. We'd mistakenly assumed that they would find the crash and come after us from there.

From a distance of about two hundred yards, we could see the erratic movements of flashlights getting closer. And, to our horror, we heard dogs. We quickly jumped out of sight, and I turned off the flashlight.

"What do we do?" Aubrey whispered in a panic.

It was possible we could stay hidden from the soldiers, but there would be no way of masking our scent from the dogs. By the moonlight I could see a small drainage ravine to our left.

"Here, let's jump in the ditch. Lay low and keep quiet," I said, pointing to the ravine. We slid into the ditch and kept still and silent. We could hear barking, but it was hard to tell if the dogs were moving toward us. I hadn't noticed while we were walking, but a warm breeze was blowing from the south. It was taking our very heavy scent of blood, sweat, and tears directly toward the dogs.

A long ten seconds had passed when the dogs suddenly stopped barking. That was not a good sign. I'd been hunting enough to know that when dogs picked up a scent, that's when the barking stopped. I could picture them raising their noses to the air and sniffing in our direction.

So what happened next was no surprise. All hell broke loose, and the dogs went wild; they had our scent. We could hear the barking intensify as they ran toward our position. I didn't know if we should try to run or if it even mattered. I was in a panic, thinking we had to do *something*, when I heard the most beautiful, gentle voice. Marti had begun to quietly sing. Her voice sounded like an angel's.

She sang in part Creole and part English. It didn't take long to understand what she was singing—it was the twenty-third Psalm, the Psalm of David.

Marti sang and I prayed. I could feel cold chills on my neck and arms. The hot jungle air suddenly turned cool and the winds above us began swirling in a vortex and suddenly changed direction.

I looked at Aubrey. She had her eyes closed. Aubrey was praying too.

Something spiritual and amazing was happening around us. After a few more seconds, the barking abruptly stopped; the dogs had lost our scent. About thirty seconds later, it started up again—but much farther away, heading in a new direction. After a few minutes, we could barely hear the dogs.

Marti stopped singing, and for a while we all were silent. It was quite apparent that for the third or fourth time in the last few days, God had wrapped us tightly in his veil of protection. Humbled and amazed, I closed my eyes again and thanked him.

Feeling it was safe to leave the ditch, we hurried up and over the hill. In front of us was an open plateau, well lit by the full moon.

About a mile away we could see the dim lights of what we hoped would be our refuge. We had to make the decision now: cross the open, exposed plateau or take the longer—but safer— route around the perimeter.

After what we had just experienced, it was a quick discussion. We chose the plateau.

CHAPTER THIRTY-SIX

We got across and made it to the highway just as the sun began to rise. It was a welcome sight. Hiding in a small patch of trees on the roadside, we kept our eyes on the highway. Only a handful of cars had passed, mostly tap-taps or trucks filled with workers. There were no signs of police or anyone who looked official. We were one step closer to freedom, it seemed.

Marti asked for Reagan's phone and placed a call to her cousin, speaking quickly to him in French. The guy must have been surprised, I thought, to get a call from his "drowned" cousin, but there wasn't time for a long talk.

"He said he'd be here in five minutes," she reported. "He'll be in a small white pickup. He said for us to jump in back when he pulls over by the road."

I started to question the wisdom of riding in an open truck bed, but I kept the comment to myself. I should just be glad we had someone to come and get us. We could probably lie down and not be seen over the sides of the back of the truck.

In exactly five minutes, a white truck appeared on the side of the road. It was an old Datsun with a high frame over the bed covered by a black tarp.

Looking in both directions, we made a mad dash to the truck. The driver, who I assumed was Marti's cousin, jumped out and met us at the back. He gave Marti a quick hug and said something to her in French, a look of joy on his face. He partially pulled the tarp back and, head first, we piled in. In the darkness, we could feel the benches on the sides of the bed. Aubrey and I sat on one side and Marti on the other. It only took a few seconds for our eyes to get adjusted to the dark and when they did, we saw that we were not alone.

Someone was sitting in a corner on Marti's side. Before we could question who it was, Marti's cousin dumped the clutch, causing the truck to lurch forward and almost tossing us out of the bed. Aubrey fell against me, and I watched, alarmed, as Marti plunged toward the back of the truck. She would have surely fallen out had a hand not reached out and grabbed her.

His face came into the light. It was Nathan who'd saved Marti.

Aubrey and Marti cried out, but I was less surprised than you might imagine. I had known Nathan for many years and sometimes I believed that he sat alone at night and thought of ways to just appear and shock the hell out of his friends. I was interested, of course, in how the heck he'd ended up in the back of Marti's cousin's truck. But one look at the expression on his face, and I knew that would have to wait.

"Where's Reagan?" Nathan asked.

No one had an answer, and Nathan had been through enough in his long career to know what our silence meant.

"Reagan didn't make it, did he?" he asked solemnly.

Marti was the one to answer. "I'm so sorry," she said as tears rolled down her cheeks.

Nathan put his arm around her, and Aubrey and I kept our eyes on the floor. This was their moment, godfather and goddaughter.

We rode in silence for a few minutes until the truck came to a stop. Marti's cousin pulled the tarp back, and we stepped out onto a small pier next to several fishing boats that were tied up to a mooring. The cousin pointed us toward what looked like a small office or storage building a few feet from the dock. We walked into a sparse room with not much more than an old wooden table with four chairs, piles of tangled fishing nets, and the strong smell of fish.

In French, Marti introduced us to her cousin, Jude Bellefontaine. He smiled and said something we couldn't understand while directing us to the table.

"He said that it's nice to meet you and to please have a seat," said Aubrey. "Also, would anyone like some water?"

When we nodded, he pulled a cooler from behind the door. He took four water bottles out and placed them on the table. We couldn't get the caps off fast enough.

While we drank, he and Marti stepped away to talk. The conversation was in Creole, and we couldn't understand. Jude was excited and speaking fast, waving his arms back and forth and pointing wildly. Marti listened and nodded, a concerned look on her face. After a few minutes, he gave her a hug and told us goodbye.

Marti joined us at the table. "He said the national police are all over Roseaux and up the coast. They've been speeding up and down the highway asking if anyone has seen or come into contact with any blancs. Everybody's wondering what has happened." She picked up a bottle of water and took two long gulps, and then she continued.

"I asked him if he thought he could get us to Jeremie in one of his boats, and he said he thought he could but that we'd need to leave real soon. Because this is the time that he leaves every morning, and it might look suspicious if he left any later. It's his normal routine to go to the port in Jeremie for fuel, so it won't look unusual for him to head that way." She paused. "The only problem is the crew. He said he would think about it, and he would let us know."

I pulled another round of waters from the cooler. Nathan reached for one, but I pulled it back. "Not so fast," I told him. "You have a little explaining to do."

He leaned back in his chair and said okay. I tossed him the water.

"After you told me that you were headed to Roseaux and that Marti was going to contact her cousin, I put in a call to Charles." He glanced at Marti, and his eyes grew soft. "I'd been putting that call off, and I'm glad I waited. I didn't have to tell him that his daughter had died in an airplane crash. I told him we'd escaped and been separated. And I explained very briefly why I had to find her cousin. Then he gave me Jude's name and his location at the pier, and I snuck into town about hour before sunrise. Needless to say, he was surprised to find me waiting at his office. But I got Charles on the phone, and he explained everything to Jude. It was all I could do to talk Charles into staying in Petionville. I told him we'd call when we were safe."

Then Nathan asked me about Reagan.

It was my turn to explain. "When we took off, we were low and slow; we made for an easy target. As we were climbing and turning away from the road, they lit up the airplane with bullets. I'm not sure how many times we were hit, but it was enough to take out the back starboard windows, and the left side of the instrument panel was gone too.

"After we got clear of the road, Marti noticed that Reagan was slumped over in his seat. When she pulled him back to check on him, he was covered up in blood. Nathan, Aubrey tried to help, but when they found the wound, it was through his chest. The bullet had come through the fuselage and entered through his back. He was barely breathing; they did all they could." I took a drink of water and a deep breath and then continued with the story.

"By the time we landed, he had passed. He not only saved Marti, Nathan, but Reagan saved us all. That bullet was on a direct path for me. It would have hit me in the chest or head, and I would not have been able to fly the airplane. None of us would have made it."

No one spoke or moved. Nathan stared at me. Aubrey had her eyes fixed on something across the room. Marti was watching Nathan. It was like we were frozen in place, locked in some kind of trance. Maybe after the roller-coaster ride of the last twenty-four hours, we just had hit a wall of emotional exhaustion. Whatever it was, it didn't last for long. The door opened and Jude walked in and spoke to Marti.

Marti stood up, the spell broken. "Jude says it's time to go."

We downed the last of our water and headed for the door. This would not be the final chapter to this adventure we were on, I thought, but we were one step closer. We still had to get to the port and to the airport and hope that Mike Moseley had managed to get to Haiti. There were still so many variables to consider, and Nathan stopped as we walked toward the door. He looked uncomfortable, and I could guess what he was thinking. We had come too far not to know what might lie ahead. He cleared his throat.

"Marti, do you mind asking your cousin how he plans to get us to the port and then the airport? I don't mean to sound ungrateful, but I'm sure the police will be checking all the incoming boats and cars."

She nodded and we watched as she asked Jude the questions. In response, he smiled; it looked like he had a plan. As he explained it all to Marti, I found myself wishing that I had paid more attention in French class during college. Aubrey had taken French as well, but she and Nathan seemed just as confused as I was, trying to follow the words quickly flying from Jude's mouth. To tell the truth, I was surprised that Nathan wasn't fluent in French and Creole. His Superman status dropped a few notches in my mind as he waited for Marti to translate for us.

Soon she filled us in. "He said that as we neared the dock he would cover us up with the tarps and nets," she said. "Since he gets fuel every morning, he doesn't think anyone will be suspicious. He's told his crew he has to leave the boat there for inspection because of mechanical issues. So he's having them take the truck to the marina so he can get back home. That way, he'll be the only one with us on the boat. As for getting us to the airport, he said he'd have to figure that out once we get there."

I thought that sounded good, but I could see that Nathan was concerned.

"Tell him it's a good plan, but we need to change it just a bit," he said. "The police will be searching everyone. They'll expect us to force some local to transport us, either by car or boat. But I have an idea that might be enough to fool them. Ask him if those tanks are full of air." He pointed to a storage rack in a corner of the room. I looked and saw hanging on the wall several scuba tanks, masks, and vests.

Marti asked Jude the question and, with a look of confusion, he answered.

"He said they are," she reported. "They use them when they untangle nets and inspect the bottoms of the boats. He said to ask you why."

Nathan smiled. He was in his element and explained the plan, and it was indeed quite brilliant. We all agreed that it might work.

After making sure no one was hanging around the dock, we took our day packs and hid them under the bench in Jude's truck. We then loaded the scuba gear onto the boat. It was just after seven o'clock when we pushed off from the pier. Jude said the port was about five miles away, and due to the choppy waves, it would take close to an hour for us to get there. There were no other boats in sight, but we all lay low and covered up with the tarps in case someone might be watching from the shore with binoculars. The boat was large enough for us to lie close to the sides and not be seen, but we didn't want to take any chances. About fifteen minutes into our voyage, with the hypnotic drone of the engine and rhythm of the boat, I drifted to sleep.

—

It was a warm summer day, and Aubrey and I were at the river house with our families. Dad and I were rocking on the front porch with tall glasses of cold tea when he glanced down the gravel drive.

"You remember the first time we drove up that driveway?" he asked, and I laughed.

"I do," I replied. "I was scared to death. We'd come to get a map of the property from Mr. Reese. If we hadn't needed that map, we wouldn't be sitting here now."

"It's odd how things work out," he said. "I always hoped that you and Aubrey would end up together. During your college years, you got a little distracted and almost missed out on this fine life that you've got right now. I wanted to tell you I thought you were making a mistake, but I kept my opinion to myself. You needed to figure things out for yourself. That's part of becoming an adult." He was still looking up the driveway, but then turned to me.

"Son, I want you to know I'm proud of the man that you've become and proud of the father that you are. I know I spent too much time at work and that I was not around as much as I should have been. If I could change that, I would. A lot of who you are you had to figure out all on your own." He smiled and reached over to gently shake my shoulder.

I was about to tell him what a great role model he had been and how much I appreciated him working so hard to provide for us when my son appeared, flying around the corner of the porch. His smile looked just like Aubrey's. He was pushing a toy race car, a gift from his granddad. It was a moment I'd never forget.

When the engine died, so did my dream. I woke to find the boat was idling. I peeked out from the covering to see we were nearing land. Nathan motioned for us to move towards him.

"We're about a half mile out now and it's time to go," he said. He slid each of us a tank, vest, and mask, and he gave us a quick lesson on how to operate them and put them on. All suited up, we crawled down into the engine room and waited for Jude to give the signal.

Less than ten minutes later, we heard the metallic sound of a wrench tapping on the door frame to the room. We put on our masks and stuck the air regulators in our mouths. Then Nathan pulled a tarp over our heads. He'd said if we didn't panic and breathe the air too fast, we should have about forty-five minutes of air.

When the thick smoke began to fill the room, I tried not to panic. Jude had poured transmission oil into the air intake of the diesel engine. He'd loosened the bolts to the exhaust manifold, causing black smoke to pour out from the engine. I could only imagine what it looked like from the pier—like we were on fire, I hoped.

Nathan's idea was that instead of using stealth, we would draw attention.

I felt the boat tap the pier and then I heard shouting as several people came on board. When the engine stopped, that was our signal to go. Nathan pulled back the tarp and opened the half door on the hull that served as access to the engine bay. Silently, we climbed out and eased into the water. Nathan shut the door, and on his signal, we went under.

The concrete, rectangular pier spanned about a hundred feet. We followed the wall to the end and swam around the corner. With the pier about two feet above the water, we could surface and stay hidden. We had no idea what was happening on the boat; all we could do was tread water and wait.

It didn't take long—five minutes might have passed—when a shadow appeared above us. It was Jude. He motioned for us to swim to the shallow end of the dock. When we rose above the pier, the old white truck was waiting.

We'd made it one step further.

CHAPTER THIRTY-SEVEN

Mike

After producing the proper papers to the Customs and Immigration official and refueling the King Air, Mike departed Miami for Haiti. His direct route would have him clipping the southeast tip of Cuba and would take about three hours. Having prior experience with Cuban air traffic controllers, he'd decided on a route that would take him along the coast of the Dominican Republic. On any given day, the Cuban ATC might permit a flyover or just as easily deny entry. They also had been known to ask too many questions.

Without any issues, he made it around Cuba and skirted the DR at Cabo Isabela then crossed over into Haiti at Monte Cristi. The sun was just rising into a cloudless sky, and no matter what, it was going to be a beautiful day.

So far, he hadn't heard any radio traffic and, with very little aviation going on in Haiti, he didn't expect to do so. What did trouble him was his route over the middle of the country. It would take him across the west bay and then back onto the southwest leg of the island. On a clear day like this one, anyone who might be looking for airplanes could spot see him easily. He thought about flying further out over the ocean and circling into Jeremie, but that was the behavior of a pilot who wanted to slip in and land unnoticed. That would arouse suspicion. He reminded himself that he was a tourist on a fishing trip and needed to act like one by staying on his present course.

After entering the bay at Grande Saline and crossing over Ile de la Gonave, he could just make out Jeremie on the horizon. His GPS reported that it was twenty miles away. Preparing for landing, he announced his arrival on the Jeremie Unicom frequency but got no response. It was listed as an uncontrolled airfield, which usually meant no monitoring, but he knew that today would be the exception to the rule.

With the airfield in his sight, he did a final pre-landing check and, with three lights in the green, meaning the landing gear had been safely extended, and with the throttles pulled back, he lined up for landing on runway twenty-seven. As in most rural airports in Haiti, the short runway was bright white, made from an aggregate of shells and sand. Contrasting with the light-colored runway were several black SUVs parked nearby on the tarmac. He smirked at the cliché of government officials in black SUVs and trucks. They were waiting for him, he knew.

He landed the King Air on the short field and taxied to the tarmac.

Just as he expected, several serious-looking men in uniforms and dark sunglasses were waiting for him. They motioned for him to park near the trucks. He took a deep breath and again reminded himself that he was just a guy on a fishing trip.

CHAPTER THIRTY-EIGHT

Jules

After the long four-hour ride, Jules Pierre-Toussaint arrived at the Jeremie airport just after seven o'clock to find the gate locked and no sign of activity. Since most flights were scheduled arrivals and since there were no permanent personnel, the airport stayed locked when not in use. As he unlocked the gate, several vehicles sped up in a huge cloud of dust. He would not be the only one meeting the new arrival.

Thinking about how to handle the situation, he decided he would simply do his job. According to Colby, the pilot knew his role as a tourist, and if he played it right, there shouldn't be a problem. He thought about the irony of the situation. Instead of looking out for others who might be trying to deceive him, today he'd be the one trying not to get caught.

As he slid back the gate, several drivers wheeled into the airport in SUVs and pulled their vehicles onto the tarmac. After securing the gate, Jules got into his truck, pulled up to the FBO, and went inside. If these guys wanted to talk, they would have to come to him.

Thinking ahead, he had already manually created an arrival notice of the scheduled aircraft and, before the men approached, he quickly entered the information onto the computer. Colby had given him the pilot's name and the type of aircraft he'd arrive in, but that was all Jules knew. It wasn't much, but he could at least show that he had been notified of the arrival. That might be enough to tamp down any suspicions they might have.

He had just finished making the entry when the door opened and four men in national police uniforms walked into the room. Looking up from the computer, Jules was greeted by a man in a captain's uniform.

"Good morning," said the man.

Jules returned the greeting.

"We need to know if there has been any flight activity from this airfield in the last twelve hours," said the captain.

"May I first ask who is inquiring?" Jules made sure to maintain a non-threatening tone.

"Of course. I'm Captain Henri Ostavien of the national police, and these men are with our special forces unit."

Jules rose from his desk. "I'm Agent Pierre-Toussaint with Customs and Immigration. Pleased to meet you." He stuck out his hand for a friendly handshake. "As for your request, I'm not sure at the moment. I just arrived and don't know of any activity from yesterday or last night. Most of our traffic is out of Les Cayes or Ile-a-Vache. I'm only in this office when I have a scheduled appointment either here or at the port."

Then the captain asked the question Jules knew was coming next.

"Yes, we do have someone scheduled to come in," said Jules. "There's a King Air from the States that should be arriving any moment." He leaned over the desk and tapped a few keys on his computer. "Mike Moseley is his name. He says he's coming down for a fishing trip."

"Is he coming by himself?" the captain asked.

"No passengers are listed, but that doesn't mean he'll be alone. It's just American customs that requires a passenger list. All we require are valid passports on arrival." He paused as if curious. "Are we expecting any trouble with this particular arrival?"

Before the captain could answer, they heard the sound of an approaching aircraft.

"We're about to find out," the captain answered as he and his men turned toward the door.

CHAPTER THIRTY-NINE

Mike

Mike shut down the engines and prepared to meet the soldiers. As he lowered the cabin door, they were standing a few feet from the airplane, waiting. He was not sure if they would be boarding or if he'd be allowed to exit. He poked his head out the door, and they motioned for him to disembark.

A few of the men had automatic weapons cradled in their arms. He noticed that they were British-made Enfield L85A-1 rifles and was immediately amused. How preposterous that he was being held by rifles commissioned by the Queen.

"Welcome to Haiti, Mr. Moseley," said the captain. "Is anyone else on board the aircraft?"

"No sir, only me," Mike answered, surprised they knew his name.

The customs agent was standing a few feet from the soldiers. Mike assumed that this was Colby's friend. But it was clear the captain had taken charge. "May we please see your passport and paperwork?" the captain asked.

Mike had them ready and handed him the papers.

"Mr. Moseley, have you ever been fishing in Haiti before?" asked the captain. The interrogation had begun.

"No, I haven't," Mike replied. "Have I made a bad choice?"

The captain couldn't help but smile. "Well, it's not the most popular fishing destination in the Caribbean, but it's not a bad one. When did you plan your trip?" He had quickly lost the smile.

"I planned it a few days ago. I was on a layover in Puerto Rico and met a chap who said the fishing near Ile de la Gonave was good and also cheap, so I booked a trip."

"Mr. Moseley, I find it odd that you planned a fishing trip to a foreign country with just a few days' notice. Most people take a lot more time with their preparation," the captain said, beginning to press him harder.

Mike was ready for him. "Maybe that's how most people do it, but I spent thirty years flying with the Royal Air Force and participated in four wars and three conflicts. I'm not used to having much time for preparation. When I'm ready to do something, I just do it. I don't piss around and think about it. Is there any reason I'm being questioned by you and not by him?" Mike pointed to the agent. "As you can see from my passport, I've flown in almost every country in the Caribbean, and I've never been questioned by the military or the police," he said, beginning to press back.

"Where are you staying and who do you plan to fish with?" the captain asked him, undeterred.

"Place Charmant and Marina Blue," Mike answered.

"Mr. Moseley, I'm not sure that I believe you. I think you might be here for other reasons. Let's step into the terminal and continue this conversation." The captain was turning to walk toward the building when one of the soldiers pointed in the direction of the coast.

They all turned to see black smoke rising in the air about a mile away. The soldier whispered something to the captain, who then pulled the agent to the side. The captain seemed to be giving him instructions.

Then he turned to Mike. "Mr. Moseley, you are *not* allowed to return to your airplane, and you need to stay here with the agent until my return. We'll also need to check that you have no weapons." He motioned for one of the soldiers to pat Mike down.

"If you're involved with some American guests of ours, you've made a big mistake," warned the captain. He then instructed the agent to take Mike to the FBO.

The agent removed his weapon from his holster and motioned for Mike to head in the direction of the terminal. Meanwhile, the others jumped into their trucks and quickly left the airport.

The agent waited until they were out of sight. "I understand we have mutual friends," he said, putting his gun back in the holster.

"And it looks like they've got themselves in one hell of a mess," Mike said. "How do *you* fit into this?"

"Come inside and I'll fill you in," he said as they walked inside the FBO. Agent Jules Pierre-Toussaint introduced himself and poured them mugs of coffee. "I'm assuming since you were military that you drink it black?"

"Yep, we all have that in common. No time to mix in all that fancy stuff," Mike replied as he took the mug. "Have you heard from them?" he asked.

"No, I haven't. Have you?" the agent asked.

Taking a sip of his coffee, Mike shook his head to indicate he hadn't. "Any idea where they are?" he asked.

"If I were guessing, I'd say about a mile down the road near the source of that black smoke." Pierre-Toussaint pulled a chair out from the table. "Sit down and let's talk."

They spent the next twenty minutes talking about how each of them had come to know Aubrey and Colby. Pierre-Toussaint told Mike about Marti and her disappearance and what her rescue meant for the future of the country. He also told Mike about his boys and what had happened to their mother.

Mike was describing his adventures in the military when the agent's phone rang. Pierre-Toussaint looked across the table at Mike and grabbed the phone off the table. The call was coming from Reagan's phone.

Cautiously, he answered. "Agent Pierre-Toussaint." He listened briefly, then put the phone on speaker mode so that Mike could hear.

"Jules, has Mike gotten there?" It was Colby speaking.

"Yes, he's here. Where are *you*?"

"We just left the port. We're in the back of Marti's cousin's pickup truck a few minutes from the airport. Tell Mike to get the airplane ready."

"Okay, will do. The police have been here, and they'll be returning soon. You'll need to board the airplane fast."

Then suddenly Colby's voice rose. "Shit!" he yelled into the phone. "The police just passed us. They're heading to the airport. I don't know if we'll have time."

"You just get here and we'll be ready!" said Pierre-Toussaint.

Mike was already on his feet and headed toward the door—but then he stopped. He turned toward the agent. "Hey, listen," he said. "You've got kids. You can't be involved in this. Hurry, take off your boots!" he yelled.

Pierre-Toussaint looked confused but nevertheless complied. Mike ripped the laces from the agent's boots and in less than a minute he had taken the agent's gun and tied him to a chair.

"Sorry mate, but it has to look real," he said, frowning, then hit Pierre-Toussaint in the nose with a glancing blow as blood shot everywhere. Then he hit him again, this time harder, and Pierre-Toussaint went limp.

Then Mike ran outside and climbed into the airplane.

Just as he started the engines, an old white truck wheeled into the airport. It stopped at the gate. Aubrey, Colby, Nathan, and some woman who must be Marti jumped out from the back. The driver got out of the truck to close the airport gate. Mike's four passengers were running toward the airplane when suddenly the woman stopped and ran back to grab the driver. He appeared to protest as she pulled him with her toward the plane.

Colby had just shut the cabin door when the black trucks pulled up to the gate. Mike didn't wait to see what happened next; he pushed the throttle and taxied quickly toward the runway.

CHAPTER FORTY

Colby

As we rolled onto the runway, Mike jammed both throttles full forward, and the King Air quickly gained speed—but there was no way that would be enough to save us. The trucks had crashed the gate, and the police were racing across the tarmac in their vehicles. They were angling to block us, and I could see no possible way we'd be able to take off.

I looked over at Mike, expecting to see desperation on his face, but he was calm and focused. We continued to build speed as we came closer to crashing into the trucks. Mike wasn't going to stop; this was a game of chicken.

Realizing they were about to be involved in a fiery crash and that they had another way to stop us, the police stopped short of the runway. I watched as they jumped out of their trucks with their automatic weapons. They were raising the guns to their shoulders when, about two hundred feet from the trucks, Mike pulled back on the yoke. The airplane barely lifted off the ground and I immediately had the sickening sense of being right back in the middle of a very recent nightmare.

Just like in the 310, we were low, slow, and vulnerable. The soldiers would have an easy target as we passed them.

It struck me then that Aubrey was sitting in the same position that Reagan had been in the night before. The bullets would be coming from the same angle as before.

I was sitting in the copilot's seat and had turned to yell at her to get down when I felt the safety harnesses pull tightly against my chest. Strangely, they were pulling the wrong way. I was pitching forward, instead of backwards. We should have been climbing, but at twenty feet, Mike was banking toward the trucks and shoving the airplane toward the deck.

Suddenly, I was looking at the soldiers eye to eye. They looked as shocked as I was. Then I felt the wheels tuck into their wells as we passed over the trucks. We couldn't have missed them by more than a foot.

I was hoping the scare would be enough to keep the soldiers from firing at us as we made our climb. But we didn't climb. Once again, I felt a forward pull on my harnesses as Mike pushed the airplane even lower. The propellers were kicking up dust and sand; we couldn't have been more than a few feet off the ground. We stayed at that altitude until we cleared the airfield and moved out over the water. I glanced at the altimeter. It was barely above zero.

About a half mile out, Mike cocked his head just enough to make eye contact and give me a slight smile. He exuded the calm of a guy sitting in his living room with the TV on.

I realized that what he'd done had been totally counterintuitive. As I had attempted to do in the 310, most pilots would have tried to gain altitude and take to the air as an escape. But Mike knew that we would have been an easy target, so he kept us low and out of sight. If only I had thought of that the night before.

Mike glanced at the yoke and then back at me. I understood the message and placed my hands on the controls then gave him a nod.

"Your airplane," he said softly over the headset.

I pulled that yoke back and we headed for the sky at over two thousand feet per minute. In less than thirty seconds, with all our troubles now below us, we were clear of Haiti.

Handing over the controls had been his way of saying that we were all in this together. I checked the compass and set our course for home.

Epilogue

It had been a few short weeks since they'd returned from what Colby liked to call the "honeymoon from hell" (but not in Aubrey's presence).

But there'd been no easing back into their old life with Aubrey taking on work assignments while Colby immersed himself in aviation and gentleman farming. Instead, the several close calls with death in the short span of two years had brought new perspective.

Sitting on the front porch in Warthen with a steaming cup of coffee, Aubrey thought about her life, which hadn't gone exactly as she'd hoped. Thinking about Colby, who was still asleep in their bedroom, she wanted to blame him. But she knew that wasn't fair. The youthful expectations she'd had for the two of them had been just the foolish dreams of a schoolgirl too naïve to know how life really worked.

But what a blissful life it would have been. Once she had imagined they'd graduate high school together and then college, then they'd move back into the house by the river that she loved so much. They would have a family and live happily ever after. Even now, she could picture herself and Colby spending Sunday afternoons sitting on the dock while their kids, daredevils every one, jumped off the big rock into the muddy river.

Those dreams began falling apart by the time she turned eighteen, and they completely evaporated after a short marriage to a man she'd never loved.

Now, as she mourned all the things that never happened, the eager faces of Simon and Sandley drifted into her thoughts. Her brief encounter with the two boys would become a turning point in Aubrey's life. With tears running down her face, she knew what she was missing. And there was no way that she could ever go back to the way things were before.

Being with Colby once again had filled a hole in Aubrey's heart, but it hadn't filled it all the way. What Aubrey wanted more than anything was to be a mother. It might be too late for the traditional route to motherhood, but there were children in the world who had no one and wanted desperately to be loved.

She smiled, thinking that she and Colby could love and care for one of them, maybe more. It was time she and Colby had a talk.

—

Colby woke up to find Bella licking his face with joy. Since becoming another canine member of the family, she'd been sleeping in their bed, and Colby didn't like that. Hannah and Savannah, Colby's twelve-year-old redbone coonhounds, never came inside and lived mostly underneath the house. Of course, he had gotten nowhere when he suggested that Bella sleep outside, or at least in the large and expensive dog bed that sat unused on the floor beside his and Aubrey's bed.

Smelling the sweet aroma of coffee, he knew now why Bella was so eager to get his attention. If Aubrey had been in the bed, the dog would have been curled up next to her.

He scratched behind her ears and thought how happy he was to be safe at home. The honeymoon had been a whirlwind of death-defying adventures that he never in a million years would have thought could happen in real life. Before then, except for one previous occasion, he had spent the last twenty-five years going to the same job every day with nothing more exciting than a speeding ticket to interrupt his dull routine.

Now, he wasn't sure how to tell Aubrey, but he longed to have a normal life again. Mostly, he wanted *her* life to be normal. And as long as she worked with Nathan and the company, that could never be.

—

Nathan and Laura casually rocked in a wooden swing that hung between two hickory trees. They looked out over a mountain that towered over a deep valley. It had been a brutally hot summer in Madison and, needing to get away from the heat for a few weeks, they'd escaped to the coolness of the North Carolina mountains.

After his return from Haiti, the solitude of their isolated home had given Nathan time to think. His heart was still heavy over the loss of his dear friend.

To him, life was a scoreboard with columns for wins and losses. Saving Marti had been a huge win, but it had come with a big loss. He'd tried to look at Reagan's death against the background of all the lives that Marti would ultimately save by bringing change and revolution to an impoverished Haiti—but he couldn't do it. Holding Tamara in his arms as she mourned her husband's loss had simply been too much.

Nathan silently got up from the swing and squeezed Laura's hand. She smiled and gently squeezed it back. He knew she understood that he had things he had to work out.

Walking down the driveway, he slipped into the woods and sat beneath a large white oak. With no one else around, he buried his face in his hands and wept. Then, after finally releasing all the sorrow he'd held in for so long, he made a decision. At almost seventy years old, he was tired of so much death, destruction, and pain. He decided his days with the company were over. Semi-retirement would now become a permanent retirement. The final chapters of their life would be the kind Laura needed and deserved.

Looking up through the trees at the clear blue sky, he felt a sudden lightness; a weight he'd carried for so long was no longer there. He couldn't wait to tell the news to Laura.

He hoped Aubrey would understand.

—

After members of the cabal had been secretly gathered up by contractors from Nathan's company, it was time for Marti to go home. When the country heard the news, they broke out in a riotous celebration as only Haitians can. Mike, with permission from his boss, flew Marti back to Port-au-Prince in his company's new Gulfstream 650 jet.

Upon their arrival, the Haitian Air Traffic Control shut down the airspace, allowing them a grand reentry. More than a hundred thousand people crammed in and around the airport to welcome home their country's new hope.

On the tarmac, Mike lowered the door of the 650. Suddenly, a cool wind replaced the hot, still air and the temperature quickly began to drop. All around the city, tree limbs and leaves shook and swayed to a new rhythm.

Marti emerged from the airplane and, like the vodoun goddess Lasiren, made her reappearance into the world.

The sound of yells and applause were carried all the way to a small pavilion on a particular beach on the island of Ile-a-Vache.

Meanwhile, in Les Cayes, in a weatherworn blue house, Tamara Flexion sat in front of a small TV and wept; they were happy tears for the return of Marti, mingled with mournful ones for the loss of the husband she loved. A few weeks earlier, Nathan had visited and explained how Reagan had come to die a hero's death. He'd asked for her forgiveness, which she'd given him without hesitation.

From a farm in South Georgia to the North Carolina mountains and across the sea to Haiti, they all made decisions on how to move forward with their lives. No one would ever be the same, as nothing goes untouched by change. It is a dynamic part of life.

Sometimes we will be the ones rescuing others, and sometimes we will need to be rescued. As choices defined the actions of Aubrey, Colby, Nathan, and all the characters in this story, so will they define us. Maybe we will choose as they did and take the leap of faith to trust and believe in each other.

James Campbell

ACKNOWLEDGEMENTS

I hope you enjoyed *Mandatory Flight* and the adventures of Aubrey, Colby, and Nathan.

I had just started writing this book, which is the sequel to *Mandatory Role*, and was planning for the adventure to take place in the Bahamas when the "real-life" Nathan suggested I accompany him on a trip to Haiti. After a day or two in the country, I knew it would be the setting for the book.

I want to thank Nathan for his help generating ideas. I also appreciate his assistance in planning the logistics for the scenes in Haiti. He is a great friend with many talents and interesting stories (some of which he can't officially tell).

I also want to thank my editor, Mary Beth Bishop. I finished writing the book in February and began the process of finding an editor. Mary Beth was highly recommended by my publisher, but she was in such demand that I would have to wait five to six months for a slot. Wanting the book to be out by summer, I considered finding another editor, but the publisher said I would not regret the wait and she was right!

Editing with Mary Beth was as enjoyable as writing the book. Her style and ideas helped enhance the story and made it so much better. She understands how to connect with the rhythm and vibe of the author, which is a must for a good outcome.

Also, most of the characters in the book are based on actual people. I want to thank them for the opportunity to use their amazing accomplishments and adventures in the story.

James

About The Author

James Campbell grew up in Atlanta and earned a degree in journalism from the University of Georgia. Although he'd planned to pursue a career in his field of study, he somehow got pulled into the vortex of the business world, but never lost his desire to write. After twenty-five years of building and operating multiple businesses, he decided to fulfill his longtime ambition to become an author. *Mandatory Role* and its sequel, *Mandatory Flight*, are both filled with action, adventure, and, most importantly, romance. In these fast-paced novels, James combines his love for flying, travel, racing cars, and the outdoors with the eternal hope that love might really conquer all. He currently resides in the Georgia towns of Madison and Warthen.

Website:
jamescampbellauthor.com

Facebook page:
facebook.com/
JCampbellAuthor